I0638400

Mrs Jones

Tommy Connell Mystery #1

B.A. Morton

Twisted Ink Publishing

Mrs Jones

Tommy Connell Mystery #1

© B.A. Morton 2011

The right of B.A. Morton to be identified as author of
this work has been asserted by her in accordance with
the Copyright, Designs and Patents Act 1988.

ISBN-10: 0992985501
ISBN-13: 978-0992985509

First edition published 2011
Second edition published 2014
This revised edition published 2017

Cover Images Courtesy of: jgolby/Shutterstock
Guitar photographer/Shutterstock

For Michael

'Soul Mate & Partner in Crime'

By the same author

Crime Fiction
Molly Brown - Tommy Connell Mystery #2
Bedlam
Twisted
Ten Green Bottles - Dark Minds (Anthology – various authors)

Historical Fiction
(The Wildewood Chronicles)
Wildewood Revenge
Bad Blood
Assassin's Curse
The Burning Boy

One

She answered the door on the sixth knock.

He knew that because he had counted.

Six knocks, thirty seconds between knocks, three minutes.

He'd raised his hand to give her the seventh, seven being his lucky number and three and half minutes as long as he was prepared to wait, but she'd beaten him to it. All the same, six knocks. These weren't palatial penthouse apartments, they were studios. What had taken her so long? Delays in answering the door in this neighborhood were usually accompanied by the sounds of hurriedly flushed toilets. On this occasion there was silence.

When the door finally opened she left the chain on, which was smart, but didn't make his job any easier or quicker. He had a prior engagement and he was already running late. He flashed his I.D. through the crack in the door.

"Detective Connell, Ma'am. New York Police Department. You called in a report about a hit and run. I'd like to ask a few questions."

He pulled his badge away just in time to avoid his hand being jammed as the door slammed closed in his face. Frustrated, he checked his watch again. His date wouldn't be waiting now. She'd be on her way home and deleting his number from her phone. That was twice he'd messed up. Unavoidable and unforgivable.

Everyone else on the squad had more important things to do on a Friday night than chase down old ladies who may or may not have seen an accident. He had more important things to do too, but his arrest rate was at an all-time low. He'd been spending far too much time on impossible cases, and on paper this one had looked like an easy check in the box. Find the old lady, confirm her statement and sign off on the case.

He was about to give that seventh knock, when he heard the chain being slid. Placing a hand on the weapon holstered under his left arm, he stepped to one side and waited as the door swung slowly inwards.

"Is your mom at home?" he asked the girl who peered anxiously at him from behind the door. She was slender and pale, with a mop of unruly dark hair and wide dark eyes. Her feet, resting one atop the other, were bare, her toenails painted a vivid pink. She wore faded jeans with holes at the knees and a baggy grey T-shirt.

Connell took in her slight frame in seconds and dismissed her. It was a necessary skill to identify and eliminate any risks - certainly in this neighborhood and she was definitely no threat. "I'm looking for a ..." He pulled out his notebook and checked the name he'd scrawled down back at the station "... Mrs. Jones, Mrs. Elizabeth Jones."

The girl nodded and opened the door wide spilling light into the hall. He realized his gift for on-the-spot identification was slipping. She wasn't a girl at all. She was a young woman who looked like she hadn't slept for a week and he knew exactly how that felt.

"I'm Mrs. Jones," she replied in a soft, British accent. "You'd better come in."

Connell wasn't often surprised, but she was definitely not what he'd been expecting. She didn't look old enough to be Mrs. Anybody and she didn't sound like the voice on the tape. The voice had been muffled, admittedly, but had sounded older and certainly not British. Either she hadn't made the call or the voice had been deliberately disguised. The first of his inner alarm bells began to chime as he followed her into the room.

It was typical of a thousand more in the neighborhood. Close your eyes, stick a pin in a map and you couldn't fail to come up with a place like this. Short-term, low-rent housing with absentee landlords who turned a blind eye and made a killing off the backs of the poor. Shabby without the chic, it consisted of a studio apartment complete with bathroom. The furniture was old, the carpet thin, and the hotplate that passed for a stove should've been condemned. There was a moldy smell overlaid by a thin scent of perfume. He knew nothing about this young woman, yet he knew that she didn't belong here.

He held out his hand, left it hanging in midair for a matter of seconds and withdrew it with an awkward shrug as she shifted her gaze, avoiding his eyes and his shake. She was nervous and he wondered why. He made allowances for the fact that nobody liked to have police at the door, that she didn't sound like a local and, most importantly, that she'd just witnessed a death.

"I was expecting someone older," he said.

"Oh."

No explanation, just 'oh', as if that was all that was required. He'd initiated this visit and it was obvious she intended to let him do all the work.

"You made a 911 call about a hit and run. I'm just here to take some more details." He tried a smile and it seemed to work as she met it with a half-hearted one of her own. "It was *you* who made the call?"

"How did you find me?" she asked. "I didn't leave my address."

"We traced your call to the lobby downstairs. It wasn't difficult."

The janitor had been very helpful, particularly when offered ten bucks. Sure there was a Mrs. Jones, third floor, apartment 13A. He smiled again - he really wanted to ask her why she hadn't used a cell phone, why she'd chosen to leave no contact details, why she seemed reluctant to be found - but decided to leave those questions for later.

"Please have a seat," she said. As there was only one, piled with books, he sat cautiously on the edge of the bed to the accompaniment of creaking iron springs. "Would you like some tea?" she asked with forced brightness, her cheeks a little flushed, her eyes over-bright. "Or perhaps you'd prefer coffee. I have both."

The stack of free sample packets on the counter top, suggested she'd filled her pockets at the local diner. "Tea is fine, ma'am, if it's no trouble." His date was undoubtedly blown out of the water by now. He had no reason to hurry and his curiosity was piqued. There was something about her manner that was odd and Connell found anything odd intriguing.

He scanned the room as she filled the kettle and turned on the gas beneath the aged hotplate. She only had one cup that he could see, and apart from the freebie tea and coffee, he couldn't see any food. Perhaps she ate out. That wasn't a crime, but again it was odd. In this part of the city people tended to stay indoors after dark.

There were three books on the chair and a small bag under the bed that he could feel against foot. No TV, no radio, not even a clock. He glanced through the open door to the ancient bathroom. A lone toothbrush stood propped on the cracked porcelain sink, her coat hung on the back of the door, but other than that, there was nothing personal at all, and certainly nothing to suggest a long stay or a Mr. Jones.

10

He took out his notebook again. "Mrs. Jones, Elizabeth. Can I call you Elizabeth?"

"Lizzie is fine," she replied. Her hands trembled slightly as she handed him his tea. "I'm so sorry I don't have any milk or biscuits."

She didn't have another cup either, so she did without, moving the books from the single chair to sit cross-legged upon it, her feet tucked in somehow in some strange yoga position, the books in her lap. Connell was pretty fit, no stranger to the gym, but he knew he could never tangle himself up like that. Respect to her agility, he would have fallen off the chair.

He liked her voice. The softness made a welcome change from the nasal New York accent he was used to. He decided it was time he heard some more of it.

"So what brings you to New York, Lizzie?"

It was one of those ice breakers. He could've chosen the weather if the weather had been remarkable in any way, or the football results if the Yankees had played recently, anything to put the witness at ease. He'd chosen the fact she was obviously a visitor because he thought it would give them a safe topic of conversation where maybe she would tell him she was taking a year off after college and was travelling the world, and he would confess in turn that it was something he wished he could have done. In the process he would size her up and get a handle on who she was and whether she was a credible witness.

But the look on her face when he asked the question told him far more than he'd hoped. She hesitated, just for a moment, and it was enough to set off his second alarm.

"You said you needed more details about the hit and run," she said, ignoring his question. "There's really not much more to tell. A man got knocked down and I called 911. That's it, really." She pulled at her hair, stretching and twirling it nervously.

He made a note in his book to check with immigration then raised his head and looked at her.

"How long have you been in the country?" he asked directly.

"Five days."

Only five days. He hadn't expected that. "So you witnessed the incident on the day you arrived? Quite a welcome, huh?"

"Quite." She drew her bottom lip between her teeth and began to chew at it nervously. And the more she chewed the more interested he became. He loosened his tie and undid the top button of his shirt.

"Why did you call it in?"

"Because it was the right thing to do. Wasn't it?"

Good answer, honest answer. He hoped it was the first of many. "Sure it was," he replied, "but not everyone is so public spirited. Some people would just turn the other way and keep on walking."

"Some people might."

"I see you like to read." He'd thrown her by his change of direction and when she frowned in response he gestured to her lap. He could see that one book was an A to Z of New York. A necessity for a visitor planning to do some sight-seeing but Mrs. Jones didn't look like a tourist to him.

She patted the paperbacks gently with her hand and shrugged. "They're just what I picked up for the journey to while away the time."

All three books were well thumbed, including the A to Z. Three books in five days was pretty good going. "So you haven't done much sightseeing yet?"

"Um, no, not really."

She glanced at the door as if she either wanted out of it or was expecting someone to come through it. Connell wasn't sure which but her edginess was catching and he found himself tensing slightly in case it was the latter. As

12

she divided her attention between the door, the books on her lap and the cobweb hanging from the light-fitting he took his time drinking his tea and studied her. "Have you been *anywhere* since you got here?" he asked eventually.

"No."

Her reluctance to answer simple questions interested him. Why she'd stayed in her room for five whole days interested him even more.

"Okay, so you flew in five days ago, from where?"

"London."

"London Heathrow? You got any I.D?"

"I.D?"

He wondered if she was being deliberately vague or maybe she was a little slow. It was hard to tell. "Identity details, drivers licence, passport?" He tried another smile. "You know how it works. I show you mine and you show me yours."

She missed the joke entirely. "Oh, yes, sorry." She unfolded her legs, and got down from the chair. He moved his feet as she slipped her bag from under the bed. The bag wasn't huge and she dug around in it quickly before pulling out her passport and handing the document to him.

He paged through it, noted the passport was new, that she hadn't travelled anywhere prior to arriving in the US, and although her photo didn't do her justice, the likeness wasn't bad. Better than his, anyway. He did a quick calculation with her date of birth and decided she looked younger than thirty, way younger. He glanced between the girl and her photo; good genes maybe. Turning the passport over in his hands, he felt the material it was made from, flicked through the empty pages again and noted the travel documents stuffed in the back. He had absolutely no reason to doubt its validity, but …

13

"I'll hang on to this, if you don't mind." He slipped it into his jacket and took note as her breath quickened with poorly masked alarm.

"Is that allowed?" she asked as she resumed her seat.

He cocked his head, trying to memorize the sequence in which she tangled her knees and feet, but she did it so quickly that he didn't quite get it.

"Sure it's allowed," he replied with a smile. "You'll get it back, don't worry."

"What do you need it for?"

"Procedure."

"But what if someone asks to see it in the meantime?"

"Are you planning on going somewhere in the meantime?" Considering her apparent reluctance to leave her room, he was interested in where that might be. But all he got was another shrug. "So, you came here straight from the airport, and on the way, you witnessed a hit and run."

"Yes."

"Were you traveling alone Mrs. Jones - Lizzie?" He could easily check but he wanted to ask, to probe a little deeper. He was interested in her reactions and was rewarded by further hesitation. Strike three on his alarm register.

"Yes, I was."

"No Mr. Jones?"

"No."

"Why here? Why, this neighborhood?"

"Why not?"

"It's pretty rough around here. We don't see many tourists. Why not go to a hotel?"

She stared into space for a moment as if she was asking herself the same question, and finding difficulty coming up with an answer. "I just ended up here ... I'm not really sure how. Does that sound odd?"

Of course it sounded odd, but there was a strange innocence about her that made him believe that, yes, she could have wandered all the way from the airport, witnessed a man's death and rented herself the nearest ghetto apartment she saw.

"Odd? Not at all. Did you get a cab from the airport?"

"Yes."

"And where did you get dropped off?"

She began to fiddle with the topmost book on her lap, folding down the corner of the first page and then unfolding it again. "I can't really remember. Is it relevant?"

Connell smiled again and shook his head. He could easily check. "No, not really, I'm just trying to understand what brought you to the spot where you witnessed what you saw. Just building a picture in my mind, that's all."

"Oh." Again that single word, which came out almost as a sigh of relief.

"Tell me what you saw."

She took a breath. "I was waiting to cross the road; it was extremely busy and noisy. I'm afraid I'm not used to so much traffic."

"Isn't London busy?"

"I don't live in London."

"Where do you live?"

"The North. The middle of nowhere." She smiled wistfully, got that faraway look in her eye that he suspected was homesickness or regret or maybe something else. In any case the smile, sweet though it was with its accompanying dimples, was fleeting.

"So you were waiting at the crosswalk."

"Yes, and everyone surged across. People were pushing and shoving rather rudely and I hesitated. The cars were still coming."

He knew what she meant. You literally took your life in your hands crossing streets in this town. Usually it was easier to go with the flow. The trick was to make sure you were in the middle, out of harm's way, and if someone pushed, then you pushed back even harder. It wasn't rude, it was survival. "And then what?"

"He was on the other side, coming toward me, and he hesitated too." She gazed into space and Connell watched her carefully, recognizing the look of someone who was choosing their words thoughtfully, walking a narrow line with extreme caution. It distracted him. *She* distracted him. "Then suddenly he stepped out and a car hit him. He…he was flung into the air and landed on the bonnet."

That part was real, he decided. She couldn't have faked that look in her eyes. He'd seen it before, many times - shock, disbelief, and a touch of fear. "So you saw him before he was hit, and by bonnet do you mean the hood, the front of the car?"

She hesitated. "Well… yes, I mean yes to both, I saw him before he was hit and yes he landed on the hood."

Out of all of those people waiting on the opposite curb, she had zeroed in on him. That was quite a coincidence. "How did he look when you first spotted him?"

"He just looked normal, a man waiting to cross the road." Her pale cheeks flushed and she dipped her head as if aware of the change, and anxious that he shouldn't notice.

"Did he look distracted, happy, scared? Did he speak to anyone waiting with him at the curb? Did he look like he was about to throw himself under a car?"

"As I said, he hesitated and so did I, so he sort of caught my eye. I didn't notice anything else about him."

He considered her reply for a moment before pressing on.

"Okay, what kind of car?"

"I've no idea." She arched one eyebrow. "A big American car."

"What color?"

"Black."

"A big black American car," he confirmed. "Could it have been a limousine?"

"Possibly."

He knew that it was. He had other witnesses who'd given the exact make and model, but he wanted to know what she'd seen and why she was the only one who'd called it a hit and run. Everyone else had simply seen an accident.

"Did you get a look at the driver?" Another hesitation and he was up to alarm bell number four.

"No, the windows were tinted."

She looked at her feet, the books in her lap, anywhere but at him. And he so wanted to squeeze, just a little, to see what she would do. But he gave a lazy smile instead, and continued.

"He didn't stop and get out, and check if the man was okay?" He knew that he had. The other witnesses had confirmed it. He even had the name of the guy who'd been driving. He'd waited around for the ambulance and police to arrive and given a complete statement.

"No, I didn't see anything else."

Connell looked at what he'd written. There were only three words, each punctuated by a question mark:

Immigration?

Fear?

Lies?

Not much, but it was enough to go on. He'd also doodled four alarm bells.

He changed direction. "I'd like to speak with Mr. Jones."

"Mr. Jones?"

17

"Yes, your husband - Mr. Jones."

"I told you, he's not here," she replied quickly, too quickly, and the corner of the page came away in her hand. She looked at the fragment held between finger and thumb as if unsure what to do next. Tucking it back inside the cover of the book, she lowered her lashes and tried to avoid his gaze once more.

Connell wondered if the husband had just left. Maybe that explained the fear in her eyes. He'd seen too much in his line of work not to jump to the occasional conclusion.

"Was he with you when you witnessed the accident?"

"No, he wasn't," she replied, and reddened a little more. She was trying very hard not to look him in the eye and he tried very hard to make her.

"Where is he now?" he asked.

"I don't know."

"When will he be back?"

"I'm not sure."

He tried again. "Do you expect him to come back?"

"Not really, no."

Connell added two more words to his list - *Mr. Jones?* and underlined them. He gave her a reassuring smile and one more opportunity to come clean. "Can you think of anything else you think I should know?"

"I'm not sure what it is that you think you should know."

He sighed, folded his notebook and replaced it in his inside jacket pocket beside her passport. As he did, his jacket opened to reveal his holstered gun and he noticed how her eyes widened nervously when she caught sight of it. British police weren't ordinarily armed, so he could understand her reaction, but despite that, he decided to leave his jacket open. It couldn't hurt for her to realize that it was a mistake to play games, and she was definitely playing something, probably him.

18

"Okay, Lizzie, let's get this out in the open." He rose from the bed, shoved his hands in his pants pockets and leaned casually against the back of the door. "I need to know why you saw a hit and run and everyone else saw an accident; why you didn't see the driver and everyone else did; and basically why you're lying to me. I need to know what you saw, and I need the non-fiction version, not the one you made up when I walked in the door."

Her mouth actually dropped open with shock. He'd never seen a reaction like that, that wasn't a con, but it looked real to him, and for a moment he thought he'd been wrong and that she'd been telling the truth after all. Then she snapped that sweet little mouth shut and he knew he was on the money.

She glanced again at the door behind him as if she was weighing up her odds and considering making a run for it. She looked at the window, but he'd already written that off as a sorry plan. It was possible that she might have the agility to make it out of the window and down the fire escape ahead of him - if it wasn't painted shut.

He studied her expression as she considered her options, counted the seconds in his head up to seven, and saw the exact moment when she gave it up.

Relief and resignation settled in her eyes as she gave a slight, hopeless shrug. "He was white, with white blond hair and sunglasses, an albino I think, and he saw me, looked straight at me–and I ran." It came out in a rush, as if she'd been hanging onto it with some effort.

"Who are we talking about here?"

"The driver."

Connell faltered, confused. "Why did you run?"

"Because he saw me and I was scared that he'd come after me."

He'd knocked a guy over. Big deal, it happened all the time, tragic, probably avoidable but an accident nonetheless. It wasn't usual for drivers to jump out of their cars and set off after innocent witnesses. "Why would he come after you? It was just an accident."

"No, it wasn't, it was a hit and run and I saw what he did."

"Do you actually know what a hit and run is?"

She looked at him squarely, raised an eyebrow, and he saw the tiniest glimmer of attitude sparkle in her dark eyes. "I'm English, not stupid. Of course I know what a hit and run is. It's when someone hits a pedestrian with their vehicle and then makes off so they don't get caught."

"But he didn't take off. He waited around for the police and ambulance."

"No, he didn't. He got out of the car and disappeared into the crowd, but, before he did, he ran over the man twice to make sure he was dead."

Connell stopped her with a raised palm. "Hang on, back up. You're saying this albino guy ran this man down, reversed over him on a busy street, then calmly got out of the car and walked away."

"No. Not reversed. The man ...." she paused as if replaying the details in her heads, "The man bounced off the bonnet, excuse me *the hood*, and landed in front of the car. The driver stopped, looked at me and then drove over him again."

Connell tried to picture it. It seemed unlikely somehow and yet .... "How did you know he was dead?"

"Sorry?"

"You said he ran over him twice to make sure he was dead. How did you know he was dead?"

The girl blinked. The colour drained from her face so quickly that he was sure she was set to faint right in front of him. "Isn't he dead?" she whispered.

"Sure he's dead, but how did you know that?"

"He ... he had no face left ... afterwards, just lots of blood."

Connell winced. Yeah, that would do it. "No one else saw what you saw. How can you explain that?"

"I can't speak for your other witnesses."

Connell wondered about the validity of the other witnesses. He'd skimmed the file, speed-read the statements but he hadn't interviewed them himself. He began to realize this wasn't going to be the easy in and out case he'd been promised. "And you reckon this guy got a good look at you?"

"Yes, he ... smiled at me."

"He smiled at you?"

"Yes, but not in a nice way, it was more of a sneer, really. He had a gold tooth. I remember now, it glinted in the sunlight."

Connell snapped to attention, all thoughts of other witnesses pushed aside. "You were so close you could see his teeth?"

"I'd started to cross the road after the others. I stopped in the middle when it happened and he looked at me."

"Did he say anything, do anything?"

She hesitated briefly and when she replied there was a catch in her throat. "He did this." She held up her right hand in the shape of a gun and Connell watched as the barrel of the gun shook. No wonder she'd run, no wonder she was holed up here like someone in hiding, she probably *was* in hiding.

Connell knew of only one albino, Mo Pater, a man with glittering teeth. He knew all about Pater and the organization he ran. But according to the file Mo Pater was not the driver who'd waited for the emergency services. The man who'd waited was a Clifford Reay, fifty-four years old, first day on the job and he was going to lose his license. He'd been so upset about the accident

21

he ended up going to the ER in the back of the ambulance. But as Connell knew to his cost, anyone could be bought with enough money, including witnesses.

He needed to look into the victim, wasn't sure whether he'd been identified yet. Why would Mo want to kill some random guy? It didn't make sense. But, then again, neither did Mrs. Jones.

Pulling away from the door, he crossed to the window. There was wonderful view, fire escapes and garbage cans.

"What are you really doing here?" he asked.

"Just waiting."

"For what?" He turned when she failed to answer. She had amassed a small pile of shredded paper on her lap.

"For someone to help me," she whispered as she drew up her knees and hugged them tightly.

He scanned the room again. Had she really been holed up for the last five days with no one to turn to? He felt a twist in his gut. "Do you know anyone in New York?"

"No."

"What about Mr. Jones?"

"I told you, he's not coming back."

She was scared and alone, and a long way from home. Not a good place to be.

"Then we need to get you out of here."

"I can't go home," she said as she scrubbed at her eyes with the heel of her hand.

She needn't have worried. She wasn't going home. If she was telling the truth - and that was one hell of an 'if' - she was the witness he'd dreamed about for the last two years. She was the witness who was going to help him close the biggest case of his career and the worst chapter of his life.

He stepped to the door, cracked it open and looked down the hall. It was empty. He crossed the landing and looked down the stairwell. He was being paranoid - there was no one there - but she'd just jumped to number ten on his alarm system, and by rights that meant she should be dead already.

"Well, you can't stay here," he said as he came back into the room. "Get your stuff, you're coming with me."

"Where to?"

"Somewhere safe"

"Is there such a place?"

"Sure there is. As long as you're with me, you're somewhere safe."

Two

Friday night, and the station was full to bursting with drunks, dealers and prostitutes. Connell nodded at George the intake officer and guided the girl, with a hand on her back, through the noise and the crowded hell of the booking hall, and up the stairs to the squad room. By comparison, this room was a sea of calm, empty and quiet. The on-duty guys had been called out, and by every right, Connell himself should have called it a day hours ago.

Dropping her bag, he gestured to a seat on the opposite side of his desk. She hadn't said a word on the ride in, spent the entire time hunkered down in her seat as if she expected the albino would reach his hand in through the window and grab her. She looked scared, as if the fear had been building slowly inside for the past five days, and now that she'd told someone, it was leaching out of her pores. He knew what that kind of fear felt like, how it could build like a flooding river if you let it.

He also knew that she wasn't telling him the whole truth.

"Can I get you a coffee?" he asked. "You want something to eat? I can send out for something."

She shook her head and looked at the floor. She needed to eat something, he could see that. She looked fragile, underfed, her pale skin almost translucent. But he couldn't force her. He needed something to eat too. He would have been well fed and preparing for dessert by now if he hadn't stood his date up.

"Okay, maybe later." He wasn't sure what to do with her later. He'd thought about protective custody, locking her in one of the cells - at least she'd be safe - but the look on her face as they'd come through the booking hall had knocked that idea out of his head. She was terrified. She was from the middle of nowhere and she'd landed like an alien in the centre of one of the busiest cities on earth. He wondered how she'd survive the witness stand if she ever got that far.

He pulled up a variety of images from his computer's suspect list and printed them out. "I want you to look at some mug shots and see if you can find the driver. If you see him, shout out. I'll grab us a coffee from the machine. It'll rot the lining of your stomach but it'll keep you awake." He needed her awake and alert, too bad that it was past midnight and she looked like she hadn't slept for the past five days.

He left her with the collection of photos spread across the desk, a motley group of criminal losers which included Mo Pater. He didn't expect this part to take long. He wasn't so sure about her statement though, and it needed it to be perfect or it would be pulled to shreds by Pater's lawyer.

Out in the hall the coffee machine was acting up, hardly surprising considering the amount of abuse it got on a regular basis. It took a few well-aimed kicks before it groaned into life.

"You still here, Connell?"

He turned at the voice from behind and adopted his poker face. Musgrave wasn't too high up on his buddy list. In fact, if he'd a minus line on the list, Musgrave would be well below it. The man was constantly sniffing around and always seemed to know what was going on in the department. Up for promotion, he spent his time doing everything possible to suck up to everyone further up the ladder. Connell didn't suck up and knew he would never move up the ladder, but that was cool. He felt fine hanging on right where he was.

He swallowed his distaste for the man. "Yeah, just tying up a few loose ends before I hit the sack."

"I hear you got the old lady. You turn anything up?"

Connell glanced at the man before dropping his gaze to the coffee machine and retrieving the Styrofoam cups. "What do you think? Old ladies, they imagine all kinds of crap. She couldn't even remember her own name."

Musgrave eyed him slyly. "So who's the extra coffee for?"

Connell straightened and stepped forward, causing the man to take a step back. He cocked his head and smiled. "I'm on a date, buddy, and you know what these girls are like. She just wouldn't sit and wait in the car. Now, I know I can rely on your discretion. Wouldn't want the whole squad to know what I do for fun when they've all gone home."

Musgrave licked his lips and Connell did well to hide his revulsion.

"'She a looker, Connell?"

"What do you think?"

"Lucky guy. Well, I'll leave you to it. Don't stay up too late, *Romeo*, you're supposed to be on early shift tomorrow – or should I say today."

"I've got some time off," replied Connell. "I called in few favors. I've been doing a lot of extra hours lately chasing down crazy old ladies."

Musgrave smiled. "Well, easy does it, Connell."

"Sure thing," replied Connell, *and fuck you too*, he added silently as he watched the man until he disappeared from view around the corner. He didn't know why he'd just lied but knew it was the right thing to do. Once Lizzie Jones got into the system she was out of his control, and he definitely needed to keep control.

With a coffee in each hand, he used his shoulder to push open the office door and took a calming breath. He didn't want to scare her more than she already was, and equally, didn't want to reveal the importance of her statement. The chance to put Mo Pater behind bars was so important to him he would gladly have sold his soul for such an opportunity. Now it had dropped in his lap he couldn't believe his luck.

He'd been gone minutes, if that, and yet the chair where he'd left her was empty. *Shit.* He slammed the coffees onto the desk and swung around, cursing as the hot liquid splashed the back of his hand. How had she gotten past him? She couldn't have. He'd been right outside in the hall. He scanned the room again and found her curled up asleep on the battered leather sofa behind the door. If she'd put her thumb in her mouth, she couldn't have looked more vulnerable, and he experienced a moment of gut-wrenching doubt. Once it was known that he had a witness, her position would become precarious, to say the least.

One arm dangled over the edge of the sofa. In her outstretched hand was the printed image of the albino, Mo Pater. The remainder of the prints were scattered on the floor. Squatting, balancing on the balls of his feet, he gathered them up into a neat pile and replaced them on the desk. He took out his notebook and the passport, slipped off his jacket and laid it gently over her. He took back Mo's picture. It was creased where she'd held it and he smoothed it out. He looked at her again, asleep on his couch. With a sigh, he resisted the urge to reach out and smooth a stray strand of hair back from her face. He had work to do. Her statement could wait.

Connell called his contact in Immigration, who just happened to be one of his very best buddies. Immigration was first on his list for a very good reason. He needed to know exactly who she was, a full background check, and he needed to know why she was here. She hadn't answered his questions when he'd asked, so he'd ask the people who ought to know, the people from Homeland Security whose job it was to know.

He woke Marty up, forgot it was the middle of the night and that other people actually went to bed. He answered on the seventh ring.

"I need a favor, Marty." He kept his voice low so as not to wake the girl but, more importantly, in the hope it reduced the chance of Marty's wife being disturbed. Charlene was a force to be reckoned with and Connell knew from long experience that it didn't pay to get on her wrong side.

Marty groaned. "Do you know what time it is, Tommy?"

"Sure I do, but it's an emergency."

"Why is it always an emergency with you, and why is it always after midnight? Haven't you got any normal cases that you can work on during the day?"

"You know how it goes, Marty, slim pickings at the moment."

"Okay," he grumbled. "I'm awake now, so make the most of it. What do you need?"

"I need a full background check on a girl who flew in from London Heathrow on the twenty-first. I need to know everything you've got and anything you can get from your buddies in England"

"Why, what's she done?"

"Nothing, but I need to know she's credible."

"As a witness?"

"Amongst other things."

"A witness to what?"

Connell laughed. "If I told you, I'd have to kill you, Marty."

"Better not tell me, then," answered Marty. "But I need some details. I'm good but I'm not that good."

"I've got her passport. I need you to do that thing you do with that cool machine of yours. Can I drop it off?"

"Tonight?"

"Sure." He glanced at his watch, twelve forty-five and counting. Rubbing wearily at gritty eyes, he added, "I can be there in an hour."

"I don't bring my cool machine home with me, Connell. It's kinda big and expensive. I don't think my boss would let me. Anyway, the passport will have gone through the checks when she came through arrivals. If there was anything suspicious about her or the passport, they'd have flagged up."

"Maybe not."

"How so?"

"She's not the type who would ordinarily arouse suspicion." Who was he kidding? She'd certainly aroused his.

"Good looking?"

He glanced at her sleeping peacefully under his coat. "Vulnerable."

Marty sighed. "Okay, drop it off and I'll see what I can do, but I won't have anything before midday."

"I owe you one, buddy."

"You owe me more than one, Tommy."

"Sure I do. Say, Marty, will Charlene be up and about when I get there?" He needed to psych himself up if she would. She was a big woman with a mouth on her and it was Charlene's baby sister that he'd just stood up.

"Well, that all depends on how quiet you are. She was worn out consoling her sister. You know how it goes. Some jerk stood her up … again."

"Ha ha, you know that girl was never going to be happy with me. I did her a favor by not turning up."

"Well, you keep working on that story, bud. By the time you get here you might sound convincing enough to get past Charlene. But I can tell you, she's been playing righteous mama bear all night and she's looking for blood."

"Mine?"

"You know, poor girl gets screwed over by an arrogant jerk …"

"I didn't get anywhere near screwing her. I stood her up, remember?"

"Okay, poor choice of words. Just be ready for a lecture. See ya, buddy."

A slow smile spread across his face as he clicked the phone down. It'd be fine - not even Charlene was immune to the Connell charm.

Okay, back to the list.

Fear …

Well, yeah, he'd be a little anxious himself if Mo Pater was after him, but he knew who Mo Pater was, knew what he was capable of, the business he was in. He'd been after him for long enough. So, yeah, if Mo Pater pointed a make-believe gun at him he might reasonably view that to be a threat. But Mrs. Lizzie Jones, from the middle of nowhere, didn't know him, so why would she have taken his gesture as anything more than a sick joke? More importantly, why would Mo Pater have considered some random face in the crowd to be of enough risk to him to warrant making a threat?

There was something here that he was missing. In fact, he suspected there was probably a lot that he was missing and he needed to find out what it was pretty quick.

A visit to Mr. Pater might shed some light on the matter but it was a tad too early to go showing his hand.

Alternatively, a visit to the driver Mr. Clifford Reay, who was presently languishing in hospital, might be just the ticket. But even Connell, who paid little heed to convention, wouldn't risk showing up at the hospital at one in the morning. Who knows when he might need the services of the emergency room himself and it certainly didn't pay to get on their blacklist.

He checked his list again.

Lying ...

Well she had been initially, but then she'd thought better of it and come clean. And his investigations would no doubt reveal how clean. He doubted she was whiter than white, but why lie at all? If she was as scared as she made out, why hadn't she left her contact information when she'd called in? Why risk not being found at all by the police if help was really what she was waiting for?

He finished the first coffee and started on the second, deciding he needed it more than her and reluctant to wake her before he had to. He had fifteen minutes tops before he needed to make tracks for Marty's, but that was enough time to pull up a list of the witnesses who all swore to Clifford Reay's version of events. He scanned the list. No names jumped out at him and the addresses were as he expected, all from the same neighborhood where he'd found Lizzie.

He ran a cross-check and only Clifford came up. Small-time really, petty theft, welfare fraud and default on child support. Connell grimaced. Now that just wasn't right. A man should care for his kids, and a man who didn't needed some pressure applied. He printed the lists and tucked the folded pages inside his notebook.

One item left on his list.

Mr. Jones.

He pondered over it for a moment, wasn't really sure why he'd thought it significant enough to note other than curiosity about why the guy had run off and left his cute little wife. There was a story there for sure, but whether it had anything to do with his investigation was anybody's guess.

One-fifteen and it was time to go. He'd much rather be going home to bed. But these days it seemed that what he wanted bore little resemblance to what he actually got. He took back his jacket and retrieved his notebook and the passport, which he slid inside an envelope before stowing in his pocket. She stirred, and he leaned over and shook her the rest of the way awake.

"We've got to go, honey."

She opened her eyes, looked straight at him and remembered with sudden clarity why she was there. He saw it, recognized the fear which was quickly guarded as her eyes focused on him. "Go where?" she asked.

"Some place else. I've got things to do, people to see. I can leave you here with the duty officer …" That's exactly what he should do, he knew that, but he didn't want to and wasn't going to. He didn't want to let her out of his sight.

"No," she replied hurriedly, struggling to her feet. She rubbed her eyes, trying for alert, settling for awake. "I only know one person in New York and that's you."

"Fine. But you do exactly as I say and stay close."

He ushered her out of the office and down the hall. "Do you need to use the bathroom before we leave?" She nodded vaguely as they stopped outside the ladies' room. "Go on then. I'll be right across the hall." He hesitated before opening the door to the men's room. "Now don't you believe everything you read on the walls in there, Mrs. Jones, those ladies have dirty minds." He grinned at her and she rewarded him with the sweetest smile.

* * *

Lizzie leaned against the cracked countertop and closed her eyes. She steadied her breathing and calmed

32

her nerves. Now what? Everything was going wrong and she hadn't a clue how to put it right. Could it be put right? She wasn't alone anymore, and after five days of living in fear, that had to be an improvement. Or was it? She had no way of knowing for sure.

The detective, Connell, didn't believe her, she knew that. She could tell by the way he'd looked at her, smiled at her, humored her. She wasn't a fool, although she guessed he suspected she was. But she couldn't tell him the truth. She was in too deep for that. He'd said she'd be safe with him and he certainly looked like he could take care of himself. He had an air of self-assurance and determination about him, and despite his undoubted charm, it gave him an edge. But could he look after her as well? And would he still want to when he worked it all out?

What alternative did she have? She was alone in a strange country, with a very real fear that she'd started something she couldn't stop. Yes, she was under police protection or, more likely, police suspicion, but it didn't diminish the fear that curled in her belly. It would take a lot more than a detective with a cocky smile to do that.

She opened her eyes slowly, caught her reflection in the mirror and shook her head sadly. It wasn't good, which was hardly surprising given the last few days. She reached into her bag, dashed some color on her lips and forced a weary smile.

You can do this, she whispered.

* * *

"What do you do for a living at home in England?" Connell asked as he forced his way out onto the freeway with much blaring of horns and raised fingers. This time of night, the roads were still busy but a whole lot quieter than during the day, and once he got across town, he'd be on empty freeway all the way to Marty's. He ran a hand across his stubble. He needed a shave and he needed to stay awake.

He glanced at her when she didn't answer, noticed she'd fixed herself up a little and smiled to himself. "Hey, come on, talk to me. You've got to keep me from falling asleep at the wheel."

"I'm a student," she yawned, covering her mouth politely with one small delicate hand.

A thirty year old student … okay, maybe she wasn't so bright. "Studying what?" He guessed English Lit, solely because she was a pretty sharp reader.

"I'm a student nurse … well, ex-student, actually. I've just finished my degree." She'd hesitated a little too long before answering but she'd surprised him with her reply and he liked surprises.

"Really?" He gave her a sideways glance. "You got a cute little uniform?"

She rolled her eyes and he caught the faintest of smiles. "Not with me."

"Shame." He kept his eyes on the road and added a smile of his own. She'd loosened up a little. He wanted to keep it that way.

"So, they were right what they wrote about you in the ladies' room," she continued a little awkwardly, as if she wasn't used to banter and was trying hard for his benefit. To entertain him or distract him? He couldn't decide. He reined himself in, unsure what her real story was and unwilling to push too hard in case she really was as innocent as she was making out. He hadn't been in the ladies' room, but had a good idea what might be written. Those ladies sure liked to vent.

"You like your job?" he asked.

"I do."

"So what are you doing here and why don't you want to go home?" He watched as the shutters came hurtling down. And actually, when he thought about it, she hadn't said she didn't want to go home, she'd said she couldn't.

Marty's house was in darkness when they arrived, apart from a low light in the kitchen. Connell took the girl's arm and guided her around the back, across a minefield of discarded toys. He cursed softly when his shin caught the training wheels of an upturned bike and she grabbed at him when she stumbled over an empty paddling pool. Her hand, flailing wildly in the darkness, inadvertently caught at his holster as she tried to stay upright. He lifted her clean off the ground with her wrist up her back and her waist in a vice grip before she could draw breath. She squeaked with fear and he released her immediately.

"Sorry. I'm a little touchy around the gun area. You okay?"

She nodded wordlessly and rubbed at her wrist.

Marty stood in the kitchen in his boxers, hair on end, feet bare. "Tommy, you didn't say you were bringing a guest along." He yanked a wrinkled T-shirt out of the laundry basket and tugged it on. "Charlene's on her way down. You want coffee? It's fresh."

"Sure, Marty, thanks." Connell pulled out the envelope. "And here's what I owe you. Thanks for the loan."

Marty looked from the plain brown passport-sized envelope to the girl, and nodded. "No sweat, bud, anytime. 'You going to introduce us?"

"This is Lizzie Jones. She's had a rough night."

"Pleased to meet you, Lizzie. I'm Marty, long suffering friend of Tommy-boy here, and this …," he turned as the kitchen door swung open and the largest lady ever swept in, a sleeping baby over one shoulder, "… is my wife Charlene, and youngest son, Milo."

Lizzie smiled tentatively and sidled close to Connell. She half-hid herself behind him and Connell wondered why. She had no reason to fear anyone here.

"Hello," she said simply. "I do hope we didn't wake you."

Charlene harrumphed loudly and zeroed in on Connell. "Why, you two-timing low-life son of a bitch, you hitting on this little girl while my poor Cynthia cries herself to sleep?"

She passed the baby to her husband and Connell backed off, hands in the air. "Now, Charlene, you've got it all wrong. This here's Mrs. Jones. She's a respectable English lady and I'm just doing my job."

She turned to Lizzie. "Honey, I don't care if you are a married lady, he don't know what respectable is. My advice, for what it's worth is, stay clear."

"Come on, Charlene," cajoled Connell, "you know the only reason I stood Cynthia up was because I knew I wasn't good enough for her, and she knows that too. Hell, she's going to end up with someone real respectable, like a doctor or a lawyer. You want that for her, don't you?" Charlene sniffed. "And so does she, so a few tears now will save her a lifetime full of them, am I right?"

"You're a bad man, Tommy," she chuckled and enveloped him in a bear hug that he returned as best he could but, at twice the weight, she had the upper hand. She released him before his chest was totally crushed and he smiled at Lizzie.

"Don't know about bad, Charlene, but I do know I could eat a horse. You got anything tempting on the stove?"

Charlene shook her head. "It's two in the morning, Connell. The only thing I got warming on my stove is Milo's bottle and I pumped that earlier, so I doubt that you'll want any of that."

"Coffee's fine, black, if you don't mind." He turned to Lizzie who shook her head. He could tell by the barely concealed grimace, that the last thing she wanted was coffee.

Marty handed the baby to Connell while he poured the coffee and Connell passed the baby to Lizzie while he helped him carry the mugs to the kitchen table. The baby stirred, aware that he was not being held in the ample bosom of his mother, and opened his mouth to complain. Lizzie cuddled him in, patted his back gently and the baby settled back to sleep.

"The girl's a natural," said Charlene as she took the bottle from the pan on the stove and tested the heat of the milk on the back of her hand. "You got kids, honey?"

"Um, no," replied Lizzie.

"No, of course you don't, you don't look old enough to have kids."

Lizzie smiled tiredly.

"How long have you been married, honey?" Charlene added and Connell paused momentarily with the coffee mugs.

"Too long," Lizzie replied. She smothered a yawn and looked for somewhere to sit and for someone to suggest that she could.

Putting down the mugs, Connell reached over, took back the baby, and passed him to his mother. He gestured to the sofa in the family room adjacent to the kitchen. "Go sit and rest awhile, Lizzie. I'm just catching up with Marty."

Lizzie nodded and padded through the dimly-lit room. Kicking off her shoes, she curled up in the corner of the couch and closed her eyes.

"Listen, guys," said Charlene, "I'm going to love you and leave you, and take this little one back to bed." She turned to Connell. "Now, you both stay as long as you want, and Marty, make sure they've got what they need.

They want fed, then you feed them, okay?" She glanced at the girl on the sofa and dropped her voice. "And you, Tommy, you just remember that you're meant to be a gentleman, you hear?"

Then she kissed her husband, clipped the back of Connell's head affectionately with her outstretched hand and left them to it.

Marty turned to Lizzie. "Milo doesn't sleep very often. When he sleeps, we all sleep, or we do without. And we've got another five kids upstairs in bed, so it gets kinda tiring."

She didn't answer; she was already asleep herself.

"I appreciate this, Marty," said Connell as he downed the hot liquid as quickly as he could. "Look, we'll be on our way and you can get to your bed."

"And where are you going next?" asked Marty as he glanced at the sleeping girl. Connell shrugged, he hadn't really thought. He knew where he was going when it got light - he was going to pay Clifford an early morning visit - but they were still some way off daybreak. "Stay here, if you like," Marty offered.

Connell was tempted but he shook his head, "Thanks, buddy, but you've got kids upstairs and I don't know what kind of shit I may be stirring up."

"Well, leave the girl here," suggested Marty.

"Nah, someone's a little too interested in her for me to leave her anywhere. I think we come as a package until I know what I'm dealing with."

"Are you going to tell me what's going on? Who's looking for her, Tommy?"

"I wish I knew what was going on. Hopefully with your help, I'll find out."

"Who's looking for her, Tommy?" repeated Marty. "Like you said, I've got six kids to worry about. I think I have a right to know."

Connell thought about bending the truth a little, but decided that he couldn't, not to his best friend. "Mo Pater," he murmured.

"Why?"

Connell shrugged wearily. The longest of days wasn't over yet. "She saw someone killed, and she's scared, but something doesn't fit and I'm hoping you can shed some light. I'll call you tomorrow. Just do the best you can with the passport."

Marty slipped the passport out of the envelope and flicked through it quickly. "I can tell you something for nothing."

"Yeah?"

"This isn't her passport." He held it open at the photo page.

Connell put down his coffee. "How come?"

"No way is she thirty years old. Come on, Tommy, you slipping or what? That girl is lucky if she's past twenty."

He grabbed back the passport and squinted at the photo. Marty was right. Of course he was right. On closer examination the photo wasn't even her. "So she's traveling on someone else's passport?"

"Looks like."

"So who the hell is she?"

"Fucked if I know, Tommy."

"But you're going to find out for me, aren't you?"

"I'm going to try, but it's not wise to drag her around with you while you're waiting. If she's a witness then you may compromise her testimony, and if she's a suspect, you'll compromise the case."

Connell knew he was right, Marty was always right about things that mattered, but there was no way that he was letting go of her. "Sure, Marty, I hear you, but I know what I'm doing."

"Do you, Tommy? Do you really? I know how much you want Mo Pater, but you need to be careful. If this girl has come in to the U.S. on a false passport, then Mo won't be the only one interested in her."

"The Feds?"

"Of course, and you don't want them muscling in."

Connell looked at her again through the darkened room. "She knows something, Marty, and Mo knows that she does."

"Then you need to find out what that is."

"Damn right I do."

"And how do you propose to do that?"

Three

The motel was a rundown, pay-by-the-hour affair and the man at reception didn't bat an eye when Connell half-carried the girl from the car to the room. He guessed the jerk had seen far worse and he certainly wasn't employed to moralize. Connell also knew as long as he paid up front and didn't trash the room, they could do pretty much what they liked. All he had in mind was sleep.

Connell woke Lizzie when the all night pizza arrived and she tried to eat some, but for reasons he couldn't begin to understand, pepperoni at three in the morning didn't hold the same allure for her as it did for him

"You going to eat that?" he asked as she pushed her share aside after a few bites.

Lizzie shook her head, glancing around at the shabby room, dismay evident in her expression. Admittedly it was worse than the one he'd found her in, but this one was safe and he knew where he'd rather be.

"I'm sorry. I'm tired," she sighed. "I'm going to get ready for bed."

"You've got to try and eat more than that," he pressed but he was wasting his time. She was beat. Any energy she might have possessed had drained right out of her. Too little sleep and too much stress, he recognized the look. Picking up her bag, she disappeared into the bathroom and he returned his attention to the pizza. He washed it down with a couple of beers and listened to the sound of running water.

Slumped in the only easy chair, his eyes drifted shut despite his best efforts to the contrary, and when the bathroom door opened, bathing the room in harsh yellow light, he was pulled awake with a start. She padded across the room in her pajamas and slid beneath the covers on the king-size bed.

Pajamas, plaid pajamas - was she for real? He'd worn plaid pajamas when he was five.

He dragged himself up and took his turn in the bathroom before switching off the light and returning to his chair. He placed his gun carefully on the arm next to him and closed his eyes again. He'd had worse all-nighters; at least there was a chair.

"Why are we here?" she asked, a small voice in the darkness, and he dragged his eyes open again.

"You mean in a spiritual, meaning of life way?"

"No."

"I thought you were tired?"

"I am, but I'm worried that something will bite me while I'm sleeping."

Connell smiled. "You got money for a five-star hotel?"

"No."

"Neither do I and this place is convenient. I'm too wrecked to be driving around." He settled down and shut his eyes again. "You'll be fine. They spray the rooms every week."

"How do you know? Do you come here often?" He couldn't see her smile, but he heard it in her voice.

"Only in the line of duty."

"Will we be safe here?" she asked.

"Sure we will. Go to sleep."

* * *

The trouble with pulling all-nighters was that, come the next morning, you ended up looking and feeling like shit. He'd slept in his clothes and felt as bad as his wrinkled suit. She, on the other hand, looked surprisingly bright-eyed and bushy-tailed, which didn't seem fair and did nothing to improve his mood.

He needed breakfast, protein and carbs and plenty of it, and nothing was going to get in the way of that, including Mo Pater. He drove to the nearest diner and guided her to a window seat where he had a good view of the parking lot and road. Connell didn't expect trouble but he liked to be prepared, just in case. Until he knew what was going on he had to be prepared for anything.

"Hungry?" Lizzie remarked as the waitress delivered an overflowing plateful of cholesterol to their table and placed it in front of Connell.

"Think of it as fuel," he said with a smile, "and it wouldn't do you any harm to eat a little more." He gestured to her toast. "That's not going to keep you going through a busy morning."

"Are we going to have a busy morning?" she asked as she studied him discreetly from behind her toast.

He shot her a glance, realized he was being given the once over and covered his amusement by taking a mouthful of bacon and eggs. "Sure we are," he answered when he'd finished chewing. "You're going to tell me why you came to New York and I'm going to decide whether to believe you."

"I thought this was about the hit and run, about what I saw."

"It is." He suppressed the smile, but the twinkle in his eyes betrayed his continuing amusement. "But I'm a thorough guy. I like to dot all the I's and cross all the T's, and at the moment, I'm just not getting a clear picture."

"I've told you everything I know."

"No, you haven't." He took another mouthful and shrugged. "But that's cool, I'm a detective - I'll just do some detecting. But, you know, while I'm wasting time trying to guess what's going on, our good friend Mr. Pater might just be getting the jump on us."

She nibbled half-heartedly at the corner of her toast, raised her head and gave him a blank look. "Who's Mr. Pater?"

"Your albino driver - Mo Pater."

"So you know him?" she asked, absently brushing toast crumbs from where they'd scattered across her chest.

Connell dragged his eyes away. "You could say that. We've met on more than one occasion, usually with a loaded gun between us. We have unresolved–issues."

"Then why don't you arrest him?"

Connell took a slug of coffee. "It's not as simple as that."

"If you can't arrest him, how can you keep me safe?" Her voice rose with alarm. "Maybe I should just go home after all. I don't want to get mixed up with criminals. I'll withdraw my statement and you can believe what your other witnesses told you, that it was an accident."

She made to rise from the seat, and he reached out and stilled her with a hand on her arm. He had no idea who she was or the extent of her involvement. He couldn't allow her to walk away.

She looked at his hand, firm against her bare skin and glanced back at him questioningly until he removed his hand with a shrug.

"You're already mixed up," he answered. "And you can't go home. I've got your passport, remember? And anyway, you haven't made a statement yet. That's what's going to keep us busy this morning." He paused for a slow smile "But first things first, are you sure you haven't got your nurse's uniform with you?"

Lizzie frowned. "It's not something I carry around with me."

"Pity, because we're going visiting, and I may need you to check someone's pulse."

* * *

Clifford Reay had a private room and lots of flowers which Connell found weird and Lizzie found fascinating. She gently plucked at the exotic blooms, sniffing their various scents. Connell dragged his eyes away as she delicately brushed a dusting of pollen from the tip of her nose. He had an urge to reach out and catch the bit she'd missed, but he picked up Clifford's chart instead. The bed was empty. The severely incapacitated patient had miraculously risen from it and snuck out for a sly cigarette. Connell passed the chart to Lizzie.

"So, what does Nurse Jones make of that? Is he for real?"

Lizzie glanced at the notations and stats, and gave another shrug. "His vitals are normal. They suspect a whiplash injury which is quite likely … if he'd actually been driving." She handed back the chart. "But he doesn't need to be here. As I already told you, he wasn't the driver."

Connell smiled at the challenge in her eyes. He was convinced there was another side to sweet little Lizzie, a side she was currently keeping under wraps. If he'd had a little more time and a few less distractions, he'd have enjoyed taking his time with the unwrapping. As it was, someone wasn't telling the truth. As yet he wasn't quite sure who.

"Okay, I want you to go wait outside, no sense in letting him see you. And, Lizzie…"

"Yes?"

"Don't wander off."

45

"Clifford, you really need to wise up here," said Connell when the man eventually returned, and after he'd been entertained by Clifford's version of events. "We have several witnesses who place Mo Pater at the scene, in the car, behind the wheel, and we're looking at first degree murder. You need to consider whether what they're paying you is enough to take that kind of rap."

Clifford squirmed, held his whiplashed neck pathetically with one hand, and denied everything. "Detective Connell, would I lie to you? Like I said, I was driving and that poor guy, well he just jumped out in front of me, like he had a death wish. No way could I avoid him."

"He was hit twice."

"Well, you know that's the weird thing, he certainly was a bouncy guy. One hit wasn't enough for him, he just threw himself head first under my wheels." He leaned forward and Connell recognized amusement in his eyes. "Have you ever heard someone's skull go pop? I can tell you that is not a sound I'll forget in a hurry. Reckon I've got that post-traumatic stress disorder now."

Post-traumatic stress! He'd give him stress. "I know you weren't driving and I know Mo's involved in this."

Clifford smiled. "Sorry, detective, but you're mistaken. Ask your forensic guys. My prints were all over the wheel and the bruising on my neck proves I was in the driver's seat. I always wear my seat belt, safety first and all that."

Connell shook his head. "You're a fool, Clifford. You're playing with the big boys, and believe me they'll stamp on you good and hard."

It seemed that Clifford was hell bent on taking the heat and it sounded like the evidence would back him up. Connell almost believed him, but if Clifford was telling the truth, then Mrs. Jones wasn't. His patience was fast running out. On shaky ground already by not reporting her as a witness, he'd lied to Musgrave and put Marty in a difficult position. He needed the truth, and one way or another, he'd get it. Maybe it was time for some Connell charm.

He pulled a few stems from one of Clifford's ample floral displays as he left, specifically choosing the blooms that she'd found so alluring earlier. He avoided the pollen, shook off the excess water and handed them to Lizzie as he placed his arm loosely around her shoulders and walked her down the corridor away from Clifford's room.

"What are you doing?"

He felt her stiffen and removed his arm and stepped away. Okay, so much for charm. Maybe he wasn't her type. He wondered why. Felt a little insulted. Also felt there was more to it, to her, than that. Another alarm bell began to peal ominously in his head and he silenced it with frustration.

"Trying to blend in," he replied, gesturing to the other visitors milling around the corridor. An assorted group, none of whom looked like they'd slept in their clothes. "If anyone in this crowd is here to see our man Clifford, I'd rather they thought we were a couple who'd been shacked up all night having a little fun, than a cop and a witness to murder." He tried another smile. If she'd been anyone else, he would have cut through the nonsense and got to the truth by now. But there was just something about her.

"So you do believe me."

"Believe you about what?"

"The hit and run."

"A guy is dead, I believe that."

She sidled back up to him, flicking quick anxious glances at the others in the corridor. Any challenge quickly subdued. Her face was a picture of apprehension. She was easily scared and that intrigued him. Secrets and fear; she seemed to balance precariously between the two and he wondered how long it would take for her to tip in the right direction.

"Do you think one of those people might be looking for me?" she asked.

He shook his head. In all honesty he doubted it, but it didn't hurt to keep her on her toes. "Mo can't know you're with me, not yet anyway." Although he knew it wouldn't take long, just as long as it took Clifford to make a phone call. Mo wasn't stupid. He knew there was only one real witness and he knew what she looked like. He gave her a reassuring smile and replaced his arm.

Time for Plan B.

"Come on, Nurse Jones, one more stop, then we're out of here."

"Where are we going?" She quickened her step as he propelled her along, the flowers clutched against her breast, pollen staining her clothes.

"The morgue."

He wasn't sure what he'd expected her reaction to be. So far she'd pretty much surprised him on most things, but when she dug in her heels and refused to budge, he was forced to stop or cause a scene in the middle of the corridor.

"W…Why?" she stammered.

He tightened his arm around her, wasn't going to let her go, no matter how uncomfortable he made her feel.

"To see if you can identify our man "

Her skin paled. "He has no face, there's no point."

She was right, the guy had been well and truly smashed, but he hoped that maybe the shock of seeing him would help to encourage the truth out of her.

"The *point* is that it may jar your memory."

"I don't want to," she whispered, her eyes brimming with sudden tears. "You can't make me … can you?"

He couldn't, but he was sorely tempted. He was guessing that one more little push and those tears would flow, along with the truth. "Come on, honey, you can't be squeamish. You're a nurse. Just take one look."

She shook her head. "No, I'm sorry, truly I am. I want to help you but I don't want to look at him." She began to shake and people began to notice them. Connell gave an apologetic smile to an orderly who had stopped beside them. *Women*, it said, and the man smiled back.

Some people were disturbed by the sight of a dead body, he understood that, but she was a nurse and should be well used to them. He didn't understand her reaction, didn't understand what was going on. But he was meant to be one of the good guys and Charlene had told him to be a gentleman. "Okay, sweetheart, you win. Let's go."

He backed her gently against the wall next to the elevator and with one palm braced against the wall, he bent his head to hers and spoke directly against her ear. "We're trying to blend in, remember."

He was counting back from ten when his phone rang, and checking the display, he saw it was Marty. He stepped away from Lizzie with a measure of confused relief. He didn't usually have to try this hard. Most women were more than happy to have him cozy on up to them.

"Hi, bud, you got something for me?"

"You alone?" asked Marty.

"Nope."

"Then just listen. I've got a little story for you."

"I'm all ears." The elevator arrived, the doors pinged open, and he stayed Lizzie with a hand on her arm and let the empty car go by.

"Okay, Mrs. Elizabeth Jones, 'Beth' to her friends, is a thirty-year-old teacher working at a school in Northern England. Currently on maternity leave, and according to my sources, the happy event is due in four weeks' time.

The person currently traveling on Mrs. Jones' passport is obviously not the aforementioned, unless she's hiding an eight month bump under her T-shirt."

Connell glanced at Lizzie, he knew she wasn't. He'd had his hands around that little waist. He wondered where this was leading.

"I got a look at the video footage from arrivals. It made for interesting viewing. You need to see it. Your girl charmed her way through customs, had them eating out of her hands by the look of it. She sure has a sweet smile. Stopped off at the diner and made one phone call. Airport cab picked her up. The driver, a Mr. Delmar Bleekwood, dropped her off one block away from the accident. She told him she was meeting someone."

"Right." Connell narrowed his eyes.

"Mrs. Elizabeth Jones, the mommy-to-be, is married to Mr. Carl Jones, an American citizen, and again, according to sources, they are estranged. Are you getting this, Tommy?"

"Sure I am."

"So your little cutie is using the mommy-to-be's passport. Maybe she lifted it. I'll leave you to find out why."

"I'll get right on it."

"That's not all."

"Go on."

"The passport, I put it through my super cool machine, and guess what? It's a phony - and it's one of Gilly Tasker's." Connell stared at the phone. Gilly Tasker was an associate of Mo Pater. "Tommy, are you still there?"

"Yeah, sure. Just wasn't expecting that."

"No? Well, when things look like a coincidence, they're usually not. One last thing, Tommy."

"Yeah?"

"You might want to start by tracking down Mr. Jones. Apparently he's another one who's been linked with our man Mo."

"You're kidding me."

"Would I kid?"

"Buddy, I owe you one."

"*Another* one, Tommy, and your list of IOUs is growing. Listen, you take care. You've got quite a tale to unravel and I'm guessing you're maybe only a day ahead of the Feds."

Connell pocketed the phone and considered his position. If he had any sense he would hand her over and walk away, but this was becoming less about the bust and more about his need to discover the truth. He needed to hear her side of the story. He glanced at her, caught her watching him expectantly, and made up his mind. There was no way he was going to let Mo Pater get away with murder again.

"Okay, Lizzie, time we hit the road. I think our boy Clifford is probably on the phone to his boss as we speak."

She pulled herself away from the wall and took a hesitant step toward him. "Where are we going now?"

"My place. I need a change of clothes."

Four

Connell's loft apartment was in a block of converted warehouses in what he'd reliably been told was an up-and-coming part of town. A change in zoning and government funding meant it hadn't quite reached its full potential. The stock market crash hadn't helped either and the contractors had gone belly-up. The project ground to a halt with only three completed apartments within an essentially derelict building. The other two had failed to sell. Perhaps he was the only one with the vision to have made the purchase? Connell liked to think of it as an investment in that when he was dead, it might just raise enough to cover his funeral.

He guided Lizzie through the entryway from what those with a good imagination might call the underground parking lot. The fact he'd parked his car there being the only clue to its designated purpose. The cavernous space was littered with the remnants of the unfinished conversion project; bags of cement long since hardened within the sack, twisted metalwork ripped from the body of the building and left to rust, and the ever-present dripping of some long-forgotten leaking pipe. He ignored the odor of damp and neglect and ushered Lizzie into the service elevator that reluctantly wheezed and clanked its way up to the top floor.

Lizzie followed him. Stepping with care from the rickety elevator, she picked her way around the clutter that lay piled in the hallway outside his front door. Though she didn't say a word, Connell could tell by the way she wrinkled her nose she was wondering whether this might actually be a step down from the motel. It lacked the necessary curb appeal to entice a favorable response from anyone. With no working light, the hall was desolate and their footsteps echoed unnervingly. He imagined how scary it would appear to the uninitiated. *Hell*, even he looked over his shoulder after dark and he knew there was nothing to fear.

The interior more than made up for the less than stunning exterior, and when he unlocked the door and ushered her in, he knew by her intake of breath that she was surprised.

The architect responsible for this large airy space had known his stuff. He'd recognized the beauty of the aged industrial bricks and the distressed oak floors. He'd acknowledged the strength and visual impact of the steel girders and massive oak rafters.

And he'd left well enough alone.

Connell agreed with his vision. Sometimes space was best left as just that. He'd continued the theme with minimal furniture, less by good design and more by lack of funds than anything else. The vast floor-to-ceiling windows looked out over the industrial landscape and flooded the internal space with light, but now, the winter sky was turning grey and the subsequent light was subdued.

Connell followed her in and closed the heavy door behind them, drawing home a variety of industrial locks. Throwing her bag onto the scuffed leather sofa, he slipped off his jacket and draped it over the back of a chair. Her eyes were drawn hypnotically to his gun holstered beneath his left arm. He felt her attention, was aware of her anxiety. He ignored it. It didn't hurt for her to have a reminder of the position she was in.

"Make yourself at home," he said. "I need to shower and change. I won't be long." He crossed to the kitchen and wound a metal handle that cranked open a skylight set in the ceiling. A silver tabby cat slid through the gap and dropped onto his shoulder. "This is Cat. There's food under the sink. Would you feed him?"

Lizzie nodded and took the cat from him as he left the room. The cat purred softly and rubbed its head against her leg as she set about feeding him.

"Good cat," she said softly and left him to eat.

* * *

Seven days before Lizzie had been in England leading a normal life, getting up late for work and staying out late with her friends. She didn't even know any policemen, let alone those who brought guns home with them, and would never have gone back to a man's apartment on a one day acquaintance. But these weren't normal circumstances and she understood quite clearly that this was the man who was going to keep her alive.

She stood with the cat snaking around her feet and surveyed Connell's home with curiosity. There were pictures stuck on the fridge, photos of Connell and his friends - men and girls having fun, the usual things. She had photos just like them - nights out, days at the beach. They humanized him. Along with the photos stuck to the fridge with Disney magnets, were drawings. Crudely fashioned crayon pictures - children's pictures, colorful and fun.

He obviously had a life outside of his job and stuff going on outside of her problem. She was intruding and knew she shouldn't. She wouldn't like it if someone poked around in her life, but she was intrigued and curious nonetheless. For her own peace of mind she needed to know that she'd hitched up to the right person.

She wandered back into the living room area and trailed her fingers gently across his things, inhaling the scent of his home, a mixture of leather and wood polish, and a faint whiff of spices. Somehow, she couldn't imagine him keeping house, but someone kept the place clean and tidy.

There were more pictures, framed in various styles - family photos, an older couple probably his parents standing with two smiling little boys; a childhood photo of Connell and possibly a brother taken at the beach on a windswept day. The children were hanging onto kites while the parents hung onto the kids. Then older, and Connell became more recognizable, the twinkle in the eye and the cheeky grin. The next, showed Connell with a little boy who shared his cheeky smile, a son maybe, with blonde hair and freckles. She hadn't even considered that he might have a family of his own, a family who might wonder where he'd spent the previous night.

Her gaze fell on the phone lying next to the photos and she turned to check that the door he'd gone through was still closed. She needed to make a call, wasn't sure whether she dared, but this was her first real chance. Beth would be climbing the walls with worry.

She could hear the sound of the shower and was sure she'd have time if she hurried. She hesitantly picked up the phone, listened for the tone and dialed.

"Hi, Beth, it's me ..." Lizzie kept her voice low and turned her back to the rest of the room.

"Oh my God, Lizzie, I've been so worried. Why haven't you been in touch?"

It was so good to hear her voice. Lizzie ignored the obvious concern in it and concentrated solely on the familiar tone. She hadn't realized how alone she'd been. She longed for home, to be held by someone who cared for her. She struggled to swallow the lump that constricted her throat and continued, "Just listen. I haven't much time …."

"Are you okay? Has something happened? Did you meet him?" Beth's concern reached down the line. Lizzie imagined how she'd be twisting the wire with worry, just as she was twisting her hair. She felt a sob struggling to be let loose. With considerable effort she subdued it.

"Yes, I'm okay, and you don't have to worry about anything anymore. It's a little complicated ... not what we expected ... but it's all sorted. He'll never hurt you again…. " She felt her own relief as she said it but couldn't rid herself of the growing anxiety that gnawed in her belly. She was in beyond her depth, caught up in something she had no real understanding of.

"What do you mean complicated? I should never have let you do this, Lizzie. He always manages to come back. He hasn't hurt you, has he?"

"No. Of course not. He didn't get the chance …." He would never get the chance to hurt her again. She wanted to say it out loud, more for her own personal belief than anything else, but doubt niggled alongside the anxiety and she had no wish to count too soon. She had the unsettling feeling that there might yet be chickens waiting to hatch.

"What do you mean?"

"I can't explain over the phone, Beth. Just trust me." How could she explain about the hit and run, and the Albino, and Connell? She didn't understand it herself - it was a jumble in her head - and her part in it, the biggest mystery of all.

"When are you coming home, Lizzie? I've haven't long to go now and I need you here."

Lizzie gripped the phone tightly and worried at her hair with her other hand. She had no real answer to give. "I don't know, Beth. I've got a few little things to sort out …"

She had to get the passport back for a start. She glanced at his jacket hung on the back of a chair. Maybe he wouldn't notice if she just took it back, or maybe he would. He was a detective, after all.

"Are you in trouble, Lizzie? Look, this is entirely my fault. If you're in trouble, let me help you."

She was in trouble, big trouble, she knew that. She had been ever since she'd stood on the curb waiting to cross that busy road. She closed her eyes and remembered it exactly.

He'd been in a hurry, looked over his shoulder, more interested in what was behind than what was on the road. Then he'd seen her and realized she was not the person he'd expected to see. There was a moment when neither knew who was going to make the first move and cross the road. So they'd both stepped out at the same time....

"I'm fine, Beth, don't worry about me. I've met someone who's helping me. I'll be okay." She glanced over her shoulder. The door was still closed.

"Who have you met, Lizzie? You can't trust people you don't know. How many times have I told you that?"

She hoped she could trust him, he was a policeman after all, but she couldn't go into that now. She didn't have time. The noise of the shower had stopped. "I've got to go … I'll call you."

Gently replacing the phone with a shaking hand, she took a steadying breath, tried to think of what to do, what to say that would make all of this go away.

* * *

"I'm going to make a sandwich and you're going to eat it, okay?" said Connell as he came up suddenly behind Lizzie. She turned with a start and he cocked his head and studied her, recognizing the look of someone who'd just been caught with their hand in the cookie jar.

He'd changed out of his suit into jeans and a T-shirt, and his hair was damp from the shower. He'd decided to cut her some slack, but now that he'd caught the guilty flush on her cheeks, he wasn't so sure.

"Is this your little boy?" Lizzie asked, gesturing vaguely to the photo.

Connell could tell she wasn't sure how long he'd been there and how much, if anything, he'd heard. He could almost hear the rapid pounding of her heart and took a measure of satisfaction in her obvious discomfort.

All she had to do was tell the truth. Was it that difficult?

"Yeah, that's my little guy," he replied as he picked up the photo.

"He looks like you. What's his name?"

He watched as she regained control, her breathing gradually slowing to normal. She thought she'd gotten away with it. "Joe," he answered with a smile.

"Does he live here with you?"

Connell traced the outline of the little boy gently with his finger against the glass and took his time replying. "No, he used to, but would you want to live here if you were four years old? No place to play and Daddy's never home." He shrugged. "He lives with my mom and dad upstate."

She followed him to the kitchen and hoisted herself up on the counter. "He's cute. Do you see much of him?"

She was trying to distract him, he realized, but he was happy to talk about his son, and if it helped to put her at ease, all the better. "Most weekends if I'm not working." He pulled out some bread and leaned into the fridge for some ham.

"I'm keeping you from him. I'm sorry."

He looked up and smiled. If it hadn't been for Lizzie and the hit and run, it would have been something else that kept him from his son. His life in general was going down the drain. "No sweat. You want milk?" He pulled out a carton and reached down two glasses. "If I have any more coffee, I'm going to have a coronary and it's too early for anything stronger."

They both ate in silence and considered each other.

"We need to talk."

"We do?"

Connell helped her down from the counter and gestured to the sofa. "Yup, and this time I don't want any fairy tales. Okay?"

"But I've told you everything I know–"

"You said that already, and sorry, honey, but I don't believe you. So here's what we're going to do. I'm going to ask you some questions and you're going to tell me the truth." He sat down opposite her, elbows resting loosely on his knees. "And if you don't tell me the truth, I'm going to hand you over to the Feds and they can get the truth out of you, okay?"

"Oh…," she stammered.

He gestured to the phone. "Who were you calling?"

"Um -"

He raised his hand to stop her and dropped it with a start when she flinched. He was intrigued and slightly offended that she thought he might strike her. "Stop right there, honey," he continued, more gently. "You see, when you start a sentence with 'Um' I get to thinking that you're trying to make up another story."

She faltered, as though she'd revealed something that she hadn't intended. Connell found her discomfort both interesting and rather sad. It wasn't his intention to frighten her or back her into a corner, but he needed to know what was going on.

"Hey, there's no reason for you to be scared of me. All I want is the truth."

She nodded slowly. "I was calling my sister, Beth. Well, she's my step-sister actually … two real sisters with the same name would be rather odd." She gave a weak smile, lowered her lashes and avoided his gaze.

"My mum married Beth's dad when I was a baby, so I became Lizzie and she became Beth."

Connell nodded, tried to imagine this weird little family with two girls called Elizabeth. "Why were you travelling on your sister's passport?"

"How did you know?" she asked.

"Come on Lizzie, your sister's what, ten years older than you?"

"Eight, she's eight years older, but she looks much younger than her age and I didn't have my own passport, and he sent that one along with the tickets, and there wasn't time for me to do anything about it."

It came out in a rush like a child forced to admit some misdemeanor. She twisted her hair nervously and shot a glance at the door. He remained sat where he was. No need to bar the exit here; no way could she get past the many deadlocks. The place was a fortress.

"Am I in trouble?" she asked.

"Sure you are. You said he sent it. Who's he?"

"What kind of trouble?"

"That depends on how cooperative you are. Who sent it?"

"Carl. Beth's husband."

Connell nodded encouragingly. Finally they were getting somewhere. "Why? Why did he send her a passport? Why didn't she just get her own?"

Lizzie shrugged and Connell restrained himself from reaching over and holding her shoulders still. What was it about that simple gesture?

"Okay, so why was Carl here in the US while Beth was in England? Hardly your average happy family, is it?"

"It's a long story."

"We've got all day."

Lizzie looked at him, looked past him at the photo of his little boy. Connell watched as she wavered. He couldn't force her to trust him, but really, she had no choice.

"Beth and Carl have been apart for some time. He was a difficult man. She was trying to get on with her life."

"You and your sister are close?" It was obvious they were. He'd heard her on the phone and he knew all about sibling loyalty. He was close to his brother too, though they'd fought like dogs when they were younger and fought even harder over girls when they'd gotten older. He'd do anything for Will, particularly if he were in trouble. He was interested to know how far Lizzie was prepared to go for her sister.

Lizzie responded with that sweet dimpled smile that told him without a doubt that she'd decided to tell the truth. "Very close. She practically brought me up when our dad died. I was ten and she was eighteen. I would have gone into care if it hadn't been for Beth."

Okay, so she'd do practically anything. "So how was Carl difficult?" He watched her face tighten. The pulling of her hair was a dead giveaway and he wanted to tell her to stop, that he was on her side.

"He had a temper."

Most people did, but most people learned how to control it. That's what the terrible twos were all about and he'd had his fill of them. Joe might look angelic, but he was a demon when he didn't get his own way. "Did he hurt your sister?"

"Sometimes," she said, though the look in her eyes belied the truth.

"Did he hurt you?" She shook her head a little too vehemently. "Why did he send the passport?"

"He wanted Beth to meet him here in New York. He asked her to bring him some stuff that he'd left at the house. He said if she came, he'd give her a divorce. He

61

just wanted to see her one last time. She desperately wanted the divorce but she couldn't come."

"Why not?"

"She's pregnant. Carl didn't know about the baby. She didn't want him to know." She glanced again at the picture of Connell with his son. "I know that sounds bad, but she's met someone else, a really nice man and she deserves to be happy. She was frightened that if he knew she was trying to make a new life for herself, he might harm the baby, or at least refuse to give her the divorce– who knows? She couldn't come but I could. So I did."

"Is it Carl's baby?"

Lizzie shrugged. "She didn't say and I didn't ask."

"Then why come at all? Why not ignore him? What's he going to do, come and get her?"

Lizzie blinked. "You don't know him."

No, he didn't, but he was going to find out. "Okay, so you took the passport he sent and you came here to meet him in place of your sister?"

"Yes."

"And what did you hope to achieve? After all, he was expecting his wife."

"I thought if I met him, I could persuade him to give her the divorce anyway and leave us all alone."

"And did you?"

"Did I what?"

"Meet him."

Lizzie gave him a puzzled looked, as if he'd missed some crucial point, and he wondered if he had because none if it made any sense to him. If the guy was such an asshole, why come halfway around the world to put yourself within his reach?

"Well, no, at least I almost met him … but your friend the albino beat me to him."

"The albino?"

"The hit and run."

"Carl Jones was the guy who got hit?"

"Yes."

Oh shit! This had suddenly got very complicated and just a little weird. "Whoa, are you telling me that you got sent a passport by a man who asked you to bring something into the country, and then, before you could hand it over, he got his face run over by an albino mobster?"

His voice was raised. He couldn't help it. Lizzie bit at her bottom lip and held her hands so tightly together, her knuckles whitened. He'd scared her and he needed to un-scare her or he wouldn't get the rest of the story, and it may as well be a story because no one else would believe it.

"Yes, I suppose so," she whispered. Her eyes began to fill with tears and her hand went straight to her hair.

He lowered his voice, calmed his own breathing and bit down on the sliver of excitement that had begun to thread its way through him. He might just be on the verge of something very big and he needed to play this very carefully. Leaning forward, he reached out and squeezed her knee gently. "Hey, it's okay. It doesn't matter what happened. You're safe here. Now what did he ask you to bring him?"

"Just a package. Something he'd left at Beth's."

"A package?" He couldn't believe that she could be so naïve. "What was in it?" he asked.

She shrugged again delicately and he just couldn't stop himself. "Quit doing that!"

"Doing what?"

"The business with the shoulders. Sit still, will you?"

She looked at him for a moment and he looked straight back at her and neither knew exactly why.

"Sorry," she said simply. "I don't know what was in the package. I didn't open it."

He shook his head and looked away, anywhere but at her. She was a liability. "You brought a package through customs and you didn't check what was in it? What if you'd been stopped, searched … detained? You've heard of 9-11, surely."

"Carl said customs was sorted, that Beth wouldn't be stopped. I believed him. He's a fixer of things, that's what he does."

Customs was fixed! No wonder she'd been able to waltz through arrivals with a suspect package and a counterfeit passport. What kind of guy could fix customs? Who the fuck was he anyway?

"Do you still have it?"

"What?"

"The package!" His head was beginning to ache.

"It's in my bag." She reached across and retrieved her bag from the end of the sofa, pulled out her cosmetics case, the books, some rather interesting underwear that she hastily replaced, and a plastic carrier bag. She threw the latter to him, "Catch," and he caught it with one hand.

"Are you telling me that you didn't even look in here once?" The bag was folded over on itself, about the size and weight of a camera. He unwrapped it gingerly. It could be a handful of plastic explosives for all he knew.

"Well I did have a peek afterwards," she admitted. "It's nothing exciting, just a portable CD player. I thought maybe it contained his favorite CD."

"Oh yeah, sure, like he would go to the trouble of paying off customs to allow some hokey CD into the country. He doesn't sound like the sentimental type to me." He opened the CD player and took out the disc. "It's a data disc," he said with sudden interest, crossing to the desk and switching on his computer. "What did Carl do for a living?" he asked as he waited for the computer to boot up.

She followed him across the room and stood by his shoulder as he sat at the desk. She almost placed her hand on his shoulder. He felt her nearness, her hesitation, and ignored them both.

"He was some kind of lawyer or accountant," she replied, stuffing her hands in her pockets. "I'm not really sure, to be honest. I know he was a bit of a whiz with numbers. I was only twelve or thirteen when he and Beth first met, and by the time I was eighteen and off to nursing college, they were already apart for much of the time."

"So where did the baby come from?" he asked. She started to shrug and stopped herself, and he suddenly wished she hadn't.

"Beth kept throwing him out, but he wouldn't be thrown. He'd come back to the U.S. on business, and then, months later, he'd turn up at the house like nothing had happened. He turned up eight months ago."

"And charmed his way in?"

"No, not charmed." She turned away. "Beth was already in a relationship with someone else. She hadn't expected to see him again after the last time. She told him she wanted a divorce. He wasn't happy. He thought he would teach her a lesson."

Nice guy.

The disc would not be read. "It's corrupted." Connell swore under his breath. Of course it wouldn't be that easy. "Did you put your bag through the X-ray machine?" He wasn't quite sure what that would have done, but knew it fucked with camera film.

"Yes, I had to."

Connell ejected the disc and studied it. He pulled open the disc player and checked whether there was anything inside that he'd missed. Carl would know the bag had to go through X-ray. Whatever it was he was so desperate to have, it wasn't in the CD player.

"Was there anything else in the package apart from this?"

"No, just the CD player."

"Well, it seems unlikely he'd go to all this trouble to have it go belly-up at the airport."

"Beth and I thought it had nothing to do with the package; that it was all about getting Beth to go to him. He was like that. He liked playing mind games."

Connell looked up. "You didn't like him much, huh?"

"No."

"Were you scared of him?" She didn't answer, so he took that as a yes. "Regardless of what you and your sister might think, this has to be more than just him wanting to bully his wife. Why else would Mo Pater have finished him off?"

Lizzie shrugged. "I don't know. That's all he asked for. He sent the passport, he asked for the package, I came to deliver it and saw him get killed, and there isn't anything else."

Connell stretched and rubbed his eyes. He was missing something obvious. Mo Pater thought something was going down, and Mo Pater had a nose for these things. Mo was sufficiently troubled by whatever he suspected that he'd wiped the face off poor old Carl. Carl might have deserved everything he'd gotten–in fact, if the look on Lizzie's face was anything to go by, he definitely deserved it–but it still didn't explain what was going on.

"The passport was a phony," said Connell, thinking aloud. "Why would he send a counterfeit document when your sister could simply have gotten herself a genuine one from the British Passport Office?"

"Am I in trouble for using a counterfeit passport?" asked Lizzie.

"Sure you are," he answered distractedly. He was beginning to lose track of the number of things she was in trouble for. In truth, he was more interested in the things that he didn't yet know, such as what the hell was going on between Mo Pater and the dearly departed Mr. Jones.

"How much trouble?" she asked as she cast an eye toward the open skylight.

He looked at her, followed her gaze and smiled. "Tons. You want a beer?"

She shook her head. "I thought it was too early for beer."

He looked at his watch, "That was then. Now the time's just about right."

He needed to know more about Carl Jones. Carl had wanted something that he'd left in England, and he wanted it badly enough to have it brought to him. Why couldn't he just go get it himself? According to Lizzie, he was back and forth between England and the US with some regularity, so why not now? And if there was a reason why he couldn't travel, why not simply have it mailed to him?

Lizzie reckoned this was all about the hold that Carl had over Beth, but Connell didn't buy that, unless the man was some kind of psycho, and reading between the lines he couldn't rule that out. And what was the story with the passport? Carl had gotten a passport from probably the best forger there was. That would've cost something, but why go to that expense and trouble when Beth could've gotten her own passport. He needed to get the passport back from Marty before the Feds started sniffing around, and he needed to have a word with Gilly Tasker, sooner rather than later.

Gilly Tasker was a seventy-five year-old Peter Pan who frequented the kind of clubs that attracted a much younger clientele. He either liked the music or the girls, and Connell figured the music was running a close second. Gilly looked good for a man of his age and he had a certain charm that, to date, had protected him from the outrage of the girls who'd discovered that age didn't necessarily dampen a man's ardor. As well as having an eye for a pretty girl, he had an eye for detail, and that's what had made him his rather dubious fortune.

Gilly Tasker was a master forger who called the shots, named his own price and mixed with the rich and infamous of the criminal world. After dark, Gilly liked to be entertained, and Connell knew just where to find him on a Saturday night.

"You got anything in that bag of yours you can wear of an evening?"

Lizzie shot him a look. "Pajamas?"

He shook his head and smiled. Definitely cute. "Maybe not. We're going clubbing tonight."

He gave her the use of his room, simply because Joe's room was special and full of Joe's stuff, and he didn't really want anyone going in there. He didn't like going in there himself. It held too many memories of other times, and sometimes those memories made him sad. So while he left her to shower and change, he took the phone with him to the sofa and called his son.

"Hi, Mom, is Joe there?" Joe led a hectic life for a four-year-old and spent most of his time outdoors with his dogs and his grandpa. There was always stuff to do on the farm and Joe liked to help out, even if his idea of helping didn't match everyone else's.

"You not coming up this weekend, Tommy?" asked his mother. He heard the disappointment barely hidden within the warm tone. It added to the guilt he already carried.

"Don't think I can. I'm working. I'm in the middle of something that I really can't leave." He grimaced. He'd used the excuse many times before, and each time it had been the truth but it didn't make it feel any better.

His mother sighed. "Joe will be disappointed. He wanted to show you how he can ride his bike. It's supposed to be a surprise for you."

Connell ran his fingers through his hair and closed his eyes. "I'm sorry. I'll make it up to him." He was a crap dad. Why didn't she just say it out loud and be done with it?

"I know you will, Tommy, but this time is precious. He'll be grown up before you know it. You shouldn't miss any of it. Did you speak to your boss about a move?"

"We've been over this, Mom. It's not that straightforward. Maybe when I crack this case I'll be in a position to ask for a favor or two."

"Mm, you've said that before."

"Look, Mom, I'm trying." He couldn't hide his frustration. "Do you think I want to be stuck down here when I could be up there with Joe?" He glanced up as the bedroom door opened and Lizzie came out, wrapped in a towel. He allowed his eyes to stray the length of her, his mind equally distracted. He gestured to where he had set up the iron at her request and turned his attention back to the phone. "Is he there?"

"He's gone out with your father to feed the horses. Try calling later."

"I'm on a job, I can't ring later. Tell him I love him and I'll catch him tomorrow. If I can manage to get up on Monday, I will, but don't say anything to Joe. I don't want to disappoint him if I can't make it."

"Are you looking after yourself, son?" Her voice softened. He dreaded her concern almost as much as her disappointment. She was a mother, of course she worried. He got that, but didn't need the burden of it.

"Sure I am, Mom."

"You found yourself a nice girl yet?"

"Not yet."

"Well, keep trying, son. God loves a tryer."

Connell doubted whether God gave a shit either way.

He put down the phone and stared at it for a long moment. He couldn't keep this up much longer, being away from Joe. It had been easier when the boy was younger, but he was at the age now when he wanted his dad there and couldn't understand why he wasn't. Connell pushed it to the back of his mind. He couldn't afford to be distracted when he had a job to do.

"Is everything okay?" Lizzie asked.

He gave himself a shake, pasted on a smile. "Sure ... kids, huh? You go get ready."

Lizzie nodded, disappeared back in to his room and Connell rang Marty and arranged to meet him downtown with the passport.

"You going to see Gilly?" asked Marty.

"Thought it might be a good idea," replied Connell as he held the phone against his ear and rifled in the laundry basket for a clean shirt.

"Are you really sure about that, Tommy? You haven't been back there since -"

"I'm sure."

"What about the girl? Are you going to take her with you?"

"Sure, she'll be fine. Mo's not going to be hanging around the club. It'd be the last place he'd expect her to be." He balanced the phone between his shoulder and his ear, and spread out the shirt on the ironing board.

"I don't know about that. Clifford discharged himself from hospital this afternoon. He left in a bit of a hurry according to the nursing staff ... had you been visiting?"

"Hey, nothing to do with me. I'm a good visitor. I just explained the position he was in." The iron was still hot and he quickly took care of the creases.

"Did he see Lizzie?"

Connell shook his head. "What do you take me for? No, he didn't see her."

"Okay, I'll meet you outside the club at nine, but don't be late. Charlene's on the warpath again. I'm supposed to be babysitting so she and Cynthia can go drown Cynthia's sorrows. You see the trouble you cause when you break a girl's heart. They're going to be back by eleven, so I've got to be back by ten-thirty at the latest."

"So who's actually babysitting?"

"Me. I'll have the kids in the car. It's the only way I can get them to sleep. She'll kill me if she finds out I've dragged them all over town in the dead of night, so they've all got to be back in their beds by the time she comes in."

"Better you than me, buddy. Nine it is."

He ducked into the bathroom to finish getting ready, and when he came out it was almost eight. He scanned the room; she still wasn't done. It'd been awhile since he'd been waiting around for a woman, and he paced and checked his watch.

He turned when he heard the door open. "Finally ..." he began and paused, taking in the sight of her. She'd put up her hair but a few tendrils were determined to escape, while the remainder was tethered in place by tiny silver pins. She'd put on some make-up and her eyes looked huge, her plum lips full, glossy and inviting. But it was the dress that finished him off. A simple black number, it hugged her figure and just covered her backside. The material shimmered as she walked.

She didn't look cute anymore. She looked all grown up and very tempting.

She was slipping her feet into sandals as she stepped into the room, and missed the expression on his face. By the time she looked up, it was gone. "Sorry, have I kept you waiting?" she asked and she gave him that ever-so-sweet smile.

"Sure you have," he replied with a grin, "but it was worth it."

He took his gun from his holster, checked the safety, and slid it into the waistband of his pants at the small of his back.

"Okay, good to go?"

Five

Connell parked a few blocks from the club and sat listening to the click of the cooling engine. Within minutes Marty pulled up in front with a car full of sleeping children. "Wait here," he said to Lizzie as they climbed out of the car. She leaned against the fender, gently rubbed her bare arms against the chill night air.

Nodding a greeting to Lizzie, Marty handed the envelope containing the passport to Connell through the open window and caught at his wrist as he was about to pull away. "For fuck's sake, Tommy, you're not taking her in there looking like that?"

Connell turned to look at Lizzie and grinned. "Sure I am. She cleans up pretty good, doesn't she?"

"She's jailbait, that's what she is, Tommy. You wanna turn around right now and take her home. Or, better still, hand her over to the Feds and be done with it."

"She's not jailbait, Marty, she's twenty two."

"That's not what I mean, Tommy. You take her in there and I can guarantee that someone will end up in jail. Because you won't like the way the guys are looking at her and you certainly won't like what they'll want to do to her. Are you armed?"

"What do you think?"

"Then go home now, Tommy, before you do something you'll regret."

Connell shrugged. "Marty, you worry too much. All I'm going to do is catch up with Gilly. She'll be fine, I'll be fine. Now get those kids home to bed." He watched as Marty pulled away into the traffic, turned and walked slowly back to Lizzie.

Marty was right to be concerned, though Connell didn't like to admit it. Sometimes he thought Marty knew him better than he knew himself.

"Okay, honey," he said with a lazy smile, "you stick close to me at all times. It's going to be jumping in there. I don't want to lose sight of you. And you definitely don't want to lose sight of me."

"I have been to a club before." A smile lit up her face, put a sparkle in her eyes.

"I don't doubt it but this isn't England, honey. You may be a little shocked by what goes on in there. I'm going to put my arm around you but don't go getting the wrong idea. I just want to make sure I know where you are. I also want to make sure the guys in there know you're with me, so they keep their hands to themselves. Do you get that? You're not going to get weird on me again, are you?"

"Don't worry, I get it and I'm sorry about before at the hospital, I didn't mean to cause a scene." She looked away. "… It's just that … things are …"

"Crazy?"

She hesitated, considered for a moment. "Weird, yes … things are a little weird at the moment."

That was an understatement. "Forget it. Just remember I'm one of the good guys."

The club was heaving and Connell only got them in the door because he knew the doorman, and the doorman knew better than to get on the wrong side of him. The man had outstanding warrants and Connell could have pulled him in and improved his arrest record. But he was after bigger fish. So, instead, he gave him the eye and the doorman did the smart thing and didn't let on to anyone that he'd just let a cop into the club.

The music was loud with a driving beat that hit them like a wall. Connell winced and Lizzie raised her hands to her ears. She took an automatic step back and Connell caught her from behind, placing his hands gently on her arms. Pausing a moment on the threshold till their eyes became accustomed to the flashing lights, Connell scanned the interior trying to quell the bad feeling in his gut.

In two years the club had undergone a makeover and the music had moved on, but the layout was the same and it was easy to see it as it had been. Connell determinedly shrugged off the memories of what had gone down on his last visit, pushed the images of flashing blue lights and blood to the back of his mind, and took Lizzie's hand in a firm grip.

Weaving their way through the mass of bodies to the bar, Connell kept her close, ignoring the jerks who sized her up, and shooting off a glare at those who leered. His hackles rose despite his efforts to the contrary.

He should have listened to Marty.

At the bar he helped her onto a stool and stood as close as he could, which was pretty close considering it was shoulder to shoulder at the bar. The bartender sized him up, recognized a cop when he saw one, and glanced at the blonde who was holding court at the other end of the bar. She acknowledged him with the slightest inclination of her head, and after making her apologies to those hanging on her every word she sashayed along the bar and offered her hand along with her ample cleavage to Connell.

"It's been a long time, Detective Connell. What can we do for you?" She raised her voice above the din. "Come to sample some of the merchandise?" She gestured to the stage where half-naked girls moved provocatively. Lizzie followed her gaze and sidled closer to Connell, who merely smiled and shook his head.

"Off duty, Madeleine, just out with my girl here. I could use a drink, though."

"The usual?"

"Sure, and a cocktail for the lady." He slipped his arm around Lizzie's shoulder, ran his fingers down her bare arm, dipped his head and breathed against her ear. "You okay?" He scanned the room as he nuzzled her neck and found himself distracted by her scent.

"I'm fine," she shouted back against his cheek. He felt her warm breath, nodded and pulled away. Madeleine returned with a Jack Daniels and some scary looking pink thing with an umbrella for Lizzie. Connell winced at its luminosity, picked up his own drink and passed the offending cocktail to Lizzie. He watched as she sipped at it cautiously. The pink liquid provided unusual contrast to her plum lips. She used the tip of her tongue to remove the excess. Maybe it tasted of strawberries. Maybe, if he played his cards right, he'd find out later.

"You looking for anyone special … while you're out with your girl?" asked Madeleine. "We're all clean here. No sense in you stirring things up."

"Stirring things up?" Connell drew his attention back across the bar and gave her a tight smile. "Now, would I do that?"

"Sure you would. You've done it before."

"I told you I'm off duty, but if I were to run into my old pal Gilly, I might stop and ask, how its hanging."

Madeleine glanced at Lizzie and sized her up with a knowing look. "I'm sure Gilly would be quite happy to shoot the shit with you and your young lady here, but I don't want any trouble, do you hear me?"

"Sure. I'm not here to cause trouble, just to talk." *Just to talk*, who was he kidding? He might have started off

76

with that intention, but now that he was here, he was beginning to feel differently. He couldn't believe how edgy he felt and no amount of fantasizing about Lizzie was going to shift it. He didn't like it one little bit, the fear of losing control.

Marty was right, coming here had been a mistake.

Madeleine gestured with a nod of her head towards the raised area at the back of the club where private booths were used by the club girls to entertain the special request customers. Gilly Tasker was seated in a booth at the far side.

"Drink up," he mouthed to Lizzie, downing his own. He felt the welcome burn as it slid down his throat, ignored the battle going on his head and the churning in his gut, and pasted on a smile. "Dance?"

Dance wasn't the correct word for what was happening on the dance floor. It was too crowded for anything but squeezing close together and moving in time to the music. It was, however, the only way Connell could get over to Gilly without pulling his gun and shouting 'Hit the floor!' And anyway, squeezing up close to Lizzie wasn't without its attractions, not while he had the image of cocktail-smeared lips stuck in his head, and certainly not while she was wearing that dress. Sometimes it didn't hurt to get distracted. Occasionally, it even helped.

Pulling her off the stool, he forced his way onto the dance floor. He slid his hands down to her hips and didn't even need to pull her in close; the crowd of people around them did it for him. Despite knowing it was unprofessional and downright wrong, he took advantage of the situation and enjoyed the feel of her against him. He felt her hands flat against his chest and he caught her raised brow. Yeah, she was right, he had said he wouldn't cop a feel, but she was so tempting. And what better way to keep his bad memories at bay? He shrugged apologetically and bent his head to her ear.

"Think undercover, sweetheart," he said with a crooked grin. "We're trying to project an image. You're my girl and I'm your hot date. Some girls would give a lot to be in this position."

She smiled "You mean Cynthia?"

He pulled a face. "You know, you could pretend that you're enjoying this. I have a reputation to uphold."

She laughed softly, placing her hands around the back of his neck, and he felt her fingers delicately skim his skin. He gave an involuntary shiver and tightened his hold until good sense overcame him and he pulled away, severing bodily contact before he ran the risk of forgetting he was actually working a case. He caught her eye and glimpsed the hint of mischief before she dropped her gaze. Maybe he wasn't the only one pushing his luck.

Resorting to brute force, and ignoring the curses of the fellow dancers, Connell forged a path to the far side of the club, and making sure that Lizzie was still by his side, he stepped up onto the raised area and approached Gilly's booth. He was stopped by a mountain of a man in a severe black suit, with an equally severe hair cut, who placed the palm of his dinner plate-sized hand flat against Connell's chest.

Connell spread his arms wide, hands in the air. "Hey, just want a word with my buddy Gilly."

The man exerted pressure with his hand and Connell stood his ground and stared him in the eye. He could do mean, if that's what was called for. "Are you going to take your hand away?"

"Are you going to make me?" replied the man.

"Sure," said Connell and he slipped his gun out from behind him and stuck it in the man's left ear. Lizzie gasped. The man lowered his hand and Connell lowered his gun. "See, that wasn't too hard, was it?"

"Tommy Connell, are you causing trouble with my boy?" Gilly roared with laughter. "Mr. Smith, kindly let them through, if you will. I can handle this." The man stood aside with a look that spoke volumes about what he thought of the situation and Connell slipped into the booth, drawing Lizzie along with him. "You've got to learn to be less defensive, Detective Connell. One of these days you're going to pull that gun and it's going to go off in your face. Then what are you going to do, hmm?"

"Point taken, Gilly." Connell smiled thinly at the old man. "Hey, listen, we need to have a little chat." He looked pointedly at the half-naked, impossibly endowed girls who were currently draped around the man, and Gilly nodded. "Later, ladies. Now go have some fun."

Disentangling themselves, they slid from the booth, making a big production of squeezing past Connell who simply shrugged at Lizzie as warm cleavage brushed his cheek.

"You going to introduce me to this delightful young lady, Tommy?" asked Gilly as he narrowed his eyes and inspected her thoroughly.

Feeling her squirm self-consciously at his side, Connell wrapped an arm around her shoulder and squeezed reassuringly. "This is Lizzie ..." He'd been about to say 'Jones', but she wasn't Mrs. Jones and he realized that he hadn't actually gotten around to asking her what her real name was.

Gilly bestowed his most charming smile. "So pleased to meet you, my dear, and so refreshing to see you back in the game, Tommy. It's been a long time. Time to put the past behind you and move on, don't you agree?"

"Sure, Gilly," Connell replied flatly, ignoring Lizzie's attempt to catch his eye. "I need to know about Carl

Jones. I understand you did some work for him recently."

Gilly's benign expression vanished. "Can't help you there, Detective Connell, never met the man."

"I think you have," replied Connell, taking the passport out of his pocket and placing it on the table. "I know it's one of yours, Gilly. The Feds might be interested if they got their hands on it, but all I'm interested in is Carl Jones and why he asked you to supply it."

Gilly glanced back at Lizzie, "I thought you looked familiar. I never forget a face and yet you look younger in the flesh. But that's old age for you. They say when the policemen start looking young you're getting old and I tell you, Tommy, you are definitely too young for all the shit you stir up."

Lizzie squeezed Connell's thigh beneath the table. He sensed her unease. Gilly seemed unable to keep his eyes off her. Covering her hand with his, Connell interlaced his fingers reassuringly. She shot him a sweet nervous smile and he returned it and held her gaze a little longer than necessary. If anyone was going to stare, then let it be him. He was one of the good guys, after all. "So what do you know about Carl?" he said finally, drawing Gilly's attention away from her.

"I know that you're digging into something you shouldn't."

"Let me be the judge of that."

Gilly sighed. "Tommy, as usual you're treading on dangerous ground. Walk away now while you have the chance."

"I can't walk away, Gilly, you know that. One man is dead and people are at risk. I have a job to do."

Gilly shook his head. "I could make it worth your while to walk away. You could take off upstate with your kid. Isn't that what you want at the end of the day?"

"Gilly, cut it out now or I'll take you down for this."
Connell held up the passport. Gilly merely shrugged and
waved his hand dismissively. "All I want from you is
information. I can deal with anything else."

"Can you? What about the girl?" Gilly glanced at
Lizzie.

Connell wished he'd taken Marty's advice and left
her at home. Gilly was scaring her and he didn't like it,
and Marty had known he wouldn't like it. "You were
going to tell me about Carl?"

Gilly shrugged. "It's your funeral, Tommy. Don't say
I didn't warn you."

"Okay, I'm warned."

Gilly leaned forward in his seat and took out a gold
pen that he twisted slowly. He picked up a cocktail
napkin from the table and scrawled in elaborate
longhand on the back. "I haven't survived in this
business for as long as I have by talking to cops, but
what I will say, Tommy, is that I like you. Always have.
And I feel bad about what happened to Marie. She was a
good kid and didn't deserve to end up like she did. But
you see, Tommy, that's what happens when you mess
with things you shouldn't. And, son, you are seriously
messing up now and you need to stop." He cocked his
head and smiled slyly. "By the way, how is little Joey? It
must be hard on him with no mommy. How old is he
now - three, four?"

Connell lunged across the table, catching Gilly by the
throat with his left hand. "You leave my boy out of this,
you fuck." His right hand was raised, fist clenched, his
heart pounding.

"You don't want to do that, Tommy," gasped Gilly,
"you really don't."

Mr. Smith grabbed hold of Lizzie's hair in a meaty
fist, twisting her neck and eliciting a squeal of alarm.

Connell let go of Gilly with a snarl and slumped back in his seat.

Rearranging his tie, Gilly considered him for a moment. "Guilt is a terrible thing, Tommy. Destructive. You need to move on." He tossed him the napkin and Connell caught it instinctively with one hand. "You want to know about Carl Jones, that's where he was living. You might find out what you want to know from there. All I know is that he was caught up in the middle of something and he figured his lady could get him out of it."

Connell glanced at the address and steadied his breathing. He wanted to kill the man, right there and then. He wanted to pull out his gun and shoot him, and the need to do that was so great he felt it run through him like electricity.

Lizzie reached out and placed her palm gently on his arm. He dropped his gaze to her hand, small and pale, and forced himself to stay calm.

"The passport - why did Carl need a counterfeit when his wife could've got a genuine one herself?"

Gilly narrowed his eyes, glanced at the girl and back to Connell. "According to what I heard she couldn't have."

"What do you mean?" He gave himself a mental shake, he needed to focus.

"She wouldn't have checked out."

"I'm not following you, Gilly. She's a law abiding citizen."

"Yeah, maybe so, but she's not Mrs. Jones."

"Huh?"

"Go check out the address. Carl was not who you think he was."

Why did that not surprise him? Was anyone who they said they were?

* * *

Lizzie was silent as they left the club. Connell could tell by her furrowed brow that she had a lot of questions but had sensibly kept them to herself. Good, he was in no mood for answers. Still shaken by Gilly, he needed to cool down.

"I'll drop you back at my place," he said curtly as he pulled out too fast into the traffic amid much cursing and honking of horns. "I need to get over to Carl's place before he's I.D'd and the cops are all over it."

"I thought you were the cops," her uncertainties were thinly wrapped in a hesitant whisper.

He shot her a quick glance.

He should never have taken her in there. Marty was right. He'd put her in danger and he'd almost stepped over the edge. Her hair was messed where she'd been manhandled. Her make-up smudged where she'd rubbed shocked tears from her eyes.

He reached out and tucked a stray strand of hair behind her ear. "Sure, I am," he said, "but there are good cops and bad cops, and like I said, I'm one of the good guys. The bad cops will go in there and walk all over everything and not understand what it is they're looking at, or what's going on."

"Do *you* understand what's going on?" she replied. "Because I don't. What did he mean about Beth not being Mrs. Jones? Of course she is. I was a bridesmaid at their wedding."

"Yeah, but maybe Carl's not Mr. Jones, and don't forget, sweetheart, as far as everyone here is concerned, you're Mrs. Jones, not Beth."

"I don't want to stay at your place on my own, not after what went on in there."

She was scared. He could understand why she didn't want to be sat on her own in an empty apartment in the midst of a derelict building. Yeah, maybe he was hot-headed and he knew he'd shocked her with his attack on the old man, but he could take care of himself, and more importantly, he could take care of her.

"I shouldn't have taken you in there. I'm sorry. I get worked up and Gilly knows which buttons to press."

"He was threatening your little boy. You had every right to get upset." She paused and glanced at him. "I don't want to cause trouble for you or your family. Perhaps it would be better if you just took me to the airport and we left this whole business alone. This is entirely my fault. If I hadn't made that call, no one would be any the wiser."

"None of this is your fault. Something seriously strange is going on, and whether we like it or not, it has to be investigated. The last thing I want to do is scare you more than you are already, but you're mixed up in this up to your neck and you simply don't have the option to walk away anymore."

Jumping the car through a red light, he put his foot down. The roads were clearer here and he stepped on the gas and Lizzie held tightly onto the sides of her seat.

"But I'd never forgive myself if something happened to your little boy." There was a quiver in her voice, and when he looked her eyes glistened with unshed tears.

"Nothing is going to happen to Joe. I wouldn't let it." His stomach rolled. He'd thought that nothing would happen to Marie, but it hadn't worked out like that. "Gilly is all mouth," he said with more confidence than he felt. "Like I said, he knows which buttons to press. He was warning me off. That tells me there's something worth finding out."

"In that case, I want to go with you to Carl's. Maybe I'll see something that will help. I know him, you don't."

It made sense but in his gut it didn't feel right. Gilly had given up the address too easily and he didn't like to think they might be walking into a trap, that Mo Pater might be sitting waiting for them with his golden toothed

84

smile and a sawed off shotgun. By rights he should be calling for backup, but he'd not done any of this by the book and he wasn't quite sure why. He should've logged her witness statement, updated the squad on events and put her in protective custody where at least she'd be safe. And he should have arrested Mo Pater. But he hadn't. He'd done his usual maverick go-it-alone routine, and the last time he'd done that he'd gotten someone killed.

If this whole thing went bad, he could kiss goodbye to his career, such as it was. In truth, that was the least of his worries. If he didn't manage to land on his feet, and if everything went wrong like the last time, he wouldn't need to worry about his career. He'd be on a slab and so would everyone he cared about. He toyed with calling Marty, his own personal voice of reason. Then he thought of Marty's kids and ruled that out.

He had unfinished business with Mo Pater. The truth was, only he could finish it and it didn't involve reading him his rights and taking him downtown.

"Okay, we'll both do Carl's, but stick close and do whatever I say."

"*Whatever* you say?"

He shot her a quick smile and saw the tiniest spark had returned to her eyes, "Well, within reason."

* * *

Carl's apartment block was high dollar and reeked of money, lots of money. The common areas were well maintained and overseen by a well-dressed and well-mannered doorman.

Connell left the car around the corner and they waited outside under the cover of a doorway. To any casual observer they appeared like any couple engaged in a little romance, while Connell waited for the doorman to be distracted so they could slip into the building unseen.

"Why don't you just show him your badge?" asked Lizzie as she sidled closer for warmth. Her little black dress, although perfect for clubbing, was less perfect for standing in icy doorways.

Connell wrapped his arms around her, ducked his head and breathed his warm breath against her ear. "I don't want the world to know I'm interested in Carl, and once I show my badge it becomes official." It was also a pretty good excuse to get up close and personal with Lizzie, which was totally against the rules–if he were the type of guy who followed rules.

They didn't have to wait long for a crowd of party goers to fill the lobby, and they snuck in with them and slipped into the elevator. Connell kept up the pretense, he was beginning to enjoy a little too much, by backing Lizzie into the corner. Obstructing the view of those who shared their car, he turned his back on them and leaned into her.

"Is this entirely necessary?" she whispered against his cheek as his hand strayed cheekily to her behind.

"Absolutely," he replied with a grin "First rule of undercover … stay in character."

"Mm," she responded as the elevator pinged for their floor.

"You see," he laughed as he led the way along the hall, checking the door numbers, "now when those nice folks in the elevator are asked to identify us, they'll say, *Uh, not sure, officer, they were just some couple making out. Don't know what they looked like, didn't like to look … embarrassing, you know how it is.*"

Lizzie smiled at him and Connell got the feeling that, despite everything that had happened, the old Connell charm was beginning to work.

"You okay?" he asked.

"I'm okay," she replied as she slipped her hand in his and hurried to keep up.

Connell had the door open within seconds. He closed it silently behind them and cautioned her to be quiet with a finger against her lips while he listened. The apartment was in darkness. He held his breath and strained his ears for any sounds of life.

"Stay here," he whispered, leaving her by the door as he slowly and carefully checked the apartment. When he was sure they were the only ones there, he switched on the lights and called her into the living room.

"Our boy Carl wasn't short of a buck. This place must have cost a fortune. Was he sending any of it home to Beth?"

"Beth never saw any of this. She has a cottage that belonged to our dad and she's always worked. She likes her job. She doesn't need his money."

Just as well, thought Connell, because this money smelled bad. "Okay, have a look around. See if you can find anything that may be useful–papers, diaries. Look for a computer, anything, and hurry. I don't know how long we've got before Gilly throws us to the dogs."

Connell was systematic; he'd done this many times before. He stacked the laptop, a digital camera and a folder full of paperwork on the coffee table to take with them, and began to rifle through the desk drawers, starting at the bottom, working his way to the top. He raised an eyebrow at the quantity of porn in the first drawer and made sure the drawer was shut before Lizzie came back into the room. The guy was a jerk. He wondered how he and Beth had got together in the first place.

* * *

87

Lizzie wandered from the kitchen into the bedroom, not knowing what she was meant to find that could be termed 'useful'. The scent of Carl hit her as she entered the room and it stopped her in her tracks, her stomach recoiling with dread. He was gone, she had to remember that, rejoice in that, if she could.

She crossed slowly to the wardrobe and pulled open the door with a shaking hand. His clothes hung limp on their hangers. The smell of his aftershave, cologne ... whatever it was he bathed in daily, clung to the garments, leaching out, a permanent reminder of the person who'd once worn them. She reached in her hand and reluctantly checked the pockets of the many jackets, fearful of what she might find. They were empty. She shrugged. She didn't know what she'd expected but there was nothing here. She shuddered and made to close the cupboard door. Perhaps Connell had been more successful.

* * *

In the second drawer, beneath a stack of sailing magazines, Connell hit the jackpot. Tied in a rubber band and stuffed at the back, out of the way, was a stack of six passports, six identities - all the same man, aka Carl Jones. He didn't have the time to study them. Adding them to his stash, he found a bag to put them all in, topped them off with a telephone address book, and called to Lizzie.

"You find anything?" he asked as he pushed open the door to the bedroom. She didn't answer.

He found her on her knees, frozen to the spot, and when he followed her gaze, he saw the inside of the wardrobe doors were plastered with photographs. Drawing closer, he realized that the photos were all of Lizzie: unmistakably sweet and innocent, a child digging sandcastles in a lemon-spotted swimsuit; then as an ungainly teenager, playing tennis, horse riding and swimming; and finally as an emerging beauty in a variety of poses, but in none of them was she looking at the camera. Everyone had obviously been taken without her knowledge. A hidden camera and a sick mind, Connell wondered just how far Carl had taken his obsession.

He got a pretty good idea when he looked at Lizzie's face.

Picking up the garbage can next to the bed, he crossed to the wardrobe and tore the photos down. Dropping them into the bin, he threw in a lit match and watched as the photos curled, blackened and finally burst into flames.

He turned to Lizzie and lowered himself beside her. Balancing on the balls of his feet, he wrapped her in his arms and held her, feeling the silent sobs that racked her body and soaked his shirt. He tucked her head against his chest and ran his fingers gently through her hair, pressed his lips against the top of her head and swallowed the fury that he felt inside.

For once this wasn't about him and his fucked-up life.

They sat for what seemed a long time together on the floor of Carl's room with the scent of the monster all around them, and Connell was acutely aware of the need for them to move soon, that the longer they delayed, the more likely they would be compromised, but he couldn't rush her. He knew that she needed to be held, protected.

"It's okay, sweetheart, he's gone now," he said eventually in a calm soothing voice that cost him dearly. Inside he was roaring with anger and frustration. If Carl Jones hadn't been lying on a slab in the morgue already, Connell would have pulled out his gun and finished him off there and then.

Of course he knew about people like Carl. He couldn't do his job and not know about the perverts who

89

preyed on children–young girls–spent years, sometimes, grooming them, just biding their time, waiting till the time was right. He wondered whether the marriage to Beth had all been about getting close to Lizzie. It had taken some courage for her to come all of this way to face him on her own.

He smoothed the curls away from her damp cheeks and framed her face with his hands, forcing her to look at him though she tried to avert her gaze. "Listen to me … listen to me." He locked his eyes with hers and the look in them almost broke his heart. "This is not about you, do you hear? It's about a man who wasn't right in the head, some psycho who's lying on a slab in the morgue and can't hurt you anymore. It doesn't matter that he's dead though, because whatever he was fucking around with, we're going to find it and finish it – for you and your sister."

She shook her head sadly, releasing fat tears from brimming eyes. "I can't do this anymore ..." A sob caught in her throat and she struggled past it, "I ... I thought I could, but I can't."

"Sure you can." He brushed his lips across her damp cheeks. Not a kiss, just the merest touch. A little comfort, an attempt to prove to her, and to himself, that human compassion was stronger than human weakness. "Come on, honey, you came all this way across the Atlantic on your own to protect your sister and her baby from this freak who scared you both. You're not on your own now–you've got me. We're a team."

She shook her head again, sniffed noisily and wiped her runny nose with the back of her hand. Her make-up was streaked, her eyes red and puffy, and she'd lost the silver pins from her hair. "I just want to go home … I'm no good to you." She turned away from him. "I'm no good to anyone."

Connell sighed deeply. That sick son of a bitch had screwed with her sweet little mind; he had to figure out a way to unscrew it. "Are you going to walk out on me, leave me to figure it out on my own?"

"You don't need me."

"I need you."

"What could you possibly need me for? You're not scared of anything." Her hand went straight to her hair, twisting and pulling. Connell took hold of it, squeezed her fingers gently and held them still.

"Sure I am. I'm scared of lots of things. I'm scared of screwing up … again. I'm scared that someone will press my buttons and I won't have someone like you there to put a hand on my arm and stop me from doing something I'll regret. And I'm scared that my son will grow up and think that I'm a shitty dad … Loads of things."

He pulled the bottom of his shirt loose and gestured to it. "Spit," he said distractedly. She spat and he used it to wipe the runs of mascara from her cheeks, the way his mom had hurriedly rubbed his face clean before church when he was small.

She locked eyes with him and the faintest of tired smiles brushed her lips. He wanted to hold her, but he drew back instead. He wanted to say that he could fix everything, but things were never that simple.

"You knew Carl. You carried something into the country for him. You know what it was. You just don't know you do. We need to work through all this stuff together so we can work out what this is all about."

"But -"

"You heard what Gilly said. I have to stop them before they get to Joe. And I need you to help me."

Six

Connell rang Marty from the car while Lizzie scoured Carl's phone book for any names she might recognize.

"Buddy, I know' it's after midnight - why break the habit of a life time - but I need your help again."

"I'm not your buddy. I'm just this poor sad sack whose life is being ruined by you. Charlene got back early, caught me with all the kids in the car, all awake and eating MacDonald's. I had to blame you, Tommy, or my life wouldn't have been worth living."

"What'd she say?"

"She says I'm associating with the worst sort of people and I've got to find myself some new friends."

"That sounds like a good plan, Marty, but don't sweat it, I'll fix it with Charlene for you, don't worry."

"I'm not worried. She's right, you are the worst sort."

Connell smiled "You going to help me, or what?"

"Sure I'm going to help you. What do you take me for? What happened at the club? You get out in one piece without drawing your piece?"

"Mm … yes and no, in that order."

"You didn't shoot anyone, did you? I'm not helping you if you've been shooting people."

"Relax, Marty. I didn't shoot anyone. Do you know any Feds?"

"One or two. What's going on, Tommy?"

"Any that you trust?"

"One or two. Why?"

Connell glanced at Lizzie. She had her head down, concentrating on the book. She looked a little more composed but she wasn't fooling anybody, least of all him. He chose his words carefully.

"Our man Carl seems to have had a split personality … six, actually, and I think that maybe he was known by at least one of them to our boys. Might have been double-dealing, which would explain why Mo was pissed at him. I need to know what they know. I think we may be sitting on something here but haven't a clue what it is."

"They're not going to give away shit for free. What have you got?"

"I've got his computer, a camera with some pictures of some serious looking guys doing serious type stuff, and a bunch of papers that mean zilch." Lizzie held up the phone book and he shook his head. He was hanging on to that. "I've also got six passports that will probably prove to be Gilly's handiwork, and a suspicion that Carl Jones was not his given name."

"You've got quite a lot."

"Enough to trade?"

"I expect so."

"Well, see what you can do. We're heading home. Call me later–and thanks, buddy."

He turned to Lizzie. "There's a pen in the glove box. Write down the names from the passports in the back of the phone book and stash it under your seat. I don't want all our eggs in one basket."

"Are we going to your apartment now?" she asked.

"Yeah, you tired?" It was after two and he was certainly beat. He was going to have to swap another shift, maybe pull a fake flu and take the rest of the week off. That would put him on the wrong side of Personnel, and they were even worse than Internal Affairs.

"Just a bit," she replied, stifling a yawn.

"Not long now, sweetheart. We're nearly there." He thought about stretching out between cool sheets in his king-size bed, then remembered that he'd given up his room to Lizzie. He thought about rescinding his offer and stretching out alongside her, but parked that idea. The last thing she needed tonight was some guy hitting on her, and no way could he stretch out in the same bed without hitting on her. Joe's bed would be fine. He wondered why he was wasting time even thinking about it, what with everything going on around them. He decided it must be some kind of male default–if all else fails, think of sex. That was cool if all else failed; he could just about manage that.

* * *

He sensed there was something wrong as they rode the service elevator, long before his brain made the connection, which was about the time that he noticed that the old piles of junk in the hall outside his door had been moved. Not moved as in thrown away by the contractors, but moved as in kicked out of the way by people with no respect for other people's garbage.

He drew his gun, and cautiously pushed with his foot at his front door that hung by one hinge. He felt Lizzie at his back and was happy for her to remain there as they slowly entered the apartment.

It had been ransacked and he caught his breath at the devastation. The sofa was shredded, the furniture upended and every dish was smashed. The floor was littered with broken glass where family photos had been thrown to the ground and stamped on with a heavy foot.

"Hi there, Tommy. You want to put your gun down?"

Connell froze.

"I've got your little lady in my sights, Tommy boy, and you know I'll pull the trigger."

Bending slowly, reluctantly, Connell placed his gun on the floor by his feet, then he rose and turned to face Mo Pater. Mo had the muzzle of his gun pressed hard against the back of Lizzie's head. She had her eyes tightly shut.

"Good man. Now then, let's sit and down have a little chat, and I'm going to want your word as a gentleman and an asshole that you'll cooperate. Will you cooperate, Tommy?"

Connell glared at him, cocked his head to one side and shot Mo a 'fuck you' look. He realized too late that Mo was not alone when he was smashed on the side of the head with an automatic weapon. He dropped to his knees with a curse, leaving what was left of his senses behind him.

When he managed to retrieve them, he was slumped on one of his own kitchen chairs and his hands were tied behind his back. He felt the stickiness of blood at his temple, blinked it from his eye and wondered how long he'd been out for the blood to have stopped flowing. He drew a ragged breath, looked desperately about the room for Lizzie, and was relieved to discover that she wasn't dead on the floor, but similarly confined and white with shock and fear.

"I believe you have something belonging to me," said Mo to Lizzie. She shrugged and Connell held his breath. Please don't do that sweetheart, he begged silently, but Mo didn't react. Maybe he was the only one who was driven to distraction by the move.

Lizzie shot him a pleading look as he strained at his bindings, but there was nothing he could do. "I don't know what you mean," she eventually stammered.

"Wrong answer, Mrs. Jones," said Mo, nodding to his associate who dealt Connell a crippling blow to his stomach. Connell drew up his knees and strained against his bindings, his natural reaction being to double up against the pain as he tried against the odds to draw in enough air to replace the breath that had been knocked out of him. He gasped hoarsely and Lizzie chewed at her lip.

"Try again," said Mo.

"Tell me what you want. What do you think I have?" Lizzie shifted her frantic gaze to Connell. *Help me*, the look implored him silently, though it was obvious to all present that he was in no position to help anyone, and that scared the shit out of him.

"You know what it is. You brought it."

"I don't," she pleaded, "I truly don't. I don't know what any of this is about and neither does he." She gestured to Connell.

"Another wrong answer, Mrs. Jones. My apologies, Tommy." This time the punch was delivered to Connell's face. His nose popped against scarred knuckles, his lip burst against his teeth and the resulting blood dripped onto his shirt. Spitting the taste from his mouth, he glared at Mo.

"He asked me to bring a CD player that was all. If you want it, it's over there on the floor beneath the desk. That's the only thing he asked for, the only thing I have." Her voice was climbing, hysterical, and Connell fought once more against the ropes that bound his wrists together.

"You fuck," he growled. "I'm going to finish you once and for all."

Mo crossed the room and picked up the machine. He flicked it open and pulled out the disc as Connell had done. "Don't get ahead of yourself, Tommy. You're tied to a chair. What the fuck are you going to do, spit me to death you sad piece of shit?"

He returned his attention to the disc and his eyes gleamed when he recognized that it was a data disc. He turned a sly grin on Connell. "You're slipping, Tommy Boy, missed the prize, because you were too busy panting after the girl. By the way, how does she compare to Marie?"

Connell forced himself to stare blankly back.

"Did we interrupt your evening, Tommy? Were you just about to get your rocks off? Or maybe you haven't gotten that far yet. Newly widowed and all. Maybe she's not quite ready for your special brand of charm." He laughed. "Maybe I should be your stand-in. After all, you're in no condition to service a lady like she deserves, are you? You've kinda missed the moment, haven't you, and you're going to get blood all over the sheets." He hunkered down in front of Lizzie, cocked his head to one side and flashed his golden smile. "Are you up for a little private party, babe?"

Lizzie shut her eyes tight and Connell tried to calm his mind and channel his rage. He racked his brains frantically for a way out.

"How about we make a deal?" he suggested. His voice came out a little nasal, his nose full of blood.

"How about no," replied Mo. He stood and turned away from Lizzie. "Why would I make a deal when I have all the cards? Take a look around, detective. I think you'll find that I'm the one with the gun and the disc and you're … not."

"Carl had a computer to go with the disc," said Connell "You want it, I can get it, but you have to let her go."

"Or how about you go get me the computer or I'll shoot her here and now." He sneered at Connell. "It won't be the first time you've let a woman take a bullet for you, will it?"

Connell felt the steady thrum of electricity building inside him again, and if he could have freed his hands, Mo would have been dead. But strangely, instead of giving in to the red mist and reacting, he managed to project an outward calmness that shocked even him.

"Fine, shoot us both, and the Feds can have the computer." Connell tried a shrug of his own, and perversely, that did have an effect on Mo who hammered another one home and split Connell's eyebrow.

"You little pussy. You think that you can play games with me?"

It took Connell a moment to recover his senses. His vision blurred. He felt a strong urge to vomit. "I'm not playing games," he gasped, "I'm cutting you a deal. You let us go and we get you the computer. That's the important thing here, isn't it? You getting back whatever Carl intended to sell to the Feds? You're not going to let an opportunity like that slip by."

Mo narrowed his eyes. "And Mrs. Jones, your star witness, you think I'm just going to let her walk out of here?"

"No, you're going to walk out of here and leave her here unharmed. She didn't see anything, she doesn't know anything. I'll put her on a plane and nobody's any the wiser."

"And what about you and me, Tommy? What about that little itch that you're just going to have to scratch? Because, let's face it, Tommy, only a coward would let a man blow away his woman and not want revenge. You telling me you're going to give up on justice if I let Mrs. Jones go?"

Connell took a long steadying breath, which difficult, there wasn't a pain free inch left on him. His eye was beginning to swell rapidly and he struggled to keep it open. "That's something else entirely, between you and me, and only a pussy would try to deal his way out of it."

"You calling me a pussy, you fuck?" Mo raised his foot and kicked the center of Connell's chest with the flat of his shoe. The force of the kick slammed Connell and the chair backwards, smashing the back of his head against the floor and crushing his tethered arms. Connell lay dazed, blood pooling from the back of his head as Mo approached him, gun raised. He squatted down next to him and rested the barrel against his forehead.

"You're a lot of fun, Tommy, do you know that? You just keep on going, regardless of the consequences. You're like one of those Ever Ready rabbits, that just keeps going like a dumb fucking animal who's too stupid to know when it's over, but you're also a dead man, Tommy, never ever doubt it, maybe not tonight, but soon." He stood and turned to Lizzie. "When he comes around, tell him to drop the computer off at the club with Gilly. He's got until midnight tomorrow."

He left his man to untie Lizzie, then they both departed and the apartment was left strangely quiet. She waited until the sound of the elevator going down broke the silence before she dared to leave her seat. Heaving the chair onto its side, she untied Connell's bindings. He was badly beaten, blood pooled on the floor. She grabbed a cloth to stem the flow and checked his vital signs hurriedly.

"Please be okay," she whispered as she pulled back his eyelids and checked his pupil reaction. "Connell, can you hear me?" She patted his cheek and he swatted her hand and rolled away, groaning. His chest heaved, his breath came in and out with an accompanying painful wheeze. He'd had more than his fair share of fights and was no stranger to coming off worst, but this time he hadn't had the chance to defend himself or fight back. He felt like shit and he was going to be sick.

With her help he made it to the bathroom, and afterwards, he sat on the edge of the bath while she cleaned up his face and inspected the gash on the back of his head.

"You need some stitches and you need a CT scan. You have concussion and the way you hit the ground, you may have a fractured skull. You need to go to hospital."

Connell tried to shake his head but the room wouldn't stop spinning. "I'm fine - quit worrying. I just need some sleep." He closed his eyes against the brightness of the bathroom light and his chin dropped on to his chest.

Lizzie shook him. "No, you don't. That's the worst thing you can do if you have concussion."

From where he was sitting it sounded like the best thing he could do. He dragged his one good eye open and gave up on the other. "I'm not going to the hospital, okay?"

"What happens if you have a blood clot on the brain? You die in your bed and I'm left to deal with the albino on my own?"

"Is this the way you talk to all of your patients? 'Cause I'm telling you it's not good. You're meant to be reassuring me, not reading me the last rites …" His words slurred to a halt. He held his head with his left hand, winced at the pain in his wrist and changed hands. He wanted to lie down, wanted to be sick again.

"Please, Connell, I'm worried. Let me take you to hospital and get you checked out."

Connell tried to reply, opened his mouth to form the words, slid from the edge of the bath and hit the bathroom floor with a thud.

* * *

The doctors all said Lizzie had done the right thing calling 911 and getting him straight to the ER. They checked him out and stitched him up, and the only

100

fractures they found were two in his ribs and one in his left wrist. They treated his concussion and asked if Lizzie wanted them to call the cops, and she'd said no, explaining that it was an accident - he'd fallen down the stairs, drunk. They didn't believe her. They knew what a beating looked like, had seen plenty after all, but they accepted her version of events because it meant less paperwork, contenting themselves with observing him for a couple of hours. When it was obvious that he wasn't going to die in his bed, or even lie quietly in it, and he'd made it annoyingly clear to anyone who came near him that he didn't want or need to be there, they discharged him, with some relief, into Lizzie's care.

"Aren't you meant to be looking after me, checking vitals and stuff?" He gave her a lopsided grin as he struggled to get out of his shirt, getting the sleeve stuck on his temporary cast. He was going to have some pretty amazing bruises in the morning, if it wasn't morning already.

"I'm sure I've got a thermometer and a pair of rubber gloves somewhere," she replied. She helped him to his room, and when it appeared he had finally fallen asleep, she checked the makeshift closure on the battered door. Leaving the lights burning in the living room, she slid between his sheets and lay next to him, listening to the sound of his breathing, checking that it didn't stop.

"Tomorrow … today … whatever, I should go see Joe," he said tiredly. He reached out his good arm and pulled her against him, wincing as she leaned up against his tender ribs. He smiled wryly when he realized she was still fully clothed.

"Do you think that's wise?" she whispered in the darkness of the bedroom. "You look a little scary."

His eye was totally closed, his lip swollen and his scalp resembled a patchwork quilt. "Do I scare you?" he asked.

"No, but I'm not four years old."

"But you are scared?"

"Of course I'm scared. You were almost beaten to death in front of me. We were both almost killed and we will be killed if we don't hand over the computer by tomorrow midnight. Aren't you scared, just a little?"

"I'm scared that you may get hurt, that people I care about might get hurt, but I'm not scared of Mo Pater. I'm just a little confused."

"A blow to the head will do that for you."

He smiled in the dark and closed his eyes wearily ... when all else fails, think of sex ... and he moved his hand down her back. The little black dress had a wonderful silky feel to it. "Yeah, but I'm confused as to why Mo let us off the hook, didn't just kill us, gave us another whole day to play detective."

"He wanted the computer."

"If he wanted the computer, he just had to look in the car. It's parked downstairs." He felt her shrug of bewilderment against him and experienced for the first time what that delicate movement felt like. It felt good and he winced with frustration. He had her where any sane man would want her but, between his broken bones, his twenty something stitches and a headache that felt like a six day hangover, he wasn't exactly firing on all cylinders, certainly not the important ones, anyway.

"You okay, honey?" he asked. He'd monopolized the past few hours, courtesy of Mo and his fancy foot and fist work, and overlooked the fact that not all injuries showed quite as obviously as his but could be serious nonetheless.

"I'm fine," she replied.

"Then go to sleep," he said quietly. If he thought about it long enough he would work out why Mo was still playing with them.

* * *

She was down to her underwear by morning, and regardless of the blow to the head, Connell knew he would have remembered if he'd had anything to do with it.

Her little black dress hung on a hanger on the back of the door. So they had something in common; she was another one who didn't like to sleep in her clothes. He leaned across her to check the time; Sunday morning and it was after ten. They'd overslept, which was hardly surprising. His headache was gone and her skin was smooth and warm against him.

"Hey, Mrs. Jones, have we got a thing going on here?" he breathed huskily against her ear.

"Only in your head, Detective," she replied with a sleepy smile.

"Mm, I promise you that's where the best things get started. Try it– imagination is a wonderful thing." He brushed his lips across her forehead, sighed and rolled away from her. He had things to do and time was running out.

He stood under the shower for some time, though he'd been told not to get his stitches wet and the short cast on his left wrist meant that he had to stick his arm out of the cubicle to keep the plaster dry. Complications - he could do without them. He looked in the mirror. Lizzie was right, he did look scary.

The doorbell rang as he wrapped a towel around his waist. He gestured to Lizzie, who had slipped his bathrobe over her underwear, to stay back.

"It's probably just Marty," he said as he pulled the door from its precariously balanced position and found Musgrave on his doorstep. He was flanked by two uniformed officers.

"Good morning, Detective Connell. Been in the wars, have we?"

Connell stared as the man brushed past him into the ransacked apartment. "*Detective Musgrave* we're a tad formal this morning, aren't we? What's up? You gone and got your promotion and started making house calls?"

Musgrave smiled. "Not yet, though I do believe it's going to be in the bag when I take you in."

"Take me in? What crap is this?" Connell ran his fingers through his wet hair.

Musgrave scanned the room, took in the devastation with some satisfaction and turned to Connell. "You've gone too far this time, Connell. Internal Affairs want to have a word with your poor broken down ass."

"In your dreams, maybe." Connell shook his head and caught the tail end of his concussion.

"Your feud with Mo Pater, Connell, it's gotten out of hand. People are beginning to worry that you're mixing with the wrong kind of acquaintances, that maybe you've gone over the edge. It wouldn't be impossible after everything that's happened. No one's blaming you exactly, in fact there's a good deal of sympathy for you, but we can't have a rogue cop running around now, can we?"

"Are you on crack or just crazy, Musgrave?"

Musgrave ignored him and wandered the room, picking his way carefully over the broken glass. Connell watched with growing unease. "You withheld a witness, which is bad enough, but maybe understandable." He stopped his wandering and considered Lizzie at length She pulled the bathrobe more tightly around her and he smiled and turned back to Connell. "You're right. She is a sweet looking babe."

"What witness? Who says she's a witness?" said Connell. "I haven't withheld anything I just haven't filed my report yet. I had a few problems." He held up his cast by way of explanation.

"Mm ... busted it playing football on the stairs while you were drunk, did you?" Musgrave turned to the two uniforms who stood uncomfortably at the door.

"Wait downstairs, would you?" The men glanced at each other, sent Connell apologetic looks and disappeared out the door.

"So, where were we?" continued Musgrave. He righted one of the kitchen chairs, noted with some distaste the brown stain on the floor where Connell had leaked blood the previous night, sat down and crossed one leg over the other. "Tampering with a witness, cultivating her for your own purposes, perhaps?" He turned slyly to Lizzie. "Mrs. Jones, please feel free to let me know if you've been tampered with."

Connell scowled. Who did this guy think he was? "You know what? You're a piece of shit. You come in to my home accusing me, insulting an innocent woman. She's got nothing to do with this."

"So you admit there is a 'this'?"

Connell tightened his fist and felt Lizzie's hand on his arm, gentle but firm. "Since you seem to think there is, I'm happy for you to maintain your fantasy a little longer. So what else you got, Detective Mutgrave?"

"It's 'Musgrave', you stupid fuck, and what I've got is this: you broke into a dead guy's house and stole evidence. Now why would you do a thing like that?"

"Says who?"

"Say the guys who followed you."

Connell shrugged. He was sure they hadn't been followed. "So your guys got it wrong. You've got nothing, Musgrave. Try it with someone who actually cares." He turned away, caught a strange look on Lizzie's face, and wished that she'd go and put some clothes on.

"You really think feeling up your woman in a crowded elevator wasn't going to draw attention to you?

Connell, you're probably the only cop I know who would try that and think it would work."

Connell shot a quick glance at Lizzie. Well, that depended on what you were trying to achieve. From where he'd been standing, it had worked just fine. "Like I said, you've got nothing."

"I've got your prints all over the apartment, and there's the small matter of what was burned in the wastebasket, destroying evidence. What was all that about, Connell?"

Connell almost glanced back at Lizzie but stopped himself just in time. No way did he want any of that shit brought up. He thought about Mo. He was one clever son of a bitch. No wonder he'd been happy to leave them be, no wonder Gilly had given up Carl's address so easily. They'd been set up.

"And you hammered an old man nearly to death," continued Musgrave. Connell spun back around. Now that was going too goddamn far. "Look at you, Connell. You're trying to make out you weren't in a fight? Oh sorry, you fell down the stairs–drunk–that's the official version, isn't it? You may be a lot of things, Connell - irresponsible, unreliable and a total psycho - but, you know what, I've never seen you drunk, not really loaded."

"Don't pretend you know me," said Connell flatly. Musgrave was wrong, he had been falling down drunk before, but only the once and only his good pal Marty had been around to witness it. It had lasted a week. He'd managed to sober up for the funeral.

"Someone worked over Gilly Tasker last night and you were seen arguing with him at the club. In fact, you were seen by a number of witnesses with your hands around his throat. You're up to your neck in something, Connell, and when you go down, I go up. It's as simple as that."

"You are so far off-base, Musgrave. I'm telling you now, this is a set up and I can prove it. You want me to go speak to Internal Affairs, fine, I'll do that, but no way am I going in with you."

"You want to hang onto what's left of your self-respect a little longer, Connell? Well, sorry, no can do. You're coming in with me and Mrs. Jones is going home to jolly Olde England this afternoon on the four o'clock flight. If she's not a witness, she doesn't need to be here, does she?" He held out his hand. "I need your gun and badge, Detective, and perhaps, in the interests of common decency, you'd both better put on some clothes."

Connell smiled and held up his plaster cast. "She's going to need to help me get ready ... you know, button my buttons, zip up my zipper ... unless you want to do it yourself."

"Whatever." Musgrave waved them away. "But don't take all day. I'm not going sit here and wait while you two get it on in the bedroom."

Connell took Lizzie's hand, pulled her with him into the bedroom and closed the door. He hurriedly discarded his towel and Lizzie looked away. "Connell!"

He pulled on his shorts and stepped into his jeans. "Come on, Nurse Jones, I'm sure you've seen worse than that."

"Worse?"

He smiled. "Well, I doubt you've seen better. Come on, you need to motor, get your clothes on." Lizzie hesitated and he shook his head. "Okay, I'll look the other way."

"No, it's not that," she said as she discarded the bathrobe and pulled her jeans and t-shirt on over her underwear. "It's him."

"He's a prick, ignore him. When we get to the station, I'll work everything out."

"No, that's not what I mean. You called him Musgrave. Is that his name?"

"Yeah Henry J. Musgrave. Can you help me here, honey?" He was struggling to pull up his zipper and fasten the button on his jeans with one hand.

She crossed the room, placed gentle fingers against his crotch, and hiked his zipper.

"Whoa, easy does it."

"Sorry. Did I hurt you?"

He shook his head. "Not exactly, no …"

"His name was in Carl's address book." She lowered her voice, glanced at the door and then back at Connell.

Connell paused, his t-shirt half on, and Lizzie pulled it down over his bruised chest. "Whose name?"

"Musgrave's."

"You sure?"

"I'm sure," she replied.

Connell sat on the edge of the bed as she helped him with his socks and shoes.

"Don't get used to this. This is just because you're still in the first twenty-four hours after your concussion and I'm responsible for you– professionally."

"What happens when we get to twenty-five?"

"You learn to dress yourself or you go naked."

Connell kissed the top of her head. "You can be my nurse anytime, but first we've got to get out of here."

"Are you two done screwing around in there? Mrs. Jones has a plane to catch, remember?" shouted Musgrave.

Connell opened the door and entered the living room with his badge held awkwardly in the fingers of his plastered left hand. "You asked for this," he said and he threw it to Musgrave who rose from his seat to catch it. Stepping swiftly forward, Connell followed it with a quick sharp punch from his right hand to Musgrave's face. It broke his nose and floored him in one. "You

108

asked for that as well." He cursed and shook his hand. "That hurt."

"Is he okay?" asked Lizzie.

"He's in better shape than I am. Better shape than he should be. He should be fucking - sorry - he should be dead, the double-crossing piece of shit."

Lizzie knelt and moved him in to the recovery position just in case. "How are we going to get past the two policemen downstairs?"

Connell glanced up at the skylight. "Grab your bag. We're going down the fire escape."

"What about the cat?" she asked.

"The cat can look after himself," replied Connell. "That's what mice were made for."

She emptied the contents of Connell's medicine box into the carrier bag along with her books and stuffed it into her bag - if he wasn't hurting now, he soon would be - and she pulled together a change of clothes for Connell from his laundry basket. Connell stooped gingerly, extracted the photo of Joe from the broken glass and slid it into his pocket. Then he stuffed his gun in the waist of his jeans and placed a chair on top of the kitchen counter. He climbed up with some difficulty and popped the lock on the sky light.

"Climb up here with me," he said and they balanced precariously on the small chair. He took her bag from her and flung it through the gap. Lizzie followed, wriggling her way seductively up his body. Connell rolled his eyes–all these missed opportunities. He was cursed with bad luck and worse timing. Someone up there was having a blast at his expense.

He helped her on her way with his hand on her shapely buttocks and a good push, and she climbed through and out onto the roof. Connell stepped up onto the back of the chair, and before it toppled, he got his elbows through the opening. Despite the pain in his ribs and the pain in his arm, he hauled himself through the tight space and collapsed against the sloping tiles. "Now that was harder than it looked," he admitted as he tried to shake the pins and needles out of his fractured wrist.

"Does it hurt?" she asked.

"Only when I laugh," he replied, and she smiled.

"Don't worry, that's normal. It proves you're still alive. When you can't feel anything, that's when you need to worry."

He knew exactly what she meant.

Seven

They picked up the car from the underground parking garage while the uniforms hovered in the stairwell, wondering why Musgrave was taking so long and whether they should go check. But since neither of them cared much for Musgrave, and both knew a bit about Connell and the business with his lady and Mo Pater, they were inclined to wait a little longer.

Connell headed out of town. He wasn't really sure where he was going but he needed to put some space between them and those with an unhealthy interest in them. An hour of driving, though, and his head was pounding and he couldn't hold his left arm on the wheel any longer. He pulled into a diner, found a preferred seat in the window and rested his head in his hands.

"We up to twenty-five hours yet?" he said wearily.

"Why, do you need me to help you at the bathroom?" she asked with a smile.

He tried a laugh but the pain in his ribs made him wince and he shook his head instead. "You can if you'd really like to, but what I need is drugs." He smiled sheepishly. His eyes were bloodshot, his face a bruised mess.

He looked and felt like shit.

"I thought you might by now." She opened her purse and pulled out a plastic bag, emptying the contents onto the table. "What would you like?" She passed him painkillers and anti-inflammatories, and he washed them down with some coffee. For once the thought of food held no appeal. "They should kick in soon. You just need to get some rest and you'll be fine."

"Is that your professional opinion?" he asked. He reached across, taking her hand and squeezing it gently. He marveled at how small and delicate it was, sitting within his palm.

"It is."

He let her hand go. He was getting distracted, and no matter how distracting he found her, or how rough he felt, there were things that needed to be done. "Well, unfortunately, I can't rest yet and neither can you. I need to check in with Marty, find out what's going on and see if he's managed to set anything up yet with his friendly Feds."

He hoped so. He needed to offload what they had before Mo and his buddies realized he wasn't going to turn up with the computer. Pissed as Mo would be, he might just get the notion to start looking for them out of town.

"I don't understand. Why can't you just call the police? You were attacked by the person you want to arrest. Does this not make it easier for you? Why can't you arrest him for assault and build a case against him for everything else?"

Connell shook his head. *Build a case.* She'd been watching too much TV. "It would, if Musgrave hadn't suddenly become a part of it. I need to know whether the rest of the squad believes his version of events, in which case we're basically on our own." And that wasn't really a place that he wanted to be, Mo on one side, cops on the other.

He leaned back in his seat, took out his cell phone and dialed.

"Well this is a first," said Marty. "A call during daylight hours. I was beginning to think you'd been bitten by a vampire."

"Yeah, well, can't be the cause of marital disharmony, can I?" Connell rubbed carefully at his eye, avoiding the stitches. He received a warning look from Lizzie and dropped his hand.

"Is everything okay, buddy? You sound wasted."

"Had a little run-in with Mo. Seems like he's got Musgrave on his payroll. I need to know whether it's a private arrangement or whether I'm on America's Most Wanted."

"For fuck's sake, Tommy, what happened? Is the girl alright? Are you alright?"

Lizzie began to gather up the various medicines from the table top. Connell watched, blinking slowly, tiredly, as she stacked the various bottles in a growing tower. "She's fine. I'm a little less than fine. But, hey, it could be worse - at least I've got my own nurse."

"Where are you - your place?"

"Nope, Musgrave is at my place … it's a little messy."

"You didn't shoot him, did you? 'Cause that would definitely put you on the *Most Stupid*."

"No, I just set some boundaries with him. You see, I do listen to all your parenting advice."

"Was he breathing?"

"Of course he was. He was so relaxed that he was sleeping when we left." He smiled at Lizzie. Her tower was about to topple. She pulled out the plastic bag and began stacking the pill vials inside.

Marty groaned. "What happened with Mo?"

"He paid me a visit, got a little physical. He wants Carl's computer, or so he said. The whole thing with Carl's place was a set-up. Fucking Gilly. I thought he was a little too accommodating. He set me up and

113

Musgrave showed up this morning and demanded my badge."

"Never mind Musgrave. Are you telling me Mo paid you a visit and left you alive?"

"Barely, he likes to play. But you know me, Marty. I just keep getting up again I'm a regular glutton for punishment."

"Okay, where are you now?"

"Fucked if I know. I just put my foot down and headed for the hills."

"Okay, so where are you going?"

"You tell me. Have you spoken to the Feds yet?" He leaned forward and stilled Lizzie's hand.

"I'm on my way to a meeting now."

"Okay, bud. Listen. I really need to get my head down and lay low for a while. I'll call you later–tomorrow even, unless you think I need to hear something urgently. Do what you can. Find out what the word is downtown. You know what I mean. I need to know if I'm fucked or not."

"You going to be okay?"

"Sure I am. Nurse Jones here says all I need is a good night's sleep and I'll be good as new."

Marty didn't sound convinced. He knew what Mo was capable of. He'd been the one who had picked Connell up off the floor the last time. "Take care, Tommy. You got me worried."

"Sure thing, bud." Connell pocketed the phone and caught Lizzie's eye. "What's with the bag?"

"What do you mean?"

"There's something written on the inside of the bag." He leaned across and tipped out her neatly packed pill vials.

"Hey, I've just packed them."

He shrugged his apology. "Turn the bag inside out."

114

She reversed the bag and flattened it out on the table top. The surface of both sides was covered in row upon row of scribbled numbers - three, two and two, separated by hyphens.

Lizzie scooted around to Connell's side of the table so she could see more clearly. "Move along," she said and he made room for her on the bench, resting his plaster cast on the seat back behind her.

"Was this the same plastic bag that the CD player was wrapped in?"

"Yes, I just used it to scoop up the medicines from your apartment. I thought you might need them."

"Then I think we may have just found the rest of Carl's package," said Connell. "They look like bank-type codes."

"British banks use three sets of two numbers," said Lizzie, shaking her head.

"And American banks have more numbers than that," admitted Connell.

"Maybe they're not bank numbers. They could be dates."

"Oh yeah, how long are months in England ...?" Okay, so maybe not dates.

"Perhaps it was meant to be used in connection with the disc," she suggested.

"And Mo has the disc that doesn't work anyway." He studied the lists. There were hundreds of sets of numbers; they had to mean something. "It's not the disc, that's too obvious. Why would he want a cd player when he could download onto an MP3 or an iPod? Why would he dress up a data disc to look like a music cd when he knew it was corrupted? Who the fuck has heard of 'Jamaica Inn' anyway? Some British band, huh?"

"What do you mean?"

"The title of the CD was Jamaica Inn. You heard of them?"

115

Lizzie grinned. "No, but I've read the book." She ducked back in her bag and pulled out one of the three books that had been on her chair when he'd first interviewed her. "'Jamaica Inn' by Daphne Du Maurier; it's about smugglers and highwaymen, and a girl who gets mixed up in dangerous stuff."

Connell raised his good eyebrow and grinned back at her. "Dangerous stuff, huh?"

"It was in the bag along with the other books and the CD player. I just never gave it a thought. I only brought them so I would have something to read on the plane. Only I didn't actually read that one because I'd read it before at school."

"Well someone's read it, and read it well, by the look of it." He picked it up and flicked through. It was dog-eared, the pages worn smooth with much handling. "Any ideas?"

"Maybe he liked good books," she said with a shrug. "It's a good book."

"Does that sound like him, in your experience?"

Lizzie shook her head, "Not really. Don't get me wrong, he was intelligent. He seemed to know a lot about a lot of things, but I don't think he would have appreciated good writing."

Connell smiled, not wanting to admit that his idea of good writing was the sports page.

"Maybe he was into smugglers and highwaymen," suggested Lizzie and Connell's smile widened.

"Or just smuggling. Guess what we import from Jamaica?"

"Drugs?"

"Among other things."

They looked again at the numbers and the book, and Connell found his attention straying. The painkillers were kicking in, and now that he was pretty much pain free, he was aware of Lizzie's nearness but he didn't have the energy to do anything about it.

"What about page numbers?" she said, "followed by line and then either word or letter. He could be spelling stuff out - a code."

Connell pulled his attention back to the matter in hand. "Try the first one - 165, followed by 14 then 10."

"How do you know it's the first one?"

He stared blankly at her. "It's the top of the list."

"But there are two sides to the bag. Which is the first side?"

Connell shook his head. "Tell you what, let's not worry about which side is which. Let's just test the theory first."

"Okay, so we've got page 165, line 14 and either tenth word, which is 'progress', or tenth letter which is 'E'."

"This could take some time," said Connell, glancing around, "but it could work. We need to move, go somewhere less obvious, and I know just the place."

He gathered their things, stuffed them with one hand into the top of her bag and nudged her out of the booth ahead of him.

"Is it far?" she asked as he propelled her towards the exit.

"About an hour." He caught her look, the hand straying to pull at her hair. "Don't worry, we'll be safe."

"Will you be able to drive that far?" she asked and he flexed his plastered hand experimentally, keeping his face neutral despite the jab of pain that shot up to his elbow.

"Sure. I just need you to give me a hand with one thing."

"Of course. Anything," she replied.

Anything. He doubted that. He sidled close, hooked his good hand around the back of her neck and whispered in her ear "I need to take a leak. Can you do my top button for me when I come out?"

* * *

They were headed upstate, but not to the farm, not yet anyway. Connell was headed for Marty's cabin, the place where Marty ran to when Charlene made life hard on him–which was quite often lately– or when the joys of six kids wore a little thin.

It was basic, a hunting and fishing cabin where a man could drink a few beers without having to think about anything. It was remote, and as life was becoming a little difficult, Connell decided it was the perfect hide-out.

It took longer than an hour, because they stopped for supplies, but also because Connell was finding it increasingly difficult to concentrate, and as a result, he kept his speed below the maximum which was about half the speed he normally drove at.

By the time they were off the highway and on the mountain road, the car was weaving and Lizzie was shooting worried looks at him. "Have we much further to go?"

"Not far. Another mile or so."

"Do you want me to drive?" she asked.

He shot her a glance. "Honey, you think that I'd let you drive my car?"

"I can drive. I'm a good driver."

"Yeah, on the wrong side of the road."

"Connell, you're on the wrong side of the road anyway."

He pulled at the steering wheel. "Well that's cool. There's nothing coming."

* * *

Connell found the key to the cabin in its usual spot under the door mat.

"Marty's very trusting," said Lizzie.

"Nobody comes this way," replied Connell, "except hikers and hunters."

"You mean prowlers and gunmen?"

"Well, yeah, if you want to be picky." He carried in her bag, setting it on the table in the middle of the room. "I need to get the generator going. What are you like at starting fires?" He gestured to the wood burning stove in the fireplace. "It can get pretty cold in here at night. I'd do it myself but ..." He held up his cast apologetically.

"I'm a country girl. I can light a fire with my eyes closed."

"Good, close your eyes and get lighting."

He walked the perimeter of the property slowly while it was still light, listening to the sounds of the forest, staring out at the woods, trying to see things that weren't there. He'd been here before with Marty and knew what to expect, knew where everything was, but he checked it all the same. When he'd been here previously, his only concern had been whether the fish were biting. He had a little more on his mind now.

There was no boundary to speak of. The property ran into the woods on two sides, the stream on the third, and on the fourth the track they'd driven in on. He crossed to the outbuildings, got the generator going at the first attempt and stood awhile listening to the hum of the motor. If anybody did decide to sneak up on them, the generator would cover any noise they might make but, if they wanted electricity, if they wanted light in the dark of the woods, they needed the generator.

He carried in an armful of logs and stacked them by the stove before heading back out to the car and bringing in Carl's stuff from the trunk, the telephone book from under the seat and a box of ammo from the glove box. Once inside, he checked the doors and windows, making sure they were secure. There were only two main rooms in the cabin: the living-kitchen and the bedroom with

119

bathroom off it. It looked like he'd be sleeping on the sofa, which was a little better than a chair but hardly conducive to his recovery.

"You okay to talk about Carl?" Connell asked as they sat and watched the logs burning. The cabin was secure, they'd eaten, and Connell had given in and taken more pain killers. He was feeling okay, surprisingly, secure in the knowledge that they were safe from those who might be looking for them. It was time for him to get his head into the game and figure out what was going on.

"I suppose," replied Lizzie, although he reckoned that depended on what he wanted to discuss. She'd been watching him in uneasy silence as he'd battened down the hatches as if preparing for a siege. He was sitting now, well fed and relaxed, with that inner glow that only good meds could provide. It appeared she didn't share his feeling of well-being.

"So how did they meet, Beth and Carl?" They seemed an unlikely match, teacher and master criminal.

"She first met him when she was at university. He was doing a stint as a mathematics tutor on some exchange program ... or so he said. He'd apparently met our father some years before. He was quite charming, initially. Beth was ... beguiled."

"He knew your father?"

"Well, Beth's father."

"And you didn't think that was odd?"

"Not then, no. Dad was a history professor. Carl said he'd met him at some conference. That's how he got talking to Beth initially. I suppose it could look a little odd now."

Connell watched her and read far more from her expression than she was prepared to say. "How long were they together before things went sour?"

"I don't really know, about four or five years, I suppose. I was about sixteen when Beth first kicked him out."

He glanced at her; that sounded about right. He'd waited for her to be old enough before he made his move. Typical predator behavior. "And did he stay in England with you and Beth for the entire time or did he fly back and forth to the US?"

Lizzie shrugged. "He went back often, maybe three or four times a year. Sometimes for just a few days but, other times, he would be gone for months. Beth would pretend it was okay, that she knew all about it." She glanced at Connell. "But you know when you just know that someone is putting on a face, pretending they're alright when really they're not."

Oh sure, he recognized that. It must be a family trait. "And Beth was never tempted to come over here with him?"

"Initially, yes, she wanted to go and meet his family but she had her studies and he tended to book flights when she couldn't go, during term time or in the middle of exams. Beth is very conscientious. She was determined to get good grades. I suppose, looking back, he didn't want her with him. Maybe he had stuff to hide."

"What about you?"

"Mm, my grades were okay. I'm not quite as conscientious as Beth. Less motivation, I expect. She had me to look after. I just have myself."

He reckoned she was underselling herself but that wasn't what he meant. "I meant did he ever ask you to go with him on one of his trips?"

"No."

He cocked his head. He didn't believe her; he thought they'd gotten past lying.

"Okay," she relented, "he asked me once, when Beth was stressed with her exams. He offered to take me with him. I was about fifteen … a little bit cocky, I suppose." Connell smiled and tried to imagine her as a cocky teenager. He couldn't quite get the image. He preferred the sweet one that was stuck in his head. "I didn't want to go. Beth didn't want me to go. He got a little touchy."

"What did he do?"

Lizzie looked away. "Nothing, I told him to bugger off and he went by himself."

"Why do you think he married your sister?"

Lizzie shrugged. "Why does anyone get married?" She pulled the plastic sack out of her traveling bag and emptied its contents onto the table. "I suppose we should make a start."

She'd had enough of talking about Carl but Connell wasn't quite finished. "Did he mention any friends or colleagues from here? Did anyone call him at the house?"

"We didn't have contact with anyone."

"And you didn't think that was strange?" Here was this guy who flew in and out of their lives, had no friends or relatives and liked hanging out with kids. He'd think that was pretty weird.

Lizzie shrugged. "I was a child. I didn't think about it. Beth may have thought it was strange but she didn't confide in me …, not then, anyway."

"But later she did?"

"I think we should get on. It'll be dark soon and it's been a long day."

Okay, so she didn't want to discuss Carl anymore. That was cool. They had plenty other stuff to work through.

Eight

Carl had six identities according to his passports, though it looked as though only three had been used with any regularity. Carl Jones traveled between England and America on a regular basis, his first visit almost nine years since and the last eight months ago, which pretty much tied in with what Lizzie'd said.

Connell stared, both disgusted and curious, at the photo, his only real opportunity to see what the guy looked like, seeing as how he no longer had a face. It was a ten year passport. The photo showed a younger man, though his date of birth confirmed him to be forty three, a good deal older than Beth. If Connell had been expecting a monster, he was disappointed. Carl was an ordinary guy: clean-shaven, well groomed, unremarkable. No hint of what lay beneath the surface. Connell figured if he were to smile and throw out a little charm, he could easily fool a vulnerable young woman.

"Is this how you remember him?" he asked, tossing the passport to Lizzie as she busied herself with the numbers and the book. She was transcribing the long list from the bag into an equally long list, this time in a notebook, and with the addition of the relevant words and letters.

She paused and marked her place on the list with a finger. Looking at Carl's photo, the color drained from her face. "That's how he looked at first when Beth first met him, when she first brought him home." Pausing, she took a measured breath. "He resembled a teacher I had at the time. He had the same kind of attitude … *Lizzie, you must learn how to behave*." She pulled her eyes away, shrugged as if she didn't care and went back to the lists.

Connell studied her. *Oh sure*. He wasn't fooled that easily.

James Cleaver looked a little different, in so much as his hair was darker, worn a little longer, and he balanced frameless glasses on the end of his nose. He was also older, the passport being a mere five years old. It showed a history that primarily involved travel between the US and the Caribbean, Cuba, and interestingly, Iceland. *Who goes to Iceland,* wondered Connell, *unless they have a thing for volcanoes and hot springs?* James Cleaver was not so well groomed and had a dangerous air about him. The intervening four years of traveling had given him an edge, an intensity directed through piercing grey eyes. Connell flicked through the pages. His last journey as Cleaver was three weeks ago. He had been to Jamaica. Connell smiled this guy was a regular Christopher Columbus.

The third passport was Canadian and had seen Colin Manson through various journeys during the last seven years between Canada, the US, the Far East and Israel. Manson's hair was cropped short against his head, he was tanned and he had a carefree laid back look about him. His eyes were brown. He had been to Kuwait regularly, the most recent visit being four months ago, and home to Canada two months ago.

Connell checked the other passports. Two were unused and recently issued in the names of Gerald

Spooner and Christopher Gideon. The last had been issued four weeks ago but used only once, when Michael Butler had returned from Ireland ten days ago. Of all of the images, it was Butler's that made the greatest impression on Connell. His dark hair was swept roughly from his face, as if he'd been in a hurry when the photo was taken. His stubble, not quite designer, made him look a little unkempt, desperate, and his green eyes had a haunted quality to them. This was a picture of a man who knew that he was on Death Row and was placing all his faith in an appeal he could never win. As far as Connell was concerned, this was the man who had been killed by Mo Pater, and he knew that because he recognized him.

"What about these guys?" He laid them out slowly on the table, open at the photo page. "You recognize any of these?" He watched her carefully as she studied them.

She trailed her finger along the line pausing at James Cleaver. "This is the Carl I remember most." She withdrew her hand and almost looked away, but her gaze was drawn reluctantly back. "This is '*Lizzie, you will fucking well do as you're told*'."

Connell blinked, shocked at the cussing. It didn't suit her, didn't fit somehow, and he realized the depth of emotion caught up in that. Carl had a hell of a lot to answer for, shame in a way that he was already dead. He'd have enjoyed asking the questions. "What about the others?"

Lizzie quickly swept her gaze across the remaining photos and stopped at Michael Butler. Reaching out with an unsteady hand, she picked up the passport for a closer look. "This was how he looked on the street before he was killed. I almost didn't recognize him ... I mean, it's obviously Carl ... the way he walked, his stature, but not Carl in the small things. Just look at his eyes. Out there on the pavement, waiting to cross, he looked scared, and that threw me because I knew it was Carl but I wasn't sure. Carl was never scared."

"He led quite a life, our man Carl," said Connell quietly, gathering up the passports and putting them to one side. He'd jumped to conclusions, which was a dangerous thing to do.

He'd assumed Carl was some low life piece of shit who ran a little illicit import and export operation, a run-of-the-mill jerk-off who'd gotten on the wrong side of the guy who yanked his chain and he'd paid the price. Maybe he'd intended to weasel his way out of trouble by selling some goods or information, but basically the guy was a nobody. Connell told himself the real reason he'd taken an interest and remained interested was because of Lizzie and what he suspected this guy had done to her. But festering beneath his honorable intention was his dishonorable feud with Mo Pater and his need for revenge.

Despite all that, he was beginning to realize this was about much more, and he wondered how far into this mess they'd actually gotten themselves and whether there was still time to get out. They said a little knowledge was a dangerous thing but, in this case, he thought a lot of knowledge might be even more dangerous. There was a whole lot more in the stuff they had if they were willing enough, brave enough and stupid enough to work it out.

He'd recognized Carl aka Michael Butler because, four years before, Butler had been the guy who'd introduced him to Marie, and two years later, he'd been the guy who'd betrayed her.

He crossed to the window, cracked the blinds and stared out at the woods. They were losing the light. It would soon be dark, and although he was confident they would be safe tonight, that they were too far away from anywhere for anyone to figure out their location, it was a temporary situation and he wasn't so clear about what tomorrow would bring.

He turned his head to Lizzie, head bowed over the lists, determined to solve the puzzle, and he sighed wearily. The pills were catching up to him. He needed to sleep.

"Look, honey, leave that. We need to get our heads down on the pillows. I'll take the sofa."

She shot him a quick glance, frustration at yet another interruption flashing briefly in her eyes. "I'm fine." She fixed a smile on her pale face. "I want to finish this. You take the bedroom. I'll be okay on the sofa. It's warmer in here anyway."

"You sure?" It didn't seem the gentlemanly thing to do, to take the bed and leave her on the sofa - and Charlene had told him to be a gentleman. He was sure she'd more in mind when she said it, and if he had more energy, maybe he'd be thinking it too. But just now, sleep was what occupied his mind.

"I'm sure. Go to bed. I'll look in later and check you're still breathing."

He raised one eyebrow and gave her a sleepy smile. "Oh yeah? Is that a promise?"

* * *

It took Lizzie another two hours to fully transcribe the rows of numbers, only to realize there was something missing. Yes, she had a list of words and letters, but they made no sense, were in no logical order and she needed the key to turn them into something that made sense. She'd numbered each entry as it had been shown originally and finally decided the first entry, by the fact that the ink from the biro was more legible on one side of the bag than the other. But there had to be a further list of numbers that would tell her in which order the words and letters should be read.

She picked up the other books and scanned through them, looking for any signs, but there was none. Maybe the key had been on the disc, or on the computer, or in the pile of papers that Connell had lifted from Carl's apartment. She turned to the passports and flicked through them, idly wondering at the many destinations. No wonder he'd spent so much time away from home. How had he managed to keep track of where he was meant to be, and perhaps more importantly, who he was meant to be?

She looked at the time and shrugged. It was very late but sleep eluded her, and in truth, the sofa didn't look that comfortable. She picked up her pen, opened up her notebook and started to make a timeline. Carl Jones or whoever he actually was, had come into her life nine years ago and left it seven days ago. Between those times, he'd traveled the world under various aliases for a reason. There was a pattern in what he'd been doing. Perhaps if she could find it, she could work out what was going on.

* * *

It was the cold that woke her sometime around two in the morning, and she raised her head from the table and rubbed at her neck. She stopped rubbing when she heard the noise. She stopped breathing when she realized the noise was outside, right outside. At about the same time, she realized the reason she could hear any noise at all was because the generator had stopped, which also explained why the cabin was in darkness.

She sat for a moment, frozen in her seat. She'd sent Connell to bed, and if she yelled for his help, whoever was out there would hear her.

She considered her position, not rationally as she would have liked, but frantically with a racing heart, and when she heard a creak on the boards outside the door, she was forced terrifyingly into action. Creeping from

128

her seat, she picked up Connell's gun from the table, padded to the window and put her eye to a chink in the blind.

Of course she realized, as she stood in the cold, her own breath misting on the windowpane, for this discreet surveillance to work she would have to open her eye.

She did so gingerly, her imagination awash with monsters and bogeymen. When she summoned the nerve to look, she was assisted by the milky light of an almost-full moon. She scanned the tree line and squinted, trying to see the extent of the porch.

Taking her eye from the window for a moment, Lizzie weighed the gun in her hand. She had no idea why she'd picked it up and no clue how to fire the thing. There was a safety, she knew that. She'd watched CSI. She turned the gun over in her hands, trying to work it out.

A further noise on the porch made her jump and a hand was clamped roughly over her mouth. She was relieved of the gun and forced, none too gently, against the back of the door.

* * *

"What are you trying to do, shoot yourself?" hissed Connell as he removed his hand.

"The ... there's someone out there..." she stammered. "They turned off the generator."

Connell pressed a finger against her lips and cocked his head, listening. He stayed her with one raised palm and crossed to the window, standing where she had stood. He peered through the blind and tried to see around the corner, as she had done. When he realized the futility of that, he took the safety off the gun and crossed to the door.

"No. Please don't open the door - Connell!" she shouted, and as he swung his head around to see why she was yelling when they were meant to be getting the jump on whoever was out there, there was an almighty roar from outside the door and the sound of something very heavy moving very quickly away.

Connell turned and exhaled. "It's a bear, a damn bear," he laughed, relieved.

Lizzie scowled at his laughter. "So, who turned off the generator?"

Connell shrugged. "Well not the bear, obviously. It probably just ran out of gas." He stood before her in his shorts and lowered the gun. "Don't touch this again, do you hear? I don't want you shooting yourself, or me, for that matter."

"Then don't leave it lying around," she countered shortly. She pulled her eyes away from him standing there half-naked. The stove had gone out and she rubbed at her bare arms with her hands.

Connell watched her. He read the fleeting expression in her eyes and smiled crookedly. "I'm going back to bed." He held out a hand. "Are you coming?"

She looked at the cold sofa and shrugged. "I suppose so." She dismissed his hand and followed him into the bedroom. "But no funny business."

Connell shot her an amused glance. "Funny business? Is that what you call it in England?"

She ignored him and he slid beneath the covers as she shucked out of her jeans. He listened while she tiptoed into the bathroom and tried to brush her teeth in the dark, and then he felt the slight dip in the mattress and the blast of cold air as she snuck beneath the covers. She was freezing. He could feel her shivering. He sighed and turned over.

"Okay, here's the deal." He reached out in the dark and pulled her back up against him. "I'll keep you warm and you go to sleep. No funny business." This was going to be torture. He'd been right when he'd told Marty that he was a glutton for punishment. Time for some Connell charm. "Or we could just get it over with and have some crazy sex. The choice is yours - sleep or sex?"

Lizzie wriggled around to face him. "I haven't had a good night's sleep for over a week."

"Yeah, but how long since you've had crazy good sex?" He gently pushed her hair back from her face.

"Does it have to be crazy?"

"Sure it does." What other kind is there? "If it doesn't drive you crazy, you're not doing it right."

"Then maybe a little bit longer than seven days."

"Just a little bit?"

"Mm. Depends how crazy good you mean."

"Pretty good."

"Then probably never."

"Aren't you just a little bit tempted?" He ran his hand down her arm and felt her skin prickle in response.

Lizzie smiled in the darkness and hesitated just long enough. "A little," she admitted, laying her hand on his chest. Connell felt the coolness of her palm against the warmth of his skin and he waited, just knowing it wasn't going to be that easy. "But, as your nurse, I don't think crazy is a very good idea. You might burst your stitches."

"I might ..." He brushed his lips gently across hers and caught the little gasp she tried to suppress. He pulled his mouth away before she could feel his responding frustrated groan.

"So, I suppose," she continued, "that tempting though the thought is, we should really choose sleep and do crazy some other time."

"Is that your final answer?" He slipped his hand beneath her t-shirt and slid it slowly to the small of her back.

"I'm afraid it is."

He kissed her again. "Don't be afraid. There's no need to be afraid of me." He pulled away and did a

131

pretty good job at hiding his frustration. "Sleep's good. We can go crazy later."

"You sure?" she whispered.

"Sure I'm sure." He closed his eyes, felt her relax and didn't know quite how to feel about the emotion welling through him. Christ, he wanted her, and for once this had nothing to do with sex.

"What if the bear comes back?"

"Then I'll wake you up and you can yell at him again."

She snuggled closer still and laid her cheek against his chest. He felt every inch of her pressed up against him. She was warming up nicely and so was he, which wasn't good, not when he'd suddenly discovered a moral conscience and feelings he didn't know he had. Did she realize what she was doing to him? He rolled his eyes in the dark. Being a gentleman wasn't all it was cracked up to be.

"Okay, goodnight, Connell," she whispered sweetly.

"Goodnight, Lizzie," he sighed.

* * *

The sound of his phone woke Connell, and the sun was already up. He felt around for it on the nightstand before realizing he wasn't at home, he wasn't alone, and the phone was in the pocket of his jeans that were slung over the end of the bed. He reached across, pulling the covers with him, and Lizzie grumbled and pulled them back. She was warm and sleepy, and her hair was mussed. She smiled when he leaned over and breathed against her ear.

"Sleep well?" he asked.

"Mmm."

"Cool, that's the next seven days taken care of. Time for some funny business, by my figuring."

Lizzie opened one eye slowly and looked at him. "That's not in the least bit funny. Answer your phone."

132

Connell grinned.

"Hi, Marty, you're an early bird. You got something for me?" Connell sat back against the pillow and let his hand linger on Lizzie's thigh as she slid from the bed and disappeared into the bathroom.

"It's not that early, Tommy, and I've been trying to reach you for the last hour."

"You have?" He couldn't believe he'd just spent another night curled up next to Lizzie and slept right through it. Man, what was wrong with him?

"What have you been doing?" asked Marty. "Or shouldn't I ask?"

"Just sleeping," and wasn't that the truth. "What you got?"

"I've been talking to my boys. They're very interested in what you have. Didn't give much away. They were, to be honest, a little guarded but they want to meet and they want you to bring the girl."

"What about Musgrave?" asked Connell. He didn't want to go meeting anyone until he knew the score and whether he was likely to be arrested.

"Musgrave is playing a little double-bluff. I called the station, asked for you, and that little red haired chick …"

"Brenda?"

"Yeah Brenda, she said you were on sick leave, said you'd taken a dive down the stairs. She sounded real upset about it. You and she been screwing around, Tommy?"

"No, we haven't. You know, Marty, you and Charlene need to get a life and leave off trying to second-guess mine. I do not screw around with every woman I know." *Just some of them*, he admitted to himself as he shot a glance at the bathroom door.

Marty laughed. "For what it's worth, she sounded genuine, said the guys were worried about you. She confided that she thought you were an accident waiting to happen, that it was about time you took some time off."

"Gee, I feel better already."

"Do you, Tommy? You sounded like shit yesterday."

"I'm fine, Marty, really. Just a few bruises. I'm more concerned about Lizzie and all this crap with Carl. It's all getting a little messed up. This guy Carl Jones was some kind of criminal mastermind, a secret agent or something. He's got all these different identities, spends his time jetting around the world and thinking up secret codes to cover his tracks. Fuck knows what he's up to, but he's mixed up with people I don't like, people I have issues with."

"And what about the girl? We already know she's not who she claimed to be."

"She's clean, Marty. Got caught up in it, that's all."

"A little more than that, Tommy. She came in on a false passport."

"Lizzie is not the problem here, Marty." He swallowed away an unwanted flash of irritation. "Mo is the fucking problem and he's not going to go away. I can't let him, Marty, not now. There's more to this than even I can work out. Carl knew Marie–at least not Carl exactly, but Michael Butler. He and Mo were involved in what happened to Marie."

"Slow down, Tommy, you've lost me. What has Michael Butler to do with this?"

"Carl and Michael are one and the same. I know it's complicated, I'm not really sure what the fuck is going on myself, but Mo knows the truth."

"Don't go thinking you can handle Mo by yourself, Tommy. You've too much history to keep a clear head. Let the Feds sort it out for you."

Connell drew a breath. Oh yeah, like they did the last time. "Where do they want to meet?"

"The Pines Motel. You anywhere near there?"

"I might be."

"You at the cabin?" asked Marty.

"I didn't think you'd mind."

"You know I don't, anytime, Tommy. I thought that's where you'd be. That's why I suggested The Pines. They want to meet at noon. Bring everything you've got, including the girl, and they'll work it out."

"Work it out?"

"Carl was involved in something that's still on-going and they need his stuff in order to see it through."

"Involved in something?"

"They mentioned National Security."

"That's what they say when they don't want to tell you what's going on."

"Hey, I'm just doing what you asked, setting up a meeting, I don't know anything about secret agents, don't want to know."

"Why do they need Lizzie?"

"They just want to talk to her."

"She can't tell them anything."

"Then it'll be a short conversation."

Connell thought for a moment and felt uneasy. "Are they cool these guys?"

"I can vouch for them, Tommy. I wouldn't have talked to them if I didn't trust them."

Connell heard the shower come on and he glanced at his watch. He did a quick working out in his head. "Can't make it for midday, Marty, got a few things to do first. Can you get back onto them? Tell them I'll be there by two. Oh and, Marty, see what you can find out about Iceland."

"Iceland?"

"Yeah, the country Iceland. Why the fuck would anybody, secret agent or not, want to go there? Maybe I'm missing something obvious. You're good with geography. See what you can find out."

135

The shower stopped and Lizzie came out, wrapped in a towel.

"You smell nice." Connell made to squeeze past her into the bathroom. Her skin was pink and glowing, her shoulders glistened with beads of water, and he fought the urge to remove those lasting droplets with his tongue. "I hope that's not the last towel."

"What if it is?"

"Then I'd have to take it off you." He placed one hand on the towel where she'd tucked it in over her breasts. "It's the law," he added with a grin.

"Then I'm fortunate the bathroom is well stocked."

She lowered her lashes, gave him a slow not-so-sweet smile, and he shook his head.

Later - he'd work it all out later ...

Nine

"Pack up your things. We've got to get moving," said Connell as he began to load Carl's stuff into the car.

"Where to?"

"Someplace else."

"You're scaring me. Why do we need to move again? You said this place was safe."

Connell stopped with a hand on the trunk of the car. "It is safe but I need to go do something, I don't want to leave you here on your own and I don't want to take you with me."

"So?"

"So I'm going to leave you somewhere else, where no one will think to look." He took her bag from her and threw it in the trunk with the rest of the stuff.

She didn't want to go anywhere without him, he could tell by the look on her face. He didn't know whether that was good or bad.

"I'd rather stay with you."

"It's not going to happen, sweetheart. I need to know that you're safe before I meet with these guys."

"The Feds? Is that who you're meeting with?"

"Yeah." He climbed into the car and leaned over to open her door. "Hop in. We've got to motor."

"Are you going to give them what we have?"

"That's the idea."

"There's a problem with that."

He started the car and turned to look at her. "What problem?"

"There's something missing from the code. I transcribed the entire thing last night but we're missing the key to tell us in what order it has to be read. Without the key, it makes no sense."

"Let them worry about that. If Carl, or whoever he was, was one of theirs, then they probably have the key anyway. I just want to get rid."

"So why can't I come with you?"

He slowly guided the car down the rutted trail and wondered how he had managed the drive the previous day feeling the way he had. "Because I don't want them thinking they can arrest you under some phony National Security shit. If they want all Carl's stuff, they're going to have to deal for it."

Lizzie looked at him and smiled. "You are a good man, Tommy Connell."

He grinned back. "I know I am. I told you I was one of the good guys."

"So, where are we going?"

"To see Joe." He gave her a crooked smile "You think I'm good. This little man is going to sweep you off your feet."

* * *

Barking dogs, and lots of them, announced their arrival at the farm, but as soon as Connell got out of the car, the dogs quieted and became pathetic wagging, licking machines. Lizzie tried to stroke them but it took a word from Connell to get them to leave her alone and put their tongues back in their mouths.

"They don't get many visitors," he apologized on their behalf, "and they like you," he smiled. "You smell nice." He dipped his head, tempted to see if she tasted just as nice, when an ear-piercing squeal had him step back with a start.

"Daddy!" The little boy rode toward them across the yard on a red bicycle, his feet pumping the pedals fiercely, the bell on the handlebars ringing like a fire truck, and Connell stood his ground and acted as a human buffer when it became obvious that Joe hadn't quite mastered the brakes.

He scooped him up and hugged him, and the little boy flung his arms tightly around Connell's neck. "You came! Grandma said you would. I've been waiting to show you my bike."

"It's a pretty cool bike, Joe, and you sure ride it well," said Connell. Lizzie watched as he closed his eyes, inhaled the scent of the boy's windswept hair and breathed out a huge sigh of relief.

"Who's that?" asked Joe as he squirmed within his Dad's arms. Connell set him back on the ground before his ribs gave out.

"This is Lizzie, Joe. She's come to visit."

"Hi, Lizzie."

"Hello, Joe. I do like your bike."

The little boy smiled proudly. "My Daddy got it for me and I been practicin'."

"You're very good." She knelt alongside him. "That's a very loud bell you've got there. I suppose you need it to make sure all of these dogs get out of your way."

"Yeah, 'cause these dogs like to run in front of me." The dogs congregated around him and he petted them, totally unafraid, despite the fact some were bigger than him.

"What you been doin', Daddy? You been falling over?"

"Something like that."

139

The little boy grinned and pulled up the leg of his pants to show off a graze on his knee. "I've been fallin' over, too."

"Whoa, that looks bad. Did it hurt?" said Connell.

"A little bit."

"Did you cry?"

"Did you?" asked Joe.

"Sure I did," he tousled Joe's hair, "but Lizzie kissed it better for me."

Joe giggled, "Grandma kissed me, but she said it was from you."

"Well, that's okay then. Hey, Joe, where's Grandma and Grandpa?" asked Connell as he lifted Lizzie's bag from the trunk.

"Grandma's in the kitchen, Grandpa's in the stable."

"Do me a favor, Joe. Run and ask Grandpa to come up to the house."

"Sure, Daddy." And the little boy took off at full speed, the dogs running alongside him.

"He's gorgeous," said Lizzie.

"A chip off the old block?" asked Connell with a grin.

Lizzie smiled. "Not quite. He's cuter than you."

* * *

"Mom, this is Lizzie. Lizzie this is my mom, Rose," said Connell as he ushered Lizzie into the kitchen and his mom wiped off her flour covered hands on her apron and welcomed Lizzie in.

"Oh, it's so nice to meet a friend of Tommy's." She glanced at her son, puzzled, and Connell shrugged in response. "You're very welcome. Please come and sit down. Would you like a drink?" She lifted the coffee pot off the stove and turned and appraised her son. "What's happened, Tommy? You look terrible."

Connell waved her concern away. "I'm fine, Mom. I fell off the curb. It's nothing."

"You've got a broken arm, Tommy, and who knows how many stitches. I don't call that nothing."

"It was a steep curb, and anyway, it's not totally broken, it's just a little bit broken. It'll be fine. Listen, we might stay a day or two, if that's alright?"

"Of course it's alright. Tommy, this is your home."

"Sure, Mom, but I've got a couple more things to finish up before I'm done, so I'm going to take off for a couple hours. Would you keep Lizzie company for me until I get back?"

"Sure, son." She looked from one to the other, puzzled. "Are you in trouble, Tommy?"

"Trouble, Mom? I'm a cop, remember? I don't get into trouble. I make trouble-for other people."

"Mm." She frowned. "Go on, then. We'll be fine here."

Connell kissed his Mom on the cheek and gave Lizzie a lingering look. "Later, then."

"You take care," said Lizzie as he left.

He crossed the yard, stopping only to talk to his father. They hugged each other, spoke for a few moments, and Connell got in his car and drove away.

* * *

"So, Lizzie," Connell's mom began, "how long have you and Tommy known each other?"

Lizzie turned her attention back to the room and sat down on the chair she'd been offered "Oh, not long."

"And you're not from around here?"

"No, I'm from England. Just here visiting."

"That's nice, so how did you meet Tommy?"

Joe came running in, followed more slowly by his grandfather who exchanged a quick glance with his wife. The little boy squirmed his way onto Lizzie's lap and she placed one arm around him to keep him still. "Um, he helped me out. He was very kind."

141

Connell's father extended his hand. "I'm Tommy's father, Harry Connell. Tommy tells me you need fattening up." He smiled at his wife. "And Rose is good at that. Now, you stay for as long as you like. It's nice to have people around the place." He glanced at Joe. "And he seems to like you."

"You got kids, Lizzie?" asked Rose.

"No, I don't."

"Well, you've got a way with them, that's for sure."

"I'm a nurse. I've been working in Pediatrics."

"Back in England?" asked Rose and Lizzie nodded.

"I've just finished my training. I'm hoping I can stay on the children's ward."

"That sounds like a worthwhile job, Lizzie. I hope you get what you want."

Lizzie smiled. They were nice people, very nice, but she wished that Connell would come back. She was scared for him.

Harry turned to Rose. "Honey, Tommy thought it might be nice if we asked Will over for dinner. Seemed sure he'd be back in time to eat. I'll go give him a call now." He turned to Lizzie, "Will is Tommy's older brother. He's a county sheriff, took over from me when I retired. You see, Tommy's not the only cop in the family."

Great, thought Lizzie. Were they rallying the troops to protect her or to keep watch over her so she didn't make a run for it?

* * *

Connell drove into the parking lot of The Pines, parked up in front of reception, and waited. He was a little early though he was sure the guys he was meeting would be there ahead of him. They weren't in the business of being spotted before they wanted to be, although they did seem to be attempting some damage limitation over Carl Jones. Connell was interested to

142

know why, but not interested enough for someone to consider him a threat to National Security. If they wanted the stuff, they could have it. The trade-off was Lizzie. He thought that was a pretty decent trade.

Fifteen minutes after he pulled in, the passenger door was yanked open and a heavy-set guy in a suit flashed some I.D in his face. "FBI Special Agent Brooks. You Connell?" Connell nodded and Brooks climbed in beside him. "Park outside number seven," he instructed.

"Sure," replied Connell. Seven - again.

The motel rooms were individual log cabins set slightly apart from one another, great for couples wanting privacy, less great for clandestine meetings where there was a good possibility that weapons could be drawn and there might be a need to call for backup.

Connell got out of the car, felt the comforting feel of his own gun at the small of his back, and hung back to allow Brooks to enter the room ahead of him. He glanced around. He couldn't see anyone lurking but didn't expect to. He half-expected to see the red dot of a laser scope dancing on his chest but didn't see that either. His attention was pulled back when the door swung open and Brooks stepped aside and nudged him forward.

There were three men in total: Agent Brooks, whom he'd already met, Agent Simmonds, who looked like he'd just got out of school with a bad case of acne, and the guy who was obviously in charge, Mulholland.

Mulholland rose and shook his hand. "Detective Connell, you've come alone. Maybe you misunderstood our instructions. You were meant to bring Mrs. Jones."

Connell looked pointedly at his hand until Mulholland released it. "Sorry, I'm not good with instructions today." He dipped his head and showed him the line of stitches by way of explanation.

"Looks nasty," said Mulholland.

"We're dealing with nasty people," said Connell with a shrug. "You want to tell me what you want and I can be on my way."

"You only just got here."

"Yeah, well I've got better things to do than hang about motel rooms with strange guys."

Mulholland smiled. "I understand you have certain items belonging to Carl Jones that you would like to hand over to our custody."

"In exchange -"

"No one said anything about exchanges. You're a serving police officer. You don't get to exchange, you get to do your job and uphold the law."

"Oh yeah, and which version of the law is that, yours or mine?" Connell stood his ground; these Feds thought they were a law unto themselves.

"You sound a little cynical, Detective Connell. Has someone been rubbing your fur the wrong way?"

"You could say that."

"Then maybe that's something we could help you with. Who's been getting under your skin?"

Connell shook his head. "Look, we could stand here all day and discuss our likes and dislikes, but it doesn't get us any nearer to fixing this situation."

"You're quite right, Connell, so what are we going to do about it, and where is Mrs. Jones?"

Connell took a seat on the edge of the dressing table and wondered distractedly why they hadn't thought to search him, and if these guys really were known to Marty or whether they were a special team sent in specifically to clean this up.

"It's a long and complicated story."

"We've got time."

"I don't."

Mulholland narrowed his eyes. "I think that blow to your head has left you confused, Connell. You're

144

obviously not thinking straight if you think you have any control over what happens in this room. We can sort this out amicably here, or I can haul your ass in and do it in an interrogation room. Can't say what that'll do for your career, though."

"Look, I don't give a fuck about Carl Jones or whatever his name was. You want his stuff, you can have it, but you need to understand that you aren't the only guys interested in what I've got. If Carl was working for you or the CIA, or some other fucking secret spook division, he was playing double agent with the other side, and they are just a little pissed off."

"Is that what happened to you, Connell? Did you run into the other side?"

"You could say that, I guess."

"I understand it's not the first time. This isn't all about your personal crusade, is it?"

Connell stood up and the Agents Brooks and Simmonds stood to attention. "You know what? I've had enough of this. I contacted you, remember. You want to fuck around, fine, but I'm out of here." He crossed to the door and heard the click of a safety being removed as he reached for the handle. He turned slowly.

"Sit down, Detective. Let's start again, shall we? I think we got off on the wrong foot. What do you want and what have you got?"

"The girl has got nothing to do with this. She doesn't know anything. I want immunity for her."

"Is that all? She came into the U.S. on a fake passport. She brought in a package at the request of someone shady. She is connected to Carl Jones in a big way, and you say she has nothing to do with this."

"She's a pawn, that's all."

Mulholland smiled slyly at him. "You want the girl?"

"I want her to be left alone."

Mulholland narrowed his eyes and considered the request. "That's very noble of you, Detective Connell. Okay, immunity for the girl. Anything else?"

"I want Mo Pater."

"Why?"

"You know why. Your man Carl Jones, or Michael Butler or whatever the fuck he's called, and Mo Pater arranged the death of someone I once knew. Carl's dead, but Mo isn't yet."

"So, you want us to look the other way while you make sure justice is done?"

"Something like that."

"That sounds illegal, Detective."

Connell guessed that Mulholland knew all about him, had done his homework before he'd agreed to the meet. If so, he would know that he was a decent cop, a little rough around the edges maybe, prone to impulsive acts and with an attitude to authority, but essentially honest. He would also know that his ex-girlfriend, the mother of his child, had been killed by Mo Pater.

"Tell me what you know and we have a deal."

Connell took a breath and settled back down on the edge of the table. "Carl Jones sent a message to his estranged British wife offering her a divorce in return for her bringing him a package. She didn't know that she wasn't really married to him, or he wasn't who he said he was. She couldn't bring him the package either, so she sent her sister."

"So the girl isn't Mrs. Jones?"

"You're missing the point. There is no Mrs. Jones, there never was. Carl arranged to meet her, and before they could make the exchange, along comes Mo and makes sure that Carl can't exchange anything with anybody."

"And the girl witnessed this?"

Connell paused, "I didn't say that."

146

"You didn't need to. Why else are you getting the shit kicked out of you by Mo, if not on her behalf?"

"She didn't see anything. She can't testify to anything, she's not important to you."

Mulholland shrugged. "There's no need to get touchy. I already said the girl was yours."

"Okay, then." Connell glared at the man, took a breath and reined himself in a little.

"I understand you have a number of passports."

"Yeah, they're in the car. Marty tipped us off to the fact that the passport Carl sent for his wife was one of Gilly Tasker's. That led us to Carl's apartment and the rest of the stuff. Mo wants the stuff and he wants what was in the package. I don't know why. I don't want to know why. Maybe you do."

"What was in the package?"

"Let me get the gear out the car and I'll show you."

Mulholland nodded and Connell brought in the computer and the passports, the pile of papers and the package. He dumped them on the table. "I haven't looked at the computer or the papers. I haven't had the time, been a little busy what with getting the shit kicked out of me and all. The passports are interesting and they're all Gilly's, so if you didn't know that already you might want to have a conversation with him." He unwrapped the package and pulled out the CD player and the books.

"The CD is a data disc but it's been corrupted. Maybe you have ways of recovering information." Mulholland shrugged. Maybe they did. "The information you really want is written on the bag." He turned it inside out and passed it to Mulholland who simply nodded. "The book works with it, I think." He tossed the book to Mulholland. "Page number, then line, and then word or letter, I don't know which; didn't get that far. In fact, it could all be nothing. Your guys will no doubt know what it's all about."

Mulholland turned the book over in his hands. "You did pretty well, Detective. Have you any idea what this is truly about?"

"Nope, and I don't want to. I just want to hand it over and get going. I don't want any follow up, I don't want to be looking over my shoulder wondering when you guys are going to pull out the National Security card and make me disappear. If you've done your homework, you'll know that I'm an honest cop. If you want a dishonest cop, try looking at Musgrave. He tried to take my badge yesterday."

"Tried?"

Connell smiled. "Not very hard, as it happens."

Mulholland smiled back. "I did hear something about it on the grapevine, along with the story of how you fell down the stairs."

"You heard about that?"

"I hear about most things."

"What have you heard about Musgrave?"

"Basically that he swings both ways, in a manner of speaking, and yesterday he walked into a door, which was rather clumsy of him. I do believe that he couldn't recall where it happened."

"So I'm not on America's Most Wanted?"

"Not yet, Connell, but if I let you loose on Mo, you might just end up there."

"I have to finish things with him."

"Then let us do it. We need to speak to him anyway," Mulholland smiled, "on a matter of National Security."

"So what happens now?"

"Well, we say thank you very much, Detective Connell, and you go back to whatever you were doing before this all kicked off. We might even have a private word in your boss's ear to remind him what a good cop you are, just in case he's forgotten."

"And the girl?"

"I'll speak with our British counterparts, explain the misunderstanding, and get her new passport and travel docs sorted out. Will that do for you?"

Connell nodded. "Yeah, but you don't need to bust a gut. I've got unfinished business there too."

Mulholland saw him to his car, watched him drive away and turned to Brooks. "Put a tail on him, Brooks. He's going straight to the girl."

Ten

Connell pulled into the yard, parked by the side of the barn and got out of the car. He was immediately mobbed by happy dogs and an excited little boy. He shushed the dogs, swung a squealing Joe over his shoulder and carried him into the stables. His father was busy with a mare that had recently foaled.

"Is everything okay, son?"

"Sure, Dad, I handed everything off to them." It should be okay now. They'd assured him it would be but it didn't hurt to be cautious. That's why he'd asked for Will to come. Suddenly he didn't want to be the maverick go-it-alone Connell from the old days. He didn't want anything to go wrong this time.

His father looked at him, read the uncertainty in his eyes and understood more than Connell gave him credit for. "And Lizzie, she seems very nice, by the way, and pretty cute too. Is she safe?"

Connell smiled and nodded. "Sure she is. Is Will here?"

"He's up at the house with Rachel and the kids. They just got here."

"Did you put him in the picture?"

"Sure I did. He hadn't heard anything. It's unlikely he would this far out. City trouble doesn't usually come this far."

Connell shrugged. "Depends on the trouble I guess."

"He's got a car sitting up on the highway, just in case."

Connell put Joe down. "Go play with your cousins, Joe, while Grandpa and I clean up. Ask Uncle Will to come and see the foal. Tell Grandma we won't be long."

Joe grinned. He liked taking messages; it made him feel grown up. He had two messages, one for Grandma and one for Uncle Will. He ran as fast as he could so he wouldn't forget.

"What are you going do about Lizzie?"

"What do you mean? Take her to the airport and put her on a plane, I guess." Once the passport arrived there was no reason for her to stay.

"Does she know about Marie, about what happened?"

"She doesn't need to know." Lizzie wasn't stupid. He was sure she could read between the lines. All the same, it was something he wasn't ready to talk about … not yet. She would understand because she had things she didn't want to talk about either.

"So, there's nothing going on between you two?"

"Why would you say that? She's just part of a case I've been working on. You know how it goes … serve and protect. I've just been protecting her that's all."

"If you say so, son."

"Dad, I'm a grown-up. I don't need a lecture."

"Maybe you do. Sometimes you don't act like a grown-up. Like I said, she seems nice. You've never brought anyone here before, not even Marie. That must mean something."

"It means this was the only place I could think of where she couldn't get in any more trouble."

"Sure, son. You keep telling yourself that …"

Connell shrugged and turned away. "Cool it, Dad."

"You two having a father-son talk?" laughed Will. He paused at the entrance to the barn, caught the strain on Connell's face and hugged his brother to him.

"You could say said that," said Harry. "I'll leave you to talk some sense into him. I'm going up to the house to wash up. Don't be too long." He winked at Will. "You both have lovely ladies waiting for you."

"So, are you going to tell me what you've got yourself mixed up in this time, bro?" asked Will as he settled himself on a straw bale and began pulling at the stalks.

"You don't want to know, Will."

"Oh I think I do. I've got two guys on overtime watching your back."

"Thanks, Will, I appreciate it." Connell shrugged, not sure whether he was making a big deal out of nothing. "It's probably not necessary. I've passed everything over to the Feds, but -"

"Is Lizzie involved?"

"Only in a roundabout way."

"Well either she is or she isn't."

"It's complicated."

"Don't tell me you're involved with a witness, Tommy. That's unprofessional. Not like you at all."

Connell grinned at him and Will thumped him on the back. "It's okay, you know, bro. You're a man, not a machine. You're allowed to drop your guard now and again."

"You don't need to remind me."

"Dad says she's cute."

"She's a sweetheart, Will, but it's not that simple."

"You have to get past Marie, Tommy, for your sake and Joe's. You've got your whole life ahead of you. What happened was terrible but it wasn't your fault."

Connell gazed into space. "I dream about it, Will. You know, not always, but lately I can't get it out of my head. All the things I should have done, or not done. That bullet was meant for me, Will. It should have been me."

152

"You can't change the past, Tommy, just learn from it. You have Joe. You can make a good life for yourself but you have to leave all this shit behind you."

"I can't. I need to finalize things once and for all and then I can let go. I want to, Will, I do."

"Finalize things with Mo Pater?"

"Yeah."

"I thought you'd handed him off to the Feds?"

"I have … kind of."

"You trust them?"

"Nope. But I trust Marty and he trusts them."

Will nodded. "Marty is a very trusting guy."

"What's that supposed to mean?"

"I mean he sees the good in everyone."

"Not everyone."

"No? Well, I'm glad I've got men on the highway. Come on, let's go eat."

* * *

Connell knocked on the guestroom door and slouched against the frame when Lizzie opened it. "You miss me?" he asked.

"I suppose so," she replied with a smile. "I was worried about you. I'm glad you're back safe." She stood aside and let him in. He leaned back against the closed door and watched her as she scanned his wounds, checking to make sure he hadn't collected any new ones.

"Is everything sorted?" Her voice was a little breathless. She so wanted it to be and he hoped that it was. Experience, however, told him things that seemed a little too easy, generally turned out to be more complicated than you imagined.

"Sure, they're sorted if you mean they're going to get you a new passport, and you'll be home in time to see your sister's baby."

"What did they say about Carl, about all the identities?"

"Not a lot. They obviously knew more than we did, but were keeping it to themselves. It's probably best we don't know any more."

"National Security?"

Connell smiled. "Yeah, something like that."

"And Mo?"

"Don't worry about Mo," he murmured and reached out his hand. She took it and he reeled her in and held her, molding her body against his. He felt her warmth, her softness. He took a breath and breathed in her scent. Relief poured out of him.

"But I do worry about Mo," she said quietly.

She'd seen what Mo had done to him and had no doubt guessed what he'd done to Marie. And right now, Connell knew she'd be imagining what he might do to her. "Just forget about him. Mulholland will take care of Mo."

"I can't forget."

Connell suppressed a slow grin. "I know something that would help you." He slid his hands down her back, cupped her buttocks and pulled her gently.

"Is that really all you ever think about? We've got a madman snapping at our heels. Just look at what he did to you." She pulled back a step, caught the amusement in his eyes and shook her head. "You're in your parent's house. They'll hear us."

Cocking his head, he sent her the smile guaranteed to hook him a tree full of birds and pulled her back. "No, it's not all I think about …."

Outside in the hall a sudden noise distracted them both and Lizzie giggled.

"What's so funny?"

"I think someone up there is conspiring against us and all we'll ever get to do is *think* about it."

"I think you're right." He dipped his head and kissed her slowly, getting a taste of what could be and probably would never be at this rate. "Mom's putting dinner out. We've got less than a minute."

"What can you do in a minute?"

He tried to think but even that took time. "Not much,"

"Then just keep doing what you're doing." She kissed him back "That'll do to whet our appetites."

Connell groaned. He'd never felt this hungry before.

* * *

Will was an older version of Connell but more sensible, thought Lizzie as she assessed him across the dinner table. Less headstrong maybe, but that deduction was based primarily on her conclusion that no one could be as reckless as Connell. She could see the likeness, though. Will had the same easy grin, and when he glanced at his wife, she saw the same charm exhibited.

She knew that Connell had discussed the situation with Will and his father, simply by the way the men regarded her as if she needed watching over, as if they thought there might still be a threat. Connell had told her everything was sorted and she wanted to believe him, but watching the body language between the men made her uneasy.

"So how do you like the U.S.?" asked Rachel, Will's wife. She was a pretty girl, maybe the same age as Beth, and she had a quiet gentle manner that she used to great effect in organizing their three children who were all under five. The twins, Louis and Ralph, were about the same age as Joe and were playing quietly under the table with their cousin while Rachel nursed the baby Mae on her knee.

Lizzie glanced at Connell. They had been exchanging looks all evening and it hadn't gone unnoticed.

"I haven't really seen much of it, but what I have seen has been great." She didn't really want to go into the details of what her time in the U.S. had actually been like. Maybe Will would update his wife later.

Rachel smiled. "You should get Tommy to show you around the farm while you're here. It's a beautiful place. Harry has some real nice horses here, if you ride."

Joe appeared from beneath the table. "I got a cool pony."

"As well as a bike? You are a lucky boy," said Lizzie and Joe grinned and decided he would climb on her knee again. "What's your pony called?"

"Flash," replied Joe with a yawn. He'd had a busy day with lots of people to play with. He laid his head against her and began to twiddle with her hair. Connell made to take him and Lizzie shook her head. He was fine right where he was.

"Is that because he's fast?"

"Yup, he's the fastest pony in the world. He can go a million miles an hour."

"You sure about that, kiddo?" said Connell with a smile.

"My pony can go faster than that," said Ralph who appeared next from under the cloth.

"My pony can fly," said Louis.

"No, it can't," argued Joe. He sat to attention and the three little boys squared up petulantly. They each had the best pony in the world.

"I once had a pony that could dance," said Lizzie, and all three little heads turned to listen. "She was called Midge and she danced to music. They call it dressage, but it's just dancing."

"Cool," said Joe, "dressage …," he sounded out the word. "They must wear big dresses."

Connell grinned. "Pretty big, Joe, but you should see the size of their shoes."

156

Joe giggled and Lizzie gripped him more tightly to prevent him from jiggling his way off her knee. "Quit messing with me, Daddy. I've seen horse shoes."

"Yeah, but not dancing horse shoes."

"Dancing's, for girls," said Ralph, pulling a face.

"Oh, I don't know," said Lizzie and she glanced at Connell. "Some men like dancing too."

"Sure they do," said Will and he turned to Connell with a smile. "Look, it's time we headed home. Get these kids to bed before they start a war. You know where I am if you need me."

Connell nodded. "Sure thing, Will. Thanks for coming."

Will and Rachel gathered up their children. "Nice meeting you, Lizzie," said Will. "You have a nice evening."

"Come on, kiddo, time for bed." Connell hoisted Joe with his good arm and Lizzie watched as they left the kitchen. She wondered if she'd be staying long enough to get her tour of the farm. She hoped she would.

She began to clear away the dishes and Rose tried to shoo her away. "Honey, you don't need to do that. You go have a seat on the porch. There's a nice sunset out there but you'll need your coat. Winter's almost here."

* * *

Connell joined her later, sat down at the other end of the seat and gave her his best smile.

"What?" she asked.

"What do you mean? I'm just smiling."

"You're up to something."

He patted the seat next to him and she budged along. "No, I'm not."

"Is Joe asleep?"

"Yeah. You want to take a walk before it gets dark?"

Lizzie smiled. "Where to?"

"Somewhere quiet."

"I'm not coming back in to the house with straw in my hair, if that's what you've got in mind."

"You're no fun," laughed Connell and he tugged at her hair.

"When do you think I'll get my passport?" Lizzie asked.

Connell sobered and shot her a glance. "Why, you in a hurry to leave?"

"Not especially, but Beth needs me there when she has the baby."

"I thought she had a new guy."

"Yes, she does. Jonathan. He's a head teacher, and of course she'll want him there, but I need to tell her about Carl face-to-face. Does that make sense?"

Of course it did. Beth had quite a lot to take in, whether she liked the guy or not, she'd been lied to for the last nine years. "Hey, don't worry about it. I'll make sure you get back in plenty of time."

Lizzie took a breath. "Connell?"

"Yeah?"

"What happened to Marie?" She said it slowly, in barely a whisper.

He didn't answer immediately. He thought about not answering at all, and when he did, it came out more sharply than he intended. "You know what happened to her. Mo killed her."

"Don't you want to talk about it?"

"Not tonight, no." He figured there were things he would much rather be doing than talking about how Marie had taken a bullet meant for him, but had the sense to realize that she'd probably guessed most of it anyway. "All you need to know is, I got her killed and I'm not going to let it happen to you."

Lizzie reached out and took his hand, laced her slender fingers between his and squeezed them gently. "I

158

know that you won't." She glanced at him "Did you love her?"

"What do you think? She was the mother of my child. Of course I loved her." He was on the defensive and he wasn't sure why he felt the need to defend his relationship with Marie.

"She was very lucky," said Lizzie quietly.

She'd opened the door on something that she should have left well alone. Whether she realized that or not didn't matter. Connell winced. "Oh yeah, so lucky she caught a bullet meant for me."

"Lucky to be loved, even for a short while. Some people go through their whole lives and never find someone special."

Connell looked at her and wondered if she was speaking from experience. He discounted it immediately. She would be very easy to love, even if she did open doors that she shouldn't.

"She must have been a good mum. Look how Joe's turned out. I bet she's up there now, looking down, thinking what a good job you're doing with Joe."

Oh yeah, sure, thought Connell. If she were up there at all, she'd be the one putting a hex on every attempt he made at getting past first base with Lizzie. "I'm not doing a good job at all. I don't know the first thing about being a good dad." He sighed and slung his arm loosely around Lizzie's shoulders. "It should have been me, not Marie."

"Why did you never bring her here?"

"Huh?"

"Your mum was interrogating me earlier," She smiled at him, "in a very nice way. She was wondering how I'd persuaded you to bring me here. She said in the two years you were with Marie you never once brought her here to meet them. I think she was a little confused. I told her you hadn't brought me to meet them, that there was stuff going on … and we kind of ended up here."

Connell took his arm away, leaned his elbows on his knees and ran his fingers through his hair. He thought for a moment and made a decision. "Marie worked at the club. She was fun, a good time–but not the type of girl you bring home to meet your mother. To be honest, it wasn't that kind of relationship. We were young. We kind of just rolled along having fun." Is that what they were doing now, rolling along having fun? He hoped not. He hoped it was more than that. "Then Joe came along and we realized we weren't exactly made the same way. Marie didn't want to be tied down and I was kind of jealous. She was a good looking woman. I was home with Joe, she was at the club with the likes of Gilly and I was juggling my job and child care. I didn't want to admit to my folks that I'd messed up. They still don't know."

He glanced at her and tried to guess what she was thinking, but her face was impassive. "Charlene and Marty were a Godsend. Joe practically lived at their home for a year. It wasn't going to work, me and Marie, and it wouldn't have lasted anyway. But yeah, I loved her in a way, I suppose, and I didn't ever want her to die."

He took a breath and felt a wave of relief that she knew the truth. He wondered what she thought of him. He was supposed to be broken-hearted but he wasn't. He was just riddled with guilt and that wasn't the same thing.

"How did you meet?"

Connell sat back, replaced his arm and pulled her closer. He had a real need to feel her against him. She slipped her arm around him and he felt her palm cool against the warm skin in the small of his back. "That's where things are starting to get a little weird."

"Oh?"

"A guy I kind of knew a little from the club introduced us. He was an Irish American called Michael Butler."

Lizzie turned to look at him, confusion clouding her eyes. "Carl?" How could that be?

"I know, it's pretty crazy isn't it. I recognized him from the photo in the passport. Things are real messed up, Lizzie, and I'm not sure which way I'm supposed to be looking at things. I bumped into him at the club one night and we got talking, like you do. He introduced me to Marie, and bam, we were an item. He even met Marty. He was an okay guy. I saw him occasionally after that, probably when he was between missions or whatever shit he was up to doing jetting around the world. The last time I saw him was the night Marie died. He was with Mo."

"You think he had something to do with her death?" Her shocked expression said it all.

"I think he had something to do with my death, only mistakes were made and I didn't die. Marie got in the way."

"What do you plan to do about it?" asked Lizzie.

He could tell she was trying very hard to wrap her head around this new turn of events. He'd been trying to do the very same thing since he'd seen the passport and was no closer to figuring it out. "Nothing. I passed everything over to the Feds."

"You told them that Carl had Marie killed?"

"That Michael Butler, aka Carl, and Mo had Marie killed."

"And are you happy with that? Do you think they'll do the right thing?"

It was a strange thing for her to say. What would be the right thing? "Well he won't end up in the federal witness protection program, if that's what you mean.

161

And no, if you want the truth, I'm not real happy about it. If someone is going to get the chance to finish Mo, I'd rather it be me."

"You'd murder him in cold blood?"

"It's not murder, it's carrying out a sentence, and it wouldn't be cold-blooded. My blood would be boiling if I eventually got him."

"Then why don't you?"

"Because we're talking about Mo Pater, a seriously fucked-up individual, and he's already threatened you and Joe. The Feds will get him and they'll have the juice to cover up anything they do. Like Will keeps telling me, I've got to stop living in the past."

"Does that not worry you?" she asked slowly, slipping her other hand beneath the front of his T-shirt to absentmindedly caress his belly.

There were a couple of things that were beginning to worry him, not least the question of how far she intended to go on his mom's porch seat. "What do you mean?"

Lizzie shrugged, her hand strayed and Connell rolled his eyes. "You keep doing that and I'm going to have to change my opinion of you."

Lizzie grinned mischievously, "Oh yes. Good to bad?"

"No good to better." He stilled her hand, kissed the top of her head and counted back from ten. "So what did you mean about the Feds?"

"Just that we don't really know what they're prepared to cover up. I mean, do we actually know Carl was working for them? If he was, why would he be trying to have you killed? You're a policeman, you're meant to be on the same side. What were you working on at the time that would concern either Mo or the Feds enough to want you out of the picture? And if you can't think of anything, maybe it wasn't you they were trying to get rid of … maybe Marie was the right target after all."

Connell stood up and took her hand. "You've got a vivid imagination."

"It's just a thought. I mean, there are so many weird coincidences. Maybe you're trying to tie too many things together. Where are we going?" she asked as they stepped down off the porch and headed across the yard.

"I need to think. We're going for a walk."

Lizzie quickened her step to keep up with him. "Maybe Carl wasn't working for anyone but himself. Maybe he was playing his own game with Mo and Marie found out, and she was going to tell you. She would know what was going on at the club, wouldn't she?"

Connell listened and his mind was filled with possibilities he hadn't considered before. If Marie had been the target, well, she would still be dead and there was still nothing that he could do about it, but at least he wouldn't feel she had taken what was meant for him. He tried to remember what cases he was working at the time. He'd been on Vice. It would have been something innocuous, hardly anything that would have attracted the attentions of the FBI or the CIA. He thought again about Carl and his apparent predilection for young girls. Maybe there was something in that. Perhaps it wasn't his international shenanigans that had brought him to the attention of others, but his secret Achilles heel that had ultimately brought him down.

"What are you thinking?" asked Lizzie.

"I'm thinking maybe we should swap jobs. You would make a good detective and I've got a great bedside manner." He pulled her with him into the stables. "You want to see something really cool?"

"Not if it involves you removing any of your clothes."

Connell grinned and kissed her gently, "You are so funny, you know that?"

Lizzie kissed him back. "I try."

"If I took my clothes off, you wouldn't be saying 'cool', you'd be saying 'wow'."

"You forget. I've seen you without your clothes."

"Okay, enough of the flattery, here's what I really want you to see." He led her to the stall that held the mare and her new foal. "Is that cute, or what?" The little filly stood next to its mother, long legs, big eyes and a curly mane. "She reminds me of someone. I was thinking of calling her Mrs. Jones. What'd you think?"

Lizzie leaned back against him and smiled, "You know, despite your preoccupation with sex, you have a lot going for you, Connell. You have a gorgeous little boy, a lovely family–and you have a horse! Now that is cool. I've always wanted to meet a real cowboy."

"Really?" He put his hands on her hips, pulled her into closer contact, then slid his hands around her waist beneath her t-shirt and kissed the back of her neck. He felt his heart begin to speed up, his blood begin to pump and he felt her skin prickle beneath his hands. Oh yes, cute ponies were almost as good as cute puppies for tugging at the heart strings. He hadn't lost that Connell charm after all.

She pulled away with a shrug, "Shame then, that you're a policeman and not a cowboy."

He narrowed his eyes and smiled at her. "You asked me before what I was thinking. Do you want to know what I'm thinking now?"

"Maybe not ..."

"I'm thinking I could be arrested for what I'm thinking, and you could be arrested for making me think it. Get the picture?"

"I'm trying to imagine it ..."

He shook his head. "Don't, just don't." She laughed and he squeezed her hand. He didn't really want to let go. "As a nurse, you should know better. When guys die of a broken heart, that's literally what happens. Forget the flowers and romance, their women mess with their minds so much they have a friggin' coronary."

"Am I messing with your mind?"

"You're messing with more than my mind."

"Would you like me to stop?"

Would he like her to stop? Was she crazy? No, he wanted to get back to the subject of crazy sex and not come out of the stables until they were so whacked they both had a coronary. "Just for now, sweetheart, my heart can't take any more." He stepped away from her, removing himself from the temptation, and wondered why he was being so chivalrous all of a sudden. "You want to know what else I'm thinking?"

"Go on then."

"I'm thinking we probably cut a deal too quickly with the Feds. We should have looked at the computer, found out a little more about Carl, tried to work it out before we handed everything over." If the Feds don't catch up with Mo soon, then it wouldn't hurt to know what was actually going on.

"We didn't hand everything over," said Lizzie, and she closed the gap again, threaded her arm through his and leaned her head against his arm. "How's your wrist, by the way?" She tapped at the cast experimentally.

He flexed his fingers. There was no pain "It's fine. I'm cured. It's a miracle. Let's take the cast off, and you can help me with some physical therapy instead." Two days and he was bored with it already.

"No, it's too soon," replied Lizzie. "If it was a fracture, it should be on for at least four weeks."

"Gee, four weeks of you helping me shower. How am I going cope? We didn't hand everything in?"

"We still have Carl's address book, all the transcribed numbers and the details from the passports."

"You kept all that shit?"

"I spent all night working on it. I wasn't going to give it away for nothing."

Why didn't that surprise him? She wasn't giving anything away for free. "Where is it?"

"In my bag in my room."

"Come on, then." He pulled at her hand and she resisted just a little.

"Is that just an excuse for you to get into my bedroom?"

Connell raised one eyebrow and smiled "Maybe. Maybe not."

Eleven

Will called at eleven. "Hi, bro, just calling to let you know my guys up on the highway have radioed in. Everything's quiet. Thought you might want to know before you took yourself off to bed."

"Cheers, Will. That's good to know." Connell held the phone in one hand as he checked the lock on the kitchen door. His parents were already in bed and he'd left the dogs to roam the yard overnight. No intruder could get past them.

"Have you been thinking about what I said?"

"What was that, Will?" Connell asked as he turned off the lights and started up the stairs. Lizzie had gone ahead of him, to get out the remainder of Carl's stuff or to get into something more comfortable, he wasn't sure which, wasn't sure what it would mean if it was the latter. He'd never really had to think much about consequences and if he were being honest, he'd tried to avoid thinking about them since Marie.

"About getting on with your life. You've got yourself a cute girl there, Tommy."

"She's not my girl, Will."

"Not yet."

Connell paused on the stairs, thought about continuing, and turned and sat down on a step. "She's part of a case I'm working on, that's all. Sure she's cute and funny, and we get along, but at the end of the day she has a life somewhere else."

"It's not like you to think so far ahead. You're usually a 'take each day as it comes' kind of guy."

"Mm, well, times change. I've got a lot on my mind these days."

"So what does she think? I saw the way you two were looking at each other over the dinner table."

Connell smiled. "Well, what can I say? I'm irresistible."

"That's more like it. Talk to you tomorrow."

"Sure thing. Goodnight, Will."

Connell checked the yard again from the window at the top of the stairs. The dogs were prowling quietly. They would settle down soon and sleep on the porch, but he knew they would sound out if anyone came near.

"Hey, babe, you ready for a long night?" He closed the bedroom door behind him and smiled. She was dressed in very little and had the remainder of Carl's things laid out on the bed. It seemed she was leaving the final choice up to him … decisions, decisions.

"Do you need some help?" she asked slowly and he rolled his eyes. Help making up his mind or undoing his buttons?

She wasn't making this easy.

"Sure, honey, you can help me anytime," he replied. She wasn't the only one who could hedge bets. She grinned and came towards him.

"Don't move." She laughed softly as she undid his button and unzipped his zipper. "Does that make it easier for you?"

"Sure does, sweetheart." He backed her onto the bed and with a sweep of his hand he cleared it of what was left of Carl. He shucked out of his jeans and t-shirt, and he watched her as she watched him. "You ready for some craziness, Mrs. Jones?"

"I think a little craziness is just what the doctor ordered," she breathed. He lowered himself beside her and ran his hand reverently down her body. Her skin felt silky and warm beneath his palm. He wanted to touch it all, wanted to kiss it all. He ducked his head, ran his lips across the sensitive skin beneath her ear and she moaned softly and moved against him.

He was about to make one of the biggest mistakes of his life or one of the best decisions, and he wasn't usually this indecisive. There was a lot hanging on this, he knew that. If he continued, he couldn't just walk away. She wasn't Cynthia. He couldn't just stand her up, leave her waiting alone in some bar. He couldn't, wouldn't, do that to her.

He pulled away and took a steadying breath. She looked him directly in the eye and smiled tentatively.

"Having second thoughts, Connell? Maybe you're not as crazy as you think you are."

"Second thoughts, absolutely not," he replied, "and I'll let you into a little secret. The best way to build up to crazy is slowly." He closed his eyes and kissed her.

He heard the door open just as he was beginning the build up and froze.

"Hi, Daddy. What you doin' in Lizzie's room? Did you pee the bed too?" Joe stood framed in the doorway, a little boy in wet pajamas.

"Shit," muttered Connell under his breath. "Don't laugh," he groaned to Lizzie when he felt her shudder with amusement beneath him. He rolled away from her with a wry grin and left her to pull the covers around herself.

"What're you doing, kiddo? You had a little accident?" He knelt down in front of his son and took his tiny hands in his.

Joe nodded. "I came for a hug."

"Sure, buddy, but you know, you can't just come into a lady's room without knocking. It isn't polite."

"I been knocking, Daddy. You was busy."

Connell glanced back at Lizzie and shrugged. "Kids, huh? Come on, kiddo. Daddy will come with you to the bathroom and then you need to go back to bed."

"My bed is wet."

"Great."

"And I need a hug."

Lizzie smiled. "Find him some clean pajamas and you can both come in for a hug."

Joe was sleeping diagonally across Lizzie's bed, pushing Connell and Lizzie together at one side. "I've changed his bed. I'll carry him back through in a minute," murmured Connell.

"Leave him," said Lizzie. "I think we lost the moment–again."

Connell wrapped his arms around her and pulled her tight. "You know, when we eventually get that moment to ourselves, we're going to have one hell of a time."

* * *

"How long since you've been on a horse?" asked Connell as he helped her onto the saddle. He'd chosen a steady gelding for her, behaviour guaranteed regardless of who was riding, but he was interested nevertheless.

"We had to sell the ponies when our dad died," said Lizzie. "There wasn't the money to keep them and Beth was off to uni, so didn't have the time to look after them anyway. I was gutted. I was ten. I didn't think practicalities when I was ten."

"And you haven't ridden since?"

"Off and on. Don't worry, I'll be fine."

"I know you will." Connell mounted his horse and turned to Joe who waited patiently on his pony. "Listen, kiddo, I want you to be smart today. No galloping off on your own. We have to look after Lizzie. She hasn't been riding for a while."

"Sure, Daddy." Joe grinned, kicked Flash and galloped off across the meadow.

"That kid–he just does as he pleases."

"Mm, well, you were the one who said he was a chip off the old block. Will he be okay?"

"Sure. He'll stop at the end of the meadow. He doesn't like the woods, thinks there's a monster in there." He nudged his horse alongside hers. "You're really good with him."

Lizzie turned to look at Joe, a little speck on a galloping pony, kicking up a dust trail. "I remember being four. Everything is exciting."

"I can't remember last week," said Connell.

"My mum died when I was four. I remember how I clung to Beth. She was only twelve. She was like a mum to me."

"How did your mom die?"

"She died giving birth to my baby brother. He lived for a few hours. Dad never got over it."

"That's rough. Is that why you went into nursing?"

Lizzie shrugged. "I never really thought about it but maybe it was. To be honest I don't really remember her. It hasn't really done me any harm, being without her, and that's what I'm trying to say about Joe. As long as he has people around him who love him, and he has you, that's all that matters."

"What about your real dad?"

"I never knew anything about him. The only dad I knew was Beth's dad, and I don't suppose he knew anything about him either."

"Does it bother you?"

"No, I was lucky I had Beth and Joe's lucky he has you. You don't need to worry about him, Connell. As long as he's got you, he'll be fine."

Connell smiled. "Oh, I don't know about that. Connells are mommy's boys. We like our hugs."

Lizzie stretched out her hand and he took it, and the horses edged closer together. "I noticed," she said with a smile. "Any excuse and he's on my knee."

"He's got good taste. He takes after his dad." He leaned across to kiss her and his cell phone beeped in his pocket. "You get the feeling someone doesn't want us to get together?" he asked as he drew back, pulled his horse to a standstill and flipped open his phone. "It's Marty. I'd better take this. Do you want to catch up to the Lone Ranger there and bring him back for me?"

"Of course," said Lizzie. She kicked the horse and cantered off in the direction of the woods.

"Hi, Marty. What's up?"

"Just checking that you're okay, bud. How did your meeting go?"

"So-so. Funny fucking friends you have, Marty."

"I didn't say they were friends exactly. I mean, we don't hang out or any shit like that. We've just done each other a few favors along the way that's all."

"Well, that's okay, then. I was starting to worry about you."

"What happened? You get what you wanted?"

"Not sure what I wanted, Marty. I gave them what I had, they said Lizzie would be okay, and that was basically it."

"But …"

"But I didn't come away exactly convinced. I think Mulholland deals from a few different decks at the same time."

"Mulholland is okay, Tommy. He doesn't give much away and he's not someone you'd want to get on the

172

wrong side of but, trust me, you'd sure want him covering your back if the shit hit the fan."

"I'll take your word for it, Marty, but I certainly didn't feel any love in the room when we met." Connell steadied his horse and patted its neck as it stamped its hooves impatiently.

"What do you expect? You're an arrogant troublemaker with no respect for authority."

"I suppose when you put it like that–"

"Anyway, are you up for a geography lesson?"

Connell shielded his eyes from the low winter sun and watched as Lizzie and Joe made their way slowly back across the meadow. "Sure, what've you got?"

"Only two things worth mentioning, although I'm sure the nice people of Iceland would disagree. Erupting volcanoes, one in particular that I can't even begin to pronounce, produced an ash cloud that disrupted international air traffic for a couple of weeks over the summer. People got stuck all over the world, because the planes couldn't fly anywhere near the ash zone. It was reported quite widely at the time. Most European airports grounded their planes, if that means anything to you or Lizzie."

It meant nothing to him but maybe Lizzie could provide an additional insight. "And the second thing?"

"Collapsed investment banks that caused a whole lotta trouble, particularly in England where people lost a lot of money."

"Is that it?"

"'fraid so."

"No secret weapons? No smuggling? No threats to take over the world, not even a little terrorist activity, nothing like that?" Connell was disappointed. Maybe Carl just liked the scenery or maybe he had another family there who also believed he was someone he wasn't.

Marty laughed. "You've been watching too many 007 movies."

"I wish. I'm spending all my time just keeping up with the Joneses."

"Oh yeah, so how's that going, or shouldn't I ask?"

Connell smiled. Lizzie and Joe were deep in conversation and whatever they were discussing, Joe found funny. He could hear him giggling from across the meadow. "It's getting there, slowly but surely."

"Since when did you do slowly?"

"Since I realized that quickly wasn't working."

"How long until she goes home?"

"I'm just waiting for your buddy to take care of her passport. I told him to take his time but she has stuff to do in England that can't wait forever."

"It sounds serious."

"No, not really, she needs to get back before her sister has her baby."

"I meant you, Tommy. You sound serious."

Connell paused. Maybe he did sound serious and he wondered if the relationship was or, if it wasn't, whether it should be. He knew one thing: he was seriously frustrated but that wasn't the same thing. "What can I say, Marty. I like her. She's cute, funny and sexy as hell, and she's great with Joe -"

"But?"

"All this crap that's going on, it scares me. I don't want her to get hurt and that tends to happen to people who hang around with me."

Marty sighed, "Tommy, you've got to stop thinking like that. Nothing is going to happen to her. You've done everything you could to make sure it doesn't. Mulholland will take care of Mo and you can get on with whatever you've got in mind for Mrs. Jones. If you think there's even the slightest chance you two could be happy together then, for fuck's sake, Tommy, don't miss out just because you can't let go of the past. Lizzie is not Marie."

Connell snapped his attention from the approaching horses and riders and back to the phone. "What do you mean, 'Mulholland *will* take care of Mo.' Are you saying Mulholland hasn't picked Mo up yet?"

"Not as far as I know. Mo has apparently gone to ground. They're busy chatting with Detective Musgrave, trying to fill in the gaps."

Connell cast his eyes around the meadow and was suddenly ill at ease. He was turning into Joe, seeing monsters in the trees. "That's not good, Marty. We can't have Mo running around."

"I'm sure Mulholland has a handle on it, Tommy. Like I say, don't worry about it. You've done everything you can."

Had he? Connell wasn't sure anymore. He'd already conceded that he'd dealt too quickly with the Feds. He still didn't understand what all of this was about, and needed to if he wanted to stay ahead. They should have spent more time last night with the information they still had but he'd gotten distracted, and that was happening all too often lately. He needed to focus. "Okay, let me know if you hear anything else, Marty," he said finally and pocketed the phone.

"Time to head back," he called to Lizzie, and despite his attempt to school his features, his taut expression and the concern in his eyes gave him away.

"What's wrong?"

Connell glanced at Joe. "Nothing's wrong, I've just got things to do. I need to touch base with Will and we need to look at Carl's stuff again." He smiled at her, attempting to lighten the atmosphere. "I think we got a little distracted last night, don't you? Come on, the sooner we get back, the sooner we can pick up where we left off." He pushed his horse into a trot, setting the pace for Lizzie and Joe, and headed back to the farm.

He had an overwhelming feeling of apprehension, and no amount of kidding about or Connell charm could lessen it. The ground had shifted beneath his feet without him realizing, and its movement left them suddenly vulnerable and at risk. He'd made a fundamental error. Despite his mistrust of Mulholland, he'd assumed the man would do his job and do it quickly. He'd had almost a full day to pick up Mo and he hadn't done it yet. Mo could go a long way, and do a lot of bad things, in twenty-four hours.

Leading the way into the kitchen, he felt the burn of Lizzie's gaze and tried to ignore it. Her hand went automatically to her hair. "What is it, Connell?" she asked. "And don't tell me that there's nothing wrong because I can tell by your face there is."

"I'm just looking for Mom and Dad. You're paranoid."

Lizzie gestured to the note taped on the refrigerator "They've gone into town. Connell, tell me what's wrong. You're scaring me."

Connell ran his fingers through his hair cursing the cast on his wrist for no other reason than the fact that it was a reminder of Mo. He turned and studied her for a moment in silence, considering his options.

He chose his words carefully. "We have to move now and we need to take Joe with us. You have to get your bag and go along with anything I say." He glanced at Joe who'd climbed on a chair to raid the cookie jar, and lowered his voice. "The Feds have lost sight of Mo. He could be on his way to Cuba or he could be on his way here. I think you and Joe would be safer if we got you over to Will's, to the Sheriff's office."

Lizzie's fingers curled her hair tightly and Connell reached out and stopped her with a hand that was surprisingly steady. He didn't feel steady; he felt he was losing control of the situation, that somehow he was being manipulated from afar and he'd no option but to follow a designated course of action. "Nothing's going to happen. You'll be fine with Will."

"What about you?" she breathed. "Will you be fine?"

Connell shrugged and forced a casual smile. Oh sure, he'd be fine when he finally got hold of Mo. But he didn't need the added stress of guessing what might happen if he didn't get hold of him quick enough. "Don't worry about me. I do this for a living."

Lizzie brushed his hand away and took a step back, the hurt as her concern was thrown back in her face evident in the rising color in her cheeks. "Oh, I'm sorry. I forgot I'm just another one of your cases, aren't I? I expect you'll be glad when my passport turns up and you can get on with your life." She folded her arms across her chest and glowered at him.

"Hey, that's not what I meant and you know it." He reached out for her again. He had more than enough on his mind and he couldn't quite understand her reaction. He was trying to protect her, to play down the risk so she wasn't scared. He was trying to do the right thing.

Lizzie shrugged him off and he shook his head, bewildered. "You've totally got things screwed up, honey, and I don't have time for this now." He scooped Joe from his perch and passed him to Lizzie.

"Yes, that's me, a total screw up," she cried defiantly, her sparking eyes at odds with the quivering bottom lip. Connell could have explained what he was worried about but he chose to ignore her instead.

"You need to get your stuff now." He made a small allowance for the outrage in her eyes. "Please."

She replied with a frustrated scowl, took Joe's hand and stomped from the room.

Shit. His heart was beginning to race, his stomach twisted. He needed to get a grip but all he could see in his mind was an image of Marie, dead on the floor.

Pulling out his phone, he dialed his brother. "Will, what've you got for me?"

"Everything's quiet, Tommy. The guys called in about an hour ago. Why, what's up? You sound spooked."

"Mulholland has dropped the ball. He's picked up Musgrave ahead of Mo, and now Mo has gone off the radar."

"You think he's coming to the farm?"

"You can bet he is."

"Is Dad there?"

"No one is here but Lizzie and Joe. We're going to head over to you, Will. Can you put your guys on alert?"

"Sure, don't worry, I'm on it. I'll see you in about twenty minutes."

Connell threw their things in the trunk of the car and strapped Joe in the back. It was only as he pulled out of the farmyard that he realized the dogs were nowhere to be seen. He shot a glance at Lizzie and said nothing. He felt the unwelcome fizz of electricity deep inside and he tightened his hands on the wheel and put his foot down.

"Where we goin', Daddy?" yelled Joe above the roar of the engine. Connell glanced at him in the rearview mirror and forced a smile. He was straining against the seat belt, trying his best to see out of the window. Joe was having fun. The grin on his little face told Connell that in no uncertain terms and the last thing he wanted was to spoil that. Fun was better than fear any day of the week.

"We're going to see your Uncle Will. I've got some stuff to do with him and you need to be on your best behavior when we get there. I want you to sit real quiet or you won't get to play with Louis and Ralph."

Joe grinned. "I'll be good, Daddy. I want to see the twins, and Lizzie can play too." He turned his head and shouted at Lizzie. "Will you play with us, Lizzie? They've got ponies too. We can play races."

"Of course I will, Joe, but you have to sit still and quiet now, like Daddy says, or you won't get to play at all." Lizzie shot a quick uncertain glance at Connell. He ignored it, his concentration fixed on driving the farm road as quickly as he could. If he'd gone any faster, he'd have rolled the car. If Joe hadn't been sitting in the back, he would have risked it.

"What did Will say?" she finally asked.

She'd calmed down some but it was costing her to be civil. He decided the least he could do was meet her half way. He switched on the radio to drown out their conversation, cocked his head and took his eyes off the road momentarily.

"You okay now?" he asked. He swung the car hard right onto the minor road and Joe squealed with delight in the back.

"I don't know what you mean."

"Yes, you do.

"You need to slow down."

"I'll slow down when you look at me and answer the question." He stepped on the gas, glanced across, saw her eyes widen with fear, and took a measure of satisfaction from it. His adrenaline was pumping and he couldn't help that some of it was spilling over onto Lizzie. She looked at him with eyes swollen with tears and he could have cut his own throat.

"I'm sorry," she said, just beating him to it. "I'm just worried. I just don't want you to go looking for Mo."

He floored the brake, braced his arms against the steering wheel and the car shuddered to a dead stop. His heart was racing and all that adrenaline was doing its thing, but he had a four-year-old in the back seat and a psychopathic killer on the loose. He took a breath, leaned across to her and stole the longest sweetest kiss he'd ever had.

"Gee, Daddy," giggled Joe, "I thought we was in a hurry."

Connell drew back with a grin. "Kiddo, I'm always in a hurry, but you'll learn that sometimes it's best to take your time." He started the car, cranked up the radio and turned back to Lizzie.

"There's nothing for you to worry about. I promise. Will's going to meet us at the station. He said there'd been no reports, no sightings, nothing strange. The guys up on the highway are sitting there bored witless…"

"But?"

"But the dogs are gone." He admitted reluctantly. His voiced lowered to exclude Joe.

"What do you mean, gone?"

"Just that. They're gone, and those dogs don't stray. Something must have happened to them."

"Do you think Mo was at the farm?" she asked.

Connell considered his reply, thought about lying and decided against it. "If I'm being honest, then yes I do."

"Then why didn't he just show himself and be done with it?"

"Because Mo is playing the long game."

Twelve

Connell headed for the highway. Will's men were stationed on the road bridge above the river where they had a wide view of the area. Anything moving on the roads, they would see it and they were saying there was nothing to see. Connell wanted to be sure, and the only way to be sure was to check it out for himself.

He pulled up in the middle of the bridge, let the car idle for a moment and then reached out, and turned off the radio and the ignition. The sudden quiet, after the noise of cranked-up music and abused motor, was quickly filled by the noise of the river flowing beneath the structure and hitting the rocks to the south of them. Connell stared at the squad car parked at the far side of the bridge, and wondered why the patrolmen inside weren't coming to meet him. He pulled out his gun and got out of the car.

"Wait here," he said, and he started walking.

* * *

Joe wriggled out of his seatbelt, climbed between the seats and sat himself in the driver's seat. "I'm going to drive fast when I'm big." He reached out and gripped the steering wheel.

"Joe, you need to sit in your own seat," chided Lizzie distractedly, all of her attention on Connell. Where were the police?

181

She didn't realize Joe had opened the car door until he was out on the road. "Joe, get back in here, sweetie." But Joe didn't want to be sweet. He was bored and he wanted to see the river. He ran around the front of the car and began to climb the guard rail at the side of the road. Lizzie caught him up, gripped him tightly by the hand and pulled him off the railing.

"Joe, that's very dangerous. You mustn't go near the edge. It's an awfully long way down to the water." Joe peeped through the railings at the water rushing beneath them.

"You like swimming, Lizzie? I like swimming," he said excitedly. "Can we go swimming with Louis and Ralph?"

Lizzie shook her head. "I never learned to swim, Joe, so you'd have to teach me." She recalled the last time she had been swimming. Carl had taken her, convinced that the best way to teach a reluctant swimmer was to throw them in at the deep end. She remembered the fear and the look the pool attendant had given Carl when he had pulled her out. He was a total stranger yet he had recognized that there was something not quite right. They had never gone back to the pool again.

"I can teach you," grinned Joe. "I got water wings and everything."

Lizzie smiled, and her attention was drawn back to Connell. He had reached the patrol car and stopped. He paused, ducked his head to speak with the driver and took a sudden stumbling step back.

Lizzie felt her stomach roll.

* * *

Connell had covered the distance between the cars at a steady pace. He hadn't wanted to alarm the patrolmen, though he was sure that Will had alerted them to his imminent arrival. His right hand hung loosely at his side, gun gripped comfortably within it. He took the time to

182

scan his surroundings, to look at the view that the patrolmen had assured Will was unremarkable just a little over one hour ago. He had to agree it did look pretty unexceptional. Apart from the patrol car and his own car, the road was clear for miles in each direction. He had no sense of unease and saw no indications that anything bad had gone down, or was about to. He wondered if he'd overreacted. Maybe the dogs had gone off after rabbits and maybe Mo was on a plane to Cuba.

He turned his head when he heard his own car door slam, and saw Lizzie and Joe up against the railings looking down at the river. That kid just wouldn't sit still– far too much energy for his own good. She had a good grip on his hand, though, which was good. Joe was a mini-escapologist, and if you didn't keep hold of him, he'd run circles around you. Lizzie had it under control.

He smiled, turned back to the car and kept walking.

These guys must be pretty cool, he thought as he approached the car. They still hadn't climbed out to meet him or to maybe ask him to drop his weapon while they checked him out. Will was running a second string crew and that didn't sound like Will.

He approached the driver's door and ducked his head.

"Hey, guys, you want to wake up and do your jobs? We've got a situation going on here."

The stench of blood and faeces and the buzzing of the flies sent him reeling back in horror. He stumbled, righted himself, and swallowed the bile that forced its way up into his mouth.

The driver's throat had been slit from ear to ear. Blood drenched his shirt and had pooled in his lap. His eyes were open and staring. His head lolled back, revealing the gaping wound in his neck like a second mouth. The second patrolman looked at first glance to be sleeping but, on closer inspection, the single gunshot wound to his forehead was clearly visible. Any doubt as to the effect of this small wound was quickly eradicated by the fact that the back of his head was spread in glorious Technicolor over the interior of the car.

Smeared in blood on the windscreen of the car was one word:

SOON

And Mo's last words to him, heard and remembered through the fog of semi-consciousness, came back to haunt him. *You're a dead man, Connell. Maybe not tonight, but soon.*

Connell backed away slowly from the car and fumbled in his pocket for his phone, the cast on his wrist preventing him from getting hold. Fuck! It clattered to the pavement, the battery bouncing out. He raised his gun and turned in a slow arc as he crouched and gathered up the phone and its battery, clumsily putting it back into place one-handed. He stood and turned back to Lizzie, mouth open, the words of warning on his lips.

And then he saw him.

Mo's large figure silhouetted against the brightness of the sky was looming up behind Lizzie and Joe. Before he could lift his weapon, the first shot rang out and he felt its sting as it glanced the side of his head, taking a few of his stitches with it. He dropped and ran, closing the gap as quickly as he could, dodging from side to side before Mo could take aim again. He stopped short when the next shot exploded the tarmac in front of his feet, and he raised his gun and looked the albino in the eye.

Mo had Joe under one arm, and for once, the child was silent and still. Mo's weapon was aimed not at Connell but at Lizzie's head.

"Well, hi there, Tommy. You took your time." He grinned and his gold tooth glinted in the sunlight. "We had a deal and you didn't keep up your part. That's not

184

good. You're putting me in an awkward position." He twisted Joe around within his grasp and Joe began to whimper.

"Let them go," shouted Connell. His gun was aimed at the center of Mo's forehead and his arm was locked, steady as a rock.

"That would be a foolish thing for me to do now, wouldn't it?" He shook his head. "You never did fully understand the concept of cards and how holding all of them tends to give you an advantage. You're not a betting man, Tommy?"

Connell said nothing, holding his tongue and his nerve. If he took a shot now, he risked hitting Joe. If he delayed, then he risked taking a shot himself and being powerless to save the two most important people in his life.

He took a silent breath and felt the sweat beading on his brow.

"Well, I *am* a gambling man, and I'll wager that you're not going to shoot 'cause you're not going to risk your kid, not even if it means losing the girl. Let's face it, Tommy. You don't have a very good record at keeping girls, do you?"

Connell glanced at Lizzie and saw her eyes widen with fear and resignation. He pulled his gaze away. Joe's lip was beginning to tremble. Any minute now he would start to cry.

Mo was not the comforting type.

"Hey, kiddo," called Connell reassuringly, "you remember what I said earlier about staying still and quiet? Well, you're doing a real good job, Joey." He fumbled with his phone behind his back, pressed speed dial and left the line open, praying that Will would pick up.

Joe tried for a smile, but it failed to appear and fat silent tears began to run down his cheeks, plopping from his chin onto the back of Mo's hand. Mo set the boy down on his feet in front of him, wiped the back of his hand against his shirt and pulled the gun away from Lizzie, pointing it instead at the top of Joe's head. "You offered me a deal the last time we met. Carl's computer for Mrs. Jones. You reneged on the deal, Tommy."

"You never wanted the fuckin' computer. You set me up."

"You're right, I didn't want the computer. As I have recently discovered, the computer is not important, but the fact remains you made a deal you had no intention of fulfilling. It doesn't make for a relationship based on trust, now, does it?"

Connell shook his head. There was no calming hand on his arm this time. "Get to the point, Mo."

"I consider myself a fair man, so I'm going to give you another chance. I don't want the computer because, as I said, the computer isn't important. Instead I'm going to trade you little Joey for what is important. You get my drift, Tommy? Have you figured out what the actual key to the puzzle is yet?"

Connell stared blankly at him. He was finding it increasingly difficult not to pull his gaze away, to scan his surroundings, check out his options, if any, and come up with a plan. He was frozen to the spot with his hand on a gun, his finger on a trigger that he was too scared to pull.

"You can have your boy, Tommy, and walk away from this, but I want Mrs. Jones."

Connell flicked his gaze between Mo and Lizzie. "What do you mean? You think I'm just going to hand her over so you can -" He didn't want to think about what might happen to her at Mo's hands. "What the fuck do you think you're going to do with her anyway?"

Mo smiled, and Connell knew instinctively that it was the same smile he had given Lizzie after he'd mown down Carl Jones. He understood now why she had run.

"Nothing bad, not if she does as she's told. I'm just going to hold her hand and pick her brains, and if you'd thought to do that instead of spending your time trying to get into her pants, then maybe you'd know the answer by now yourself."

Connell caught the confused look on Lizzie's face. It matched his own, and yet, despite that, he felt the unwelcome sliver of doubt as it began to unwind within him. Had she told him everything she knew? Was she still hiding something from him ... and did Mo know exactly what it was?

"So, what's it to be, Connell, the kid or Mrs. Jones?" He swung the gun like a pendulum between them and at each swing of the gun toward Joe, Lizzie took a small step away.

Connell looked at her and willed her to give him something, anything that would explain what was going on. She smiled at him, that sweet little smile, accompanied by the slightest shrug of her shoulders and the mere suggestion of a shake of the head. He saw the tears welling in her eyes and he knew what she was doing, what she was saying. She wouldn't let him lose his child.

"Let Joe go," she said quietly. "I'll go with you. I'll do whatever you want. Just let him go."

Mo smirked. "Why, Tommy, I do believe Mrs. Jones has some balls." He gripped Joe's collar. "Now lower your gun and you can have your son. Try anything and I'll shoot you in the gut and leave you to bleed out screaming while you watch me kill the boy. This is a one-time chance, Tommy, for you to leave in one piece with your kid. Do it and don't look back."

"Do it, Connell," pleaded Lizzie, and she took another small step away from Mo toward the railings.

Connell lowered his gun.

"Drop the gun to the ground, Tommy," instructed Mo. Connell stooped and leaving the safety off, he placed it at his feet. He closed his eyes and expected to feel the sting of a bullet, but instead he heard the sound of running feet and the wail of a terrified child.

He caught Joe as he barreled into him and in the same movement, he scooped up his weapon and swung the child behind him. Mo had Lizzie pressed against the railings. She had backed herself against them in an effort to put as much space between herself and Mo, but now she was trapped. Mo's gun was pressed against her temple.

"I'm not going to shoot you, babe," said Mo with a sneer. "I'm going to shoot him."

And he swung around, raised his arm, and fired.

* * *

Mulholland and his men had arrived too late to witness the murder of the patrolmen and were therefore unaware of the horror Mo had indulged in while waiting for Connell to appear. They'd tracked him from the city, lost him for a while when they'd hit the rural roads, but they hadn't been worried. They knew he would end up at the farm because that was where Connell had taken the girl and everyone wanted the girl, including them.

They'd waited in the wooded area above the road for Connell to appear, knew the disappearance of the dogs would spook him and the only place for him to go would be the safety of the sheriff's station. They hadn't wanted a confrontation at the farm and similarly, didn't want a confrontation at the station house. They didn't want any witnesses to what they intended because what they were about to do wasn't completely legal.

They had held Will back with red tape and plenty of FBI testosterone when he'd arrived to check on his men. They'd watched the evolving situation on the bridge with interest from their vantage point, and when Will's cell phone had taken Connell's call, they'd listened as the drama unfolded. They'd restrained Will, whose natural inclination had been to act, to do his job and try to stop a tragedy.

When Mo raised his gun against Connell and there was a real risk the girl might be caught in the crossfire, Mulholland decided it was time to intervene and gave the order. His men fired simultaneously, delivering three shots into the center of Mo's fat back with their high-powered rifles. The force of the shots lifted Mo off his feet, barreled him into Lizzie, and his weight and momentum propelled them both clean over the railing and into space before their own weight dropped them into the water below.

"Fuck!" shouted Mulholland. "Get some men down there. Get divers in the water if you need to. I want that girl."

Will pushed past Mulholland and skidded down the grassy bank to the road and to his brother. Connell stood frozen in the middle of the bridge, his shoulders slumped, his eyes on the rail where Lizzie had last stood, Joe clinging desperately to his leg. He rocked ever so slightly and dropped to his knees. Raising his head, he looked once at Will and with a final shudder, fell forward onto the ground.

Joe screamed and Will began to run.

Connell had taken a hit, not in his belly as Mo had promised, but in his chest, and by the time Will got to him, he was pumping blood and fighting the inevitable.

"Help me up," he grunted as he tried to raise himself from the ground. The world was spinning and his limbs seemed unwilling to respond. He was falling down a deep dark well and Lizzie was just out of reach. He was swirling around and he kept missing her outstretched hand, despite his best efforts.

"Stay down, Tommy. You've been hit. Help is on the way." Will ripped off his shirt, bundled it up and stuffed it under Connell's T-shirt in an attempt to stem the blood flow.

"I've got to get Lizzie ..." His words were slurred and he cast about wildly, trying in vain to push Will away, to fight him off.

Will held him and kept pressure on the wound. "She's gone, bro. I'm really sorry but she's gone."

"No, she'll be fine. We've just got to go get her ..." He felt the pain then, intense and unrelenting. The blackness was drawing in, his eyes were closing, and he fought to keep them open.

Joe backed away, traumatized by the sight of the blood. He hopped from one foot to the other. "Lizzie can't swim, Daddy. I'll go get her," he yelled and he turned and ran towards the railings, his little backpack bouncing madly as he ran, dodging the policemen who had appeared from nowhere and were moving around on the bridge. They all tried to halt his progress by stepping in his way and reaching out a hand to grab him, but Joe was far too nimble, and he was half way up the railings when Will caught up with him. "I've got to get her for Daddy," he wailed, pressing his face against the railings and staring down at the river.

Will pulled him off the railings and wrapped him in his arms. "It's okay, Joe. There are men down on the riverbank. They'll find Lizzie. You have to take care of your daddy."

"No!" he wailed and he strained to keep his eye on the river as Will carried him back.

Connell heard the muffled sounds of the approaching helicopter as he lay on the ground, each breath becoming more painful. His head was cushioned on Will's lap and Joe's tiny hand clung tightly onto his. He knew they were there and was comforted by the fact, but he was distracted by the sounds of a chaotic crime scene, men shouting, barking commands, car doors slamming, and approaching sirens wailing. He was frustrated by his inability to respond, to make sure they all understood quite clearly that they had to find Lizzie. He had failed her and he continued to do so, as he had known all along that he would.

He felt the thrum of the rotor blades as he was carried away, and he tried to fight against the ever increasing pull of darkness, but whatever the medics had given him made that impossible, and he remembered nothing of the flight to the ER. He had fragmented memories: the whine of sirens, the lights on the ceiling as he was rushed on a gurney straight into the operating room, and the sound of desperate sobbing that could have been Joe but was more likely to have been his own as he realized the finality of his situation.

* * *

The waiting room was lit by a dim light, as were the hallways and rooms. It was late, most patients were asleep, and most visitors at home in their beds. Outside Connell's room there was a small gathering, all of whom had been there off and on since he'd been brought in twenty-four hours earlier. They had gathered tonight because, earlier on, Connell had finally woken up.

"How is he?" asked Marty, the last to arrive. His face was ashen. He hadn't slept much the past few days. Will stood back against the wall, hands in his pockets, so like Connell it was uncanny. He looked at his feet, considered his words, looked up and shrugged.

"Physically I'd say he's the luckiest guy alive. Another fraction of an inch or so and the bullet would have hit his heart and we wouldn't all be standing here.

The round went straight through him, managed to miss anything vital, and sure he's got a hole in his chest and he's going to have to let up for a while so's he can recover." He smiled wearily and glanced at his parents who sat hand-in-hand patiently waiting as they'd done for the past twenty-four hours. "And letting up is not what Tommy does best." He sobered and lowered his voice "But emotionally, Marty, he's a wreck. It's like Marie all over again but ten times worse. The bullet may as well have hit his heart, 'cause he's totally fucked up."

Marty nodded "Has he said anything?"

"Didn't have to. You just need to look at his face. He's blaming himself again but, Marty, I was there. If anyone was to blame, it was Mulholland for holding back for so long. He could have taken Mo out any time."

"Why did he hold back?"

Will shook his head bitterly. "He's up to something, Marty. I know you figure he's okay, but that guy has a look about him. He's playing a double-hand. All he was interested in was Lizzie, and not in a good way."

Marty looked at the ceiling, thinking about Lizzie, remembering how she'd looked outside the club, how Connell had looked at her. She was just a kid. She didn't deserve what had happened. "Have they found any bodies yet?"

"Mo washed up the far side of the river. There's been no sign of Lizzie. The current is pretty strong there, so I'm guessing she's either caught under water somewhere or they'll find her downriver in a day or so."

Marty sighed; this was one hell of a mess. "Does he know?"

"The doctors advised us not to go into detail, not yet, and he hasn't asked. But he knows … he's not stupid. He knows she couldn't swim. If she was going to be pulled out, it would have happened immediately. We're looking at twenty-four hours, Marty. She's long gone."

Marty scanned the waiting area and recognized the look on the face of Connell's mom. She might still have her son, and she'd be thanking God for that, but there was a long way to go before she got the son she knew back, if she ever did.

"I hear you lost two good guys, Will. I'm really sorry," said Marty.

Will nodded and looked away. He still hadn't recovered from the visits he'd paid to their families. He'd been the one who'd sent them out to the bridge. Tommy wasn't the only one carrying guilt.

Joe was pressed against the door to Connell's room, trying to catch a glimpse through the crack in the door. He was wearing a Spiderman suit and had his matching backpack over his shoulder. "Has Joe been in?" asked Marty.

"Not yet," said Rose. "We didn't think it was a good idea, though it's breaking his heart. He won't take the suit off until his daddy's seen it."

"You should let him in," said Marty. "If it hadn't been for Joe, Tommy wouldn't have come back the last time." He pushed open the door. "He can go in with me."

He took Joe's hand and closed the door gently behind them. Connell's eyes were closed. Attached to a variety of machines that beeped and buzzed, he had IV tubes in his arm and an oxygen tube taped to his cheek. The left side of his chest was heavily bandaged, with a drainage tube snaking out and disappearing beneath the bed. A dressing was taped to the side of his head where the first bullet had grazed him. The white dressings looked stark against what was left of his tan but, despite the tan, he looked pale and beaten.

Marty lifted Joe onto the right side of the bed and pressed his finger to his lips. Joe nodded sadly and curled up next to Connell, his head resting on his

193

outstretched arm. Connell dragged heavy eyelids open and closed his arm around his son.

"Hiya, Spidey," he whispered hoarsely, and Joe smiled beneath his mask.

"Hi, buddy. How you doin'?" asked Marty, pulling a chair up to the side of the bed.

Connell shook his head slowly but couldn't find the words to describe the desolation and guilt that he felt. Marty simply nodded and waited while he composed himself.

"Hate to say it, Tommy, but you look like shit," said Marty with a smile.

"Thanks, bud. I can always rely on you," muttered Connell. His voice was flat and emotionless. There was no Connell spark left in there.

"What've you been doing? Not like you to fall for the bullet-in-the-chest routine."

Connell stared at the ceiling "Just doing' my job, Marty, but doing it badly, as usual."

"You think?"

"Doesn't everyone?"

"That's not the way I hear it."

Connell turned his head and looked at Marty for the first time. "No?"

"No, but I've had my orders. I'm not supposed to talk to you about what happened in case you lose your shit. Are you going to get weird on me, Tommy?"

Connell frowned "They're tiptoeing around me like I'm ready for the psych ward already. Mom looks like she's going burst into tears at any minute."

Marty smiled at him. "Maybe they have good cause. Do you want to tell me why there's an armed guard outside in the hall?"

Connell tried to shrug and winced at the pain. "Maybe something to do with the fact that I just got another girl killed."

Marty sat back on his seat and rested one foot across his knee. "Don't give me that shit, Tommy. I've been there, remember? I'm not doing it again."

"You don't like it, you know where the door is."

"Oh sure like I'd leave you to wallow in your own self-inflicted pity pool." He smiled. "Anyway, I've got my orders from Charlene. She's says if I want to keep you as one of my friends, I've got to talk to you. I haven't got many friends left, Tommy, so you're stuck with me."

Joe sat up, pulled his mask onto the top of his head, and rubbed his eyes. "Who got killed, Daddy?"

Connell looked away. He wasn't ready for this - couldn't do it.

"Lizzie fell in the river and she couldn't swim. You remember, Joe? You were there," said Marty.

Joe nodded, crossed his legs under him and slid his Spiderman backpack off his shoulders. "I was going to get her. Uncle Will wouldn't let me."

"Sure you were, Joey," said Connell quietly. "Uncle Will was just looking out for you. That's what uncles do."

"But I didn't need to, 'cause the man pulled her out anyway, and it was a long way down, and I was scared, and I didn't have my water wings." Joe took a big breath, unzipped his bag and pulled out a box of crayons and a notebook.

Connell and Marty both looked at each other. Connell felt his stomach tighten. His heart quickened and the beeps on the monitor responded accordingly.

"What man?"

"Can I have some of those, Daddy?" Joe dropped the crayons onto the bed and leaned across Connell, clumsily trying to grab a handful of grapes, and only Marty's intervention prevented him from landing on Connell's chest. "Please? I'm really hungry. I've been here for days and days, and Grandma won't let me have burgers."

"Sure you can, kiddo," said Marty, pulling off a handful and passing them to him.

"What man?" repeated Connell, and Joe grinned with a mouthful of grapes, the juice running down his chin.

"Mommy's friend." He wiped sticky hands on the clean white cotton sheet, dropped the remainder of his grapes amongst his crayons and squirmed around to retrieve them.

Connell looked at Marty, shrugged painfully and tried again. "Mommy's friend?"

"Mommy's friend. He pulled Lizzie out. I saw him."

"Joe, you can't even remember your mommy, let alone her friends, but that's okay. You were very brave and you did what you could." Connell sighed and closed his eyes against the pain. Lizzie was gone. He had to deal with it and so would Joe eventually.

"Come on, Joe. Time to go now. Daddy's tired. He needs to sleep and so do you." Marty lifted him from the bed and took his hand firmly.

Joe stiffened against him. "You going to get Lizzie, Daddy?"

"Lizzie's gone," said Marty quietly and Joe started to twist.

"Daddy, Lizzie will be waiting for you–"

"Joe, enough, come on now, you be a good boy." Marty picked him up and opened the door.

Joe twisted around in his arms and looked back at Connell through the doorway. "I am a good boy. I been waitin' and waitin' to tell Daddy what Michael said."

Marty stopped and Connell's eyes shot open "Michael?"

"Mommy's friend, Michael."

"Mommy's friend Michael?" repeated Connell. This couldn't be right. Michael, Carl or whoever the fuck he was, was dead.

"Yes. I been telling you, Daddy. You silly or what?"

"When did you see Michael?"

"I don't know, at the farm the other day, when the foal was born."

The day that he'd arrived with Lizzie. "What did he say?"

"That he was lookin' out for Lizzie." Joe grinned. He remembered. He was good at remembering messages. "He said it was a surprise and I wasn't s'posed to tell her. I like surprises. When you come home, can we have a surprise party for Lizzie with ice cream? I like ice cream and burgers, but don't tell Grandma 'bout the burgers."

"Are you sure, Joey, really sure? This is real important. This isn't one of your stories, is it? Maybe you just heard grown-ups talking and got a little confused?"

Joe looked hurt. "No. He pulled Lizzie out of the water. I saw him. He was looking out for her, like he said."

Connell looked at Marty. "Buddy, you have got to get me out of here."

"You've got a hole in your chest. You're going nowhere." He lowered his voice. "He's a kid, Tommy. Kids make things up, that's what they do."

"Yeah, but what if he's not? I believe him, Marty. He couldn't possibly remember about Michael unless someone told him. Lizzie is out there somewhere with that guy and we have to go get her."

"Michael, or Carl or whoever, is dead, Tommy. Lizzie saw it with her own eyes."

Connell shook his head. "Yeah, well, maybe she was mistaken." She'd lied to him from the start, but he couldn't believe that she'd lied about that. "We have to do this - I have to do this, if there's even the slightest chance."

"Like I said, there's an armed guard out in the hall."

"Yeah, and why do think he's there? What is it I'm supposed to have done? All of a sudden I'm a fucking' master criminal? I don't think so. This whole thing is screwed and everyone but us knows what's going on."

"Maybe you've been played, Tommy. Have you thought about that? Just because you've been getting it on with her doesn't mean you know anything about her."

He'd considered it, was considering it now, but he just couldn't buy it. Okay, she'd lied because she'd been scared, but he'd known exactly when she'd been doing it because it was written all over her face. She just didn't have the capacity for elaborate deceit. "I haven't been played, Marty. I'd know if I had, and I haven't been getting it on either."

"You kidding me? Is this the Tommy Connell I know and love? Have you had a blow to the head as well?"

"One or two, Marty, but, hey, Charlene told me to be a gentleman. I've just been doing like I was told." He smiled and Marty saw a glimpse of the old Connell.

"Since when do you do as you're told?"

He shrugged, "Okay, well, it wasn't for lack of trying, but things kept getting in the way." He recalled how trying he had been.

"What things, or shouldn't I ask?"

He raised his left arm by way of explanation and realized that the cast was gone and been replaced by strapping. He flexed his wrist experimentally. "Bad guys and bad stuff, I guess. I've been a little busy, as you know."

Marty laughed "That never stopped you before."

Connell forced a smile. "Yeah, well, I'm a reformed character. I decided it was time to grow up."

Marty looked at him and smiled "So what're we going to do?"

"Get Dad and Will in here, and ask Mom to take Joe. We need to do some planning."

"'Are you feeling better, Tommy?"

"I'm getting there."

"Good, I'm glad to hear it, but you're still not getting out of here."

Connell winced, pulled himself into a sitting position, and swung his legs over the side of the bed. "Says who?"

Marty shook his head. "Tommy most of your body is still attached to hospital property. What are you going to do, drag it out the door?"

Connell sucked in a ragged breath and pulled out the tube from his nose, tearing off the tape that held it in place across his cheek. "Whoa, that stings."

"Wait till you pull out your catheter, that's really going to leave a mark."

Connell lifted his sheet, "What the fuck have they done to me?"

"They've kept you alive, Tommy."

* * *

"I spoke with the doctor, son," said Connell's dad when he and Will came back into the room. "You're going to be here for a few more days yet. Get used to it."

Connell glanced at Marty "Where's Joe?"

"Gone with your mom to the hotel. They didn't want to go all the way back to the farm on their own."

"You told them what's going on?"

"Yep, but you still aren't getting out of here, Tommy, not yet. Your drain will come out tomorrow and if you're lucky, a nice nurse will come and take out your catheter. If you're real lucky, she'll do it painlessly, and by then maybe you could sneak out without setting off all of these machines simultaneously." He waved his hand at the electronic hardware taking up room at the head of the bed. "You lost a hell of a lot of blood. You can't just jump up and take off as if nothing's happened."

"What about Lizzie? While I'm laying around in here, the trail is getting cold." He turned to Will, "What about Mulholland? What does he have to say about this?"

Will glanced at the other men and didn't answer immediately.

"What?" He knew when he wasn't being told the whole truth, and he expected the whole truth at the very least from his brother.

"Mulholland is dead, Tommy. They found his body along with his two special agents up by the Pines Motel."

Connell struggled to sit up, setting off the alarms, and Marty pushed him firmly back against the pillow. Connell ripped the contacts from where they were stuck to his chest in frustration and winced as he took some hair with them. The machine continued to shrill and Marty reached over and switched it off. All three men stared at him and Marty shrugged.

"We don't need a machine to tell us he's alive and kicking."

Connell sat back up. "Fucking Carl. Do you see now we've got to get out of here and start looking for Lizzie? The guy's a total head case. There's no way of telling what he wants or what he'll do."

"It's not that simple, Tommy. Why do you think there's a guard outside in the hall?"

"Huh?"

"Mulholland was found at the Pines just after you met with him. They think you killed them, Tommy."

Connell paused, stunned. Either the injury to his head was worse than he thought or he was being given some weird and wonderful drugs through his IV.

"He was alive when I left him," he said bluntly.

"And he was alive yesterday on the bridge when he and his pals took out Mo," said Will. "I know because I stood right next to the guy."

"So what's going on?" Connell turned to Marty. "You set up the meeting. Have you spoken to him since?"

Marty shook his head. "The last time I spoke with him was to arrange the meeting, I tried calling him back when you said you were going to be late, but I just got his voicemail."

"And you thought he was one of the good guys?"

"Sure. I wouldn't have spoken to him otherwise."

"I didn't meet with a good guy, Marty," said Connell, remembering the meeting and the feeling of mistrust that stayed with him after he'd left. "He fucked up with Mo. He should have picked him up immediately. He spent his time chatting with Musgrave instead." Musgrave the crooked cop.

"The Mulholland on the bridge would have let you die, Tommy. All he was interested in was Lizzie."

"So where is he now?" Connell looked from Will to Marty.

"No idea. Haven't seen him since."

"What do you mean?"

Will thought about it for a moment. "After the shooting, I ran straight over to you and Joe. Mulholland and his men disappeared. I assumed they'd gone down to the river to look for Lizzie–I'm sure they did–but I was the one who called for backup, for the helicopter and then things got a little hectic."

"So who's running the investigation? Who put the guy on my door?"

"Captain Gerald Gesting from Internal Affairs is the guy in charge."

"Fuckin' Gestapo Gerry." Connell shook his head. "Well, that figures. He would just love to nail me for three murders. But, Will, you and I both know that

Mulholland the good guy must have been dead long before either of us ever met him."

Harry Connell had sat back quietly listening to the younger men. With a sigh he pulled himself to his feet. It was about time he offered the benefit of his experience.

"This is a whole pile of shit you boys have got yourselves mixed up in, and here's what I think you should do."

Thirteen

She'd had the presence of mind to take a frantic gulp of air before she hit the icy water, but the weight of Mo's lifeless body sent her plummeting through the frigid depths to the river bed. By the time she'd struggled out from under his body and fought her way to the surface, her lungs were screaming and panic threatened to send her straight back down again.

She felt air against her face and gulped at it, taking river water along with much needed oxygen, causing her to splutter and choke, and sending her beneath the surface once more. The current pulled her along and she tried to fight it, desperately scrabbling at anything that might slow her inevitable journey to the maelstrom of the weir. She had no idea what lay in wait but felt with great dread the pull of something evil. Dropping beneath the surface again, she kicked her feet and found she was propelled back up and could take another gulp of precious air.

Floundering, she tried with growing desperation and failing strength to stay afloat and steer herself to the river bank, but the force of the current beat her back, played with her, tantalized her, pushing her almost within reach of safety then spinning her back towards the weir. She began to weaken, overcome with fear and losing the will to fight. She'd seen Connell in the split second before she was knocked over the railing. She'd seen him shot and knew he must be dead. She tried for a last breath, swallowed river water instead and slipped below the surface.

Strong hands took hold of her, pulling her clear of the equally strong current. Dragged from the water, her soaked and listless body was hefted onto the sandy bank before she was rolled onto her back and the water was expelled from her lungs. Hauled back from the brink of oblivion, she began to cough and shiver.

Her rescuer sat back on his heels and considered her. "Lizzie, you really have to learn how to swim!"

And Lizzie opened bleary eyes to a ghost.

* * *

When she woke again, she was wrapped in darkness and the gentle hum of a motor. Music playing quietly and intermittently, on a radio that was having difficulty finding a station, interrupted her fuzzy disjointed thoughts. She felt the oppressive warmth of the heater.

Under normal circumstances she would have balked at the heat, but these were far from normal circumstances. As a result she kept her eyes closed, and remained still and quiet beneath the rough blanket on the rear seat.

Her clothes had partly dried against the blanket but remained damp against her skin which indicated how long she had been confined. She felt chilled despite the heat, as if a virus threatened. Her stomach churned and she jammed her mouth closed and bit down on her lip, fearful that some involuntary response might alert the driver of the car to the fact she was no longer sleeping. She'd no idea where she was or where she was headed. The only thing clear in her head was the fact she'd made a terrible mistake.

Carl Jones was not dead.

Cocooned within the blanket, she tried to imagine what Connell would have done in her position. Something heroic and foolhardy perhaps. Maybe he would have launched himself at the back of the driver and caused him to crash the car, or waited until the car stopped, overpowered the driver and taken control of the situation. He'd have known what to do and he'd have done it regardless of the consequences. He certainly wouldn't have lain frozen with fear while the car was driven further and further away.

She recalled her last glimpse of him standing on the bridge, his gun raised. She saw it in slow motion, the moment when the bullet hit him, the jolt of the high powered missile as it collided with his chest. He'd recoiled but he hadn't fallen, and the expression on his face as he'd locked eyes with hers had been one of absolute dismay.

With his last breath he believed he'd failed her.

She would never see him again. Everything they'd nearly had would never be. She'd never known such grief. She felt it in every part of her. Every nerve ending tingled with it. She understood the guilt Connell had carried around for the last two years. He'd believed he was responsible for Marie's death. Lizzie knew she was responsible for his.

There was no one to come after her now, no one to protect her, to save her. If she wanted to be saved, she would have to take control of the situation herself.

She sat up slowly and pulled the blanket from her head, adjusting her eyes to the dim interior. The road outside was black–no approaching headlights and no street lights. The scudding clouds released a clear moon into the night sky and illuminated a highway lined either side by never-ending forest.

"Where are you taking me?" she croaked. She swallowed painfully and controlled her wince.

"Somewhere safe," replied her captor. He glanced at her in the rearview mirror and studied her as much as a quick glance would allow before dragging his eyes back to the road.

"I was safe with Connell," she replied. She tried not to betray her emotions but even the sound of his name on her lips caused her to falter.

"Ah yes, Detective Connell. I've no doubt he was doing his best. He always does but, from experience, I know that his best isn't always good enough. Did he tell you about his failure to protect the mother of his child?" He glanced at her again in the mirror.

"He told me she was murdered. I expect you know more about that than me."

He laughed humorlessly and after checking the rear-view mirror again, he pulled into the side of the road and stopped the vehicle. Lizzie readied herself. If she was going to escape, this seemed a likely opportunity. If he were going to attack, it was also a likely opportunity.

But he didn't get out of the car. Instead, he merely switched on the interior light, turned in his seat and appraised her.

Lizzie stared back at him in total confusion. He may look like Carl and sound like Carl, but this was certainly not Carl.

"Who are you?" she asked and he smiled back at her, a crooked, dangerous smile.

"You know who I am. I believe you took my passport."

She stared into deep green eyes. "Michael - Michael Butler?"

He nodded. "Pleased to meet you, Mrs. Jones. You're not in the least what I was expecting."

"But you're supposed to be Carl. I saw you knocked over and killed. I don't understand." She shook her head slowly, rubbed at eyes that felt gritty and looked back at him. She could see the differences now she was looking for them. Carl had a blank uniformity to his features; he could show pleasure and cruelty, but little in between. This man had a little more character to judge from his eyes and his slightly off-center smile. From a distance, and perhaps to someone who didn't know Carl, she could understand how this man could be mistaken for him.

What she didn't understand was why.

"No I don't expect that you do. It is a little complicated. Don't worry, you haven't gone crazy. You were correct in your initial observation. You did see Carl Jones knocked over and killed by Mo Pater. Where you and Detective Connell made a mistake was in assuming we were one and the same."

Lizzie shook her head again. If Carl was dead, that should be good news, but if that was the case, what did this man want with her? "If you're not Carl, what do you want from me? I don't even know you."

He glanced at his watch and back at her. "No, I don't suppose you do, but I know all about you, Lizzie, and that's what counts." He paused to scan her flushed appearance. "You don't look well. Are you ill?"

She was having difficulty swallowing but that was the least of her worries. How did he know all about her and why was that important?

"I … I'm fine," she croaked. "I've been thrown off a bridge, half drowned, and kidnapped by a man I don't know. Of course I'm fine. How are you?"

He gave a slow smile. "I see you've picked up some bad habits from Tommy. When someone asks how you are, you don't need to come on with the smart reply. It's not a trick question. I'm merely concerned you might be suffering some ill effects from your near drowning."

Near drowning. She would have drowned if it hadn't been for him. How had he known to be there? Why was he there at all? "You know Connell?" she asked.

"You know that I do. I'm sure he mentioned how we met."

"You sound as if you were friends."

"Not exactly, although for a time I suppose we were."

"Yet you had him killed."

He cocked his head. "What makes you say that?"

"You and Mo murdered Marie, Connell told me. Now you've had him killed. Are you going to kill me too?" She wondered why he would go to the trouble of hauling her out of the river if he intended to kill her anyway, but as she understood nothing of what had gone on since she arrived in the U.S., she accepted that anything was possible.

He tightened his jaw, lost the slightly amiable expression he'd offered so far, and when he spoke, his American accent was heavily spiced with Irish brogue. "I think you've have been slightly misled, Mrs. Jones." He turned back in his seat. "No matter, fasten your seatbelt, we have a way to go yet."

"I don't want to go anywhere with you."

He shrugged. "Do you want me to leave you at the side of the road in the dark, to be eaten by bears?" Lizzie narrowed her eyes, wondered at his reference to bears, and considered the fact that he may have been following them for some time. "As I said before, I'm taking you to safety."

"Why? Mo is dead. I'm already safe."

He shook his head and started the motor. "It's not Mo you need to worry about. It was never Mo you needed to worry about."

"What do you mean?"

"Get some rest. I'll wake you when we get there."

"Get where? Where are we going? What are you going to do with me?"

"Get some rest," he repeated as he hiked the volume on the scratchy radio and turned his attention to the road.

* * *

Michael Butler decided to risk pulling in to the gas station. He'd been thinking about it over the last hour, weighing up the options in his mind. An early morning mist hung in the trees that hugged the road. It would burn off as the day progressed, but at the moment the sun was still sluggishly dragging itself along, and he knew how that felt.

He'd driven through the night in an effort to put as many miles between them and those they'd left behind. He needed sleep but he also needed gas. He figured this time of the morning the teller would be as wasted as him and wouldn't remember what he looked like if asked at a later date. That was his plan. There was too much at stake to make a mistake.

He smiled and thought of the little *mistakes* he'd already made, the little signs he'd left, the bigger signs that no doubt she would attempt to leave, none of which were actual mistakes, just part of the plan, the plan that would ensure the necessary people were assembled at the required time and place.

Lizzie had slept for most of the journey, and he'd turned down the radio and listened to her ragged breathing. She'd picked up a chill from her time in the river, and laying in wet clothes had done her no favors. It could have been much worse. If he hadn't managed to grab her, she would have drowned. She was all but done-for when he'd pulled her ashore, but not quite. That little spark left in her had spluttered into life at his hands. Perhaps she didn't fully appreciate that he'd saved her life.

She stirred in the back when he switched off the engine, and he turned to look at her. He wondered if he'd done the right thing interfering in the natural order of things. Butler supposed that Lizzie Jones hadn't yet had the opportunity to experience much of life, but he suspected she'd influenced a good proportion of it all by herself. Marie, on the other hand, may have lived a little longer in years, but none of that had been of her own design or making, and Butler digested that thought and considered where the blame for the injustice should rightly lie: with the circumstances that forced Marie into the life she chose to live? With the man who fired the gun that killed her? Or with the man who inadvertently placed her in that perilous position?

He had no answer.

"I need you to stay quiet and refrain from drawing attention to yourself," he said quietly, his Irish accent even more prominent now, as if he'd given up any pretense at an alternative identity.

* * *

The pump attendant was already at the car fiddling with the cover on the gas tank. With an iPod in his breast pocket and earphones connecting him to the music, he whistled softly to himself. Lizzie judged him to be maybe fifteen or sixteen, fitting in a job before school. He looked like he should have stayed in bed; his eyelids were dark and heavy and his hair tousled. His school work would soon suffer if he kept this up.

Lizzie heard the sound of the gas as it filled the tank and the steady thrum as the gas pump did its job, and she opened her mouth to respond to her captor. Butler placed a finger against his lips and shook his head. The boy finished filling and tapped on the window to let Butler know. As he did, he glanced at Lizzie and gave her a nod, a courtesy really, nothing more, nothing less.

Butler moved the car from the front of the station into a rear parking space and turned to look at her. "Good girl," he said quietly. "Now here's the deal, I'm going in to pay and you need to stay in the car. There's an outdoor store next to the gas station. I'm going to go in there and get you a change of clothes, and then I'm going to go get us some breakfast. I don't believe you'll stay in the car while I'm gone, so I'm afraid I'm going have to make sure that you do."

He leaned over the back of the seat, clipped handcuffs around her left wrist and fastened them to the door handle. "Don't make a noise and don't make a fuss. I know you don't want to cause any trouble for the young lad at the pumps, and believe me, you cause trouble for me and that's exactly what would happen."

Lizzie stared at the cuffs in disbelief. "You'd hurt a boy? He has nothing to do with this. You don't even know him." Her voice was cracked, her throat still sore.

"No, you'd hurt him, Lizzie. Every action has a consequence. Think about that while I'm in the store." She looked at him and he looked back at her. Neither blinked. "What size boots?" he asked eventually.

She shrugged, thrown by his question. "Boots?"

"You have nothing on your feet. Your shoes were lost in the river."

She recalled vividly the swirling water, the absolute fear and the feel of his strong grip as he'd pulled her to safety. "4. U.K. size 4," she replied quietly.

He nodded and left her.

* * *

He paid for the gas, picked up a selection of over-the-counter cold remedies, a couple of coffees and breakfast muffins to go, crossed the parking lot and went into the outdoor store. He scanned the interior from the doorway. The franchises were all laid out to a similar plan and this was no exception. He went straight to the ladies

211

department and quickly picked up boots, jeans and a hooded sweatshirt, some thermal underwear and socks, and a padded jacket. When he went to the till, he found the same boy waiting to serve him.

"You running a double shift, son?" he asked pleasantly.

"Yes, sir. Saving for a car." The earphones were gone. The boy was paying attention.

Butler smiled, paid for his purchases and left him a handsome tip. "You keep up the good work. I hope you get your car real soon."

"Thanks, mister," the boy called after him when he realized how much he'd been given. And then he followed him to the door and watched as Butler crossed the lot and returned to his car.

Butler threw the clothes onto the back seat, set the coffees down on the dashboard and unlocked her handcuffs. "I guessed at a size 6 in clothes. You want to put them on?"

Lizzie's hand strayed to her hair nervously. "Not here, no."

He shrugged. "Fine, stay in damp clothes, but it won't do you any good and it's going to get a whole lot colder where we're going."

"I need to use the bathroom. I'll get changed in there."

"Good try," he replied, "but there's no way that you're going anywhere without me."

"I won't do anything stupid. I remember what you said about the boy."

He assessed her shrewdly. "Okay, put your boots on and come with me. I'll wait outside." He took her arm and walked her quickly across the parking lot, averting his gaze from the security cameras positioned high up above the pumps, and ignoring the boy who watched them from the store doorway.

The ladies room was small, with barely enough room to do the necessary, let alone change clothes. Lizzie frantically checked for something she could write with to leave a message. Her bag was in Connell's car and her notebook was with the rest of Carl's things in Joe's backpack. She had nothing but the clothes she stood up in.

"Hurry up, we need to get moving," called Butler from outside the door and Lizzie checked her reflection in the mirror. She tried to comb her hair with her fingers. She was a mess, and seeing just how wretched she looked made her desperation grow. Would anyone even notice that she'd gone? Would they realize she'd been taken, not lost in the river but taken against her will by a man with a reason for doing so? Or would they be so distraught at the loss of Connell they would merely give up and go home?

She would never know unless she tried. She leaned towards the mirror, breathed her moist breath across it and used her finger to tell it how it was. *Lizzie Jones wuz here Wed + MB please HELP!* And then she bundled up her old clothes and dumped them in the trash.

"Where are we going now?" she asked as he took her arm and led her back to the car. She couldn't hide the hopelessness that crept into her voice. She'd played her only shot and she very much doubted its success.

"Somewhere safe," he replied as he put her in the passenger seat and handed her breakfast.

"You said that before."

"Then it must be true." He smiled, pulled out of the gas station and back on to the highway.

"And I said I was already safe and I didn't want to go anywhere with you."

"Eat your breakfast," he said. He turned up the radio and settled down behind the wheel.

Behind them at the gas station, the boy watched them leave.

Fourteen

Gerry Gesting had heard all about Tommy Connell and knew him to be irresponsible and cocky, with no respect for the rules and regulations that should, by all rights, govern the life of a police officer. By most accounts though, he was a likeable guy, a charmer who managed to get by pretty much on a grin and a joke. For the last two years he'd been sailing close to the wind and was perilously close to losing his job.

He'd read his file, every line of every page, which was surprisingly thick for such a young man, and even read between the lines where he believed the interesting details were usually found. He thought Connell's commanding officer deserved a medal for putting up with him. He also figured he was essentially an honest cop with more than his fair share of bad breaks who'd gotten mixed up in something decidedly ugly.

His job was to determine who murdered three well-respected agents up at the Pines Motel. One thing he was certain of; it wasn't Tommy Connell. No matter how much he might be irritated by Connell's approach to life, Gerry Gesting was an honest cop too and he would do his job.

Gesting studied him now as he slept. It was obvious he'd taken a recent beating in addition to the gunshot wound to the chest, and Gesting thought it would be a while before he was out and about. Which was just as well, because Gesting figured ordinarily Detective Connell would be a hard man to pin down and if he wanted to get to the bottom of this mess, he was going to have to spend a fair bit of time in his company.

"Good morning, Detective," he eventually said. Connell dragged open bleary eyes and took a moment to focus. Gesting noted the IV, recognized the slow pupil reaction and decided Connell had needed some help getting to sleep. Maybe he wasn't as cocky as he liked people to think.

"We need to have a talk. You up to that?"

Connell shrugged, sat himself up painfully, and reacquainted himself with his situation. The others had left sometime after midnight, chased out by the night nursing staff. When he'd demanded to go with them, tried to explain quite heatedly that he was well enough and perfectly able, they'd taken it upon themselves to administer a little sedative, and any fight left in him had quickly dissipated.

His dad and Will were heading back to the river to check for any tracks or signs Mulholland's imposter may have missed. Joe said Lizzie had been pulled from the river and he'd seen it happen. He was a little guy and his view from the bridge would've been substantially restricted, which narrowed the search area considerably. If Lizzie had been taken from the river and removed from the scene so quickly that the searching police had been unaware, whoever had taken her must have used a vehicle. If that was the case, the soft mud of the embankment would be bound to offer up some clues.

Marty had been sent to follow up on the shooting up at the Pines. Someone had intercepted Marty's call to reschedule the meeting, and Connell suspected it was the guy who'd pretended to be Mulholland. Who he actually was, and who he was working for, were beyond Connell whose current capacity for serious cognition was more than a little impaired.

He rubbed at his eyes, ignored what felt like a bad hangover and gave his visitor a long look. Until a nurse with gentle hands decided to pay him a visit and disentangle him from hospital property, Connell was pretty much stuck. He decided, as he'd nothing better to do, he may as well pass the time of day with Gestapo Gerry.

"Sure, fire away." He smiled wryly. "Not literally of course. Been there, done that."

Gesting narrowed his eyes. "You look a little wired. Have they been looking after you, Detective Connell?"

"Oh yeah. They come in every so often and juice me up. You should try it." He blinked slowly and would have happily closed his eyes again, such was the strength of whatever it was they were pumping into him.

"Are you going to tell me what's been going on?"

"I would if I could." Did anyone actually know what was going on? He doubted it. Shifting awkwardly, pain shot through his shoulder.

"Perhaps you could try."

"Sure, where do you want me to start?" he drawled, forcing his eyes to stay open, distracted by the fact that Gesting reminded him of someone, though for the life of him he couldn't recall who it was. Someone off the TV maybe. He was easily distracted these days.

"At the beginning would be a good idea, around the time you got the job of interviewing Mrs. Jones. How come you ended up there?"

Gesting took out a notebook and stumpy pencil and Connell thought back to his first meeting with Lizzie. He knew Gesting was trying the same trick he had, coming on all official to get the upper hand. It might have worked with Lizzie, but it didn't work with him.

216

"I swapped with one of the guys." He tried to concentrate, struggling with the chronology. So much had happened in such a short space of time. "I was doing extra hours so I could get time off with my boy."

"So you were just there by chance. It could have been anybody from the squad?"

"I suppose." Connell recalled how the job had been bounced around a few times amongst guys who had better things to do. He'd taken it because he was sick of Charlene's matchmaking.

"And if you hadn't gone, who was next on the list?"

"Who knows? Musgrave was the only one still there when I got back, so I guess it would have been him …" Connell digested that fact slowly, rolled it around in his foggy mind, and recalled Musgrave's interest at the coffee machine. Maybe he'd inadvertently jumped the line and lifted Musgrave's job. Or perhaps he'd been deliberately maneuvered into it without realizing.

"Why didn't you report in afterwards, file your report, you know, the usual things? I know you brought her into the station house because you were seen and yet you decided to play it alone. Why?"

"I don't know, I got caught up. She was interesting." Connell's mind was still on Musgrave, how he'd been going to take Lizzie from the apartment the day he'd tried to take his badge. He'd said he was going to put her on a plane. There was no plane. There'd never been a plane.

"*Interesting*. So that's what they call it these days."

Connell swung his attention back. "I figured I'd do a little detecting first. That is my job after all, and to be honest," he added with a shrug, "I needed the bust to keep my boss off my back. The girl was scared. I wanted to know why, and until I did, I figured she needed protection."

"From whom?"

"I don't know - the bad guys. If I had all the answers, I wouldn't be lying here with a crater in my chest."

Gesting paused. "So it had nothing to do with your feud with Mo Pater?"

Connell rolled his eyes. "Of course it did, I'm not going to lie to you. Suddenly after two years of waiting, I had a witness land in my lap who saw Mo murder a guy in cold blood. I wasn't going to pass on that, even when Musgrave started sniffing around. It was personal. I expect you know why."

"I do know why," replied Gesting as he settled back in his seat. "Tell me, Connell, since you've brought it up, how do you feel about what happened back then?"

"Are you shitting me?" Connell shook his head. "How do I feel about a guy getting away with murder? How do you think I feel?"

"I understand there were no witnesses to Marie's shooting apart from you, and your testimony was found to be unreliable." Gesting had acquainted himself with the case notes.

"There were plenty of witnesses. They just weren't willing to testify." He glared at Gesting. "And since when was the testimony of a serving police officer found to be unreliable?"

Gesting shrugged. "Maybe when you're keeping dubious company, when you're in a relationship with the victim, and when you're accusing her boss of murder."

"Mo wasn't her boss."

"Mo Pater owned the club where she worked. In my book that makes him her boss."

Connell took a breath. If Gesting was trying to work him up, he was succeeding, and Connell didn't want to give him the satisfaction. "I know Mo killed Marie, and he's dead now. So, if that's all you're interested in, you may as well leave. I've got nothing more to add, except maybe, if you'd done your job back then, you might have prevented what just happened."

Gesting sat for a moment in silence. Connell guessed what the man was thinking. He'd been over it himself a hundred times and still couldn't make sense of it. There'd been something odd about Marie's death and the premature closing of the murder case. The investigators had bought the story Mo had given, that an unknown third party had fired the shot. It was bullshit and the sooner Gesting understood that the better.

"Why do you think Marie was killed?" asked Gesting eventually.

"You know what I think. It's all in my statement. If you'd bothered to read it, you wouldn't need to sit here wasting my time."

"I know what you thought two years ago when you made your statement. What I'm asking is what you think *now* in light of current events."

Connell wondered just how much Gesting actually knew. Okay, so he was beginning to doubt he'd been the primary target, but he had no real idea why Mo would have wanted Marie dead, unless, as Lizzie had suggested, Marie had information that she'd intended passing on, information Mo didn't want passed.

"I'm not sure where you're coming from," stalled Connell. "Why would I have changed my opinion? What connection do the current events have to Marie's murder?"

"Well, all the key players for one thing - Mo, Gilly Tasker, Carl Jones, yourself and of course, an innocent girl."

"Lizzie has nothing to do with Mo."

"You mean other than the fact he wanted her dead? Come on, Connell, you're not stupid and neither am I. There are too many coincidences for there not to be a connection. Look, I can understand you might feel cheated and that maybe justice wasn't served two years ago. Nevertheless, I'm a little surprised you'd risk the life of yet another young woman in pursuit of your own revenge agendas. That doesn't sound like you at all, if in fact she was innocent. Or was she another employee of Mo Pater?"

Connell was instantly deflated; Gesting was right. He'd been too obsessed with his need for revenge against Mo to think rationally. He'd sat in Lizzie's apartment watching her squirm with apprehension and he'd harnessed her fear for his own ends. A sense of self-loathing settled in his gut. "I didn't think she was in any real danger, not at first. She was naïve, told me she got scared crossing the street. I just thought she was exaggerating, over dramatizing, which shows how wrong I was."

"And you believed her about Mo Pater?"

"I had no reason not to. She described him perfectly. She didn't know who he was. She'd just got off a goddamn plane for fuck's sake. The first time out of her own country, the proverbial innocent abroad."

"Yet she was using a false identity and a counterfeit passport, so not that innocent."

"I didn't know that initially."

"And yet you were sufficiently suspicious to have her checked out by your good friend in Immigration."

He'd been suspicious of her the minute he'd walked in the door when his first alarm had gone off. "As I said, I'm a detective. I was doing my job. I had to make sure she was credible if I was going to use her as a witness." He glanced at Gesting, "Have you spoken to Marty?"

"Not yet, but I will."

"He's a good guy. He hasn't done anything wrong. I asked him to do some checking for me, part of a legitimate case, and that's all he did."

Gesting nodded. "So why didn't you do your job when you discovered her deception?"

Connell knew what he meant. What made an honest cop turn a blind eye? He wasn't sure he had the answer, wasn't sure he was entirely honest either. He'd had more than one thing to hold her for and using phony ID was the least of them. "I did my job. I investigated, and when I realized I'd uncovered a whole pile of crap, I handed it over to the Feds."

"I'm sure there's more to it than that," said Gesting.

"It's a complicated story," conceded Connell, and he wasn't up to telling complicated stories. He wasn't even sure he understood what had gone on enough to retell it. He'd been there and it made no sense. How could he possibly explain it to someone else?

"So I understand. Would you like to enlighten me?"

"You sound like you already know," muttered Connell. Everyone seemed to know what was going on but him. Gesting's interest in Marie's death had blurred the edges even more and Connell was finding it increasingly difficult to separate the two events.

"Maybe, maybe not, but I'd still like to hear what you have to say, your version of events."

"I can tell you one thing for sure: I didn't kill those guys at the motel."

"That wasn't what I asked," replied Gesting, "but now you've brought it up, I believe you."

"You do?"

Gesting shrugged. "You sound surprised. I'm a reasonable man and you're an honest cop, so why wouldn't I believe you?"

Connell appraised him slowly. "You have a certain reputation."

Gesting smiled. "That makes two of us."

"You shouldn't believe everything you hear about me."

"Likewise," replied Gesting. "But, fortunately for you, I do believe some things I hear about you, and murder just doesn't fit your profile. If it did, you'd have taken out Mo Pater two years ago. What I'm having difficulty believing is all this nonsense about Mrs. Jones."

"Like I said, it's a complicated story." And Connell was done telling it. "You want my advice? You need to spend your time checking out Carl Jones, or whoever the fuck he really was, instead of sitting here keeping me awake."

Gesting narrowed eyes, betrayed his irritation at Connell's lack of respect for a senior officer. "Thank you for your advice, Detective Connell. I have men doing just that as we speak." He rose and crossed to the window. "I need you to look at some mug shots, see if you can identify the men you met with at the Pines. Your brother will be asked to do the same. We also need to talk about the evidence you took during your illegal search of Carl Jones' apartment. It's unfortunate you gave it away so quickly. Maybe, when your mind is a little clearer, you might recall some details."

Connell ignored the reference to his visit to Carl's. He already knew he'd dealt his hand prematurely with the evidence; he didn't need Gestapo Gerry to tell him that.

"What if they haven't got any form, the guys at the Pines? They did a pretty good impersonation of Feds. Maybe we need to be looking closer to home."

"And where would you start, Detective Connell?"

"I'd start with Musgrave. He was taking his orders from Mo."

"You don't like the man?"

Connell smiled unpleasantly. That was an understatement. "Not particularly. He set me up, and tried to take my badge and Lizzie. He said you'd sent him."

"Maybe I did."

"If you're in bed with Musgrave, I may as well give up now."

Gesting smiled and stooped to pick something up from under the bed. "Have you been throwing your toys out of the bed, Connell?" he asked, handing over Joe's Spiderman backpack, a handful of crayons and a notebook. "You like to think you're a superhero, do you?"

"Sure," said Connell distractedly. The backpack and crayons belonged to Joe, but the notebook was Lizzie's. As he put them back in the bag, he discovered Carl's address book sitting at the bottom along with an assortment of action figures.

"When are you out of here?" asked Gesting, taking in the paraphernalia surrounding the head of the bed and the fact that Connell was still connected to some of it. "Connell!" he repeated when it became obvious he wasn't listening.

Jerking his attention back, Connell was glad he wasn't still linked to the heart monitor; it would have given him away for sure. "A while yet," he lied. He'd be out of there as soon as Gesting left the building.

"Good I'll see you later, when there's a little less juice in your veins. And Connell …"

"Yeah?"

"Don't go anywhere."

"Sure thing," replied Connell.

* * *

As soon as the door closed behind Gesting, Connell buzzed for assistance.

The nurse who answered his call wasn't exactly as he'd imagined in his crude schoolboy fantasies. She was twice the size of Charlene, had hands like shovels and one hell of an attitude. He should've expected they'd send in the heavy artillery after last night when he'd lost his shit again, but this woman was scary. The thought of any of his important parts being within striking distance of those paws of hers made him shudder.

"You the tough guy who thinks he's ready to leave?" she grizzled, and Connell wondered if she was really a guy and someone was playing a joke on him.

"That's me," he replied. "I just need to be unhooked or whatever, then I'll be out of your way."

She checked his IV and chuckled. "Still on morphine and you think you can manage on your own?"

Connell smiled. So that's what it was. "Sure, just give me a couple of aspirin and I'll be fine."

She checked his pulse and shook her head. "I tell you what. I'll do you a deal, tough guy. I'll unhook you, and if you can manage without anything for the next couple of hours, I'll speak to the doctor about discharging you."

"Sure," said Connell. He would agree to anything that meant he could take a piss the way God intended.

"Okay, honey. Now, you want to look away while I do this?"

"Will it hurt?" he asked. "'Cause I may need to use that again."

"Funny guy. You want to try childbirth, now that hurts." She whipped out the catheter, and he had the good grace to look embarrassed at his own cowardice. "If it stings when you pee, come tell me, particularly if you're planning to use it for anything other than peeing anytime soon."

"Do I look like I'm going to be doing much of that?" Connell grinned.

"Well, hey, what do I know, but I'll let you into a secret. You don't need to go getting a bullet in the chest if you don't feel like it. Take it from me, a headache works just as well."

She checked there was no more fluid leaking through his drain, snipped the stitches holding it in place and slid it slowly from his wound. "I think we can change this dressing for something a little less bulky," she said, and she opened her sterile dressing tray and set too. "You doing okay?" she asked when she was done, and Connell nodded. He still had morphine pumping through him, he was fine. She crossed to the I.V., turned off the flow and gently removed the line from his arm. "That's it, tough guy. It's all up to you now. You're going to start feeling some pain and you'll probably need something in a couple of hours. Give me a holler if it gets too bad."

"Where are my clothes?" he asked.

"Clothes weren't part of the deal," she replied, and headed towards the door.

"Come on," he cajoled. "I just want relearn how to dress myself so when I'm released into an unforgiving society I can fend for myself."

"Good try, but you're wasting your time. Your clothes were cut off you in the ER. If you're planning an escape, you'll need an accomplice on the outside." She winked at him. "Unless you want to play doctor?"

"I like the sound of that."

Narrowing her eyes, she glanced at the door. "There's still a guard in the corridor. What have you been up to? I'm not aiding and abetting a criminal."

"He's just there for protection in case the guys who did this come back for seconds."

"So you're not some criminal scumbag type?"

Connell grinned. "Absolutely not."

"You go pee. I'll see what I can do."

* * *

Dr. Connell walked out of the hospital two hours later in surgical scrubs with a Spiderman backpack over one arm and a bottle of aspirin in his pocket. He'd passed the pee test with flying colors but he'd lied about the pain in his chest. He needed to sit down and he hoped his accomplice was punctual.

His getaway car was waiting in the no parking zone and the driver looked slightly flustered when he opened the passenger door and slumped into the seat.

"Hi, Mom, thanks for coming."

"Tommy Connell, you're seriously out of control, son. You're going to get your own mother a criminal record."

"Fine, I'll sit myself on the *thinking about it* chair when we get home. Just get me out of here for now."

Joe squealed with delight in the back of the car. He spent most of his time on the naughty chair; it would be cool to share it with his dad.

Connell twisted around with some difficulty. "Hiya, Spidey. I see you're still dressed for action. You going to change outa that suit sometime? You're getting a little stinky, kiddo."

"No way, Daddy," said Joe with an expert flick of his wrist. "You might need my special powers."

Connell caught the imaginary web with one hand. "Cool, kiddo. I'll let you know if I do," and then he slumped back into his seat and closed his eyes against the pain.

* * *

Four cars behind, Gesting pulled out into the traffic and smiled. Connell had guts, he'd give him that, but he was so transparent. Gesting wondered how he'd survived this long as a cop. Gesting had known he would bolt as soon as his back was turned, would have put money on it and that was fine. He'd just made sure his back wasn't turned. Now at least they could cut the crap and get down to what was really going on here.

Connell had lost his heart to Mrs. Jones, it was written all over his face, and he should be broken-hearted at her death. He wasn't broken-hearted which, in Gesting's experience, meant she wasn't dead, and Connell knew it.

226

Fifteen

Connell hadn't wasted the two hours he was forced to wait before being allowed to sneak out the back door of the hospital. The stitches were removed from the back of his head and he'd spent a little time regaining his sea legs that were naturally wobbly after two days flat on his back. But the majority of the time he devoted to Lizzie's notebook and Carl's address book. Although his powers of concentration were suspect at the best of times, and even more so when his brain was addled with drugs, he was determined to make sense of what she'd painstakingly transcribed.

He turned it over in his mind on the drive back to the farm. Lizzie had said they were missing the key to unlock the code. Connell couldn't accept they could be so close to the answer and yet not have it, and he couldn't believe Carl would have overlooked something so important. If it wasn't contained within the package Lizzie had brought, it must either be in the evidence that he'd handed to Mulholland's imposter - in which case it was lost - or it was still somewhere at Carl's apartment. There was another possibility that Connell didn't want to think about: that Carl didn't need to note the key anywhere because it was locked in his own brain and was something he knew he couldn't forget. If that was the case, they'd never get to the bottom of what was going on. Connell had an unsettling feeling he needed to do exactly that if he wanted to recover Lizzie.

Lizzie's notebook held pages of words and single letters, and he didn't even know which list was correct. He veered towards the words simply because that was easier, and he favored easy over complex. Carl's choices, however, being an extremely complex character, could not be as easily predicted. The address book was new to him. Lizzie had been the one who'd looked at it initially and found Musgrave's name. Perhaps he'd find something she'd missed.

The yard was quiet when they got back to the farm. "Still no sign of the dogs?" asked Connell. His mother glanced at Joe and shook her head.

"Them dogs have run off, Daddy. Grandma says they've gone off on an adventure. Dogs do that. Grandpa says they've gone to the North Pole to see Santa."

"Cool," replied Connell as he climbed unsteadily from the car. He hung onto the door, swayed a little, then blinked away the dragging pain and turned to Joe. "Are you sad about that, kiddo?"

"Nope, 'cause Santa's coming soon and Grandma says I can ask him for a new puppy. I'm going to call it Spidey." He ran off in the direction of the house and Connell and his mom crossed the yard more slowly.

"What happened to them?" he asked.

"Your dad found them behind the barn. They'd been poisoned."

Connell sighed. Sadness and anger vied for position in his gut. He didn't have the stomach or energy for either. "All of them?"

His Mom nodded sadly. "They were a greedy bunch. Any sign of food and common sense would have gone out the window."

"I should never have come back here," muttered Connell, "I've brought all this trouble home and I never

228

intended any of it. I'm so sorry, Mom." His voice broke and she put her arms around him and held him.

"This is your home, Tommy, where you belong, and that includes when you're in trouble. What happened to the dogs was terrible, but what's happened to Lizzie and Will's men is far worse. There are bad people in the world and I guess that's why your dad, your brother and you do the job you do. Never apologize for standing up for what's right."

He hugged her back before pulling away with a weak smile. "You are one push-over."

"How come?"

"A puppy called Spidey? You realize he won't stop till he's replaced all six of those dogs."

Rose smiled. "He has a gift for getting his own way, he reminds me of his father." She led the way into the kitchen and pulled out a seat at the table. "Sit down before you fall down."

With his first cup of coffee under his belt, Connell began to feel normality returning. He downed a couple of aspirin and took out Lizzie's notebook. In the background he could hear his mother as she set about preparing dinner for later and Joe as he played with his figures on the mat in front of the stove. Behind that comforting noise he heard the patter of rain on the porch roof.

It had been threatening rain all morning and they'd been chased by heavy clouds all the way from the city. He hoped his dad and Will were making good progress. This storm would eradicate any tracks that might have been left behind by Lizzie's abductor, and without tracks, they'd have no starting point to begin their search.

Connell was asleep with his head on the kitchen table when Will and Harry returned. It was after dark and the storm had blown itself out, leaving swampy pools in the paddocks and branches littering the yard.

"You go on in, Will, while I check the stock," said Harry. "I'll be in soon. Ask your Mom to get the supper out. I could eat one of my own horses."

"How is he?" asked Will as he shucked out of his wet weather gear on the porch.

"He's tired," said Rose, "and still a little mixed-up. I think Captain Gesting gave him a hard time this morning but he's okay, and he's been working on something belonging to Lizzie. I told him to go to bed but he wanted to see what you'd found." She paused. "Did you find anything? Please tell me you did."

"Sure we did, Mom, but we need to tell Tommy first."

* * *

"Hey, bro," said Will, as he sat down alongside his brother, "it's nice for some people, sleeping on the job."

Connell dragged himself upright and took a moment to register where he was, his eyes revealing confusion and pain before he blinked them away and forced a smile.

"So, you got some news for me, or what? Did you pick up a trail?"

Harry came in, hugged his wife and warmed himself in front of the stove. Will waited until they were all seated and supper was served before continuing.

Connell sat back and pushed his food to one side. His gut still churned and he had no appetite.

"Joe was right," began Will. "Lizzie was taken out of the water. We found tracks from a pickup leading away from the bank. The driver reversed in. Looks like he'd been sitting there just waiting. Afterwards he headed out onto the country road and turned west. Just before he hit the pavement, he had a little trouble in the mud. It's a narrow entryway and our boy had to work his truck around a little to get it through. He lost some paint on the gatepost, blue metallic paint."

Connell nodded slowly and imagined the scene. Somehow Carl, or Michael, or whoever he was, had known something was going to happen on the bridge and had been sitting there waiting for it to happen. The cops on the bridge had been used merely as bait. Whoever had taken them out had known he would stop and relied on that fact, and now Connell wasn't entirely sure who'd set up the scene or who'd murdered the patrolmen. He hoped it was Mo. He didn't want to think that it might have been Carl.

Will was speaking and Connell pulled his attention back to the room. "You remember old Parker Williams? He farms in the next valley." Connell shrugged. He had too much going on his head to sift out memories from his misspent youth, but he had an idea the old guy was some kind of hermit he and Will had terrorized when they were kids.

"The guy with the scary dog?"

"It was only scary when it saw you, Tommy. It was a sweetie to everyone else but, yeah, that's the guy. He's hanging onto that piece of land of his to the bitter end. Too old to farm, too stubborn to sell," replied Will.

"So?"

"So Parker was driving home from town–"

"The guy's still driving? He must be in his nineties."

"Sure he's driving and yeah, he probably is in his nineties, and his hand-eye coordination is a little suspect. Put it this way: he needs both lanes on the highway."

No sweat, thought Connell. He was a long way off ninety but he'd needed both lanes on the way to the cabin.

"Old Parker, he has eyes like a hawk and he swears he had to swerve outa the way of a metallic blue, extended cab pickup headed west. He said the guy

231

driving was mid-forties, collar-length dark hair and wearing shades. He said that the guy's hair was wet."

"Michael Butler?"

"You tell me. I've never seen the guy," said Will.

"It's him, but what about Lizzie? Did he see Lizzie?"

"No, Tommy, he didn't see Lizzie, but that doesn't mean anything. She'd just been pulled out the river. She wouldn't be sitting up waving. She'd probably be on the back seat under a blanket."

"Okay, so where's he gone? Have we put out a bulletin?" Connell snapped. His stomach churned and the pain in his chest taunted him. He needed to be doing something; he needed to be out there.

He rose from his seat more slowly than he would have liked and Will put a hand on his arm. "Take it easy. What do you think we've been doing all day while you've been sleeping? You need to take something? Mom, has he got meds he should be taking?"

Rose shook her head and shrugged. "Don't ask me. I'm just the getaway driver."

"Quit worrying, I'm okay," muttered Connell.

"You're not okay, son," said Harry. "Your brother's right. You've been shot in the chest and you've got to take it easy."

Connell scowled. "You're making a big deal over nothing. It's more of a shoulder wound than a chest wound," he argued, gesturing to the site. "If it was in my chest, it would be through my lung and I'd be dead. Another couple of days and I'll be fine."

"Chest, shoulder; it makes no difference to me. The bullet went in the front and came out the back, and in my book, that means you still have to take it easy, son."

"I'll take it easy when you tell me what's going on. We haven't got time for this."

"Okay," said Will, raising a palm to calm things down. "The pickup drives through the night and

Wednesday morning it pulls into a gas station. Jess Taylor is earning a few bucks on the pumps– good kid, nice and polite. Mom, you'd like Jess. He's staying in school, saving up for a car. Our boy Carl asks him to fill up the pickup and he does just that. He sees a girl in the back, sleeping under a blanket. She wakes up when he knocks on the glass. He said she looked a little wrecked– his words, not mine. Sixteen year-olds think anyone who looks tired must be wrecked. All they think about is drinking and sex, probably because they're not getting any of either."

Connell raised an eyebrow. He'd finally discovered his true age.

"Anyway, our man pays for the gas and gets a whole bunch of cold remedies and then goes next door to the clothing outlet and lucky for us, good old Jess is covering that register as well and is able to tell us that our guy gets a change of clothes, girl's clothes, size 6. Does that sound about right, Tommy?"

"I suppose," said Connell.

"So Jessie boy is starting to wonder, and then the guy gives him a hundred buck tip, and now he's really starting to wonder. He watches him go back to the car and he thinks there's a bit of a discussion, not a fight or an argument, but maybe a difference of opinion. And Jess sees the guy unfasten what look like handcuffs and he realizes this girl isn't there of her own volition, thinks maybe he's a cop and she's his prisoner, but he's not sure. Then he watches our suspect escort the girl to the ladies' bathroom and waits outside. When she comes out, she's dressed in blue jeans and a red hoodie, and Jess figures she doesn't look like a criminal."

"But she's okay? She's walking? She's not injured?" Connell could feel his heart quicken, that familiar thrum of electricity beginning to make its presence felt.

"Sure, she's okay. When they leave, Jess thinks about going into the ladies' room, thinks about it for a little while. Hey, he's a sixteen year- old boy; he doesn't want the guys at school to think he hangs out in the little girl's room. But eventually he goes in and this is what he finds." Will took out his phone and found the photo the cops up there had sent him of the ladies' room mirror, and handed it to Connell.

The photo was a little hazy. It had taken the cop a few attempts to capture the words, but Connell clearly made them out and grinned. Despite everything, she'd had the presence of mind to leave a trail they could follow. They were there on Wednesday morning. It was now Thursday evening. A lot could happen in two days. He zeroed in on the word HELP and his stomach tightened. She was scared and he'd seen her scared before. He didn't like to think of her being scared without him there to protect her.

"She left her clothes in the trash can," said Will. "See if you recognize anything."

Connell clicked through the remaining photos, recognized them all and tightened his jaw at the underwear. "The cops have sent them for analysis, see if they can find anything …"

"I know what analysis is, Will," grunted Connell. "You don't need to explain." He thought of the other photos, the ones he had burned for Lizzie at Carl's apartment and his stomach twisted even more. Why would she trash her underwear unless - he didn't want to go there.

Will read his mind. "Her clothes were damp from the river. He bought her dry ones, that's all there is to it. Don't read more into this than you need to."

He ignored him. "Do we know where they're headed?"

234

"Maybe. Butler bought her some thermal underwear, an all-weather parka and some heavy-duty boots."

"Huh?"

"So I don't think he's going to Cuba; he's going somewhere cold."

Connell handed back the phone. "Well, we've got two choices, Canada or Iceland."

Rose pushed Connell's plate back in front of him. "And before you even think about going anywhere, you need to eat."

* * *

Marty turned up an hour later.

"It's about time. What've you been doing'?" said Connell.

"Your job, and don't you forget it," he replied with a grin as he dumped a bag on the table and nodded a greeting to Will and Harry. "I went over to your place. Thought you might need some stuff. Fed the cat. You weren't kidding when you said you'd left a mess. I left Charlene cleaning it up. The contractors have fixed the door."

"Thanks, buddy. You didn't need to do that."

"Sure I did. Any news?"

Rose set a plate of food and a mug of coffee in front of him, and Connell brought him up to date, describing the message that Lizzie had left on the mirror. "She said she was with MB, So, it's got to be Carl aka Michael Butler."

"Or she's run off with Bullwinkle the moose. He's Canadian, isn't he?"

Connell smiled. "I love you Marty. You always say the right thing."

"I try."

"Okay, what've you got?"

"Now I know how you love all that espionage shit, Tommy, but this reads like something out of

235

spyware.com. Carl Jones was recruited by the government because of his mathematical genius and his total lack of moral conscience, perfect material to be raised up right-or wrong."

"The government?" said Harry.

"I'm not talking local government guys, librarians or tax inspectors. I'm talking spooks."

"Raised into what?" asked Will.

"Undercover operative, spy, call it what you will. Carl led a double life for over twenty years."

"How do you know this stuff? Who've you been speaking to?" Connell looked at him with new respect.

"Don't ask. I've been pulling in favors and listening at doors."

"Marty, you're in the wrong job–how many passports do you have?"

"Just the one," laughed Marty. "So anyway, Carl was recruited straight from college and he worked on a number of low-level assignments in various places throughout the US, even did a little stint in London at the embassy. Then he moved into overseas work when his skills were identified and appreciated at a higher level. By the time he was sent to work undercover as Mo's money man, he was already running a number of other jobs that required him to adopt a variety of aliases. In essence, that means he was responsible for the moving, hiding and retrieving of all the ill-gotten gains for a number of illegal organizations, including Mo's."

"People actually do that?" Harry asked. "I mean, I've seen it in the movies. Didn't realize we employed guys."

"In the beginning, he was fed information by his bosses to ensure Mo and his associates were suitably impressed at his financial prowess, and in return, he fed back information that allowed certain associates to be intercepted. Within a very short time he didn't need to be fed and before long, he was cultivating his own associates."

"So what did the government get out of it?" asked Will.

"They got inside organizations, got to know where the money came from and where it went. If you follow the money, you understand how it's being generated, and that's what they wanted."

"Huh?"

"In Jamaica or South America, it may have been drugs, and DEA would have worked with Carl, or whoever he was on that job. DEA get the drugs and the bad guys, and Carl changes his coat and his name and moves onto the next location."

"Sounds good," said Connell.

"Sometimes he may have run a few jobs at the same time - drugs, weapons, people trafficking, which would explain why he spent so much time hanging around the place."

Sounds like he had a lot going on."

"Yeah, sounds like your kind of job, Tommy. Flying around the world, mixing with the rich and infamous, and he didn't need to know anything about the merchandise. He just needed to know how to move the money and he was pretty good at that."

"So where did it all go wrong. Why did Mo knock him off and why is he not dead?"

"From what I hear from spy central, Carl went native, he was left on the wrong side of the line too long, and started believing his own hype and saving for his own retirement. Let's face it, he was good at what he did. Why make money for the mob and for the government when he could be making it for himself?"

Connell knew all about the line and how easy it was to get confused about which side you were meant to be on. He had wavered along that line for the last two years, and every time he had come close to Mo Pater, he had wanted to cross it.

Marty was still talking and he dragged his attention back. "His handlers decided to tug on his rope and bring him in, and about the same time Mo and his cohorts were starting to get a little suspicious. Both sides realized that Carl had managed to climb to the top of the tree and knock off all the lower branches so nobody could follow him."

Connell was confused. "Never mind them not following him, I'm not following you."

"You still have happy juice in your veins, Tommy?" asked Marty with a smile.

"No, maybe that's the problem." He ran his fingers through his hair, trying not to show how tired he was.

"Carl was the money man for over twenty different organizations. Within each of those he managed maybe ten or twenty separate funds. He had the account details, the passwords, everything - and he was preparing to disappear."

Connell thought of the lists, the numbers. They'd had the answer all along. It wasn't a code to be read in its entirety; each set of numbers referred to a separate fund, each word a password ... it had to be.

"So where does Lizzie come into it?"

"You tell me, Tommy. Suspicions were first raised about nine years ago when he returned to London."

"That's when he got together with Beth."

"He'd been on the payroll over ten years doing a good job but suddenly he was distracted, reluctant to fly far from the coop. Something was keeping his attention in England."

Connell tightened his jaw. He knew exactly what had distracted Carl and it wasn't his new wife. He avoided Will's questioning look.

Marty continued, unaware of the heightened tension. "Then five years ago they started getting jumpy. Carl was going AWOL, not keeping his bosses notified of where he was. There were gaps appearing where he would disappear and couldn't be located using any of his alternative identities. He'd created another life somewhere and he was getting ready to jump. His handlers had him watched."

"What do you mean 'watched'?"

"Well, I don't know. They probably have spies that spy on spies - super spies. Only these things take time. They can't just pull a guy out if he goes bad. They've got to ease someone else in to replace him, otherwise they lose everything they already have."

Connell had the urge to look over his shoulder. This was getting weird.

"The cracks really started to appear about eight months ago. Apparently Carl started to behave a little strangely, erratically, aggressively. His handlers and the bad guys were all busy shaking that tree and good old Carl was hanging on for dear life."

"Eight months ago Beth told him she wanted a divorce," said Connell. "Lizzie said Carl wasn't a happy man when he left. Reading between the lines, I think Carl had been a problem for some time. They were both scared of him."

"What did she tell you about him?" asked Will.

"Nothing," Connell replied sharply, "nothing important." He rose from his seat. He needed to stretch his legs, to put some space between himself and his inquisitors. He crossed the room, rested his hands on the counter and hung his head wearily.

"Everything is important, Tommy. You know that," said his father quietly.

Connell turned. His father was right. He considered his words carefully. She hadn't actually told him

239

anything. "It's not what she said, it's what she didn't say - those pauses, awkward silences, that you expect should be filled but aren't. Avoiding questions or changing the subject. It's probably nothing. You know what it's like in our job, you read things where there's nothing to be read." He glanced at his mother. She was fussing around the stove, wasn't listening, but he felt uncomfortable even thinking about what he suspected of Carl while she was there.

Harry followed his gaze. "Rose, I think I hear Joey upstairs. You couldn't just go up and check on him, honey?" He smiled at her and she nodded.

"To be honest, boys," said Rose, "I was thinking of turning in, if you don't mind. All this has got me plum worn out. I'm not cut out for any of this cloak and dagger stuff."

"You did great, Mom," said Connell quietly.

She smiled. "Well, I'll leave you to talk and I'll see you in the morning."

"Goodnight, Mom," said Connell. He hoped he was as wise when he was her age but he doubted it.

Harry rose, kissed her cheek and saw her to the door. "I won't be long, honey."

She turned back into the room. "Marty, why don't you take Tommy's room. He seems to have taken over the guest room and you won't be going anywhere tonight."

"So," said Will when his mother had left. "What did you think the pauses and silences meant?"

Connell looked him in the eye. "I think Carl liked little girls. Beth tried to protect her little sister and suffered because of it."

"But Lizzie didn't actually tell you that?" said Harry.

Marty shrugged. "I certainly didn't pick any of that up from my sources."

240

"She didn't need to tell me. The guy was weird, their relationship was weird. He was obsessed with her."

"How come?" said Will.

"When we went to his apartment, he had photos of her, I mean a lot of them, stuck on the inside of his closet door. Like a shrine he kept hidden from everyone else."

"What kind of photos?" asked Will.

Connell thought back. He hadn't looked that closely. She'd been so upset he'd just wanted to get rid of them. "Nothing obviously nasty, just odd, really. Photos of her as a little girl, through to quite recently, all taken without her knowing about them. If there'd just been one or two, then I probably wouldn't have thought anything of it. We all have family pictures lying around the place. But it was the quantity and the way he'd displayed them. Lizzie was really freaked out. Like I say, she was scared of him."

"And yet she was ready to face him. She must have some nerve," said Will.

"She has."

"So the net was closing in and his plans were coming apart. He must have been using Beth's home like a safe house," said Harry in an attempt to pull the conversation back and give Connell some breathing space.

"Yeah, and suddenly Beth was over it. She had a new man and was moving on and Carl needed his list of numbers so as he could get to the money," added Will.

Marty shook his head. "Not exactly, he didn't need the lists to access the accounts. I think he needed all that stuff because he was about to run and was given an offer he didn't want to refuse. He was going to hand over the lists in return for his life. What I'm not sure about is whether he meant to deal with his handlers or with Mo and his associates. The fact it was Mo who tried to kill him makes me wonder if it was the government who he'd been dealing with."

"That doesn't answer the question of who shot Mulholland," said Connell.

"I think it does," replied Marty. "Think about it. Mo represents the bad guys. He knows Carl has sent for something from England because Gilly had told him about the passport. He also suspects he's going to hand it over to the Feds, so he kills him on his way to the meeting and then sets about getting hold of the person who brought his stuff, which is Lizzie. In the meantime, Tommy, you come along and screw everything up by poking your nose in."

"Thanks, Marty. I'd call it investigating."

"You decide to hand it over to the Feds and the bad guys take it first."

Connell thought for a moment. "If all they wanted was the package, and I'd already given it to them, why did they follow us to the farm? Why did Mo follow us and why did they shoot Mo if they were all on the same side?"

Marty shrugged. "I'm not a genius. I don't know everything."

"They were after Lizzie," said Will. "They only took out Mo when it looked like she was going to get caught in the crossfire. You should've seen the panic on their faces when she went into the water."

"So back to square one," said Connell, "what does Lizzie have to do with all of this? She's only involved because she did a favor for her sister."

"And she's the only witness to Carl's death," said Will. "Only Carl isn't dead, is he?"

"What are you trying to say, Will?" Connell turned on his brother with a snarl. "'Are you saying this was all planned, that they were in this together?" He recalled how she'd stayed up half the night copying the lists into her notebook. Was she just ensuring she had a copy when the original was handed over? He pushed that to the back of his mind, along with all the other crap he didn't want to think about.

"I'm not saying anything of the kind, Tommy. Calm down. No one is saying she's complicit. All I'm saying is there are things about this situation which don't add up, and whether you like it or not and whether she knows it or not, she *is* involved."

Connell took a step forward. "Yeah, she's involved alright, and while you're fucking around here, she's being held by some freak she's terrified of."

Will rose to meet him and Harry put himself between his sons, palms up. "This isn't helping. Tommy, you need to calm down. Take a pill, get some sleep. We're trying to help. Will's just thinking aloud, that's all. That's how cases get solved, son, by everyone throwing their hat into the ring. Will doesn't know what's going on, and neither do you. The only person who does is the guy who has Lizzie."

Connell glared at no one in particular. He wanted to lash out but didn't have the energy. "Okay, okay, but we have to stop talking and fucking *do* something."

Will approached him hesitantly, put an arm around his shoulders. "It's okay, bro, we'll find her, but we've got to do this right. We can't afford to miss something important. Go get some sleep."

"I'm not tired and we're wasting time."

"Tommy, Tommy, listen to me. Go put your head down, just for an hour. We'll go over everything again, and as soon as it's light, we'll go get her. We can't do anything now, you know we can't. But tomorrow, when you're firing on all cylinders again and we've figured it all out. It'll be easy and we'll wonder what we were fighting about."

Connell pulled away and shrugged. "I guess," he muttered. He looked at his brother and forced a weak smile. "Sure, Will."

He climbed the stairs wearily, trailing his hand along the banister, reluctant to leave the discussion in the kitchen but suddenly desperate for his own space. He had too much information rolling around in his head. He entered the guestroom and eased himself down on the edge of the bed, the bed he'd shared with Lizzie - maybe not in the way that he'd intended - but shared nevertheless. He was totally exhausted and not for the first time, he doubted his ability to fix anything. He dropped his head in his hands and wept silently.

"Don't cry, Daddy," said Joe softly as he slipped his hand in Connell's. Connell looked up, wiped his eyes roughly with the back of his hand and hugged his son.

"What're you doing', kiddo? It's late. You should be sleeping."

"I've been waiting for you."

"Good, I'm glad you did, but you should be in bed."

"You need a hug, Daddy?"

"I sure do," said Connell, and he lifted Joe onto his knee and held him close.

"You been falling over again?" asked Joe, and he traced his finger gently across the wound on Connell's head where the first bullet had grazed him.

"Something like that, Joey."

"Mrs. Hooper at the store says I'm a rascal 'cause I'm always getting into trouble. Are you a rascal too, Daddy?"

Connell smiled and ruffled Joe's hair. "I guess so."

"I done a picture for you." Joe proudly held up a crumpled sheet of paper.

"Cool, Joe." Connell tried to make out what the crayon squiggles were meant to be. "That's a really great picture."

"It's you and me and Lizzie. And Spidey." He pointed at a little smudge in the corner.

Connell smoothed out the paper and turned it over. "We should put your name on the back."

"I'll get a crayon," said Joe and he slid down off Connell's knee and padded back to his room.

Connell looked at the back of the paper, realized it was a page out of Lizzie's notebook and saw there was something written on it. He turned it this way and that and held it up to the light. It was a timeline. Lizzie had created a timeline incorporating all of Carl's identities and locations as they had been represented in the passports: where he had been and when he had been there, starting nine years ago and ending with Michael Butler's arrival from Ireland. Connell realized there was something very wrong with it.

Unless Carl had figured out how to be in two places at the same time.

Sixteen

The next morning saw the first frost of the year and the puddles in the yard had a thin coating of ice. Rose helped Joe put on his hat, coat and rubber boots, and he made it his personal mission to stomp his way through every frozen pool. Connell watched from the kitchen window and smiled. He'd slept and he'd eaten. He felt as good as he was likely to get and he was ready to go. The fact that Will and Marty were going with him made him feel even better.

The realization that Michael Butler was a person in his own right and not an alter ego of Carl Jones had helped to put some pieces into the correct places. More importantly for Connell, it had proved to Will that Lizzie had been telling the truth when she said she'd witnessed Carl's death. The fact that she was not being held by the man she'd feared for so long was good news, but in no way explained what Michael Butler's role in all of this was. Connell had remembered him as an okay guy and Joe had said that Michael was looking out for Lizzie. But the last time Connell had seen him, he was with Mo and Marie was dead on the floor.

Connell saw the car drive into the yard at the same time as his father, who set down the feed bucket he was carrying and raised his shotgun. The driver eased the car across the icy surface, carefully avoiding Joe, and parked up alongside Marty's car beside the barn. He sat for a moment with the engine running, and then, with a slow shake of his head, switched off the motor and got out, hands raised. Connell swore under his breath. He'd forgotten all about Gestapo Gerry.

"I thought I told you not to go anywhere, Detective." Gesting stood in the cold, his breath misting as he spoke. He kept one eye on Connell as he approached; the other he kept on Harry's shotgun.

"Dad, put the gun down, he's on our side," Connell pulled on his jacket as he crossed the yard, fumbled his arm into the sleeve and felt the resulting pain radiating into his shoulder. He was determined not to show the discomfort. He was done with feeling sorry for himself.

Harry lowered his weapon and narrowed his eyes. "You sure about that, son? Seems to me these sides are getting pretty mixed up."

Connell grinned. "Well, Dad, if this guy's one of the baddies, we might as well all give up and go home. He's cool. I'm fine. I can manage." He turned to Gesting. "You can put your hands down. He's not going to shoot you."

Harry gave Gesting a long measured look, noting his suit and tie, his city shoes and the bulge of a weapon beneath his jacket. Connell knew his father's long-held opinion of city people. He figured life would be a whole lot simpler if they stayed where they belonged. He turned and nodded to Connell. He may not be sure about the man but he trusted his son's judgment. "I'll be in the barn if you need me."

Gesting watched him go. "I don't think he trusts me."

"What do you expect? People are dead."

"You promised me you'd stay put," continued Gesting.

Connell shoved his hands in his pockets and tried a smile. "What can I say? I lied."

"And here's me thinking you were an honest cop. As I recall, you were going to look at some pictures for me."

"I was and I will, but the thing is, Captain, I'm just on my way out. Maybe I could call in on you when I get back."

Gesting smiled back at him, hunched his shoulders, pocketed his own hands and turned to watch Joe's puddle-jumping. "Or maybe you could cut the crap and invite me in out of the cold. I have a message for you from Michael Butler."

Joe spread his arms wide and began circling the puddles, whooping loudly. Connell remembered playing airplanes with Will in exactly the same spot when he was Joe's age. It was a good way to keep warm on a cold morning. All that running around kept the blood pumping. He turned back to Gesting. "You know about Butler?"

"Oh yeah, I know all about Michael. I know he has your girl and I know that you've been tracking them. While you were running home to mommy, I was getting acquainted with his file."

"He has a file?"

"Everyone has a file, Connell. You just need to know where to look."

Connell scuffed at the icy gravel with his boot and shook his head wryly. "You and Marty should get together. You have a lot in common."

Gesting leaned back into the car and pulled out a battered briefcase. "Lead the way, Detective Connell."

Will and Marty were at the table finishing breakfast when the two men entered the kitchen. They had a map spread out between them and were debating strategy. Sources had placed Butler's car at a gas station twenty miles from the border, heading north, and Marty had established that Carl had previously used an address in

248

Montreal. The sighting was from the previous day. He'd had plenty of time to cross the border. The debate was whether they should anticipate his next move and fly straight to Montreal.

Gesting raised an eyebrow. "I see you have your troops assembled. Expecting some action, Detective?"

"That depends on what you have to tell me, and how quickly you tell it."

Gesting glanced over Will's shoulder at the map. "I can tell you that you're looking in the wrong place. Our guy hasn't left the country yet. He has unfinished business - with you, Detective Connell."

"With me?"

"I believe you're integral to the plot, as they say, but I digress, and as I have all three of you together, perhaps we can look at those photos now."

Will looked at him and shook his head. "And while we do that, our kidnapper is doing what exactly?"

"You said you had a message for me," interrupted Connell.

Gesting ignored them both, looked at his watch and checked it against the clock on the wall. "Is that coffee I smell, Mrs. Connell? I could sure do with a cup to warm me up."

"The message?"

"Later, Connell. There'll be time for that later."

"Hey, we got a situation here …"

Gesting sat down and took the mug offered by Rose. She was flustered, embarrassed that she'd waited to be asked before offering her hospitality, but Gesting merely smiled. "Thank you, ma'am, that's much appreciated." He took a sip, placed the steaming cup to one side and pulled open his briefcase.

"I guess you already know about Carl Jones and his career," he said as he shuffled papers.

249

"I guess we do," agreed Connell as he pulled up a chair and sat.

"And you know about Mo Pater, the man who killed him?"

"So it was definitely Mo - the hit and run? What about the crap with the other witnesses? What about Clifford Reay? He was ready to take the rap for that."

"He was until he heard that Mo was dead and then he had second thoughts. He's going to be convicted on accessory instead." He took another sip of his coffee and warmed his hands on the mug. "Do you know why Carl was killed?"

"Sure, because he was selling out to his handlers. He was going to hand over everything that would sink Mo and his buddies."

"And do you know why Mo was killed?"

All three men looked at each other. "It's got something to do with Lizzie," said Will. "The guys who shot Mo were after her, and didn't want her to get hit."

"On the bridge ..." Connell shook his head slowly and tried to remember. "Mo said that he didn't need the computer, he just needed Lizzie. He asked if I'd figured it out yet. I didn't know what he meant and I don't think Lizzie did either."

"Are you sure that she didn't?" asked Gesting.

Connell frowned. "You're as bad as Will. Haven't you heard of 'innocent until proven guilty'? She doesn't know anything. If you met her, you'd understand."

Gesting paused and shot a puzzled glance at Will who merely shrugged. "You okay, Connell?"

"I'm fine."

"Are you sure about that? It's not that long since you were hooked up in the ER. Should you be up and around?"

"I'm fine," repeated Connell flatly.

Gesting assessed him shrewdly. "Okay, why don't we look at those photos?"

"Why not?" replied Connell and he turned to his mother with a smile. "Hey, Mom, would you mind keeping an eye on Joe while we do this?"

"Sure, son, we'll go and see if your father needs a hand with the horses. You all just take your time." She turned to Gesting. "And help yourself to the coffee, Mr. Gesting."

"I will, ma'am," replied Gesting as Rose pulled her coat from the back of the kitchen door and went out to Joe.

The men who Connell had met at the Pines Motel, and Will had stood alongside on the bridge, were not law enforcement officers, as Connell had suspected. The guy who'd pretended to be Mulholland was identified by his mug shot as Vincent Sawyer, a major player in the people trafficking business. His associates had happily played the supporting roles.

"Who intercepted Marty's call?" asked Connell.

"Musgrave. He rolled over rather quickly on interrogation," replied Gesting. "And I must say, Connell, your dislike of the man is reciprocated. For some reason he does not hold you dear to his heart."

"I'll get over it," muttered Connell. "How long had he been on Mo's payroll?"

"Since Mo took possession of some interesting photos of Musgrave and a woman who isn't Mrs. Musgrave."

"Blackmail?"

"Looks like it, though I'm guessing money also changed hands. Musgrave drives a very nice car and dines at all the finest places."

"Have you picked up Sawyer yet?" asked Will.

251

"Not yet, though we expect to do so soon. They may have Carl's lists thanks to you, Connell, but they still want the girl and we've been leaving them a trail."

"*We?*"

"What do you know about Michael Butler?" asked Gesting.

Connell didn't answer immediately. He was still thinking about Musgrave being set up by Mo, wondering if Mo had used one of the girls from the club. He was astonished at Musgrave's stupidity. He hadn't viewed him as a stupid man - an irritating prick maybe - but not stupid.

"Connell," Gesting drew Connell's attention back. "Michael Butler, what do you know about him?"

Connell wondered at Gesting's question, where it was leading. And then he cast his mind back and remembered the man. He was good at poker. That was how he'd first noticed him. As someone who sucked at cards himself, he'd been impressed. He'd bought him a drink. Michael drank Guinness and always had one in front of him, though on reflection, never seemed to drink it. He'd seemed like an okay guy. "Not a lot. I met him at the club. He introduced me to Marie."

"What did he do there at the club? Was he a customer? Did he work there? Come on, Connell, you know more than that. In fact, what were you doing spending all your time at the club?"

"My job. I was on Vice, checking out leads, checking up on the girls. I wasn't posing for photos, if that's what you're trying to imply."

"And Michael Butler appears out of nowhere and suddenly he's your best friend?"

"Not exactly, no. He was just a guy at the bar and he knew a few people. I figured he might be useful."

"So you cultivated his friendship in order to find out what he knew?"

Connell wasn't sure where this was leading. "I suppose."

"And in return, he introduces you to Marie?"

"Yeah."

"And she was what exactly - a dancer? Did she work the bar or the booths? Do you usually hook up with girls you're investigating, Detective Connell?" Gesting cocked his head and looked at Connell questioningly. "Don't answer that, Connell. We already know that you do, and now you've gone and done it again?"

Marty and Will exchanged concerned glances and both looked at Connell. He glared at Gesting. He imagined Lizzie's hand, warm and gentle, on his arm and controlled himself. "What are you trying to say, in your roundabout way, Captain Gesting? Don't you approve of my choice of women?"

"I'm not saying anything of the kind, Connell. I'm sure you're very selective in your choices but I do wonder at your apparent naïveté."

"Huh, you've lost me, Captain. I thought we had gathered here to catch a kidnapper, not carry out a post-mortem on my love life."

Gesting smiled. "And that's why I'm a Captain and you're a plain old detective." He shuffled his papers into a neat pile, replaced them in his briefcase and glanced once more at his watch. "Michael Butler will be calling in exactly two minutes. He wants to speak with you, Connell, to arrange a meet. Please do not make the mistake of thinking that you're speaking to an old friend."

"Oh yeah, so who am I speaking to?"

Marty rose from his seat and poured himself another coffee. "I think we might have just discovered our super-spy, Tommy."

"Finally," said Gesting, "someone with his finger on the pulse. I'll have a refill, Marty, if you'd be so kind."

Gesting's cell phone rang as he took his coffee and he switched it to speaker and passed the phone to Connell. There was a jumble of static initially - reception in the area was lousy - and Connell held it at arm's length while the line cleared.

"Tommy Connell ... it's been a long time," said Michael Butler. He didn't attempt to disguise his Irish brogue and Connell was initially thrown. He could not quite reconcile the strong accent with the man he'd known, and he certainly wasn't in the mood for small talk.

"What do you want, Michael?"

"What do I want? A happy ending, Tommy. A satisfactory conclusion, that's what I want."

"Well, you're the only one who can make that happen," replied Connell coldly. There was something very odd about this whole situation, but for the life of him he couldn't figure out why. He just knew that somewhere along the line he was being played.

"I suppose you might think that under the circumstances, but you'd be wrong, Tommy. You see, you underestimate your own influence in this situation, just as you did two years ago. You need to get your brain in gear, Tommy, or you're going to lose - again."

Connell scowled at the phone. "Cut the shit, Michael. Put Lizzie on."

Gesting shook his head in dismay and made to take the phone back, but Will stopped him with a hand on his arm. "Leave him. He knows what he's doing."

Michael laughed, "That's no way to talk to an old friend."

"Is that what you are, an old friend?"

"Sure I am, Tommy. Don't you remember it that way? I introduced you to the love of your life. You do remember Marie, don't you, the mother of your child?

254

Sorry I couldn't be there for the funeral. I understand it was very moving."

"I remember a lot of things, Michael, good and bad. Put Lizzie on or I'm putting the phone down."

"Calm down, Tommy, all in good time. We've got some catching up to do."

Connell rose to his feet and crossed the room, taking the phone with him. Leaning casually against the window he watched Joe running about in the yard. "You want to catch up? Sure I can do that - after I speak with Lizzie."

"You sweet on Mrs. Jones, Tommy?"

"I'm concerned for her safety, Michael, that's all. I need to know she's okay."

"You think I'd hurt her?"

"I don't know, Michael, and that's the whole point. I don't know what you want and I don't know why you have her. You need to put her on so she can tell me that she's okay."

"I don't need to do anything."

"You do if you want me to play along."

"You think this is a game?"

"I know it is, Michael, because if I remember anything at all about you, it's how you like to play games."

Michael laughed into the phone. "Then you'll also remember I always beat you."

"This isn't poker, Michael."

"No? Pretty high stakes though, Tommy, wouldn't you agree?"

"Put her on," repeated Connell, and he pulled back from the phone as another moment of static screamed into his ear. He pressed it back when he heard her voice, barely audible. He strained to hear it, thinking perhaps he'd imagined it, then the static cleared and her voice filled the room.

Hoarse and faltering, her breathing labored, Connell now knew why Butler had been buying aspirin at the gas station. She sounded like she had a major case of laryngitis, but despite that, he would have recognized her voice anywhere.

"Connell? Is that really you?"

He heard the catch in her voice that had nothing to do with her state of health, and he wanted to reach down the line and hold her. "Sure it is, honey. Are you okay?"

"I'm fine," she croaked. She didn't sound fine to him. "I thought you were dead … I saw you … I thought I'd lost you …" Her voice broke and he could only imagine how scared she must be.

Connell turned away from the room, switched off the speaker and leaned into the phone. "Don't cry, sweetheart. I'm coming to get you, don't you worry, babe. Just sit tight, I've got this."

"I know you do. I'm just sitting here waiting - watching out for bears." She sniffed loudly. She sounded desolate and he felt a pain in his chest that had nothing to do with his gunshot wound.

"You sound rough, honey. You sure you're okay? He hasn't hurt you?" He would kill him if he had. Maybe he would kill him anyway, the way he was feeling, he had a real need to wreak vengeance on someone, and not just for what had happened to Lizzie. Things were adding up in his head. Michael may have saved her life and he needed to remember that, but there was something else going on here.

"He pulled me out of the river, Connell. He hasn't hurt me. He saved my life. I have a sore throat, that's all. What about you? I saw you shot."

"You know me, I just keep getting up."

There was a pause as she took another painful breath. "He says you have to meet him, to sort things out …"

256

She began to cough, the phone descended into static again, and Butler was back.

"See, Tommy, she's fine. You should be thanking me for hauling her out of the river. She's a cute little thing, even with a runny nose, and you've got to agree she's got a sexy little voice going on at the moment. You know, if I wasn't such an honorable guy, I might just be tempted to go a-courting. But you know, Tommy, that's the difference between you and me."

"Difference?"

"Honor, Tommy. Some of us have it …"

"Michael, you're pissing me off now. What the fuck do you actually want?"

"Tommy, you need to watch your mouth. We've got a well brought-up young lady here. She doesn't need to hear that kind of language. Didn't your mother teach you any manners?"

"What do you want?" repeated Connell.

"I want the notebook."

Connell turned back to the table and shrugged. How did he know about the notebook? "What notebook?"

"The notebook that belongs to little Lizzie."

"I don't know what you're talking about."

"Tommy, cut the crap. She told me all about it when we had our little chat, how she stayed up all night copying the code. We got ourselves a regular little detective here. In fact, I bet she could run rings around some cops I know."

Connell recalled how scared Lizzie had been when Mo had tried to get information about the package from her, and warning bells began to peal ominously in his head. Michael would be more subtle. He was no thug, but all the same, Lizzie was no match for him. If he had hurt her or forced her to do anything, he would make sure that he suffered for it. "What kind of a chat?"

257

"A cozy chat. I want the notebook and I want you to deliver it on your own. We can discuss the finer details of interrogation techniques when you get here."

"Deliver it where?" No way was he going anywhere on his own. The guy had unresolved issues, personal issues. Connell hadn't a clue what they were and wasn't about to be led on some wild goose chase without back-up. If Michael was Marty's mysterious super-spy, and he'd been turned, then potentially he was a dangerous man. Far more of a threat than Carl had ever been.

"You got a GPS?"

"Sure."

"Then get a pen and I'll give you the zip code."

"What's this all about, Michael?"

"I'll tell you when you get here."

"Tell me now."

Michael laughed again. "What, and spoil the surprise? I've been waiting two years for this, Tommy. I'm not going to spoil it all by rushing. But what I will say is that you should keep your wits about you. Sawyer and his goons are closing in and they're not going to give up without a fight."

"Whose side are you on, Michael?"

"The right side, Tommy. I've only ever been on the right side."

"So why don't you just come in? If you did save Lizzie's life, what have you got to fear?"

"I have nothing to fear, Tommy. All I'm trying to do is finish what Carl Jones started and clean up a few loose ends in the process."

"So why are you holding Lizzie against her will?"

"I'm not holding her against her will. I'm protecting her from herself."

258

Seventeen

"He'll check for a wire," said Gesting. "He wouldn't be doing his job right if he didn't."

"This is him doing his job?" Connell raised a brow. "What part of the CIA super-spy job description says he has to kidnap innocent women?"

"He obviously thinks she's important, crucial in fact, to the successful conclusion of the case," said Gesting, as Connell stood stripped to the waist and he considered the best place to tape the microphone. "We can put it under your bandage. He probably wouldn't think to look there."

"Neither would I," said Connell. "Who in their right mind would stick a microphone in an open wound? All you'll hear is my heart going ninety miles an hour."

"We need to know what's going on," said Will. "If we can't get right in there with you, we can maybe get close enough to hear you call for help."

"Fine," said Connell, gritting his teeth as he peeled away the corner of his dressing to reveal an ugly wound, stitched and beginning to heal. "When my heart stops, you'll know I need help."

Gesting expertly taped the tiny microphone away from the center of the wound, ensuring it would be contained and hidden when the dressing was re-applied.

"If he pats you down, you're going to yelp," said Gesting, "but at least we'll be able to hear you."

"Tell me about it," replied Connell, downing a couple of aspirin while he had the chance.

"Are you boys all sure about what you're supposed to be doing and where you're supposed to be?" asked Harry, who'd come in while Connell was being wired. His accompanying scowl made it quite clear that he was far from happy about Gesting's plan.

"Dad, we'll be fine," said Will. "This guy has asked for Tommy for a reason. If he wanted to kill him, or Lizzie, he could have done it days ago."

"Are you forgetting that Tommy *was* almost killed days ago?"

Will shrugged. "Yeah but, Dad, that was a different bad guy."

"Gerry, I need to know you're not holding back on me," said Connell as he pulled his T-shirt back on over the Kevlar vest that Gesting had insisted on. "Why does Michael need Lizzie, and why does he want me? If you know anything you haven't told us already, you have to give it up now." He struggled back into his jacket and zipped it up. "And you can start by telling me who you really are."

Gesting didn't answer immediately and Connell watched and waited as indecision flitted across his face. "You know who I am, Internal Affairs."

"Oh sure, and you do this kind of thing every day? Play spy shit and carry state-of-the-art listening devices around in your bag." He gestured to the battered briefcase and shook his head. "You're not fooling me. You probably got a command center in the trunk of your car. Hey, that's who you remind me of. You actually look like 'Q'. Do you have an exploding pen for me?"

Gesting smiled indulgently. "I work for the government, same as you, and I root out bad cops. That's all you need to know."

"I need more than that."

Gesting shrugged. "Okay, I can tell you what I know but I don't expect that it's much more than you know already."

"Let us be the judge of that," said Connell. He twisted around considering where to put his gun. He had tried the small of his back but knew that in the shape he was in he would never be able to get at it in time for it to make a difference. He double-checked the safety and carefully placed the weapon in the front of his jeans. No way did he want that going off accidentally.

"You know all about Carl Jones, the money man?" Connell nodded though he doubted that anyone, Gesting included, knew all there was to know about Carl. "And you know about the accounts where he held the money. Yes, of course you do because that's what you handed over to Sawyer. What you gave away, however, wasn't the whole story."

"Lizzie said there was something missing," admitted Connell.

Gesting cocked his head. "Did she say what it was?"

"She didn't know. She said there should be some kind of key to unlock the code, that it didn't make sense on its own. She didn't know about all the separate accounts when she said that. She thought the code was meant to be read in its entirety."

Gesting nodded. "She was correct, there is something missing. The code details the account numbers but it also provides us with the location of the accounts, the bank where all the accounts are held. Michael knows how to read the code. He was being prepared as Carl's replacement after all, and we believe that Sawyer has also worked out the location of the bank. They are both

261

in a race to access the accounts and divert the money, but what they both lack is the key."

"The key?"

"The password, the means to bypass the bank's security. Think about it, guys, you all have bank accounts and you give out your account numbers to various third parties - payroll, direct debits, even your favorite charities - but what you don't give out is your password or pin number."

"So where is the key?"

Gesting rose from his seat and crossed to the window. The sky had a strange yellow hue. Snow was in the forecast and when snow fell here it made its presence felt in a big way. If the snow made its appearance anytime soon, it would seriously jeopardize their operation. Any discreet surveillance and back-up to Connell would prove problematic when every tire track was outlined in snow.

He turned and looked directly at Connell. "When Lizzie changed clothes in the ladies' room at the gas station, she dumped them in the trash and the cops sent them for analysis."

"So?" Connell didn't get the change in direction.

"That was how we knew for certain that Michael was involved. We found traces of blood on her T-shirt, his blood. He must have injured himself when he hauled her out of the river and naturally, as one of our agents, his DNA was on record. We also found traces of vomit. Presumably when he pumped the river water out of her system, she threw up."

Connell imagined the scene and realized how very close she'd come to drowning. Michael had saved her life and whether he liked it or not, he owed the man. "Hang on, so what you're saying is that even though he's one of your guys, he's doing this on his own initiative."

"It would appear so," replied Gesting.

"A simple yes or no would do," grunted Connell.

Gesting ignored him. "Of course, gentlemen, as you all know, in our job we never presume, and the vomit and associated saliva was tested. We didn't expect to get a match. Why would a young woman from England, who'd never stepped foot in the US before, be on our database? In truth we didn't get an exact match, but we did get an interesting result, a close enough match to someone who was on our database to set us to thinking."

Connell looked at him blankly. He didn't get the connection or where Gesting was leading him.

"Connell, did you know that Carl Jones was Lizzie's father?"

"Her father?" Connell's face didn't change, didn't reveal his stunned reaction, but in his head his mind was racing, replaying every mention she'd ever made of the man. He recalled the fear on her face when he'd tried to discuss Carl. She couldn't have known he was her father, it just didn't fit. "No I didn't, and neither did she. She was scared of him. He had this weird obsession with her. Are you sure?"

"Of course I'm sure. Are you sure she didn't know, that this wasn't all planned from the beginning?"

Connell took a step toward the man and Gesting had the good sense to take a step back. "How many times do I have to say this? She is not involved. She doesn't know what's going on."

"Calm down, son," said Harry. "He's just doing his job. He doesn't know her the way you do." He turned to Gesting. "Are you absolutely sure? Seems pretty weird if he was her father, and all this time he never lets on. Goes so far as to marry her sister and live in the same house; what kind of a man does that? What was he trying to achieve?"

"Since we came up with the DNA result, we've had guys checking this out, checking him out. You're right it is a crazy story, and what I'm going to tell you all is classified." He glanced at each of the men in turn. "I know I don't have to tell you what that means." The men nodded and Gesting continued. "Carl was spotted early on and recruited straight after graduation. While he was at college, he spent a semester in England as part of an exchange package. He had a relationship with a fellow student, an English girl named Natalie Watson."

"Lizzie's mother?"

Gesting nodded at Connell. "At the end of the semester he returned to the States, got picked up by the CIA and never saw her again. He didn't know he had fathered a child until eight years later when he was back in England on a job and just happened to bump into a guy who'd gone to the same university. They bought each other a drink, got talking, and the guy updates him on Natalie, how she'd had a kid, married a history professor and died in childbirth four years later.

"Lizzie told me that her mom died giving birth to her baby brother," said Connell. "She also told me she knew nothing about her real dad."

"Suddenly Carl had an eight-year-old daughter and he apparently became obsessed with reclaiming her. He tried to convince the professor that he was her father, wanted DNA testing, the works. The professor, quite naturally, became alarmed and did actually report his concerns to the British police. He wasn't taken seriously because, by then, Carl Jones was a man of many identities and was adept at disappearing. When Carl wouldn't let up, the professor threatened to take his concerns to the US. He met with an untimely death."

"Carl killed him?"

"Not officially, though it appears very likely. He took an overdose. Official story - He supposedly never got over his wife's death."

Connell shook his head. "Are you telling me this guy killed the professor so he could get hold of his daughter?"

"Well that seems to have been the plan, but he didn't anticipate British social services and a very protective sister."

"So he married the sister so he could stay close to Lizzie. That's kind of extreme."

"More or less. Of course we all know now the marriage was a sham. His main aim, we believe, was to retain control over his daughter's life. He'd led a double life for many years and mixed with scum, maybe he felt she needed to be protected from the big bad world."

"Toughened up, more like. He was a bully. He beat up on her sister and probably Lizzie too. She wouldn't talk about him. Like I said, she was scared of him." Connell tried to imagine how Lizzie would react when she discovered the man she and her sister were so scared of was not only her father, but had killed the only man she'd ever thought of as a father.

"So what you're saying, and what Michael and Sawyer are guessing, is that Carl hid the key with Lizzie, the only person he cared about in his own sick way, that the password has something to do with her and whether she knows it or not, she holds the key to the bank?"

"That's basically it," replied Gesting. "And I think I should stress that we're talking mega bucks. Sawyer and his goons will stop at nothing to get back what they believe is theirs."

"What about Michael? Why does he want the key? Who's he working for?" asked Connell.

"Michael was supposed to be working for us, keeping Lizzie safe from Sawyer until we worked out how to get access to the accounts."

"So, if he's working for us, why am I wearing a wire?"

Gesting smiled wryly. "Because, we're talking big money, and anybody can be turned."

"So you don't trust him?"

"I don't trust anyone."

"What's to stop me from ripping off the wire and disappearing into the sunset with the money and the girl?"

Gesting gestured to the other men with a wave of his hand. "Because I think you're an honest guy and you wouldn't let your buddies or your family down. You're not interested in the money. You're just interested in the girl."

"So why does Michael want me?"

Gesting shrugged. "That I can't help you with, but reading between the lines, I'd reckon it's something personal. Have you pissed him off?"

Connell shook his head. "Not that I recall. We weren't best friends but we got along okay. All I can really remember is him standing next to Mo Pater when Marie was shot. How can you explain that if he's one of your guys?"

"I can't explain it, but then the whole business of Marie's death is shrouded in mystery as far as I'm concerned. As I said, all that was before my time."

"Do you have any idea at all what kind of a key we're looking for?" Connell asked.

"Unfortunately not. Perhaps Michael will be able to explain more when you meet him." He looked at his watch. "And speaking of which, it's time you were leaving."

* * *

The forecasted snow began with a few scattered flakes as Connell crossed the yard. He swept up Joe and hugged him. "You be good for Grandma. I got to go see a man about a dog."

266

Joe's face lit up. "Daddy, it's got to be brown with white patches and a red collar," he took an excited breath, "and sticking-up fur and a wet nose."

"Sure thing, kiddo."

His mother frowned at him. She'd kept Joe out of the way the entire time while the men discussed the case but, unlike Joe, she hadn't kept warm by running around in circles. She pulled her coat tightly around her. "Don't promise him something you can't be sure of."

"I'll get him one."

"Just come back in one piece, son. You and your brother and Marty, that's all I ask."

Gesting followed him out to the car and leaned into the open window. "You know where you're going. Marty will be following. Will's coming in from the west and I'll take the east."

"How will I know when you're in position?"

"Leave your phone on vibrate. One ring for Marty, two rings will tell you Will has you covered, and three will let you know that I've got your back."

"Will that be enough? Sawyer is a determined guy."
"I have extra backup who can close the net. All you need to concern yourself with is meeting Michael and coming away safely with the girl. Your guys are here to help you with that. Leave Sawyer and Michael to me and mine."

Eighteen

Gesting was correct. Michael Butler hadn't crossed the border but he had led them on a chase, leaving sightings at various locations that had stretched resources to the limit. According to the GPS, he was actually holed up less than forty minutes from the farm. And the knowledge that Lizzie was so close grated on Connell. He was being played and he acknowledged reluctantly that Michael was a master at the game.

The snow turned gradually from infrequent flakes to a steady flurry, and although it was still morning, Connell switched on his headlights as the sky grew heavier and darker, with more snow to come. Michael had never intended going anywhere cold, he'd simply read the weather forecast and knew the cold would come to him.

Connell was ten minutes from the agreed location when his phone began to vibrate. When it got past seven rings, he decided someone actually needed to speak with him and he pulled in and answered.

"Change of plan, Tommy," came Michael's amused voice. "Can't have a tail following you, buddy. You're meant to be alone."

"I am alone," replied Connell. Michael was bluffing; no way could he know about Will and Marty.

"Nevertheless, I want you to take the next right."

Connell checked the rear-view mirror. He didn't see anyone on the road but him. "How do you know which is my next right?"

"Because I know exactly where you are."

"Oh yeah?" The guy was guessing. He must have worked out exactly how long it would take him to drive the whole route and judged his whereabouts.

Michael laughed. "Come on, Tommy, you really do need to wake up. You left your car in the yard overnight didn't you?"

"You put a tracking device on my car?"

"Of course I did. Did you expect any less?"

"You were at the farm last night?"

"No, I was at the farm a few days ago when you were out playing cowboys."

"You poisoned the dogs?"

"What do you take me for? I like dogs. All that undying loyalty and love and all those wagging tails, dogs are way up on my list, Tommy."

Connell started the car and looked for the turn, keeping the phone to his ear. The guys wouldn't be able to call in but Gesting should be able to hear his end of the conversation via the hidden mike.

"So, Michael, this next right turn, you mean the one after the silos?"

"Yeah, that's the one."

"I got it." Connell turned off the blacktop onto a farm road that was already coated in snow. "I don't have winter tires, Michael. This road better not get any worse."

"You worry too much. I got here."

"Yeah, in a pickup and before it started snowing."

"What makes you think I'm in a pickup?"

So, he'd changed cars. Why did that not surprise him? He would have done the same. "Okay, how far do I need to go?" The road wasn't good and the visibility was getting worse. The car was struggling to retain traction.

"Until you can't go any further."

"Then what?"

"Then you walk."

A walk in the snow was exactly what he didn't need. "Thanks, Michael, you do know I have a hole in my chest?"

"Yeah, I heard about that. A little exercise won't kill you."

"You sure about that?"

Michael laughed. "Come on, Tommy, grow some balls. You're meant to be the hero coming to rescue the damsel in distress and instead you sound like my grandmother."

"Yeah very funny, do you even have a grandmother?" The car veered, and Connell fought to straighten it, failed miserably and it nosed in slow motion into the ditch. "Fuck," he muttered as he turned off the motor. There was a sudden deep silence and without the motion of the wiper blades, he was gradually entombed in driving snow.

"Oops, sounds like you're done driving, Tommy."

"I guess so." He pushed open the car door, grimacing at the snow. He wasn't looking forward to the walk.

"Okay, just follow the track. You've got maybe a mile to go. I'll put the coffee on."

"A mile?" This certainly wasn't what the doctor had ordered. He'd be puffing like a train by the time he got there. Round one to Michael.

"Sure, if you'd been a better driver, you'd have less to walk. Go figure."

Connell was glad of his fleece-lined jacket as he set off. Although the snow wasn't particularly deep, it was slippery underfoot and the wind had picked up, whipping the snow in tiny shards against his face. He tucked the notebook inside his coat and pushed the phone back in his pocket, hopeful it would vibrate the required number of times to let him know he wasn't on his own. Then he ducked his head against the wind and headed up the lane.

Halfway, he stopped to catch his breath and survey the landscape. The air was icy cold and each intake of breath was raw and painful. The dull ache in his chest was also beginning to make itself known as the painkillers wore off. He recalled Lizzie's words, *'Hurting is normal, it proves you're still alive. When you can't feel anything, that's when you need to worry.'*

There was a collection of farm buildings ahead, and from a distance, he could see no signs of life. Connell knew from experience that meant nothing.

"Gesting, if you can hear me, you'd better be in the right place or I'm fucked. I'm headed for a derelict farm about three miles from the turn-off after the silos." He swung a three hundred and sixty. "Woods to the left of the lane, fields to the right. My car's in the ditch and I'm walking - and it's snowing, if you didn't already know."

He set off again, and when he spotted a red scope dance across his chest, he used considerable self-discipline not to react. "Gerry, if you or your guys have got a bead on me, make damn sure no one has an itchy finger. If it isn't one of yours, then someone has me in their sights and I'm just hoping it's not Sawyer."

The red dot stayed on him and his heart began to thud. Gesting had insisted he wear a vest this time, believing he was a little accident- prone, although that wouldn't save him from a head shot.

"Don't want this to come out the wrong way, buddy, but you want to vibrate my cell? I'd really appreciate that." The phone stayed silent and still in his pocket, and Connell ducked his head and kept going.

The farm buildings were gathered loosely around a yard. Connell felt the hairs on the back of his neck prickle as he crossed it and headed for the farmhouse. He was being watched, and though he could no longer see the laser scope, he was sure it was now trained on his back. Whoever was out there could have taken him out at any time during his walk. They'd chosen not to … for now.

The door opened a crack as he approached and he faltered for the first time, his hand straying to his belly, hovering uncertainly over his gun. He didn't want to pull it unnecessarily and lose any advantage he might have but, similarly, he'd be no good to anyone lying dead on the threshold.

"That you, Michael?" he called softly.

"Sure is, Tommy, and don't you look a sight. Come on in." He briefly pulled the door ajar and dragged Connell in by his sleeve.

"You're a mite jumpy, Michael. Are you expecting company?" Connell shook the snow from his hair and stood shivering, unwilling to move any closer to the fire while Michael's handgun was trained on his forehead.

"Oh yeah, I'm expecting a few people to drop in, and you're the first to arrive."

"Are you sure about that?" Connell knew there were men outside. What he didn't know was whose side they were on and he didn't want to give them away if they were on his.

"Hands in the air, Tommy. You know the drill." Michael patted him down with one hand. Making a half-ass attempt at it thought Connell, as he came nowhere near the gun and didn't notice the vest. He should have gotten him to take off his jacket if he was doing the job properly. Maybe Gesting had got him wrong; maybe he wasn't as good as he'd thought. Or maybe he was playing a different game.

"Why the gun, Michael? I thought we were both working for the same side."

Michael narrowed his eyes. "What day of the week is it?"

Connell paused. "Friday … I think. It's been a hell of a week."

"Well, Tommy," said Michael with a smile, "on Fridays I work for myself." He stepped back, lowered his weapon, and the two men sized each other up.

Michael hadn't changed and Connell found that disarming. Knowing what he now knew about the man, he'd expected him to look different, to look more like the super-spy character he apparently was, but he didn't. He looked the same as he had two years ago.

He flicked his gaze around the room, checking for escape routes, possible weapons, the usual things. It appeared as though the farmhouse had been empty for some time and he wondered why when real estate was so valuable. He remembered the stock market crash and foreclosure sprung to mind. He wondered about the family who'd been forced off the land, whose possessions still littered the place, but only for a moment. He wasn't here to worry about the victims of the rich bankers. He had other things on his mind.

He returned his focus to the man with the gun. "Where is she?"

Michael gestured to a seat by the fire. "Warm yourself, Tommy. Can't have you catching your death on my shift. I gather you've already dodged the grim reaper once this week."

Connell stood his ground but the mere mention of his gunshot wound reminded him of the throbbing pain he'd pushed to the back of his mind. "Where's Lizzie, Michael?"

"All in good time. She's somewhere safe, where the bad guys can't get her. That's what you want, isn't it?"

"I need to see her now."

"Sorry, but that's not going to happen. We've got some business to attend to first." He raised his gun again. "You brought what I asked for?"

Connell stared at him, debated on whether he could realistically disarm him, and came to the conclusion he would be stupid to try. Michael wanted something other than the notebook and he may as well find out what it was. "Yeah, I brought it." He crossed slowly to the fire and warmed his hands.

"Are you going to give it to me or am I going have to take it, Tommy?"

Connell gave a shake of his head. He was tired of it all. "It's in my jacket. I'll reach in and get it. Don't get excited." He weighed the option of pulling his gun and decided that the time wasn't right. While they were able to talk, that's exactly what he would do.

Michael took a step back, keeping the weapon trained on Connell, and waited while he extracted the notebook.

"Good man," said Michael as he took it, "now sit down and let's have that catch up; two years is a long time. How's little Joey doing? I saw him the other day, did he tell you? Yes, I expect he did. Little boys can't keep secrets, can they, Tommy?"

Connell didn't answer, glancing around the room instead, checking for signs of Lizzie. There was none, and he felt a growing sense of unease, of having missed something important.

"Where is she?"

"Later."

"No, now. I did as you asked. I brought you the notebook. Feel free to fuck around with your secret codes, if that's what you want, but you're going to give me Lizzie. That was the deal."

Michael cocked his head and looked at him. "Was it? Did I say that? Did I make a deal with you?"

274

"I don't care what you did or didn't say. That's what's going to happen."

Michael pulled up a chair opposite Connell and weighed the notebook in his hand. "I don't need the notebook, Tommy, I never needed it," he said with a smile, and he tossed it into the fire amid a shower of sparks.

Connell lunged toward it. "What the …?"

Michael stopped him as he removed the safety from his gun with a click. "Hey, I'm a super-spy, remember? I already worked out the name of the bank. All I needed was the key and that's pretty much in the bag."

"Then what's this all about? Why did you ask me to bring the notebook?"

"We have unfinished business, you and I. That's why you're here."

Connell shook his head wearily. "Michael, I don't have a fucking clue what you're talking about. I've come for Lizzie. Where is she?"

Michael paused and let the silence between them grow, and although Connell knew exactly what he was doing, had done the same himself when he'd been trying to up the ante with a suspect, he still found it getting under his skin and he hated himself for his own lack of self-control.

"It's a terrible feeling, isn't it?"

"What?"

"Knowing the woman you love is in danger and there's not a damn thing you can do to save her."

"Where is she? What have you done with her?"

"It gets you right in here, in the pit of your stomach, and it curdles and boils until you can't think straight because of the pain. Pain like that can make a man do things he wouldn't normally do."

Connell clenched his fists, felt himself starting to lose control, and didn't even try to stop it. "I asked what you've done with her. If you've harmed her in any way, I'll …"

"You'll what, Tommy, kill me?"

"I'll fucking tear you limb from limb."

Michael acknowledged him with an incline of his head. "Hmm, I suppose that would be justified if I were responsible for her death. I suppose most people would agree you'd done the right thing under those circumstances."

Connell shrugged bewildered. "Just tell me where she is, Michael. You're starting to freak me out here."

"Good, that's good. You should be freaked out, Tommy. You just gave me permission to tear you limb from limb."

"What the fuck are you talking about?"

"I'm talking about Marie. You remember Marie, the mother of your child? Marie, who was shot and killed two years ago. Marie - my wife."

"Your *wife*?"

Connell stared at him. He felt each slow beat of his heart as the world, as he remembered it, crumbled and fell apart. Fragmented into a shower of separate memories, each one an event or an occasion that had seemed unremarkable in its innocence at the time, but now each one screamed his stupidity back at him.

He recalled the moment he'd been introduced to Marie. Michael had almost pushed them together. The many occasions when Michael had been there stood out now in his mind. The way Marie had always held something back from him, despite what they'd shared, and the way she and Michael had looked at each other. He remembered how she'd wanted to terminate her pregnancy. The only reason Joe was alive was because Marie had been a good Catholic girl and Connell was very persuasive.

He hadn't liked her spending time at the club, leaving him home holding the baby. He'd thought it was because of Gilly but realized what he'd known all along but had closed his eyes to. It wasn't Gilly or the club who'd pulled her away from him, it was Michael.

"You set me up with your own wife?" he whispered. He didn't feel he could say it out loud.

"It wasn't like that."

"You introduced us - what else would you call it?"

Michael narrowed his eyes and the vein at his temple began to pulse. Connell's gaze was drawn to it and for a moment, there was no sound but the crackling of the fire.

"We worked together," began Michael, "Marie and I, which you might say in hindsight was a bad idea for a married couple. It wasn't by choice, just the way things turned out. She was meant to distract you, keep you from getting too close to what was going on at the club. Mo had a lot of stuff going down and you were becoming a nuisance, nosing around, un-settling the girls. You were jeopardizing my cover and there was a lot riding on it. I had to establish myself before Carl was taken out, and Carl was starting to look pretty flaky."

Connell shook his head. This was crazy. "You couldn't just have a private word with me?"

"At the time it was difficult to know which side you were on, Tommy - a loft apartment on a detective's salary."

"I take it you haven't seen where it is. Haven't you heard of the recession? I could afford that place on a street sweeper's salary."

"Nevertheless, you tend to balance rather precariously on the line, Tommy. Most of the time you've got one foot just over, you're known for it. You're doing it now with sweet little Lizzie. You can't help yourself."

"I'm just doing my job, same as I was then. Maybe I don't always play by the book but I know what it says, which is more than can be said for you."

"Doing your job - oh yeah, you were sure doing that. Mo wanted to get rid of you. You were wrecking business. The influential customers, the clients with the big bucks and the useful connections, were starting to keep away. They didn't want to get hammered by Vice." Michael smiled at the recollection. "Mo didn't like it and he really didn't like you, Tommy."

Connell shrugged. "The feeling was mutual."

"But I couldn't let him kill a cop. For one thing, my boss wouldn't allow it, no matter how much of an arrogant prick you are, and I couldn't blow my cover by stopping him. So they sent in Marie to distract you. And they were right, it worked. It seems that you're easily distracted by a pretty woman, Tommy."

"And you were okay with that, with using your own wife, with her sleeping with another guy, just so you could keep good with your buddy Mo?"

"What do you think?"

"You pushed us together, encouraged it. I imagine you can guess what I'm thinking."

"I had a job to do and so did Marie. I'm good at my job and so was she. She was a professional."

"And you were her pimp?"

Connell didn't see the punch coming but figured that somehow in the mess his life had just become, he probably deserved it. He dragged himself up off the floor slowly and shook the scramble out of his head. One day soon he hoped he could go twenty four hours without getting on the wrong side of somebody's fist, or at least be in a position to give one back. But still, he couldn't stop himself.

"What do you expect? You pimped your wife out to keep your fucking psycho boss happy. What did you do, agree how far she was meant to go before she left the club with me and swap details when she came back? What did you do when she moved in with me, pay her overtime and have her call in every night before we went to bed?"

"Be very careful, Tommy," said Michael raising his weapon. The gun was steady as a rock but his nerve wasn't, and Connell sensed it. Michael might be playing the cool, in-control, spy-around-town, but he wasn't fooling anyone. He was on the verge of a major implosion. He'd waited all this time for it and Connell just had to press the right button.

"Why? Why should I be careful? This is your fault, Michael. We were together for two fucking years and all that time it was all an act. I tell you, Michael, she was some actress, that wife of yours, she sure had me fooled."

"I said be careful." There was a slight tremor now in the hand that held the gun, but still Connell kept on. He couldn't leave it alone, not now that he'd started.

"No, Michael. No way. I'm way past careful. What about Joe? Was that all part of your little plan? Sure was a good way to keep me away from the club, babysitting while mommy played with the clients and you did your secret agent crap. Did you know she wanted to abort him? That I persuaded her not to? I bet that really pissed you off."

Michael took a long breath. "You have no idea how pissed I am. He should have been mine, Tommy, and he would have been if you hadn't come along." He noted the look on Connell's face. "Oh, don't worry, Tommy, there's no mistaking your kid. He has the same lousy attitude as you do." He smiled sadly. "He tried to roll me for candy when I met him the other day."

"He's a good kid," said Connell defensively. "Marie would be proud of him."

"Sure, Tommy, but the whole point is that she's not here to be proud of anybody, and I've waited more than two years to explain to you in person just how I feel about that. I can tell you, time is not a great healer. Marie died and someone has to pay for that."

"You were standing right next to Marie when she was shot, Michael. You know as well as I do that Mo killed her. Mo's dead now. What more do you want?"

"Do you know why she was killed, Tommy?"

Connell shrugged. He'd come to the conclusion that he didn't know shit about anything. "No, but I guess you're going to blame me right, Michael?"

"She'd been turned, Tommy, by you. Two years of cozying up with Mr. Charm and you got into her head. She started off trying to stop you from causing trouble. She ended up trying to keep you safe. She began to wonder whether she'd chosen the right team. Didn't like the fact that for my job to be successful, Mo had to be left to do what he did. She was going to turn everything she knew about Mo's dirty dealings at the club over to her favorite cop and Mo couldn't allow that to happen. He knew you would blow the lid off the place."

"I don't follow you. You said you worked together. If she was a cop, if she was undercover same as you, why would she jeopardize that by giving it up to me?"

"Because she knew Mo was going to have you killed and she didn't want that to happen. She knew that you were a better father than she was a mother. She blew her cover for you, Tommy, and for Joe, and I had to stand there and watch her die so that I wouldn't blow mine."

Connell shook his head. "So you blame me for her death and you want your pound of flesh?"

"Something like that."

"Who put her in that position, Michael? Who sat back and allowed it to happen? Certainly not me. You could have saved her. You had a choice and you chose your job. It's a little late to start blaming other people, isn't it?"

"You fucked my wife, got her pregnant and got her killed," snarled Michael.

"You're right. I'm not denying it and I've spent the last two years carrying a shit load of guilt around with me. But it only happened because you allowed it," replied Connell. "You knew who she was and I didn't. You could have stopped it at any time and you didn't. Why didn't you just let Mo finish me off when he wanted to and be done with it?"

"Because the time wasn't right. There was too much at stake."

"More than your wife, Michael?"

"We're talking National Security, Tommy."

Connell laughed. "Not that old chestnut, Michael. This is fuck-all about National Security. This is about money and lots of it, and you wanted to get your grubby paws on it. Only you couldn't, could you, because good old Carl was one step ahead of everybody."

Michael sighed and looked at the floor, allowing his gun to drop until it rested against his knee. Connell scanned the room quickly. This couldn't just be about revenge. Surely there was more to this whole thing than that, but if it was, Lizzie might just end up paying the price. He had to keep the momentum going. He needed to get control of this.

"This is a mess, Michael, there's no denying it, but regardless of how you feel about me you still have a job to do, the job that Marie died for. Otherwise, what was the point of her death? Sawyer and his goons are out there somewhere and Lizzie is still in danger. She has nothing to do with this, you must realize that. You want to kill me - fine, I can get that, but I can't let you take it out on her. You need to hand her over and let me get her

281

to safety. Then we can end this, whichever way you want."

Michael looked up. "Of course. We mustn't forget Lizzie, must we? Poor little naïve Lizzie, caught up in the middle of an international incident, dodging bullets and bad guys with no clue as to what's going on. Do you think she'll forgive you, Tommy, for failing to protect her? Do you think she cares about you as much as you appear to care for her?"

"Like I said, she has nothing to do with this."

"Yet she is Carl's daughter, and she arranged to meet with him. Doesn't that make you wonder? You're a cop after all; you're paid to wonder."

Connell scowled at him. "It makes me wonder when you're going to cut the crap and tell me what we're doing here in the middle of nowhere."

Michael smiled. "Okay, so love is blind, but don't say I didn't warn you." He turned to the fire, threw on another log and watched the resulting sparks for a moment. "I've spent the last two years trying to decide who's responsible for Marie's death: the man who put her in danger, the man who killed her, or the man she died for?" He stood up slowly and walked to the window. He stood to one side and glanced out at the snow. "As you said, the man who shot her is dead, but let's be honest, he's not the man who killed her, is he?"

"What are you saying?"

"I'm saying that you're right, Tommy, and that's probably the one and only time you'll hear me say that. Yeah, I'm the one who put her there, kept her there and allowed it to happen. I weighed the risks and I put my job before her. Actually, no, I didn't even consider the risks. I just thought about the job. I think I've probably known it all along. I just needed to say it out loud."

Connell wasn't convinced. Michael's body language was all wrong. This whole situation was wrong. The man hadn't waited two years for revenge to give up without a fight.

"So what happens now?" he said slowly. He felt his heart rate begin to hike ominously. For the first time since he'd come into the room he felt nervous, fearful that he wouldn't be able to turn this around.

Michael turned back and gave a resigned shrug. "The man responsible has to pay." He raised his gun and turned it to rest against his own temple."

"Whoa." Connell stood slowly, spreading his hands wide. "Michael, that's not going to help. It's not going change anything."

"It's going to change things for me."

Connell tried frantically to think his way out of this one. There was no way he could allow Michael to take his own life. He had Sawyer and his men at his heels and only Michael knew where Lizzie was.

"What about the money? Carl's money? What about Sawyer? He's outside right now. He's already killed some of your FBI buddies. Are you going to let him get away with that while you wallow in self-pity?"

Michael gave a hollow laugh. "There is no fucking money, Tommy. Haven't you figured that out yet?"

Nineteen

Michael moved away from the window, removing himself from the line of fire should Sawyer decide he'd waited long enough, but kept his own gun at his brow.

"What do you mean there's no money?" said Connell. "Isn't that what everyone's chasing?"

"Oh sure, everyone is chasing it, but they're too late, it's gone. Why do you think Carl was running? He wasn't trying to make off with the loot or make a deal with his handlers. He was trying to save his own life."

"I don't follow you." Just when Connell thought he understood what was going on, the ground was shifting again.

Michael lowered the gun slightly. "You had all of the clues, Tommy. You just didn't follow up on them."

"It wasn't my job to follow up on them. It was my job to protect Lizzie."

"Oh yeah, and you did a great job there, buddy, didn't you?"

"I'm not your buddy."

"No, you're right. You're the guy who stole my wife."

Connell refused to go down that road again, not while Michael still had the gun. Maybe if he could keep him talking, Gesting might actually show up. "You were talking about the money, about the clues I missed. Will you please for the love of God enlighten me?"

"You saw Lizzie's timeline?"

"Yeah," said Connell.

"You noticed all the places Carl traveled to?"

"Sure."

Michael shook his head at Connell's blank look. "Carl was preparing to disappear, that part was correct. He started planning some time ago by moving the money from various accounts around the world into a high-interest internet account offered by a bank based in Iceland, siphoning off a little here, a lot there, depending on whether he thought it would be noticed. He thought he had it figured. When the time was right, he'd relocate and be able to access the funds from anywhere." He eased the gun away slightly and got a faraway look in his eye. "Only he didn't figure on the collapse of the Icelandic bank. The money he'd so carefully transferred was gone and his bosses were starting to get restless, suspicious. They were also beginning to put two and two together. Mo and Sawyer were the two biggest players. They knew about each other and that Carl was doing business with both. Only Gilly Tasker knew the full extent of Carl's business."

"Why? Because he came up with the passports?"

"Shit no. The originals were done in-house. But when Carl decided to start double crossing, he needed documents unknown to his handlers and so he went to Gilly. When he needed the passport for his wife, he also went to Gilly and Gilly filed it all away up here." Michael tapped his head with the end of the barrel.

"He's a clever man," agreed Connell. Gilly had attempted to warn him off, Connell realized that now. The old man had been trying to do him a favor, even though he hadn't seen it at the time. In the future, he'd say thank you very much when someone tried to save his ass, supposing he still had a future. "So Carl's ill-gotten gains vanished into thin air. Well that sucks. What next?"

"He travelled to Iceland in a bid to salvage what he could, set up one last account in a private depository, and moved the last of the money from a Nigerian account. He planned to be in and out. People were starting to notice he was going off the radar and were getting spooked." Michael laughed humorlessly. "Poor Carl, he couldn't even get that right - a fucking' volcano blew, and all the flights were cancelled. So there he was, stuck in Iceland while the world and its granny was hunting for his ass. Sawyer was following the money. He knew it was in Iceland but what he didn't know was which bank until you gave him the code."

This was getting confusing. "So the codes are for the depository?"

"No, the codes were for the online accounts."

"Which have gone?"

"Exactly."

"And does Sawyer know the money's gone?"

"He knows that Carl lost most of the money. That's why Carl was killed. He thought the codes would reveal where Carl stashed the Nigerian money."

"And do they?"

"Sure they do, but they're useless without the key."

"The key?"

"Mrs. Jones. Sawyer has come for Lizzie because without her, he can't access the depository."

Connell sighed. He wondered if his recent knock on the head had left him with some lasting damage because he was having serious trouble following this. He raised his hands in a gesture of defeat. "If you could just tell me …"

"When Carl set up this final account, he went in person because he had to supply a unique key - a set of finger prints. He didn't use his own though, he used

Lizzie's. He took her prints when he was last in England, probably engineered a situation where she left her prints on a suitable surface. She didn't know, still doesn't. And that was the beauty of it. No one knew she was his daughter, no one would link them. He had no intention of going anywhere near her until he was home and dry."

"And then she shows up in New York."

"Yeah, he sends for the codes, expecting his long-suffering wife to run on over with them. He intended to throw down a smoke screen that would cover his escape, give his handlers the codes, buy himself some time, but things never go as we plan them, do they, Tommy? Suddenly the codes and the key are sitting there quite literally in the hands of this little girl from England who has no idea of the danger she's in."

"And that's where I came in," said Connell.

"Hmm - that's where you were pushed in."

"Huh?"

"We had to make sure that Musgrave didn't get hold of her."

"We?"

"Gesting and I."

"You and Gesting?"

"Gesting pulled a few strings, made sure you were the only one available to take that call, to go take her statement. I knew once you saw her you wouldn't let her out of your sight. You're a sucker for a pretty face and it was a given you'd keep her safe until we worked everything out."

"But Gesting fucking interrogated me about how I got the job, what I knew about her, what I knew about everything. Why would he do that if he set me up in the first place?"

"Because you're still on that damn line, Tommy, and we had to be sure you didn't know too much, that you didn't already have your eye on the money."

"And are you sure?"

"Yes now I'm sure. I'm sure that you're a fucking idiot who, given the choice, will always go for the girl."

"No, Michael, not an idiot. Just honest."

Michael shrugged and turned his attention back to the window. "There are people moving around out there. I think they're getting impatient." He still held the gun with the safety off, but it seemed to Connell that he was less interested in taking his own life now and more interested in finishing his story.

"So let me get this straight," said Connell. "The only money that's left is in a depository in Iceland, and the only way to access it is by using Lizzie's fingerprints. Sawyer knows Lizzie is the key but he doesn't know how, he just knows that he needs her and that's why he's outside now."

"Yeah, Sawyer is here for Lizzie, and no, he's not sure why, but it's all too late anyway. You see, the depository has already been cleared. The money was moved and the account closed six days ago."

"But how could the money be accessed without Lizzie?"

"The same way that it was set up, I suppose, with a set of her prints."

"By whom? Who has a set of her prints?"

"If you'd done your job and arrested her for using a phony passport instead of trying to get into her pants, you'd have her prints."

"Well, I didn't and I don't, so that rules me out. What about you?"

"Oh sure, you think I'd be sitting out here in this godforsaken place, freezing my ass off, if I had twenty million in my back pocket?"

"That much?"

"At least."

"Then, yeah, I figure you would. I think you would go through all the motions, draw Sawyer into the net and disappear with the cash, just like Carl planned."

"You have a fertile imagination, Tommy, but I don't have the money."

"Well, someone has it, someone who knew how to get at it. Who else knew?"

"Your guess is as good as mine."

"Can't it be tracked? I'm assuming that much money would leave a trail."

"We've tried. It seems to have disappeared into cyberspace."

Connell cracked a wry smile. "So the money's gone and Carl's gone, so what the fuck are we doing sitting here?"

"Waiting for Sawyer."

"Where's Lizzie?"

"I told you, somewhere safe."

"I need more than that, Michael."

"That's all you're going to get, Tommy. You see, we've all played a part in this. Mo, as you rightly said, is already dead. Sawyer, well, he's going to be dead soon. And that leaves you and me. We both know what I'm going to do. What about you, Tommy, how are you going to atone for your part in all this?"

Connell took a step back just as the first shot shattered the glass in the window and embedded itself in the wall to his left. He dived to his right and forgot about his wound until he hit the floor with a groan.

"You hit?" called Michael from his position to the left of the window.

"No," grunted Connell. "Not this time."

Michael edged to the window and glanced quickly through the broken glass. "Our other guests have arrived."

"Sawyer?"

"That's right."

"What do we do?"

"Suddenly we're a team, Tommy? I know what I'm going to do." He raised his gun back to his temple. "What're your plans?"

"To stop you from taking the fucking coward's way out," said Connell, and he pulled his own gun and shot Michael in the leg. The force of the bullet spun Michael away from the window and sent his gun skittering across the floor.

"You fuck," roared Michael, clutching at his thigh to stem the flow of blood.

"Quit whining." Connell scooted across and retrieved Michael's gun. "It's a flesh wound. You want pain, try getting shot in the chest, now that hurts." He knelt beside Michael, unbuckled his belt and slid it free before tightening it around Michael's leg above the wound. "Hang onto that, you Irish shit. I don't give a fuck about the money, or your freaking life, but no way are you going to die on me before you tell me where Lizzie is."

Another round of shots came through the window, shattering everything in its path, and Connell pushed Michael down and shielded him. He felt shards of glass and splinters of wood as they rained down on his back and he waited for the gunfire to stop.

"They're coming in, Michael, and we have to stop them somehow." He looked about, saw two doors, the one that he'd come in through and another. "Where does that door lead?" He shook Michael when he didn't answer immediately. "Michael the other door - where does it lead? Is Lizzie through there?"

"Let them come in," Michael smiled grimly. "It's all part of the plan."

"What?" Another shot rang out and Connell ducked. He grabbed Michael by the collar and began to drag him across the floor. He could feel the pull on his wound and could almost hear the stitches tearing. He gritted his teeth and ignored it. "You might have a death wish, Michael, but I don't."

"We're all going to die anyway," hissed Michael.

"Not if I can help it." Connell opened the door with one hand and peered through it. There were wooden stairs leading down, presumably to a cellar. "Gesting, where the fuck are you?" he hissed. "Now would be a real good time for you to show yourself and bring in the troops."

"No one can save you now, Connell. You can shout as loudly as you want. I told you, we'll die here together. Do you think I'd leave something as important as revenge to chance?"

Connell ignored him. "Is Lizzie in the cellar? Is that where you put her, down there in the dark?"

Michael shook his head, and with a sneer raised his left hand. Clutched tightly in his palm was a tiny trigger device, the size of a matchbox. A small green light flashed from one end. As Connell watched, the light turned red. "Poor little, Lizzie, all alone with no one left to find her. What will she do, I wonder?"

"What've you done?" growled Connell as he followed Michael's gaze to the kitchen door and saw for the first time the incendiary devices placed either side of the frame.

A volley of gunfire suddenly split the air, the door burst open and Michael let go of the trigger.

The explosion was centered at the doorway and Sawyer and his men stood no chance. Barreling through and bearing its full force, they were quite literally blown apart. The blast radiated into the room, obliterating the nearest furniture, bringing down the ceiling and still finding the impetus to hit Connell in the back as he instinctively turned away. The force sent him tumbling head first down the cellar stairs into the darkness below.

He lay stunned beneath the debris, deaf to the roar of the fire raging in the room above, his ears ringing, his coordination and balance shot. Aware of something heavy pinning him down, he had a brief moment of blinding panic, believing the floor from above had collapsed on him and he was going to burn to death. He slowed his breathing, calmed himself, and using what strength he had left, he wriggled out from under the door that had been blown down the stairs behind him. When he was free, he pulled out his phone, sent up a silent prayer that it was still in one piece, and with an unsteady hand, he punched out Marty's number.

"Buddy pick up," he gasped as he peered frantically about in the darkness. His chest heaved with the exertion of pulling himself out and his heart pounded with fear and adrenaline. "Lizzie, you in here?" he shouted, but as his hearing returned painfully, all he could hear was the crackling of burning timber.

"Tommy!" The disembodied voice filled the room and initially he thought that the voice was coming from upstairs, that someone up there had survived, then he realized that Marty had answered his phone.

"Shit, am I glad to hear you. Where've you been? I've been calling for help. Where's Gesting?" He leaned over, braced one hand on his knee and tried to draw a breath in the smoke-filled atmosphere. It caught in his throat and he fought to contain a cough that had tears streaming from his eyes.

"We just pulled into the yard. We had trouble with the snow. We lost your signal and thought we'd lost you. What's happened, Tommy? There were shots and an explosion. Where are you?"

"In the cellar. The whole place has gone up. Fucking Michael went crazy and blew up Sawyer. I can't find Lizzie. I think she might be down here but I can't see a thing. There's too much shit lying around. I can't move it

292

on my own and it's getting hot. I need some help, buddy." He couldn't hold onto the cough any longer. There was an acrid smell of burning furniture and burning flesh, and Connell gagged and spat the taste from his mouth. He cast about wildly and his hand found a body - Michael's body. He must have followed him down the stairs, unable to resist the force of the blast. He found his neck and shook him, but there was no response.

"We're coming, Tommy. There's a trapdoor to the root cellar at the back of the building. Try and make your way towards the rear of the cellar. Can you move? Are you hurt?"

"I don't know. I'm okay, I think." He felt a searing pain in his leg where the door had hit him and he struggled upright. "I can't leave her down here, Marty," he wheezed. There was so little air.

"Tommy, hang on."

The sound of hammering and splintering wood spilled into the space, along with sudden light that illuminated the dust and smoke. Connell watched with overwhelming relief as Will and Marty clambered down the rough ladder, scarves pulled up over their faces. He scanned the room through streaming, stinging eyes. Lizzie was nowhere to be seen. Michael lay in a heap at his feet.

He felt a jolt as Will grabbed his shoulder, dragging him back to reality. "Come on, kiddo, this way." And together they struggled through the debris and up out into the snow.

"She's not here. He's left her somewhere else." Connell turned in desperation to his brother. "Where did he leave her, Will?" The snow was bleaching and he dashed it out of his eyes. "In this weather, she'll freeze to death before we can find her."

"Gesting's got men checking the buildings," said Marty. "You're sure she's not in the house - upstairs maybe?" They all turned to look at what was left of the house, and Connell shook his head. Leaning over, he braced his hands against his thighs and took a laboured breath. He looked down at the trampled snow beneath his feet and swung his gaze back to Marty. He couldn't have gotten this close only to fail.

"If she'd been in the house, I'd have known." He would have sensed her and he hadn't. She wasn't at the farm.

"We need to get you under cover, Tommy," said Will and he nudged him in the direction of the cars parked haphazardly in the farmyard entrance. "You're a mess again."

Connell ran his fingers through his soot-blackened hair and dragged his sleeve across his face. "I'm fine." He limped to Marty's car, pulled open the door and flopped wearily into the passenger seat. "We're back to square one again. Michael's dead. The fucker had the last laugh. He said he was going to kill himself and he bloody did."

"He shot himself?"

Connell shook his head "No, I shot him."

"Tommy, I told you what would happen if you started shooting people." Marty looked at Will for support. "Tell him, Will."

"Chill out, Marty, I didn't kill him. I shot him to stop him from killing himself."

"Well, that makes sense," said Will, "seeing as how he's dead."

"He's dead because he blew up the fucking house. He already had it wired. I couldn't stop him. He had it planned all along."

Twenty

"So, what have you got to say about all of this?" said Gesting when he finally got his men organized and made his way over to where the cars were parked. "It had better be good," he added.

The fire had burned itself out. The farmhouse stood blackened against the heavy sky and body bags lay one against the other in the white snow. He rested his arm on the roof of the car, leaned in and considered Connell. "Did I make a mistake in trusting you?"

Connell sighed and looked up, and Gesting got a first glimpse of just how furious he was. "You've got a fucking nerve. Trust! You've been playing me for a fucking idiot from the very beginning."

"I wouldn't call it that. I'd say that I was giving you the benefit of the doubt. Was I right to do that, detective, or have you just crossed the line big time?"

"I'm where I've always been, Gesting, on the right side." He clenched his fists and felt his heart rate rise. "Can't say the same for your buddy Michael."

"We just pulled a body out," said Gesting. "Pretty much mangled. Looks like someone shot him. You care to tell me what went on in there?"

"Oh, so you want to share information now?"

Gesting frowned and said nothing.

"I thought you were meant to be listening." Connell gestured to where Gesting had so carefully placed the wire and pulled his fingers away, stained with fresh blood.

"We lost your signal," said Gesting. "Now I see why. You need to see a medic?"

"Why didn't you tell me that Michael and Marie were married, that I was fucking his wife?" asked Connell as he carefully wiped the blood from his hand onto his jeans.

"That's a joke, right?" said Will.

"Jesus," muttered Marty.

"Because I didn't know," replied Gesting.

Connell shot him a hard look, read the lines on his brow, the denial in his eyes and decided he probably didn't, but that it didn't change anything. As far as he was concerned, when it came down to them and us, Gesting was definitely one of them.

"You'd all better get in the car and out of the weather," said Connell wearily and he waited until all three were seated before he turned in his seat, slammed the door shut against the snow, and began. "This whole set-up was basically the Michael Butler freak show. It wasn't about the money." He turned to Gesting, who was sitting behind him. "Sorry to ruin your parade, Gerry, but the money's gone. Someone took it six days ago and it's disappeared into the ether. Maybe you already knew. Did he tell you about it when you had your cozy little chat?"

"No, he didn't."

"No? So where were you six days ago, huh?"

"Checking up on you, Detective Connell," replied Gesting sharply.

"Well, you should have been checking out your man instead. He wasn't working for you or the government. He was working on revenge. He was setting the scene to take out everybody he blamed for Marie's death, and that

296

included himself. He planned to put a bullet in his head, had the barrel at his temple. I couldn't let him do that, not without knowing where Lizzie was."

"So you shot him first?"

"A flesh wound, just to keep him from doing something stupid, and to remind him we had unfinished business. And then what does he do? He blows the whole goddamn place up." He sucked in a fresh supply of cold air and turned on Gesting, hackles raised. "How come you didn't know about Marie? How come someone allowed that to happen? You guys - you're fucking with people's lives, with people's heads. Maybe you don't realize it, or maybe you do, but either way it's not right. I was with her for two years, had a child with her, and all the time she was taking orders from her husband, from the government, from spy central. How fucked up is that? How do you think that makes me feel?"

"I knew nothing about it, Connell. I told you, that was way before my time," replied Gesting calmly. "But, Michael must have gone along with it at the time and so did Marie. I'm sure it wasn't meant to be personal. It never is. You just happened to be the guy who was in their way. It could have been anyone."

"It wasn't meant to be personal? Oh gee, that makes me feel tons better. I'll remember that when my son asks about his mom."

"I'm trying to say, *give yourself a break*, it wasn't your fault."

"Don't you get it, Gerry? It doesn't matter whose fault it was or who knew about it. The fact is that *your* lot, the people whom we naïvely think are looking out for us, used that girl and then, when she was killed, you covered it up. You buried my evidence and let her killer walk free. No wonder Michael was pissed. I'm fucking pissed. She was the mother of my child, a decent girl who was trying to do her job and keep herself honest, and you let her down."

Gesting looked away. As far as Connell was concerned, there was nothing he could say to justify what had happened.

"So what now?" said Will into the uncomfortable silence that filled the car, "The bad guys are dead and the money's gone?"

"Now we need to find Lizzie," said Connell, turning to his brother. "I need to borrow your pickup, Will."

"You need to get checked out by the medics before you go anywhere," said Gesting as he climbed out of the car and pulled his coat around him. "You're bleeding and you're wheezing like a two pack-a-day man."

"I don't have time for that."

"And then I need you to sit down and write me a decent report."

"I told you, I don't have time."

"You'll find the time if you want to keep your job," said Gesting shortly.

Connell returned his attention to his brother. "Keys, Will."

Will shrugged and threw them to him. "You have any idea where you're planning to go?"

Climbing out of Marty's car, Connell stretched his legs and flexed his shoulder carefully. He took a deep breath of cold crisp air, filled his lungs and turned and winked at his brother. "I'm going looking for bears."

* * *

The cabin was wrapped in a snowy blanket and Connell was reassured by the fact that the snow-covered ground surrounding it was untouched. He eased the pickup to a standstill and turned off the ignition. There were no signs of life, no smoke at the chimney, no face at the window, no welcome at the door. He felt a

298

churning in his stomach. Maybe he had misunderstood Lizzie's message.

Maybe there was no message. She'd told him on the phone that she was waiting, watching out for bears, and this was the only place where she could have seen a bear. But he'd been clutching at straws, and now that he was here, he was reluctant to get out of the truck and find out he'd been wrong - again.

He approached the cabin warily, gun in hand, all too aware of Michael's propensity for planning nasty surprises. The whole building might be wired to go up, but there was no way of knowing and he couldn't stand outside all day debating strategy. He stepped up onto the porch, felt the timbers creak beneath his weight, and he recalled with a smile the night the bear had come to call. Lizzie was so scared, and so indignant when he'd laughed at her. He remembered how he'd held her close and kept her warm that night, recalled how wonderful she'd felt and how frustrated he'd been.

He stepped to one side of the door and glanced through the icy window. There was no movement inside. The stove was unlit and the room was in darkness. He hesitated and rested his head momentarily against the rough wood of the cabin wall, suddenly fearful of what he might find inside. Michael had been consumed by his need for revenge. He had lost the woman he loved, and he might just have decided to pay the favor back and do the same to Connell. He knew he'd only find out if he went inside.

Slowly he turned the handle. The door was unlocked and swung in gently under his direction. He felt his anxiety begin to increase. If the door was unlocked, it could only be because Michael knew the occupant would not - could not - escape. He raised his gun and slowly entered the cabin. The first thing he noticed was how cold the room was. His own breath misted as he exhaled.

Crossing to the stove, he placed his hand against it. The cast iron was icy to the touch. It had not been recently lit.

The second thing he noticed was a faint floral scent. Lizzie. It meant nothing. She'd been here with him a matter of days ago. The cabin had remained closed up. Of course the scent would linger. Please God, he pleaded silently before slowly opening the bedroom door.

The room was in darkness, the drapes drawn tight across the small window. He stood in the doorway while his eyes adjusted to the gloom. His gaze was drawn to a bundle of bedding tangled in a heap in the middle of the bed, as if someone had called a party and all the guests had thrown their coats on the bed. Only there wasn't a party and the only sound was that of his own ragged breathing.

He approached the bed slowly, reluctantly. From one corner of the mound a thin rope was tautly stretched and tied to the wooden bed post. Reaching out with an unsteady hand, Connell carefully drew back the blankets, revealing that the rope was tied to a pair of tightly bound wrists. He stared at the sight of her, bound hand and foot, blindfolded and gagged.

She was curled in a fetal position, still as a grave.

"No - no," he groaned. His gun slipped from his hand and hit the wooden floor with a clatter. He knelt on the edge of the bed beside her, reached across, removed the blindfold, tore off the gag and frantically felt for a pulse.

"Sweetheart, please, I'm right here. I said I would come get you and I have." Her skin was cold beneath his hands. "Lizzie, come on, honey, open your eyes."

He fumbled with the rope, released her hands and pulled her limp body against him. He held her tight, breathing the scent of her hair and struggling for control. Pulling back, he smoothed her hair away from her face and kissed her lips gently. "Sweetheart, please wake up."

And then, slowly, so slowly that he thought he'd imagined it, her eyelids parted and she looked straight at him. He watched, mesmerized as her pupils attempted to focus and he saw the precise moment of recognition.

"Well, hello," she whispered slowly, her words a little slurred as if she had been dragged back from someplace else and hadn't quite caught up with herself. "You came for me."

Her eyes brimmed with sudden tears.

Connell thought his heart would break in two. He felt his own tears of relief, wet against his cheeks.

"Baby, don't scare me like that. I thought I'd lost you." He pulled her tightly into his arms and just held her. He felt his heat transfer slowly into her chilled body and he sent up a silent prayer.

"Are you hurt? Did he hurt you?" he asked, and she shook her head, reached out her hand and traced his face gently with frozen fingers.

"I've been sleeping for a long time. Am I dreaming now? Are you really here? You were shot, I saw it - how did you get here? You're meant to be dead." She blinked slowly, releasing the tears, her voice wobbly, and he wondered whether she'd had help with the sleep. Perhaps Michael had drugged her before he'd left or maybe it was simply the cold that had numbed her senses.

He smiled at her. "Hey, I'm a hard case. It'd take more than a bullet in the chest to keep me down."

"You have soot in your hair," she said distractedly, her eyes betraying her continuing confusion, still not sure he was real.

"It's a long story. I'll tell you all about it later." He wasn't looking forward to that, explaining about Carl and the real reason for his obsession with her. "For now, though, we've got to get you warmed up, and we need to get you out of here before the weather gets any worse."

"Is it all over?" she asked. "Are we safe now?"

"Sure we are, honey. The bad guys are all dead." At least he thought they were. He had seen them killed in front of him, but as he had no clue which side was which, he didn't want to sign his name to it.

"Is that good, that they're all dead?" she asked as she gently rubbed at the redness left behind by the rope.

"Well, that depends on your perspective. As far as we're concerned, it's excellent, but I don't suppose they're too happy about it."

She pulled up her feet, snuggled closer and slid her hands under his T-shirt, warming them against his skin. "Did you kill them?" she asked.

Connell flinched, her fingers were freezing. "Not exactly. Michael decided to play with some explosives." He gave her a lopsided grin. "You could say they went out with a bang."

"Is that what happened to you?"

"You could say."

He felt her sag against him, overwhelmed by everything that had happened.

"I think I need a hug …" she said, her voice breaking on the last word.

"I think I can manage that," he whispered, and he held her tight and let her cry against him. His phone vibrated as he pressed a gentle kiss on the top of her head. "Oh, sure, now you decide to make contact," muttered Connell, and he pulled out the phone and checked the display. He moved Lizzie onto his left arm, reluctant to let go of her for even a moment, and took the call. "Hiya, Marty."

"Tommy, you were meant to call in, Gesting's having a coronary here. What happened? Is she there? Did you find her?"

He'd promised he would keep in touch. That was the only reason they'd let him drive away on his own in the condition he was in. "I found her, Marty, right where I thought she'd be, and she's fine. She's cold and a little spaced out, no thanks to Michael, but fine. He left her tied up, no heat in the place, no intention of coming back." He didn't need to say any more about what he thought of the man who'd left her to die. "We're going to head back to the farm now."

"That might be a problem, Tommy. Take a look out the window. We've got a blizzard going on. If Lizzie doesn't need medical care, I think you might want to stay put and ride out the weather."

Connell could detect both relief and amusement in his voice, and smiled back at the phone. "Are you telling me we're stuck here in the middle of a blizzard, with only ourselves to keep us warm?"

Lizzie looked up at him, dried her tears with sleeves that were pulled down over her hands, and smiled weakly.

"That's about the size of it, buddy. Plenty of wood in the shed if you run out of ways to keep warm."

"What about Gesting?"

"Gesting? Who's Gesting?"

"Oh, you know, the guy who has me and my job by the balls."

Marty laughed. "Gesting's got enough to keep him busy explaining to his bosses how he lost the money and blew up their not-so-secret agent."

"Ouch."

"Exactly. Probably best to stay out of his way until things cool down."

"It's not that bad, we might have lost the money but we did save the girl."

"No, Tommy, you saved the girl. Take credit where it's due."

"So Gesting is pretty pissed, is he?" He knew he'd pushed him, just wasn't sure what the repercussions would be.

"He'll live. He's a pretty cool guy, plays things close to his chest. For what it's worth, I don't think he knew about Marie." Marty paused, leaving an awkward silence. "I'm real sorry about what happened, about what they did …"

"Thanks, bud," replied Connell. He didn't much want to talk about it either. "Yeah, well, I didn't really think he knew about it. I just needed someone to yell at."

"He's going to need to speak with Lizzie, and he's still bitching about your report, but, hey, if you're stuck, you're stuck. You can't be held responsible for the weather."

"I suppose not. How long are they predicting it to last?"

"A couple of days, maybe more."

"Will's got winter tires on the pickup and chains in the trunk. I think I could get us out."

"Do you want to?"

Connell let his gaze stray over Lizzie. "Not especially."

"Then I'll catch you later, buddy."

"Sure thing, Marty."

Connell switched off his phone, reached over and laid it on the night stand. No way was he switching that back on; he was done with being interrupted. He turned back to Lizzie. "Sounds like we're going to have to make our own entertainment, we can't get out and no one can get in."

"Oh," she replied, a little more awake, a little less upset.

"Oh?"

"Did you pay him to say that?"

Connell grinned, ducked his head and kissed the end of her nose. "Here's the deal. I'll play Nanook of the North, haul my ass through the snow and go get the generator started. Then I'll get the logs and light the stove, and we can cozy on up and wait out the storm. Will you be alright on your own while I do that?"

"I know a quicker way to warm up," she said.

"Oh, yeah?"

"Yes, a nice hot shower." She closed her eyes and wriggled her shoulders in anticipation.

He could see how that could also work. In fact, it had great possibilities, not least the opportunity to rid himself of the soot and grime he'd managed to acquire. "What're we going to do while we wait for the water to heat up?"

"We ... I've no idea. Maybe you can think of something."

He laughed, cupped her face in his hands and kissed her. "I love you, Mrs. Jones."

"And you're not so bad yourself."

"Hey, am I going to catch your sexy little voice if I keep doing this?" he asked.

Lizzie raised an eyebrow with amusement "Maybe, but if you're worried–"

"Do I look worried?"

She reached up and kissed him back. "No, but maybe you should be."

"That sounds like fighting talk, Mrs. J."

"I'm too tired to fight."

"Yeah?"

"Mm," she said as she snuggled against him.

"Hey, you've just done telling me that you spent the whole day sleeping."

"Go sort out the fire, Connell," she said and she pushed him gently. "I'll be fine 'til you get back."

"You sure about that?" he kissed her again, a little slower.

"You taste of soot," she said, and wrinkled her nose.

"That's what happens when a crazy guy lights the barbecue." Connell laughed. "Whereas you taste real sweet ..."

"Well, of course. Sugar and spice are what all little girls are made of." She kissed him back.

This was getting interesting and she was sure warming up. Maybe he could save himself a trek in the snow.

"Whereas you - slugs and snails and puppy dogs tails," she giggled softly.

"Shit." He drew back and pulled a face.

"What?"

"Puppy dog tails. I told Joe when I left the farm this morning I was going to get him a puppy. If I don't go back with a brown and white dog, I'm dead meat."

"Then you'd better start phoning around."

"Now?"

"Well ... maybe later."

"You kill me, you know that?"

Lizzie smiled at him. "I love you too, Detective."

Twenty One

Lizzie sat cross-legged on the bedroom floor, her hair in a towel and a dressing gown wrapped around her slender frame. The fire in the cast iron grate flickered, creating patterns on the wall. Lizzie watched them for a while and hugged the mug of cocoa in her hands. She'd been home for fourteen long days but it might well have been fourteen weeks. She was missing Connell so much in ways she couldn't have imagined.

She understood why she'd had to come home and why he couldn't come with her, but that didn't make it any easier. She'd spent the night before at the hospital with her sister and now had a beautiful new baby niece. But even that hadn't made her feel any better. She was alone, she was lonely and unsettled. So much had happened and all she could think about was a detective on the other side of the Atlantic.

She recalled the look on Connell's face when he'd sat her down and told her the truth about Carl. She hadn't wanted to hear it, hadn't believed him at first, but he'd no reason to lie to her. She'd lashed out at him and he'd let her, and when she'd cried on his shoulder, he'd held her. When she was done, he'd told her about Michael and Marie, and it'd been her turn to hold onto him.

They'd stayed at the cabin as long as they could before the real world pulled them back and the endless

307

round of questions began. She knew Gesting was just doing his job, but he couldn't quite grasp that she had nothing to tell. She knew nothing about Carl's secrets or his plans. She didn't want to know, either. She wanted to forget all about it, but she didn't want to forget about Connell.

She put down her mug with a sigh and picked up the pile of post redirected by her flat mates. Her days as a carefree student were over. Now she had to think about the rest of her life.

The first letter she opened was dated four weeks previous, and she shook her head as she looked at the date. Four weeks ago she'd never even stepped on a plane, never met Connell, and she hadn't known the awful truth about her real father. She looked at the postmark and realized it was from the U.S. Four weeks ago she didn't know anyone in the U.S. but Carl.

With trembling hands she tore open the envelope.

Her biological father had written three pages in which he detailed his regrets for the past and his hopes for the future. He was deluded enough to imagine they actually had a future.

Lizzie read the first two, screwed the letter into a ball and threw it into the flames. She had only one father, Beth's father, and he'd been killed by Carl. She was glad Carl was dead. She wanted nothing from him, not even his words. She felt the familiar knot twist in her stomach and her hand strayed to worry at her hair. She wondered whether she'd ever be able to think about him without feeling such dread. She couldn't allow him to ruin her life and she couldn't allow him to ruin Connell's.

Connell was facing an enquiry over his handling of the case - her case - and although he'd told her it was a steal, and he could charm his way out of anything, she knew it wasn't that simple. He'd broken the rules for her and could lose his job because of it. He wasn't concerned about his job, she knew he'd rather be with Joe any day of the week, but he was concerned about his honor. He was a good cop, an honest cop, and life at the moment seemed stacked unfairly against him. He might have saved the girl but the government didn't really see that as a result. They saw it as an embarrassment. They were still reeling over the loss of the money and the ineptitude of Carl's handlers.

She quickly scanned the remaining mail, circulars mostly, reminders about her store card payment that was overdue, and an invite to a party that she was two weeks too late to attend. She wouldn't have gone anyway; she wasn't in the mood for parties.

The last was from an unfamiliar bank, probably an invite to open an account. Since she'd graduated, there seemed to be an assumption she might actually be solvent. More fool them, she thought wryly, as she opened the envelope. She scanned the contents quickly and then read it again more slowly just to be sure. "Oh bugger," she whispered and picked up the phone.

* * *

"It's the middle of the night," murmured Connell, "this had better be good, and Marty, if this is your idea of payback, you're a dead man."

She'd forgotten about the time difference. The sound of his voice, thick with sleep, gave her a warm feeling. "Hiya, cowboy," she said softly.

"Lizzie?"

"I know we agreed to cool it until things calmed down a little but …"

"Hey, I missed you too."

"Really?" her stomach gave a little flutter. She wondered whether he meant it or whether he just couldn't help the Connell charm.

"Yeah."

"Is Gesting still giving you grief?" She heard Connell's sigh as it whispered down the line and imagined him adjusting the pillow behind his head.

"Gesting's got grief of his own. I think he's taking responsibility for what amounts to a major fuck up. By comparison, I guess we're pretty small fry."

"Will you keep your job?" she asked.

"Not sure," he replied slowly. "Not sure I want to keep it. Will offered me a job at the sheriff's department but hey, that would be like stepping in dead men's shoes, and seeing as I put his men in the ground, it just wouldn't sit right."

"You didn't kill those deputies."

"No, but they were only there because of me."

"Because of Carl and Michael, Connell. It was nothing to do with you."

"Yeah, sure, sweetheart, but it still doesn't feel right. I told him, 'No, thanks.' Mom was a little pissed. She wanted all her boys together."

"How's Joe?" she asked.

"Joe's missing you," said Connell with a smile that transmitted down the line along with his words. "In fact, he's curled up here beside me now. It's gets to two a.m. and here he is, regular as clockwork. I need to get him trained to stay in his own bed."

"He does like his cuddles …"

"Sure he does, but now he brings the puppy with him, and that dog leaves more wet patches than Joe."

Lizzie imagined all three vying for space in the bed. She had an idea who would end up with the most room. "Are you still at the farm?"

"Yeah. No point in going back to the city while I'm on suspension. I've just been helping Dad out with the horses and spending time with Joe. I'm going to try and get rid of the apartment, pull together a deposit and see if

I can convince old Parker Williams that he's too old to be nursing that land of his."

"Sounds good."

"It is." He paused. "Hey, sweetheart, it's the middle of the night, and although it's great to hear your voice, I hear a little bell ringing in my head here. So why are you really calling?"

Lizzie smiled. "Connell, you know how you always insisted you were one of the good guys?"

"Yeah."

"And that you would look out for me, no matter what?"

"Sure."

"Did you mean it?"

"Sure I did." She caught the uncertainty in his voice, knew his mind would be racing, trying to second guess her.

"Well, I think I may need your help."

"How come?"

She lowered her voice. "I think I may be in trouble." She recalled vividly the two days they'd spent holed up at the cabin. She had a good idea what he'd be thinking.

"What kind of trouble, honey?"

"Um, big trouble, actually."

"Hey, no trouble is too much for me to sort. Just call me Mr. Fix-It. What's up, sweetheart? You got me worried phoning in the middle of the night."

"I'm sorry. I didn't mean to wake you, but I didn't know what to do." She couldn't help the catch in her voice. Knowing it would worry him, she took a calming breath.

"Well, neither do I until you tell me what's wrong."

"Have you ever been to Geneva?"

"Geneva?"

"Yes. I just got a letter and I've got to go and see the bank manager."

311

"You need some money, babe? You couldn't wait 'til morning to ask for a loan?"

"Um, not exactly, no."

"You know, honey, I think I've maybe said this before, but when you start a sentence with 'um', I get to thinking you're not telling me everything."

"Can you meet me in Geneva?" It came out in a rush because she didn't really know how to explain.

"Why? I mean yeah, sure, like I can just drop everything, hop a plane and scoot right on over there ..."

She smiled, imagining the look on his face, the wry grin and the way he cocked his head when he found her puzzling. She paused and looked again at the letter. "Because I just got a statement from a bank account I didn't know I had."

"And?"

"And it's pretty healthy."

"Lucky you. So you want a vacation? I could think of some places I'd rather visit. Somewhere hot would be a good start. It's still snowing here, remember."

"Over twenty million dollars, actually."

"Shit."

" Am I in trouble?" She held her breath.

"Well, I suppose that depends on what you're going to do about it."

"You mean what *we're* going to do about it."

"We ..." Connell grinned and there was no hiding it from his reply. She heard it wrap around his words. "What are you thinking?"

"I'm thinking an honest cop wouldn't keep it, and the daughter of a dishonest man wouldn't want anything to do with it. I'm thinking maybe we should do the decent thing and bail out poor old Gerry Gesting. I reckon twenty million might fix those career problems you and him seem to be having."

"Yeah, I reckon it would."

"So what do you suggest I do?"

"Pack a bag, sweetheart. I'll meet you in Geneva."

"What are you thinking?"

"I'm thinking that there's no such thing as an honest cop…"

* * *

Please enjoy the opening chapter of the next in the series

Molly Brown
Tommy Connell Mystery #2

A child to save - A killer to catch.

When a strange little girl disappears into the night and no one seems to care, Tommy Connell figures someone should take another look.

The good cops are hunting down a madman.
The bad cops are hunting down Connell.
And a serial killer is stalking his next victim.

Amidst the chaos of a major investigation, Connell must find Molly Brown and keep her safe. But as ghosts from his past threaten both the case and those he loves, he struggles to stay on the right side of the line.

Protecting Molly is a challenge that will test him to the limit, particularly as she's keeping a deadly secret of her own.

"Run ... Run ... As fast as you can."

Molly Brown
Tommy Connell Mystery #2

One

The child's bedroom sat at the end of the hall, where the draft from the badly fitting front door and the smell from the filthy bathroom mingled, filling the tiny space and creating an odor of neglect.

To call it a room was an exaggeration. It was little more than a closet. If he'd stretched out his arms he could have touched each wall with ease. The ancient floral wallpaper was peeling, there was a growing pool of water around the decaying window frame, and black mold flourished like an indoor garden. Connell inhaled. He could almost feel the microscopic particles invading his lungs.

Within the miniscule space, a neatly made bed squeezed itself against the wall. The worn, patchwork comforter was tightly tucked between the sagging mattress and frame. The stained pillow still bore the imprint of a small head. A badly painted closet half-blocked the tiny window, its door hanging from one hinge. Despite the lack of drapes, the room was dim, the morning sun struggling to make it through the grimy glass. He tried the light switch, and glancing up, realized the futility. An empty wire hung where the bulb should be.

The remaining floor space was occupied by books, a whole bunch of books. Connell picked his way carefully between neat piles stacked knee-high on the wooden floor, unwilling to disturb the arrangement. There was method to it, though he couldn't quite grasp what it was. It took conscious thought to create order, and he needed to understand the order, because he needed to understand the mind that had arranged this sad little room.

He pulled open the closet door. There wasn't much in it; a child's winter coat with sleeves that had been let down, two pairs of jeans with holes in the knees and a selection of faded t-shirts. A shoe box on the floor held rolled up graying socks that had started life white. A pair of black school shoes lay neatly by the box, dusty and scuffed. He checked the size. They weren't much bigger than his son, Joe's, and Joe was a little kid.

Squatting down by the side of the bed, he gently pulled back the cover. The sheet beneath hadn't been laundered recently and gave off a sour odor. He lifted the pillow, found pink pajamas, grubby and worn out, but folded neatly nevertheless. He sighed and felt an immense sadness deep inside. A child should be cherished. This child was obviously not.

Carefully wrapped inside the pajamas was a dog-eared paperback book - *The Wizard of Oz*. His sadness was joined by an inexplicable stirring of unease, as if something very strange and very bad had just whispered cold breath against his skin. Connell gave himself a shake. He was giving himself the creeps.

He stood and glanced around. For a ten year old, she was an advanced reader. Some of the books were pretty thick and all seemed well read. There were no toys. No mess, just books. How many books could a child read? Judging by how many were crammed into the room, she must have read a book a week since she first learned how. This kid was starting to look a little odd.

Picking up the paperback, Connell opened it where it was marked by a homemade bookmark. Dorothy had just met the cowardly lion. He wondered briefly if that was significant, then discarded the book and studied the strip of card. She'd written her name in elaborate script, colored it brightly with magic markers and edged the card with silver glitter. On the back she'd printed her name and address in small, neat, even letters and after her name, in brackets, she'd noted her age - ten and one quarter. He smiled. He remembered being eight and a half. The half had been very important. He'd been four years behind his brother, couldn't understand at the time how he would ever catch up. Maybe this kid wasn't odd, maybe she just liked make believe. He got that. Sometimes the real world was all too real.

He replaced the bookmark and slipped the book inside his jacket. Stuffing his hands into the pockets of his pants, he stood in the center of the sad little room and wondered. The local cops had been and gone; he knew because he'd sat outside in his car and waited for them to leave. They'd taken their statements and made up their minds and he'd a good idea what they'd thought when they'd seen the room. This whole situation was odd. Ten year old girls didn't just walk out the door and disappear, not without a very good reason.

Catching a whiff of stale, sickly-sweet perfume he turned slowly and realized he wasn't alone. The girl who hovered in the doorway was maybe fifteen or sixteen and trying to look older. Last night's makeup overdone. Lashes clogged together, lip stick smeared comically and hair tousled. With a too short skirt, and a too low neckline, she attempted a ridiculously provocative pose.

"Hiya," she slurred. "Who the hell are you?" She blinked slowly, eyelids heavy, more than a little hung over.

"One of the good guys," replied Connell. He weighed her whole life up with one glance and swallowed his dismay. Here was a kid headed for trouble.

"Oh yeah, we're pretty short on good guys in this neighborhood. What do you want?"

He shrugged, held her gaze and asked himself the same question. "What do you think?"

"The cops have been and gone. They didn't find anything. There was nothing to find." She blinked again even more slowly than before and he thought for a moment that her eyes weren't going to re-open and she'd fallen asleep in the doorway. He was about to reach out and prod her awake, when she pulled herself back with a start. "You need to get out and look for her. She's not here. She's not hiding under the bed."

She had a good point. He should have looked there first, and would have done if she hadn't interrupted him. "Does she do that often?" he asked, and the girl raised a quizzical brow and stifled a yawn.

"Huh ... do what?"

"Hide?"

She was a little slow on the uptake. Her pupils were dilated and her movements deliberate and exaggerated. She scowled at him. He recognized teenage attitude when he saw it, along with the scent of marijuana.

"She's no reason to hide. I told the cops all this already."

"Maybe you did, but I'm not the cops." Not exactly, anyway, but it was too complicated to explain to a kid with mush for brains. "I'm just here to help find your sister. You can help me by telling me about the last time you saw her." Which again, wasn't entirely true - he was supposed to be checking up on the cops, not the kid, but something wasn't quite right here and he'd sensed it the minute he'd stepped in the room.

"I just got done telling the cops."

"You said that already."

"So why repeat myself?"

Tommy Connell smiled and settled down for the long haul. It seemed it was his lot in life to get lumbered with people who had something to hide? "Humor me, kiddo, we're on the same side." He gestured with a sweeping hand to the interior of the small room. "Why all the books?"

"She likes to read."

"No kidding. What about friends?"

"Molly doesn't have friends, not regular ones, anyway."

A ten year old without friends was odd. His own little guy Joe was only six, but he had friends and fellow mischief makers by the dozens if the sound level at his last birthday party was any indicator.

"Why not?"

The girl gave a noncommittal shrug and the movement caused her to overbalance slightly on her stiletto heels. She attempted to correct the wobble by shuffling her feet and leaning heavily against the door frame. She was wasted. Maybe that was why the child's disappearance hadn't been reported sooner. Connell bit back a sharp comment. She was a kid. Kids did stupid things. He remembered doing plenty when he was her age. Difference was, he'd never mislaid a sibling while he was busy doing it.

"I dunno," she said finally. "She's not the friendly type. She doesn't mix. The other kids think she's weird."

"Weird?"

"Yeah ... you know ..." She crossed her eyes and tapped at her own head. "Crazy. They're scared of her and it doesn't help that she stinks." She wrinkled her nose to add weight to her words.

Maybe she was a little odd. Who was he to judge, he'd never met the child. But if the poor little kid

321

smelled bad it was because she slept in a dirty bed and nobody cared enough to make sure her clothes were clean.

"You don't have a washing machine?"

"Huh?"

The whole setup was off-center. The parents were out of town and they'd left their ten year old in the care of a spaced-out teenager. They hadn't even come home when their youngest disappeared. Maybe this wasn't unusual. Maybe little Molly regularly slipped on her sneakers and sneaked out the door.

"What about you," he asked, "do you think she's weird?"

"She's my little sister. Of course I do."

He couldn't argue with that. He was a younger sibling himself, and his brother, Will, still thought that he was from another planet. He'd certainly done some pretty crazy stuff in his time. "You were the last person to see her. Can you tell me what happened?"

She stuck out her chin belligerently. "I already told the cops everything I know. I'm done with it."

Connell had just pulled an unpleasant all-nighter, following up on a pair of low-rent cops who thought it was cool to play around with the law to their own advantage. Connell didn't agree with their philosophy and he didn't much like all-nighters. And he certainly didn't have the time or the energy to negotiate the twists and turns of the teenage psyche.

"Okay. I get it. You're a little distracted this morning, but just to keep you focused, here's the deal, Lydia. It is Lydia, isn't it?" He made a big deal of pulling out his notebook and flipping the pages as if he had her whole life history in front of him. "You tell me what you argued about with your sister, you tell me what made that little girl run off into the night, or I'll haul your ass downtown and book you for possession, and believe me you'll be done with it then."

"I thought you weren't a cop," she replied belligerently, unfazed by his threat.

"I can still make things happen that you might not enjoy." He frowned, gave her his *don't-mess-with-me* look, but it had no effect whatsoever.

"I don't know what you're talking about," she exclaimed with exaggerated indignation.

Everything about her behavior was over-the-top, loud and brassy, as if she'd read up on how to be as annoying as possible and was trying it out for size. Connell found it irritating. He'd also had about enough of it.

"Fine, have it your way. I'm done with it too. Which is your room? You got your stash under your pillow?" He watched as she weighed him up, realized he wasn't kidding around and was totally immune to any feminine charms she might have imagined she possessed. He made to brush past her in the narrow doorway and she caught at his sleeve and stopped him.

"Okay ... okay, chill out. Jeez, what's the big deal? You never smoked a little?"

He was starting to feel old and he was barely thirty. He looked pointedly at her hand on his arm and she removed it with a dramatic sigh.

"Okay, so we had a fight ... I mean I yelled at her a little bit but Molly doesn't argue. Molly doesn't fight back. Molly doesn't do much of anything really." She pulled a joint from her pocket and stuck it between her lips. "Got a light?"

Connell shook his head in weary disbelief, pulled the weed from her mouth and dropped it to the floor, grinding it beneath his shoe.

"Hey, I had to pay for that," she whined.

"You were telling me about Molly."

She shrugged. "She's a pain, the toothache of my life, always bugging me. We told her to get lost. We didn't mean it literally but Molly takes everything literally. She sees things as black and white, right and wrong, good and evil, nothing in between. It's all the reading she does, it's messed with her head."

Somebody's head was definitely messed, but standing there listening to Lydia's explanations, Connell wasn't entirely convinced it was little Molly's.

"She believes real life is the same as in her books - every story has a happy ending," continued Lydia. "But life's not like that, is it? Life is one great big toilet and one way or another we all get flushed down the pan."

She had issues with her baby sister and a sizeable chip on her shoulder. She'd also said 'we' not 'I'.

"So what did you say to her?" Connell asked.

"Does it matter?"

"I think you know it does. We have a little girl who's been missing over twenty four hours. Everything matters."

Lydia's pouty mouth snapped shut, bravado instantly deflated like a burst balloon. Suddenly she stopped trying to look older and looked very young indeed. Connell cut her a little slack.

"Look, you're not in trouble. You want to fry your brain with weed? Go ahead, knock yourself out. You want to have underage sex with your boyfriend? None of my business. I just need to know what was in your sister's head when she left. Whether she intended to take off and maybe hide out to give everyone a scare, or whether someone else is involved."

Lydia pulled herself together with a final, half-hearted *see-if-I-care* shrug. "Who said I'm underage?"

"So she caught you with some boy and was going to tell Mom?"

"Not exactly."

"So tell me, exactly."

"She wasn't supposed to come out of her room. I told her not to - not when I had company." Lydia paused, dropping her gaze to her feet as if reliving the events was more painful than she'd imagined it would be. Guilt was a killer. Connell knew all about that. "She's only little ... in here." She tapped at her head. "Like I said, weird, you know. She's not exactly sociable, she gets scared at loud noises and crowds and she does this funny thing with her eyes like she's a fucking crazy person, it's scary, embarrassing. I was going to have people over and have some fun, smoke a little, mess around a little, and she was supposed to stay in her room and out of my way."

"But she didn't?" Connell was starting to see the picture and didn't much like it.

"No, she didn't. The battery in her flashlight died, she couldn't read her book. She came in to ask for another - like I carry a pack of batteries around with me."

"And?"

"And she kinda interrupted us." She gave him a knowing look. She was a child pretending to be a grown up and he found the whole situation disturbing. "She just stood there ... staring ... like she does, and Terry got mad and shouted at her. Scared her, I guess."

"Terry?"

"Yeah." She checked her pockets, seemed to realize he'd destroyed her last joint and crossed her arms nervously across her chest.

"Who's Terry?"

"Just a guy."

Connell didn't like guys who scared girls, no matter what how big or little they were. "How old is this guy?"

"Huh?"

"How old is your boyfriend?" It was hard work, much harder than it should have been. He bit at the inside of his cheek to sharpen his focus and to stop him from snapping back at her.

She shook her head. "I'm not sure. He's older than me."

"You're not sure? Well, does he go to school, college? Does he work?"

"I dunno."

Connell sighed. "Where does he live?"

"I dunno."

"You don't know much."

"Whatever ..." she replied, bored again.

"Did you know him before you brought him home?"

"No. I'd seen him before, around the bar, but I didn't *know* him."

She had the grace to look a little shamefaced and Connell wondered if she had any idea how dangerous the game she was playing actually was. Maybe he should take the time to explain. Somebody definitely needed to. He checked his watch. Time was something he was short of and he doubted she would appreciate a lecture from him.

"So let me get this straight, your mom and dad are out of town, you decide to have a party and you go out and score drugs. You pick up some strange guy in a bar you shouldn't be in because you're underage, then you bring him home and score a little action while your little sister sits in the dark alone in her room."

Lydia hung her head, studied the cracked patent leather on her shoes and the chipped polish on her toe nails. "I guess."

"Pretty shitty, huh?"

"I guess."

He was glad she thought so, even if it was in hindsight.

"What did this Terry guy say to her when she caught him with his pants down?"

She stifled a quick smile. Connell met it with a scowl and the smirk disappeared as quickly as it came. "He wasn't very nice."

"*He wasn't very nice,*" repeated Connell, slowly. What was she doing with guys that weren't very nice? "What did he say?"

She looked away again, to compose herself maybe, and he wondered if she was actually as wrecked as she made out or whether it was an act she was hiding behind.

"Terry told her she was a little freak and he'd burn her books and slit her throat if she didn't disappear."

Definitely not nice. "And do you think he would've?"

"Would've what?"

"Slit her throat."

She shook her head. "Come on. It's just something you say when you're mad, isn't it?"

Maybe in the world according to Lydia Brown, but not in any world he knew. He recalled wryly the times when Joe had interrupted him at an inopportune moment. That little guy had built-in radar, but slitting of throats didn't come into it. "How'd he know about the books?"

"Huh?"

"How did he know about the books? Did he go into her room?"

She shrugged. "I dunno, I guess so ... I was pretty whacked out."

Connell tried to remain calm. He wasn't sure whether his alarm bells were ringing because she was hiding something or simply because the whole situation stank.

"Did Terry stay all night? Was he still here when you noticed that Molly had gone?"

"I don't know what time he left. When he was done, I guess. I was high. It was about lunchtime when I realized she'd gone, and I gave her till dinner to come home. When it started to get dark, I began to get a little worried because Molly doesn't like the dark."

She didn't like the dark and yet there wasn't even a light bulb in her excuse for a room. God. He knew deep down this could only get worse. He just didn't want to think about it.

He thought instead of Lizzie and the feel of her warm restraining hand on his arm. He needed her, but maybe it wasn't such a good idea to think of the love of his life when he was caught up in a case and hadn't been home in four days.

He returned his attention to Lydia. "What about the other guests?"

"There were no other guests."

"Some party ..."

She pulled a face. "We had fun."

"Sounds like it. You didn't call your folks?"

"No."

"Why not?"

"Because I don't know where they are."

Sadly that didn't surprise him; she didn't know much at all.

That was last night and Molly had probably been gone twelve hours already by then. He added it up in his head, whichever way you looked at it, that little girl had been gone a long time.

"You phoned the cops and they came straight over?"

"No," she replied in a voice that suggested she thought he was as stupid as her crazy little sister. "They came this morning, said they'd look out for her, and to let them know if she turned up."

Connell had sat outside in his car and watched them leave. He'd assumed it was a return visit, hadn't realized it was the first response. "They weren't worried?" Since when did cops think it wasn't a big deal when a child went missing?

"Kids go missing. Most of them come home on their own ... that's what they said. Maybe there was a game on, or a sale at Dunkin Donuts. They were in a hurry."

Oh yeah, they'd be in a hurry when he caught up with them. "Did you tell them about Terry?"

"They didn't ask."

He glanced back at the pathetic little room and thought of the child who'd slept in that bed, imagined how she must have felt curled up under thin dirty covers with no light and no comfort. He couldn't bear the thought of Joe in similar circumstances.

But that wasn't why he was there or what he was getting paid for. He should just leave it to the locals and back off, but he'd never been very good at backing off, even when he'd been told to.

He turned back to the girl with a sigh. "Have you been smoking today?"

"Some."

"You need to stop now. You need to get your head in gear and go get cleaned up. You need to be ready when your sister comes home. Is there someone who can stay with you until your parents come back?"

"I'm doing okay on my own."

Connell looked her up and down and shook his head sadly. "No, sweetheart, you're not. You let strange guys into your home. Think about it, you let me walk in off the street and you still haven't asked for I.D. Strange guys have a habit of doing strange things and they usually won't be good things. How long have your parents been gone?"

She shrugged and he suddenly realized they weren't on a trip. They'd been gone for some time and Lydia had been left playing mommy, unsuccessfully as it turned out. "Who's been paying the rent?" he asked, though he already guessed the answer.

"I have," she answered with a defiant glare.

329

"For how long?"

"I don't know, weeks, months, maybe two months."

Two months! What'd they do, go out to the store for cigarettes and forget to come back? It wasn't uncommon for guys to run off and leave their women, or ladies to take off on their men, but it was unusual for both to walk out the door without saying goodbye to their kids.

"They happen to mention where they were going?" asked Connell and she answered with a shake of her head. "Or when they'd be back?"

"They left in a hurry. I guess they'd had enough of her too."

"Enough of who?"

"The bookworm, who else?"

"And what did Molly think about that?" She was a little kid, vulnerable by all accounts. Her mom and dad had disappeared and her sister was selling herself to pay the rent.

"Molly doesn't say much. Like I said, she reads a lot."

"But she does understand that they've gone?"

"Who knows? She doesn't exactly sit around making small talk."

"Do you think she may have gone to look for them?" He hoped not. The thought of a little girl wandering around the city on her own, did things to his gut that hurt.

"I doubt it. We're better off without them." Lydia reached down, and with one hand securing her to the door frame, she undid her shoes, slipped them off and shrunk by four inches and a couple of years.

"Why? Because they're bad parents or because they walked out on you?"

"Both."

Connell nodded. Good parents didn't walk out on their kids. Of course that was supposing they *had* walked out and weren't currently laying unclaimed in a drawer at the morgue. He shot a final glance at the little room. "Where do you think she is?"

The girl cocked her head and snorted softly. "Well that's pretty obvious."

"Huh?"

"Haven't you been paying attention? Didn't you notice?" She gestured to the books. "Some cop you are."

"I told you already, I'm not a cop. What should I have noticed?"

"They're all the same shitty story." She tapped her head again. "Don't you get it? Molly lives in the wonderful world of Oz and right now - she's off to see the Wizard."

* * *

Psychological Crime by the same author

Bedlam
Love hurts. Obsession kills.

Joe loves Kit. Everyone thinks she's dead. Joe knows she's not.

If you lost the love of your life, how far would you go to get them back?
Detective Joe McNeil would do absolutely anything.
When Joe breathes life into a crime scene victim, he discovers what *anything* really means.
Nell will use whatever is necessary to ensure she survives, including Joe. Is she really a victim or merely the weapon being wielded by a much more cunning foe?
Against the background of a multiple murder investigation, Joe struggles between his love for missing Kit and his growing obsession with the enigmatic Nell.
Plunged headlong into a spiralling nightmare of kidnap, murder and betrayal, his relentless search for the truth jeopardizes his career, his sanity and his life.
But for Nell, the risk is even greater.

A haunting tale of obsessive love, ultimate sacrifice and deadly consequences

"Bold ... *Different* ... Scary."

Psychological Crime by the same author

Twisted
A felon on the run. A hostage from hell.
A game with no rules.

Jack Miller's been playing a dangerous game and the stakes are about to be raised.

A spate of audacious bank robberies leave police frustrated and crime boss Otto smiling, but for ruthless robber Miller it's simply the means to an end. Wounded while making his escape, Miller has half a million in used notes and a hostage that wasn't part of the plan. As police close in, Otto wants his cash and the mysterious McKenzie wants Miller silenced - forever.

With a deadly agenda of her own, misfit Spook, isn't your typical hostage. Unstable and fearless she'll go to any lengths to get what she wants. When judge's daughter Jazz O'Hanlon also disappears and evidence points at Miller, the manhunt escalates and Miller discovers just how crazy Spook really is.

Amid the tabloid frenzy, DI John Samuels realises he must catch his man alive before the game ends in disaster.

"Quirky ... *Fast* ... Funny."

A Crime short by the same author

Ten Green Bottles

A vicious serial killer is prowling city streets, preying on working girls. Can Detective's Zoe Harte and Neil Fuller catch the monster before he catches them?

Included in:
Dark Minds
You think you know darkness? Think again.
Bloodhound Books presents Dark Minds – a charity collection of stories by authors who have come together to produce an anthology that will lure, tantalise and entertain.
All profits from the sale of this book will be donated to Hospice UK and Sophie's Appeal.

About the author

B.A. Morton writes across a number of genres, from her home in Northumberland, England. She lives with her husband and a variety of animals in a listed cottage with a unique medieval history

Success in the international literary competition 'The Yeovil Prize' with debut crime novel, 'Mrs Jones', launched her writing career. A member of the Crime Writers Association and the International Thriller Writers, she is published by Twisted Ink Publishing, Caffeine Nights Publishing and Bloodhound Books.

Discover more about current and future projects at the following links.

http://bamorton.weebly.com/
https://www.facebook.com/TwistedInkPublishing